Somewhere
Over Engla

Margaret Graham has been writing for thirty years. Her first novel was published in 1986 and since then she has written fourteen novels. As a bestselling author her novels have been published in the UK, Europe and the USA. *Somewhere Over England* was previously published as *A Fragment of Time*.

Margaret has written two plays, co-researched a television documentary – which grew out of *Canopy of Silence* – and has written numerous short stories and features. She is a writing tutor and speaker and has written regularly for Writers' Forum. She founded and administered the Yeovil Literary Prize to raise funds for the creative arts of the Yeovil area and it continues to thrive under the stewardship of one of her ex-students. Margaret now lives near High Wycombe and has launched Words for the Wounded which raises funds for the rehabilitation of wounded troops by donations and writing prizes.

She has 'him indoors', four children and three grand-children who think OAP stands for Old Ancient Person. They have yet to understand the politics of pocket money. Margaret is a member of the Rock Choir, the WI and a Chair of her local U3A. She does Pilates and Tai Chi and travels as often as she can.

For more information about Margaret Graham visit her website at www.margaret-graham.com

Margaret GRAHAM

Somewhere Over England

arrow books

Published by Arrow Books 2014

2 4 6 8 10 9 7 5 3 1

First published in Great Britain in 1990 by
William Heinemann Ltd as *A Fragment of Time*

Arrow Books
Random House, 20 Vauxhall Bridge Road,
London SW1V 2SA

www.randomhouse.co.uk

Addresses for companies within The Random House Group Limited can
be found at: www.randomhouse.co.uk/offices.htm

The Random House Group Limited Reg. No. 954009

A CIP catalogue record for this book
is available from the British Library

ISBN 9780099585824

The Random House Group Limited supports the Forest Stewardship
Council® (FSC®), the leading international forest-certification organisation.
Our books carrying the FSC label are printed on FSC®-certified paper.
FSC is the only forest-certification scheme supported by the
leading environmental organisations, including Greenpeace.
Our paper procurement policy can be found at:
www.randomhouse.co.uk/environment

Printed and bound by CPI Group (UK) Ltd, Croydon, CR0 4YY

To Maggie

Acknowledgements

My sincere thanks to Sheila Doering, Nancy Copas, Daphne Folyer, Thelma Kazda and Margot Loomis – all now of the United States – without whom this book could not have been written. My thanks also to Sue Bramble, Martock Branch Librarian with Somerset County Library, whose advice and help has been, as always, above and beyond the call of duty.

Somewhere
Over England

Part One

CHAPTER 1

The lichen was dry beneath her fingers, dry and warm. It crumbled as she rubbed her hand along the top of the old bridge; some had caught beneath her nails which were cut short and square as her mother insisted. Helen smiled because soon it wouldn't matter what her mother thought. It was 1931, she was eighteen and at last it wouldn't matter.

She lifted her face to the sun. It was hot although it was early May and through her closed lids she could see only red but she felt Heine near her, next to her. She could hear his breathing, smell his skin and here was his hand, firm on hers. Through her closed lids she could picture him; tanned, his hair golden.

'I love you, Heine,' she said and it was not until she felt his lips on her neck, his breath on her skin that she turned, looking into his face, touching the lines beneath his eyes, kissing his mouth, stroking his hair. Although he said there were grey hairs she could see none, he was too blond.

'And I love you, Helen,' he said. That was all but it was enough.

She turned back to the parapet, her arm in his.

'I used to come here with my father,' she said, the index finger of her other hand tracing the figure six, round and round in the lichen. 'Before he died, of course.'

Heine nodded, leaning over to look down into the stream. 'In the trenches, I suppose?' His voice was tense and Helen lifted his hand to her lips. There was dirt on his palm from her fingers.

'Mother wishes that he had. It would be so much more proper somehow but no, it was the flu. In 1919 when I was six. But I can remember coming here with him, I know I can, although Mother says I can't possibly. I was three the first time when he was on leave.' She stared hard at his hand. 'I can

1

remember coming here while she stayed at home to cook the joint on Sundays. He would hold my hand as we walked from the Avenue, across the fields, along by the hazel trees to this exact spot.'

She turned and smiled at Heine. 'To this exact spot,' she repeated, 'and the lichen was here then too. The weather always seemed warm and dry and the minnows darted in and out of the shadows just as they're doing now.' She paused. 'I haven't been back for years.' She thought, but did not add, that she could not face coming alone, or with her – her mother.

Helen leaned over the parapet, her shoes digging into the stones and turf of the lane which had never been tarmacked. There was no need, no traffic, just us, her father had said. The minnows were darting and now she remembered how they would each drop a stick into the water from the other side of the bridge and race back. Her father would lift her so that she could see whose had won and although her head and body had been well over the water she had never been afraid. He had been thirty when he died and she hadn't been back since then.

Would he be pleased at her news, she wondered, as she looked again at Heine, and felt that he would because she could remember him saying, Be happy, to her in that room, the spare room where her mother had moved him the moment he had become ill. Just be happy when you can, life is so short.

The room had a wet blanket soaked in disinfectant draped in the doorway day and night. Her mother had said it was to stop the germs and Helen was not to enter; on no account was she to enter. But on the first Sunday of his illness she had pushed past the heavy Army issue barrier. Its wetness had soaked into her blue summer dress, staining it darker where it had touched. Its smell had saturated the room. She bent forward and kissed him by his eyebrow. He was so hot and dry and there was a pulse beneath his skin. I love you, Daddy, she said, and he smiled. I won't let you die. Every day she had crept into that bleak room and kissed him there and said, I will not let you die. But one day he was dead, and she was alone with her mother.

Now she couldn't remember what he had looked like, though there was a photograph on the mantelpiece in the dining-room of him in his Pay Corps uniform. But somehow it was not the father she had known, the father whose smile had been slow and whose voice had been kind.

2

'We also had the flu in our land, Helen.' Heine's voice was gentle and she nodded.

'Yes, I know, my love.' But she pushed the thought of his land away, just for now. There would be enough said about that when they arrived for tea in the house in the Avenue where she still lived.

'Are you sure your mother will receive me?' Heine asked, the lines deepening around his eyes and across his forehead.

'Of course she will.' But she looked away because she did not want him to see her face as she said those words. She touched his arm. His sleeves were rolled up and his hairs were golden in the sun, thick and golden, and she wanted to bend her head and press her lips against his flesh and forget her mother as she always could with him.

She turned then and ran down from the bridge squatting beneath the hazel trees which grew almost to the banks, looking over her shoulder as she scooped her grey cotton skirt clear of the ground.

'Let's drop sticks into the water and see who wins the race,' she called. 'Come on, Heine. Choose your own or I'll pick one with branches which will snag on the rocks and you'll lose.'

She watched as he limped down to her and flushed. She hadn't forgotten that Heine could no longer run, it had just got lost somewhere in her head, just for a moment, the moment when she had smelt his skin, wanted his body. She turned away, seeing the roots which rose from the bank and then the field beyond. It must be hard when the sun was so warm, the grass smelt so fresh, the birds sang and the breeze wafted. It must be so hard not to be able to run but then – and now she paused as she searched for a thick straight twig – but then perhaps men of thirty were too old to run. Had her father ever run? She could not remember.

Heine stooped, his leg would not bend. 'That one, my darling. It is short and thick and will race and win.' He pointed to a stick just to the left of her foot buried in long grass. She picked it up; it was cool and the bark was damp, torn and pungent. She handed it up to him, narrowing her eyes as she looked into the sun.

Why had he chosen her? Of all the women he must have met, why had he chosen her? Helen reached for a stick, any stick, it

3

didn't matter now. She felt foolish, a child beside his maturity, his beauty, his intelligence.

She pushed herself up, not looking at him now.

'Let's not do this. You must think me such a child and I'm not. I might be younger than you but I'm not a child.' The sun cooler now, she rubbed her arms with her hands and the stick streaked her skin with mud. There was a mark on her new pink blouse. She moved out from the grass, from the hazel trees, looking across the fields to the backs of the houses half a mile away. Her mother would be waiting.

'You are beautiful and I wish to race our sticks,' Heine said.

He smiled as he looked at her short dark curls, so gloriously dark, not like the heavy gold plaits of the women of his land. She was so young and fresh and strong, all that he no longer was. It was this which had drawn him to her when he had photographed the new premises of the bank where she worked. In her, this young girl, he could see no harshness, no brutality, no reminders of the land he had been forced to leave. He knew he must have had a childhood but somehow he could not see past the darkness which was crawling in the streets of the towns where he had once lived. Would he regain the sights and sounds of youth with this girl whose skin was flushed and smooth? Ignoring the ache in his leg, he held out his hand and smiled as she took it. Together they walked back to the bridge and dropped their sticks far out into the running current, then hurried back over to the side which still had a number six rubbed in the lichen.

Helen leaned over, seeing again the small child, feeling her father's hands as he lifted her. Heine's was out first, the short thick one, and he laughed and kissed her and said into her hair, 'Faster on water than on land, my darling.'

And she wanted to ask him yet again how he had been injured, for it was not in the war, that much she knew, but he would never tell her. The girls in her office thought the limp romantic and she smiled at the feel of his arms around her, not embarrassed as his body pressed against hers, though she had felt awkward when she had danced with the boys at the St Matthew's Christmas dance five months ago. She remembered the hot sweating hands which had made her skin wet through her gloves, the conversation which had spluttered and died. Heine made her feel safe, made her feel full of love.

4

'Isn't it time that we faced your mother?'

Helen put her face against his jacket, not wanting to think of the world in the Avenue, her mother, the past.

'Just a little longer. It's not quite three-thirty,' she replied, knowing that today there would be meringues. On this occasion there would definitely be meringues and she shivered.

It was a million years since her mother had bought her ribbon and green knickers in the large store two weeks after her father had died. They had travelled in a lift to the restaurant where mannequins had paraded and a chamber orchestra had played on a small stage fronted by imitation palm trees. Her mother had ordered tea for two and one meringue and one toasted teacake. A waitress dressed in black with a small white pinafore had served the large meringue on a bone china plate with a white paper doily.

It was as white as her father's face had been the last time she had seen him.

Her mother's teacake oozed butter. She cut into it with a knife, carrying it to her pursed mouth with her small plump fingers, watching the mannequins, listening to the music, her head nodding in time, her black felt hat firm on her head. Helen had watched the butter drip on to her chin and wondered how her mother could eat when her own heart seemed to fill her body with the pain of loss, leaving no room for food, leaving no room even to breathe properly.

Helen had dug her fork, prongs first, into her meringue and it shattered, spraying the table-cloth and her lap, and she had been glad to see it destroyed, because that was how she felt too. Daddy, she had thought silently.

Her mother leaned forward then. Eggs and cream are good for you, she had said, and Helen could smell the tea on her breath. Eat it, or I shall put you in the cupboard. And her mother had smiled a strange smile, one that did not reach her eyes. Mother knows best, she had said, and I am all you have now. Now he is dead.

Her stomach had swayed in the lift but she had not been sick until midnight and then she had cried out, 'Daddy'. Her mother had come and taken her downstairs and put her in the cupboard, the dark black cupboard under the stairs. She had cried into the blackness, holding her father's coat against her face until it was wet, because her mother must not hear her sobs.

Every holiday her mother had taken her to the same restaurant and if she was displeased she would buy her a meringue and the darkness of the cupboard would be close.

'Oh yes,' Helen said as Heine touched her arm. 'Oh yes, perhaps we'd better go now.'

She turned and rubbed out the number six on the lichen, rubbed and rubbed, then shook her hands, smiling as Heine gave her a crisp white handkerchief. She handed it back before taking his arm and walking at his pace down the lane towards the houses they could see over the two fields. He was her sunlight, but she would have to struggle for him.

Lydia Carstairs brushed the table-cloth with the silver-plated crumb brush and dustpan which she told people had been a wedding present but which she had bought in Kingston-upon-Thames after her husband had died. There had been some money then, for the first time ever. Clerks did not earn a great deal but he had been very wise, she had to say that for Ernest, very wise in the matter of insurance. Perhaps that's what came of dealing with little bits of paper for a living. So in a way it was as well he had died of flu and not in the line of duty, because she wasn't sure just how his insurance would have stood in those circumstances. Mark you, there was no telegram, was there, with flu? No valour.

Lydia moved across to the mantelpiece and dusted the photograph of Ernest with a corner of her flowered apron. He had been a very ordinary little man, but steady, her mother had said, and he had of course owned this detached house and on a corner too, which made it rather better than the neighbours'. There was also a bit of extra land at the side which Ernest had used to grow cabbages and potatoes. He had liked potatoes straight from the soil; small and translucent, he used to say, with the scent of nature in every bite. What nonsense he talked. She stood back from the photograph. Good, no dust.

She hadn't missed him, and no, she didn't feel that was a sin. As her mother had said, no woman liked a sweating body in her bed. Men were better dealing with wars, better at being with other men. When they were home they interfered. And she'd been right. They spoilt their children, came between mothers and daughters. She looked again at the photograph. No, she didn't miss Ernest because she had Helen.

Lydia turned and looked at the table. The best cloth was on, the white cotton covered by the white over-lace. Scones, sandwiches, but not those with egg yet because they smelt so. Lydia smoothed her hands down her apron and then touched her hair, looking in the wrought-iron mirror over the sideboard. Her grey hair was in place, her face powdered, but very lightly. She wished her eyes were not such a pale blue and her face was not quite so plump. She sucked in her cheeks. Perhaps she should have less jam on her scones. There was dust on the mirror frame and she licked her finger and ran it round the wrought-iron edge.

The clock in the hall chimed three-thirty and Lydia took her apron off, carrying it through to the kitchen, hanging it on the hook which Ernest had put up on the inside of the pantry door when he seemed a little better from the flu. And while he was doing that it had seemed sensible that he should just finish off the shelf for the new meat safe. He wouldn't do the second one though; stubborn, yes stubborn. He had collapsed the next day.

She moved to the sink. Where was Helen and why had she invited this friend? The girl knew how she felt about the weekends. After all, the weekends were family times, they always had been and they always would be. It was lonely when she was away in London during the day. She was becoming a selfish girl again. Lydia picked up the dishcloth and polished the splash marks from the cold tap before looking up at the clock. She should be back from the station by now. She polished harder, pushing the rage down, pushing the fear of loneliness down. She did not want to think of the word that Helen had used, that had taken the breath from her body. Him, she had said. I will go to the station to meet him.

Helen rang the door bell because she was not allowed a key. Her hands were cold now and the porch seemed foreign to her. There was a broken tile in the right-hand corner, and the lead which swept upwards on the stained glass window was thinner at the top and cracked with age.

The door was opening and her mother stood motionless, her smile fixed, her hair newly permed. Helen could smell it from

7

here. It was crimped and tight, hard like her mother's eyes as they looked past her.

'Mother, I'd like you to meet Heine.' She could only move slightly aside in the cramped porch but her mother had not yet opened the door wide enough for them to enter.

'Heine, this is my mother, Lydia Carstairs.'

'Mrs Carstairs,' her mother said, still with a fixed smile. 'How do you do. You had better come in.' She shook Heine's outstretched hand but looked at Helen. 'Go through to the dining-room.'

They walked down the dark hall and through the first door and Helen wished that she had been able to be honest with her mother. She had wanted to tell her that Heine was her life now, that at lunchtimes she had been walking in the park or sitting in a Lyons Corner House with him but she had been unable to. She had been too afraid that it would all end, that she would not be strong enough to fight for him.

She heard her mother go on into the kitchen. She could hear the kettle humming through the hatch, then its whistle, abruptly halted as her mother lifted it from the gas and poured water into the teapot. It would be the silver one, she knew.

Helen smiled at Heine who raised an eyebrow.

'Do sit down,' she said and wondered why she whispered.

'Did your mother not know of my existence?' Heine also spoke quietly, his face serious.

Helen flushed. 'You don't understand how difficult it can be. I am all she has. She depends on me too much.' She was still whispering. She rubbed at her hands, at the lichen dust, the dirt from the stone parapet, the bark stain.

'My darling girl, you are not that frightened of the situation are you, or of her reaction? I didn't realise.' His voice dropped almost to nothing. 'I should not have put you in this position, you are too young, too fresh.'

Helen caught one of his hands. 'I am not too young. Just nervous, that's all. It needs to be put to her gently.' Her voice was still a whisper but she must not think of herself as frightened or she would be lost.

'Then I will be careful, but I just wish it need not be this way. There seems to be no end to obstruction.' His voice was still low but it now sounded tired. 'Go and wash your hands now, leave me alone with her for a while.' He kissed her hand, holding it to his mouth for a moment. 'And now I have dirt on my lips?'

'No, my love.'

In the bathroom Helen scrubbed her hands and then her nails and soap sprayed on to her pink blouse and even when she wiped it with the towel the marks still showed. He had spoken to her as though she were a child and she was, inside she still was. He was right, she was frightened; so frightened that it would all be destroyed, that he would go and leave her here with her mother. Alone with her mother whose voice was not kind, whose hands had never shown her the stream but had pushed her into the darkness.

She held the towel to her face. She must not cry, she never cried, and today if she did it would show in her eyes and her mother would say that all men did this to you; that mothers were the best companions. She looked in the mirror, she could not go down yet. She opened the window and stared out across the garden, across the fields they had just passed through, breathing in the spring air, letting the breeze cool her face.

They were both sitting at the table when she re-entered, her mother pouring tea from the silver pot.

'So your father is a solicitor, is he?' she was saying, her face stretched into a smile. 'And you have a studio just a few yards from the Underground station. Cannon Street did you say? Alton Mews? Most convenient.' She turned to Helen. 'Do take a scone, Helen. Heine says that he has not tasted anything like them ever.'

'Indeed they are quite delicious, Mrs Carstairs.' Heine smiled at Lydia and then at Helen. 'Really, Helen, you did not tell me you had such a talented mother. I should have insisted on visiting you before at this . . .' he paused and looked around the room. 'At this comfortable and tranquil home.'

Helen watched her mother smile, not at her but at Heine. She could see that he had already eaten three sandwiches and she knew he did not like egg.

'Yes, my father is a solicitor and of course is kept extremely busy. And my mother too because unfortunately our home is not as cosy as yours. It is big, too big.'

Helen watched as her mother looked again at Heine, her face thoughtful, but Helen knew she was just waiting.

'And how large is your studio in London, Mr Weber?'

'It is integrated into the flat I have. There is a pleasant garden and in the flat there is a spare room for guests. And of course I am not very far from Waterloo.'

'And they're bringing those new trolley buses in soon, aren't they, the ones they use in Yorkshire? You know, Helen, those trackless trams. They're cheaper, the paper says, and don't interfere with the traffic so much. That will make it easier for you won't it, Mr Weber? For your business?'

'You are quite correct, Mrs Carstairs,' Heine took a sip of tea from the bone china cup with pink flowers. Her mother's best, Helen noticed. He set the cup carefully in the saucer, before looking up at Helen and her mother.

Helen also looked at her mother who was patting her mouth with her napkin then back at Heine. His smile was sincere, his voice anxious. She felt warmth flood over her. Perhaps it would be all right. Perhaps Heine was going to make her like him.

'Helen, the meringues are on the kitchen table. Now pass me your cup and I shall refill it for you, Mr Weber.'

Helen rose, looking from her mother to Heine. It would not be all right. She understood her mother's words. Helen carried the plate back into the room together with the silver-plated cake tongs and placed it beside her mother. She could not look up.

'Now tell me more about yourself, Mr Weber,' her mother asked as she chose the largest meringue for Helen and placed it carefully on a small white plate and then passed one to Heine. 'I think from your accent you must be Dutch.'

Heine did not falter, he did not look at Helen who had stopped and turned. Her chair was still two paces away from her.

'I was born in Germany, Mrs Carstairs.'

Her mother held the plate quite still, her fingers whitening. She said nothing but she smiled and there was satisfaction in her eyes. It was the smile she used when Helen came out of the cupboard.

Steam was coming from the spout of the teapot, a slash of light caught the lid. Heine reached forward and took the plate from her mother's grasp, saying as he did so, 'Do you mind if I begin? It looks too delicious to ignore.'

Her mother said nothing. Helen moved to her chair now but

did not eat her meringue. Didn't Heine know what had just happened? Couldn't he see from her mother's eyes? But no, of course not, no one could but her.

Heine looked at Mrs Carstairs, his face gentle, his voice firm. 'I know that it is difficult to divest ourselves of the past. Of the pain that both our nations experienced. There are some who cannot forgive or forget but I know that those of us with compassion and tolerance, such as you, Mrs Carstairs, can see beyond that. I have chosen to live in England because I prefer it to my own land. I prefer its people, its tolerance. Its essence. I know that you will understand what I mean.' He was holding her mother's arm now.

Lydia Carstairs was looking at him, feeling the weight of his hand, hearing his words, hating him for thinking that he could take her daughter from her. She is mine, she wanted to shout into his face, but she said nothing.

'I wish to marry Helen, Mrs Carstairs. I love her and I will take care of her but I will not marry without your approval.' He looked at Helen who still did not eat. Heine smiled at her but she could only look at him and then at her mother who had still not spoken, still not moved.

Heine pushed back his chair. 'I feel it would be too impolite to smoke in your home, Mrs Carstairs. I shall go into the garden if I may.' He rose and smiled again at Helen but his blue eyes were dark and the lines were deep across his forehead and around his eyes and as he left the room his limp seemed more pronounced.

When his footsteps could no longer be heard her mother turned slowly to Helen, her lips thin.

'How could you do this to me? After all your poor father's suffering you expect me to accept a German into my life, into the Avenue.'

There was no steam coming from the pot now, or was it just that Helen could not see it in the fading light, for the sun seemed to have vanished. There was no gleam to the silver, just this hard lump in her throat which obstructed her breathing, her vision, her words. She clenched her jaw, pushing away the plate with the meringue as far as she could reach.

'Mother, I love Heine. Even if he were English you would not be pleased. You would not let me go. I know you are using his nationality as a reason to stop my marriage. You can come and stay often. We are not too far away. He is of the right sort of family to please you. Mother, I love him.'

She could feel her throat thickening, aching, and knew that tears were near but she must not cry. There was no time in her life for tears, she had told herself that years ago.

'You love him more than your own mother?' Lydia's voice was harsh, her hand had bunched into a fist.

Helen sat back. She picked up the crumbs around her plate, one by one, placing them in a neat pile along the blue painted edge then she looked up at her mother. The ache in her throat was gone and there was a coldness in its place, a strength, and she spoke clearly as she picked up the plates, laying the knives side by side, neatly, quietly.

'I love Heine as a woman loves a man. You must let me go, Mother.'

'You are disgusting.' Her mother was shouting now, opening her hand and striking the table. 'He is so old. You are only eighteen. The neighbours, what will they say when they know he is a German? Mrs Jones lost Albert, Mrs Sinclair her husband.'

Helen stood up now, standing above her mother, realising that she was taller than the other woman. 'Tell them he is Dutch.'

She wanted to strike her mother for daring to use the grief of her friends to hurt her daughter. The grief of Mrs Jones who had once been plump, of Mrs Sinclair whose eyes were deep set now when they had not been before.

'Tell them he is Dutch,' she repeated, suddenly tired. 'I shall come and see you often, you must come and see us but I shall marry him, and I shall do so in the autumn.'

Her mother spoke again. 'But . . .'

'Mother, I will marry him, even if I have to become pregnant in order to force you to agree. It is your decision.' Helen's mouth was hard and set. Heine would not marry without her mother's consent and she had spent too many years waiting to be loved, waiting to be free. She would say and do whatever was necessary.

Heine stood beyond the patio, on the grass. It eased his leg to stand on something which accommodated the difference in length between the right and left, slight though it was. He drew on his cigarette before holding it away, watching the ash as it fell. He could feel and taste a shred of tobacco between his lips. He removed it with his thumb and forefinger.

He looked at the forsythia which grew up against the wooden fence surrounding the garden and at the two apple trees near to the gate which led out across the field. Had Helen walked through that with her father, he wondered.

It seemed strange that there were no lime trees as there were in his garden. He corrected himself – in his parents' garden. Momentarily he could smell their scent. He drew on his cigarette again and the memory dissipated but at least it had existed and he felt warmed. For the first time for what seemed like years he had found his way back beyond the darkness.

He turned and looked back at the house. A dog barked somewhere in the neighbourhood. The tea had been difficult. Helen should have told her mother, it was not correct to approach their marriage in this way and fear rose in him that he would lose her, this girl who pushed shadows away. Should he go back in? But no, it was for the mother and daughter to decide, as he and his mother had decided.

Yes, you must leave Germany, she had said, her face pinched and anxious, her voice low as they sat before the tiled stove. You must leave for the sake of harmony in this house. Your father is a good man. You are also good, but impulsive. He will not change and you will make his position awkward. We love you, Heine, but you must leave.

Heine walked across the lawn, across the path to the forsythia. He threw his cigarette in an arc on to the damp earth to one side and bent to the shrub. There was no scent.

He had left Germany.

He turned and stood, his hands deep in his pockets, his jacket rucked beneath his arms. The dog was still barking in one of the gardens further down the Avenue. He looked up at the sky, it was still blue though the sun was going down slowly. And then he remembered how his own dog had barked like that when his parents had taken him as a child on holiday to one of the North Sea islands. It had barked and barked as his parents waded into the sea in red swimming costumes which reached to their knees. His mother had clasped his father's short sleeve as she tried to keep her balance against the waves but she had brought him down as

13

well. He and his cousin Adam laughed until they ached, and his father and mother had laughed too.

Heine took another cigarette from the packet, tapping it on his nail before lighting it. This time there was no shred of tobacco to become caught between his lips. Again and again he heard that laughter and he knew that his father was a kind man, a precise man, but a man who could not see that the order he craved would only be achieved at great cost. That such order would only be achieved through black boots and brown shirts kicking and pulling and punching until the most common German words would be '*Vorsicht*' and '*Leise sprechen*'.

'Careful and speak softly,' he repeated aloud in English, turning again to the house. Still there was no sign of Helen, but she was here with him, because it was through her that his love for his family had come back to him, for a moment at least.

If they married – but then Heine corrected himself – when they married, for he could not bear to think that they would not, he would take her to Germany because she had made him promise that he would. He touched his leg. He would take her to Hanover, his home town. He would take her to the forest near his home. They would walk beneath the elm, the ash, the beech and the linden and his leg would be less painful there, walking on the softness of mulched, shaded, ground. He would take her to one of the rest houses which were scattered through the forest. They would eat food cooked by the woodsman's wife. Maybe they would see elk, or deer. Yes, he would take his '*Frauchen*', his little wife, to the beauties of his land while they were still untainted.

He drew on the remains of his cigarette, the heat of the enflamed tip warmed his fingers. He would take her to the Kröpcke as he had promised today by the stream and they would sit within that glass-domed café and he would order her coffee topped with whipped cream and shavings of chocolate and watch while she ate enormous cream cakes. He would relax in her pleasure and her youth.

And yes, Helen, he said silently as he ground out his cigarette on the path, yes, I will take you to the land of my birth but I will not take you to Munich where my friends live; where something else is being born which will go far beyond law and order and decency, unless we protest again and again. And I am not there to do my share, because my mother made a decision for me. Or did she, my love? Was I just scared of being hurt again?

The sun was fading now and still Helen had not come for him and so he moved to the low wall which edged the patio. Yes, his father was a kind man and would welcome the wife of his son even though she was English because, after all, she was Aryan. Yes, he was a kind man but was he still proud of his National Socialist membership? Did he still quote Herr Hitler's every utterance as the Austrian toured the country electioneering? Heine was not sure whether he had spoken aloud, shouted aloud.

'*Vorsicht, leise sprechen!*' This time he knew that he spoke aloud but only in a whisper.

Then he heard the back door opening, and turned but did not move, could not move as he saw Helen coming towards him, because he could not tell from her face what their future would be.

CHAPTER 2

Helen waited in the car as Heine walked to the German customs office carrying their passports and the international carnet. They had driven at a leisurely pace for several days through Belgium and it had been the honeymoon they had not yet had time for because Heine had been inundated with work. Only nine months late. She smiled as she ran her hand along the walnut dashboard of the motor car Uncle had lent them for the trip. She had not known life could be like this, that such happiness existed; that there were such nights of love, such days as gentle as a stream in full sun.

The wedding had been quiet. It had not taken place in Hemsham but in London, away from the neighbours. Her mother had not smiled even when Aunt Sarah and Uncle Harry had said how much they liked Heine.

He looks a good steady sort, they had said, with a damn sight more breeding than most and it's something to have a thriving career these days. Helen had seen her mother looking at Heine, her pale eyes hard, but it did not matter now, she had Heine and their future, so full, so good. It swept memories to one side.

Now the birds sang from the branches of the trees, which were too far from her to give shade as she watched Heine talk to the German border officials. He had become quiet as they approached the customs post and she had watched as he gripped the wheel, his face becoming still, and she had heard him say through lips that barely moved, 'So my darling, we enter the land of my countrymen, most of whom seem to have pebbles for eyes and cauliflowers for ears.'

Helen turned now to look at the slender pole which hung between two posts and barred their entry to Germany. What was this country like? What were his parents like?

She heard his uneven footsteps on the road and turned,

watching as he walked back to the car, his limp rather less noticeable than it had been last year. She smiled because he was smiling, the tension gone from his face, his body. The hot June sun was burning in through the windscreen of the car but it did not matter for soon they would be moving again. And soon she would meet the woman who had sent letters greeting her into the family and bone china handled fruit knives as a wedding present which her mother had sniffed at and polished up on her apron. Heine would meet his father again, and last night beneath the light sheet she had said that he should be gentle, for, after all, it was only politics which divided the two men, not years of struggle. She had not understood his silence but he had promised, and said bless you for being nineteen.

. Heine eased himself behind the steering wheel and drove her past verges full of poppies, cornflowers, brown-eyed Susan and Queen Anne's lace and entered villages down avenues bordered by orchards flushed with cherries, apples and pears. They swept through streets of black and white houses with window-boxes of petunias or geraniums. They stopped and ate sausage and bread in the car watching girls with coiled blonde hair throwing corn to geese, before easing themselves from their seats and walking to the village ponds, throwing their crusts to swans and brown ducks.

They stayed overnight in a room with a balcony and the next day they drove alongside fields of tall rye which swayed in the breeze and darkened as the clouds swirled briefly between earth and sun. Over to the east of the road hay was being pitched into wagons drawn first by horses on the lower slopes then oxen as the fields became steeper. Helen wished that she could take photographs as Heine was doing and he promised that on their return he would show her. He pushed strawberries into her mouth and kissed her and she could taste the strawberries on his lips too.

Soon they drove through sugar beet fields where women and children hoed between the rows and Heine said that they would be at his parents' home soon and fell silent. But Helen would not let him sink again and made him tell her of the beet women. He told of how they had come after the war from the East; from Poland and Silesia to work on German farms during the beet harvest, for here they did not starve – not quite. He told of how they had married farmworkers and settled in

17

condemned farmhouses where they were secure as long as they stayed bound to the farmer. He stopped the car and pointed to a plot of land on which a woman and two children worked.

'I used to watch them before I went to Munich, wondering how they could bear it. In the spring they single out the small plants. In the summer they hoe the weeds as they are doing now and in the autumn they pull out the beet.'

Helen peered forward, trying to see past him but there was no room so she opened the door and stood looking. She preferred the fresh air, it made her feel less nauseous but she would not tell him about that, not yet. The wind was brisker now, across the flatter lands. Heine turned off the engine and he too came and stood and looked.

'I took many photographs, especially of the children. They start work at the age of six and here our winters come early and are not like English ones. I would see them tossing the beets into the carts in the snow and ice and hear their coughs. I exhibited the photographs in Munich but what can be done? It is, and was, work in a time of no work. It is food in a time of no food.' He looked over to a clump of cottages in the distance. 'I took photographs inside too, of the one large stew pot in the centre of the table, the spoons which were dug in all at once by thin armed, thin faced people.'

He turned again to the beet fields. 'I felt so fortunate that I was not a beet picker, that I had the time and energy to think; something which is denied to these people. But now I wonder.'

Helen grasped his arm. 'Come along, my love, the sun is out, this is our honeymoon. Or would you perhaps like us to move back here; pull beet, hoe, plant?' She shook him and smiled, willing him to laugh and he did, and he kissed her and said against her mouth that no, no one in his family would ever have to hoe or pull beet and that while she was with him she kept the shadows from him.

The village where his family lived was to the west of Hanover and his mother met them at the door, holding Heine to her, her blonde-white hair folded into a pleat, her face buried in his shoulder.

'Mutti,' he said. 'Oh Mutti.'

Helen knew then just how much Heine loved his mother because he cried.

She turned and looked over the village, at the church, the

18

barns, the tall poplars, the houses, the window-boxes and wondered what a mother's soft arms were like. She looked to either side of Heine's tall house and saw the lime trees, those same trees that Heine had talked about throughout the winter and as spring approached.

She looked up at the long eaves which he said dripped heavy thawed snow in the spring and knew that when they entered the house they would go into the sitting-room and sit on red brocade settees with carved wooden arms, and that there would be a portrait of his grandfather above the sideboard. She knew too that the room would be dark because of blinds drawn halfway down the window to protect the red carpet from the sun. And it was just as she imagined it would be when they followed his mother into the room from the hall except for the muslin curtains which she had forgotten would be hung in the summer.

That night they slept in the room which had always been Heine's. The bed was large and there was a shelf full of lead soldiers.

'Painted by me,' Heine said, 'when I was nine.'

'So clever, my love,' she murmured against his neck. The moonlight was bright in the room and she could see the stove clearly but not the colours of the tiles. The brass knobs of its doors gleamed as she listened to him telling her of the *Zuckertüte* he had carried to school on his first day and she imagined the rolled cone of cardboard filled with sweets and laughed when he said it had not lasted much more than an hour. 'Pig;' she said and laughed again when he told her how he and his cousin Adam had hunted for acorns to feed the pig which was growing larger and larger down in the orchard at the edge of the village.

He did not talk of his father who was away until tomorrow night but of the forest he wanted to take her to and then he kissed her, then again more strongly, and she felt passion rise in her until it matched his because she no longer heard her mother's words. You are disgusting.

The moon was behind cloud while Heine slept and she lay full and relaxed, with the feel of him still on her skin. She stretched, and knew that Heine had been right to marry according to old German country customs. She had laughed when he had insisted that a rising moon promises good fortune while a moon on the wane drains it from you. How Wednesday and Friday were reserved for widows, and she had said that Saturday had been in her mind anyway.

So they had married when the moon was rising and she knew without doubt now that good fortune was to be theirs; her pregnancy had been confirmed before they left England. But it was news which was hers alone for she had waited to tell Heine until they arrived. He would hear in his beloved forest tomorrow.

At breakfast his mother smiled at Helen and spoke in slow but clear English.

Ilse, who helped in the house, brought a jug of coffee, smiling and greeting Heine.

He smiled at her. 'How is Hans?'

'Very well, Herr Weber,' Ilse replied, placing the coffee jug before Frau Weber. 'He keeps the garden as nicely as ever, I think. Still a few weeds but not too many.'

They all laughed.

'You slept with comfort?' his mother asked as Ilse left the room. She poured coffee into large cups and held her hand to Heine's face as he stopped to kiss her.

Helen answered. 'Oh yes, thank you. The bed was fine and we didn't wake until we heard the cart go down the lane. It is very quiet here.'

There was cream for the coffee and Helen poured it from the white jug, watching it sink then swirl as she stirred. The coffee was hot and strong and the steam dampened her face as she drank.

Frau Weber turned to Heine. 'My dear, your father rang late last night. He will not be back now until tomorrow. He is sorry, so sorry, but he has a meeting.' She paused and Helen watched her place her hand over her son's as he stretched back in his chair which was at her right hand, opposite Helen. Her full sleeves were gathered at the wrist and a Zircon brooch was fastened at her throat. 'Just a meeting, you understand, but one he cannot miss, the election is too close, you see.' She paused as Heine nodded but did not speak and then she smiled at Helen.

'And now you still take your beautiful young wife to show her our forests, our woods?'

Heine looked at his mother. 'No, Mutti, not now. We will go

tomorrow. Today perhaps we shall go by train to Hanover. As you say, the day for casting votes is close and maybe my English wife should see how we in Germany conduct our elections, while we still have them?'

'Heine.' Helen's voice was loud, for she could see the darkening of his mother's eyes, the tension in her full face. He was so like his mother; the same lips, the same blue eyes, blond hair, proud face. The same lines around the eyes and mouth.

'Heine,' her voice was softer now. 'Yes, I should love to go to Hanover, to drink coffee topped with cream as you promised a year ago, do you remember?' She remembered the parapet, the sticks racing on the current and from his softening face she knew that he did too. Perhaps her news should not wait until the forest, it was needed today to lift the darkness which was easing into his face.

The train journey took little time and as they rattled and jolted he pointed to the forest in the far distance through a window which was dust spattered. She could not see the trees, just a darkening of the horizon but there was such longing in his face.

'Why don't we go there today?' Helen urged. 'You want to go so much.'

'No, I will need the forest on the day that I meet my father again. It gives me strength, I think.'

Helen grasped his arm. 'I'll be with you, my darling.'

'I know, and for that I thank God. You are my lightness, a breeze that sweeps the dark shadows away.' Suddenly he laughed, a loud long laugh and the old man who sat in the carriage with them lifted his head from the paper but could not follow their conversation for it was in English.

'I think perhaps I get, how you say, carried away. Dark shadow is altogether too poetical, my love. Let us just say that I look forward to seeing my young wife drinking her first glass of coffee at the Konditorei.'

Helen laughed now, poking his arm. 'Just because you want to see me with a white moustache, you bully.'

Hanover was busy, but not as busy as London and there were no trolley buses, just trams and cars which, it seemed to Helen, barely missed one another or the pedestrians, especially this nervous English girl. They crossed the Ernst-August-Platz and then the Georgstrasse and Helen pulled at Heine to make

21

him hurry because of the noise and speed of the traffic. She could not adjust to looking for cars coming towards them on the right-hand side of the road.

There was no free table at the glass-domed Kröpcke but Heine spoke to the Manager who smiled and shook his hand, because, Heine told her, Herr Busch knew that in the past he had brought many beautiful young women here and had greatly increased the profits of the Kröpcke. They all laughed and the Manager's eyes darted about the room until he saw a movement to their left. He signalled to a waiter, and bowed, and they were ushered to a table whose occupants were leaving.

It was so light beneath the glass dome – for that is all that the building was, just one large glass dome – and Helen thought that her father would have loved it for his vegetables. As she smoothed the napkin on her lap she noticed the women at the surrounding tables; so groomed, so immaculate, smoking cigarettes in ivory and jade holders through pursed red lips. Their perfume thickened the air. Helen felt young and gauche until she saw Heine watching her and heard his words.

'You will always be more beautiful than a hundred of these women put together.'

How did he know what she was thinking, how did he always know? But she was glad that he did. The waiter brought coffee heaped high with whipped cream and topped with shavings of chocolate and Helen laughed, using her spoon to scoop some into her mouth.

'But no, Frau Weber, with the mouth. It must be with the mouth.' Heine's smile was broad.

'You are a cruel man, Herr Weber,' she replied but she did lift the glass by its silver-plated handle and drink, feeling first the cool cream and then the hot coffee. She knew that she had a white moustache because Heine laughed and leaned across, wiping it with his napkin as he told her of his first such coffee, when he was young and in a sailor suit. Young and clean to begin with, young and dirty when he was finished. His parents had laughed too and this time his face did not tense as he spoke of them. They ate cakes which squeezed cream but left some because they were too large.

Later they walked past shops which were smart and rich and in the Post Office she dampened a stamp with a small sponge

22

before writing a card to her mother: 'Having a wonderful time, Love Heine and Helen.'

She did not put, 'Wish you were here'. They walked on towards the Markthalle, a large building with yet another glass roof where it was also light and so full of noise that it seemed to ring around inside her head.

Heine bought her an orange from a stall which had citrus fruits piled high in precise displays. Vegetables were scrubbed and placed in neat rows unlike any she had seen in England. Sausages were hung above the delicatessen counter and Heine told her of the smoking room in the attic of his mother's home and the sausages which she made herself.

'She will take you up there tomorrow to cut some sausage for the picnic before we go to the forest.'

There were lobsters, and shiny black smoked eels which made Helen turn away. There were *Kieler Sprotten* packed as tightly as she and Heine were in the flowing and ebbing crowd.

'My favourite,' Heine said. 'Smoked spratts to you, my non-German-speaking wife.'

Helen stopped and pulled him round. 'But you won't let me learn your language,' she protested.

'I know.' His face was tense again and she wished she had not spoken. 'I do not wish you to become German in any way.'

They walked again, out of the market to a café with a small orchestra playing where Heine ordered *Fleischsalat*, which Helen discovered was meat salad. She was tired now but he was smiling again. It was early afternoon and soon she would tell him of his child; but not here, it should be when they were alone. Heine drank beer with his meal; too much, she thought, as she asked for more coffee. People sat at other tables talking, laughing; the men with napkins tucked into their collars and beer foam around their mouths. Fans whirred lazily above the room, lifting the hair gently on an old man's head. He patted it with a blue-veined age-spotted hand.

As she stirred her coffee discordant sounds stabbed at her thoughts, intruding into the background music, and through the window Helen saw a van with posters on its sides. She heard a metallic voice, distorted by speakers, shouting harshly, but could not understand the words. It moved slowly down the street before pulling in further along into a small square. And now she looked up, shaken, as Heine, his lips drawn tight, suddenly shoved his chair back, scraping it across the tiles. He threw money on the table and pulled her up.

'Let's go and hear too, shall we? Perhaps you should listen to some German.' It was not a question but a statement and his voice was harsh and rapid, as discordant as the metallic voice had been. He stared at her but did not see her.

Helen held back, reaching for her handbag on the table. People were looking and now the fan disturbed her own hair.

'Whatever's wrong, Heine?' she asked, but quietly because they had already created too much fuss.

'For God's sake, just come on.' He grasped her hand, knocking the table as he brushed past the waiter, and now she followed because silence had fallen in the café.

He did not let go of her as he rushed along the street towards the crowd that was gathering around the parked van. He did not let go even when they were standing amongst the crowd which stood still and listened as the man with short hair spoke. But her hand hurt because he was holding it so tightly and he did not hear when she asked him to be gentle. She could smell the beer as he breathed hard.

'What is the matter, Heine, for heaven's sake?'

He looked at her then but his eyes were not seeing her.

'Nazis are the matter.' His voice was low and cold.

'Heine, you promised. Your mother. Our honeymoon. You must not cause trouble.' Helen clutched at his sleeve but only with one hand for he still held on to the other.

No, I must not cause trouble, Heine thought. No, none of us must cause trouble, or we get hurt. Yes, we get very badly hurt. He could hear Helen, he could feel her hand and he must not let go, no. He must never let go because she was sanity in this world which was around him again and which was reaching out, engulfing him, suffocating him.

He started to return through the crowd, turning from the man who spoke of a Germany that had been betrayed in 1918 from within. Who spoke of the armistice which meant that the war was not at an end for Germany. Heine pulled Helen along too but there were more people now. He pushed, twisted and turned, always moving towards the thinning edge that he knew was there. He could still hear the voice, even though he did not want to.

'Germany will regain its lost territories. Herr Hitler will end

24

unemployment, end despair. End the contamination of the Aryan race by the *Juden* traitors. You voted for us in 1930, you gave us a National Socialist landslide in the Reichstag elections. Vote for us again so that we can restore law and order. Restore economic stability. Cleanse our nation.'

But they were through now, there was room to breathe, there was light, and Heine moved quickly, still holding Helen's hand until he could no longer hear the man who told people what they wanted to hear. Yes, that was the danger; jobs, stability, pride – but at what cost? Dear God, surely they would not gain more power? Surely to God, that could not happen?

Heine turned now and looked at the growing crowd standing silently around the speaker.

'It's all the other things,' he shouted at Helen, holding her shoulders now. 'It's all the other things that are written, all the brown-shirted thugs who kick and push and kill. It's that maniac Hitler. If they vote for him in July then it is the beginning of the end. There will be no more freedom, no more Germany, just brutality.'

His breath was full of beer and Helen shouted back.

'You're drunk. You're drunk. Why can't you stop being so serious? We love one another, think of that. This is all just politics. Only politics.' Fear stirred deep inside her because she was outside his life when he was like this. She could not reach him. She was alone.

There was silence then between them until Heine held her to him. 'I'm not drunk, Helen. But you are right. I should think of love more often. You are also right that this is just politics. Please God, that it stays just that.'

They walked on back to the station now, with the sun lower and the breeze cool and Helen did not want to tell him of the baby, not today, not like this. Perhaps tomorrow.

Heine held Helen's arm, feeling her warmth, her flesh beneath the blouse, and loved her. With her he could learn to laugh as he had once done and was beginning to do again. And after all, she was right, it was just politics and he was living in England now. He wouldn't think of Munich. Perhaps, after all, it had not really been as he remembered it, perhaps there had not been any violence, perhaps the *Kampfzeit*, the Nazis' time of

25

struggle, had been just a nightmare he had imagined but his leg ached as they hurried for the train.

The next morning Helen followed Frau Weber up steep stairs to the attic which ran the width of the large house. The windows at either end let in the light from the fine June day and as they entered Helen breathed in the smell of stored fruit from the orchard which she could see when she peered through the window. The village looked so small, the trees even smaller and she could hear no noise.

'Through that small door is the linen cupboard,' Frau Weber said, smoothing her hands down her apron. 'It is there that we keep the winter quilts and over there in that corner is our store for all that we need each year for Christmas. Perhaps you can smell the candles. They are special; they are honey wax.'

Helen smelt them as she approached the corner; their scent hung rich on the air.

'One day perhaps you can come back to our land for Christmas. I would like that. This . . .' Frau Weber paused. 'This difficulty between father and son cannot go on. Their squabble will die as the politics die. It is just a silliness between them.' Helen stopped, she could not go where the eaves sloped. It was too dark, like her mother's cupboard. She turned, holding on to the post, feeling its roughness, wanting cool air.

'Yes, it will pass. You're right, I'm sure it will pass,' she said, breathing deeply, watching as the older woman took down a small muslin bag which hung from a hook secured to a beam.

'These apple slices will make a cinnamon tart for you tonight. It is Heine's favourite, but then you will know that, my dear Helen.'

Helen eased herself over to the window; it was light here, so light. The window ledge was warm, the grained wood worn smooth. She rubbed her hands along it, pushing the darkness away. A butterfly was beating its wings against the glass and she opened the window, cupping her hand around it, feeling it fluttering against her skin. She opened her hands and threw it out into the windless air, watching as it flew its jagged path to safety.

'Come now, my child. I will take you to the smoke room and then we shall cut some sausage for your picnic. I am glad that you go to the woods. It is good for his soul.'

Helen shut the window, still looking at the butterfly until it disappeared against the green and brown of the lime trees; only then did she turn and follow her mother-in-law.

She was glad that today they would be far from other people.

They drove the motor car to the forest and walked down clearly marked paths. Heine carried the rucksack with two folding canvas chairs strapped to it but Helen knew that she would lie on the ground when they stopped and look up at the sky through the branches of the chestnut, beech, elm, lime and ash. They passed beech trees which had been felled in November and left to bleach. She climbed over a newly hewn pine and her shoes and stockings became coated with sawdust which brushed off easily for it was so dry, and the trees' scent, so fresh and clean, clung to her hands and clothes. She lifted them to her face and breathed in deeply.

Heine laughed and kissed her and his happiness loosened his face. He showed her where the plantations of spruce were being grown for Christmas trees and she hoped that one day they would come for Christmas. But she said nothing because she did not want to draw any shade close to him today.

He reached into the rucksack and pulled out two apples, tossing one to her. She bit into the crisp flesh and juice ran down her chin. He reached forward and wiped it with his finger before taking her hand and walking on again, limping less on the soft ground.

'The Germans care deeply for their forests,' he told her. 'In ancient times we stripped our land almost bare but the wind punished us and blew away soil and seed, as is now happening in the middle of America. We learned that we must restore our forests to coax the wind to drop its rain. The forests then held back the water so that it did not rush away and so now the trees have a special place in German hearts.'

'Especially in yours, my love,' she said as she took another bite, watching his face as he looked at the sawn logs neatly stacked in piles to their right.

'Yes, I have always loved the forest. It is cool, and no matter how many people there are, it is quiet. I love the mythology also. Did you know, my English Helen, that the beech is Wotan's tree and the oak belongs to the god of thunder? Then there is the raven who has the task of flying through the trees

27

warning both man and beast that the gods are about to ride past and they must flee to their homes and not intrude on holy secrets.'

'And you of course have seen this raven?' Helen laughed.

'Indeed, everyone has seen the raven, and heard it too. It comes in the form of a storm, with wind blowing and the skies exploding in thunder and lightning. And who stays out to see the gods? No one.' Heine had lowered his voice and now swung round. 'Do you?'

His arms were round her, and he blew into her neck, dug his fingers into her ribs until she pleaded for mercy. They ate their picnic beneath the trees, not at one of the rest-houses, and then Helen lay on the ground, her green skirt and shirt dusty and spiked with pine needles, but she did not care and neither did Heine, for he lay with her. They had not used the canvas chairs.

He stroked her hair, pulling at the curls which sprang back as they had been.

'I love your dark, dark hair, your dark, dark eyes, your lips, so full, your skin so smooth,' he breathed into her neck.

'And I love your blond hair, your eyes, your mouth,' she whispered, looking up at the sky through the conifer branches. The raven was far away today, she thought. Far far away.

'I am having our baby,' she said into his hair. 'Will he have blond hair and dark eyes, I wonder?'

Heine made no movement. She could not even feel his breath on her neck and then he gripped her tightly.

'I should have known. How stupid of me, my precious darling. I should have known.' He sat up then, looking down at her, his eyes taking in the darkness beneath her eyes, the thickening waist. And then he held her so that she should not see his face, because how could this child, this girl he had married, have a child? It was a miracle somehow, a joy, an anxiety. Would she be all right? Was she strong enough?

He gripped her tightly, seeing the trees and the shadows that played beneath their branches. He had never thought in terms of a child. Just in terms of Helen. How could he bear to share her?

She turned to him then. 'I love you so much.' She looked into his eyes and saw pleasure, but something else as well. She kissed his lids, his cheeks, his lips. 'Are you pleased my love?'

28

She waited as he turned on to his back, throwing his arm over his eyes. 'It's just that it's such a surprise. And of course I'm pleased.' He paused then turned and kissed her again with his eyes shut.

Later they walked slowly back to the motor car. Helen loved the feel of his arm around her. Would it be a boy or a girl, she wondered, able now to think of the baby, now that she had told Heine, now that it was a shared joy. They passed a rest-house and flaxen-haired children were running round the hewn tables and chairs: their parents were drinking beer and watching. Helen turned to Heine who was also watching.

'In December, my love, we shall know our child. We shall hold it and know it,' she said and he bent down and kissed her.

Heine's father kissed her on both cheeks and shook his son's hand, holding his arm, squeezing it. They sat down at the heavy oak table in the dining-room. It was a dark panelled room which seemed to suck away the light from the yellowed shaded lamps set above the table and on the walls. They ate soup made from locally grown asparagus, though not from their own garden, Herr Weber told Helen. He asked if they had seen the *Jagdtrophäen* in the rest-houses. The antlers of the buck and the elk, Heine explained when she turned to him, puzzled.

Herr Weber told of the time he had been *Jagdkönig*, the Hunt King of the day, but that now he had little time, and at this point Frau Weber broke in.

'Heine has some excellent news, Wilhelm. There is to be a grandchild in December.'

Herr Weber placed his spoon back in the bowl and pulled down the serviette from his neck. 'My dear son, this is marvellous news. Quite marvellous. We shall drink brandy after the meal but not the little mother, I think.' He smiled at Helen and his face was gentle and kind and she saw a look of Heine in him. Flowers filled a large blue vase on the sideboard behind him.

They ate veal and there was too much for Helen so she sat back and listened to the talk between the father and the mother which she could not understand because it was in German. She looked at Heine who was watching her and she smiled and mouthed, 'I love you. I love you.'

And Heine knew that she did and smiled as he drank the dry

cool wine, feeling the crystal against his lips, remembering the clear ringing sound the glass had made when he had licked his finger as a child and run it round the edge. In that moment his anxiety faded and all that remained was joy, for she had opened up his past to him through her love and would continue to do so. It was a love which would expand to include the child rather than dividing itself into two.

The cinnamon tart was good, very good and Helen knew she must learn how to make it.

Herr Weber had been speaking to his wife and now he turned to Helen but spoke in German until he corrected himself. His wine glass was empty and he reached for the bottle as he began again, this time in careful English. He also refilled Heine's glass.

'I was saying before I so rudely forgot your language, my dear, that it is important for an English person to appreciate that Herr Hitler is very concerned with the legality of his actions because, of course, we Germans are a very correct race. I am a solicitor after all. His rise to power will only come about through the due process of law. By the vote. Look at the landslide in 1930.'

Helen looked at Heine. He was holding his glass to the light, turning it round and round in his fingers. She drank some of her own wine.

'I know nothing of politics, Herr Weber,' she replied.

'Indeed, my dear. Helen is too tired to think of such things.' Frau Weber intervened. 'Will you have a little more of the cinnamon tart, my dear? You are eating for two, I think you say in England.'

Heine smiled at Helen and hoped that his father would not now turn to him but he did.

'Heine, you and I have had our differences but even so you must now see that it was through pursuing the legal line that Hitler won over one hundred seats in the Reichstag.' His speech was eager, his face concerned. 'And you must see that he offers us what we need. Law and order, progress, stability. July is going to be a month of greatest importance for us. We expect over thirty-five per cent of the vote, my son. Is that not saying something to you? The people want it, Heine. Six million unemployed, a world slump. Strength is what we need.'

30

'Yes, Father,' Heine said for he had promised his wife, his mother.

'A strong man who is mindful of legality.' Herr Weber paused, sitting up straighter, his hand reaching out towards Heine.

'Yes, Father,' Heine said but his thoughts replied that until now there was no punishment without law. Will it be the same when your leader is in power? Will there even need to be a crime? Won't there just be punishment? I can remember Munich too well and I think you do too. That is why you are speaking to me like this. Trying to make sense of it too. I hope so.

'You see, dear boy, there is anarchy on our streets. We need strength to combat the unions, the dissidents. Our young people are leaving as you have done. We will become a land of old people, defenceless against our enemies both inside and out.'

'Yes, Father.' But silently he groaned. Don't you know why I left? And can't you see, can't you read? What about the solution Hitler propagates for racial purity? What about *Lebensraum*; living space? What about another war? What about Munich? What about the exhibition which was defiled by your brownshirts because my brilliant photographer friend is a *Jude*, a Jew? What about my arm which is still stiff from the beating they gave me because I interfered?

What about the socialist meeting I attended in Munich? what about the iron bar wielded oh so legally by your party members? It broke my leg in three places, Father. How can you excuse that? It was a real question which Heine asked in his mind. One that he had asked his father in January 1930 which was when his mother had sent him from Germany.

His father's kind, honest face had been confused, had been desperate because he had not been able to excuse what had happened, but neither could he believe that it was anything more than an aberration. He would not listen when Heine told him it was the norm.

Heine leaned over to his father now and covered his hand with his own. 'I love you, Father. Be careful. Be very, very careful.' He rose. 'Helen, you look tired, my darling. I'll take you up to bed now.'

He turned to his mother and father. 'Please excuse me from

31

the brandy. I also am tired and I have my family to think of now.' He smiled at them, at Helen, at his child.

Helen held him close and at last he slept, but she could not for he had told her about Munich and now at last she understood the reality of politics. She did not want to though. Oh God, no, she did not want to, because she was nineteen and in love and pregnant. She wanted her husband for herself, she wanted the peace of their lives to go on. She wanted the photographs they took, the child they had, the walks, the laughter to be everything. She held him tighter still. How much of his life would it take?

CHAPTER 3

In England in August 1932 Heine received a letter from one of his Munich friends telling him that German voters had handed Hitler's brownshirts an election victory on 31 July and the Nazis now formed the biggest party.

'But he doesn't have a majority?' Helen asked because she had been listening to Heine since they had returned to England and now understood the political situation.

He put down the letter on the kitchen table. 'No, at least he does not have that.'

'So, there is still hope,' she insisted, shaking his hand, leaning over and stroking his face. 'Come on, Heine, you must be brave, you must go on. We must go on.' Because she had decided that whatever battles had to be fought they would fight them together. She paused. 'Listen, you were telling me about the changing mood of photography. If you want me to be able to help with the work, we must concentrate.'

She rose from the table and moved round to him, putting her arm along his shoulder. 'This baby is getting bigger and bigger. He won't wait for something that might never happen. And it might never happen, you know. Hitler can still be defeated – contained. If he's as bad as you say the German people won't let him take power.' She held his head against her. 'Now, my love, what were you saying about imagery.'

She felt his hand on her swelling abdomen and then his voice, muffled as he spoke into her body. 'I try for a greater range of imagery. I like strong direct photographs with the emphasis on design instead of soft focus and tranquil scenes. Now is a time for realism.' He sat up straight now and used his hands to express his ideas and Helen felt relief ease into her. She had caught his interest, kept him away from the shadows for now.

He told her that he had been taught to use an overall soft focus to provide atmosphere, to use a sombre tone for mood landscapes, to use soft and subtle nuances of light and shade, but in Munich he had become interested in the 'New Objectivity' which he thought had grown out of the harsh reality of the war. He told her that Martin Weiss, his Jewish friend whose photographs had been defiled, considered it wrong to allow the ego of the photographer to come between the camera and subject and, though others thought that this technique was too cold he did not.

'I would want a picture to say something about myself, my views, my feelings, the feelings of others involved,' Helen said.

'Well, that is another style and a successful one. Perhaps it is as well that we have different opinions,' he said.

They walked to the darkroom which had originally been the dining-room. 'We should have another lesson with the Leica. I have no appointments scheduled for this afternoon so we shall do it then, but now, my darling, let us go through again the procedures of developing and printing.'

He stood at the door as he waited for her to repeat all that she had learned throughout the last two weeks.

'You must understand the principles, you must have knowledge,' he told her as she protested.

And so she explained how black and white films contain light-sensitive crystals which darken after exposure, and how development is required to make the image visible.

'The longer the exposure the greater darkening of the crystals,' she added. 'Development is required to make the image permanent and visible.'

'Good girl.' Heine moved into the darkroom showing her the wet and dry areas, the enlarger, the processing equipment, the dryer, pausing at the print finishing area. There was still some work left to do on the photographs he had taken last night at the introduction of the trial floodlighting of some London buildings. He told her how he had concentrated on the traffic chaos because it was important to see a situation from an unusual angle.

'You can help me,' he said, setting the working surface at thirty degrees. 'I want to get them delivered to the magazine office at lunchtime, then we can spend the afternoon in the park with the camera.'

34

'Remember Mother is coming to stay for the weekend. She will be arriving tonight.' Helen settled herself on to the stool, peering at the photograph of black cars and angry drivers. She reached for the trimmer from beneath the bench, confident, sure, eager to begin work, work that she could share with him. She eased her back which ached more each day as her child grew within her.

'My love, how could I forget that your mother comes?' Heine shook his head but his smile was visible in the dim red light of the room. 'Every time I go into the spare room I am reminded of her.'

Helen laughed and had to put the photograph to one side. 'I know, she has certainly staked her claim, but how could I say anything?'

She pictured the dressing table with her mother's brushes, her photographs, her pots for hairnets and pins. She had stayed on their return from Germany after Helen had written to ask her, saying she was to become a grandmother and they would like to see her. It had seemed impossible to do anything else. Her mother had turned the spare room into a replica of her own bedroom, saying as she did so that it was as well to be comfortable since she would be spending so much time here, especially now there was a grandchild on the way. She had been brisk but not unkind and Helen had remembered Frau Weber's soft arms and wondered if there would be a future after all for mother and daughter.

Christoph was born on 1 December and Heine looked down at his son and marvelled at the perfect fingernails, the perfect feet and the softness of his skin, the lightness of his hair, while Helen looked at her husband and saw love in his eyes for his son and wondered if her father's eyes had been the same.

When Christoph was nearly two months old, on 30 January, Hitler became Chancellor of Germany, and while Helen held the baby, stroking skin she could hardly feel, kissing hair which was gossamer fine, she reminded Heine that all was not bad in the world. Hadn't the British Prime Minister ordered a review of the Government's policies on unemployment after the marches and riots? Hadn't Roosevelt won the United States elections with a landslide and promised a New Deal? Hadn't two of his photographs been taken by an American magazine? And after all, in Germany it might all pass.

'And look,' she said, 'Christoph is smiling, I'm sure he's smiling. Here, hold him and see for yourself.' She pushed the baby towards Heine who took him and looked but did not seem to see, and Helen touched the fine crocheted shawl, feeling its pattern, its warmth. 'I'm sure he's smiling,' she said again, touching her husband's hand, feeling him at last lift hers and put it to his lips, but despair still remained in his eyes and Helen knew that she was still outside his pain.

When Christoph was nearly four months old the Enabling Act was passed in Germany allowing Hitler, rather than the President, to rule by decree.

'It sets him above the law, you see,' Heine said, his voice flat, his eyes dark, and Helen wondered what Herr Weber must be feeling but Heine would not write to him; he would only pace the flat, leaving work unfinished so that Helen felt she must work until midnight in the darkroom to complete his assignments for him after she had put Christoph to bed.

When Christoph was nearly six months old books were burned in the streets of Germany, unions were harassed and in London the blossom bloomed and Helen printed and developed films and delivered them because Heine did not have time. He was too busy writing letters to Munich and meeting friends in dark pubs.

When Christoph was seven months old he reached forward and pulled Helen towards him and laughed but Heine did not notice because opposition parties had been ousted from the Reichstag in June and a month later Hitler announced plans to sterilise imperfect Germans. Helen took a Leica and carried out two of Heine's assignments and the results were as good. And so, increasingly, she took over his workload too and did not mind because she had told herself that she would join the battle if that would help this man she loved so much.

In August her mother came to stay and Helen had to take her out to photograph damage caused by the gales which had hit England, and that night, when the wind blew again and the thunder roared and her mother was asleep, she crooned to Christoph and told him of the raven who was warning them to stay in in case they saw the gods go by. She looked up and smiled at Heine when he came home wet and cold.

'Did you see the gods going about their holy business, my

darling?' she whispered, lifting her face for his kiss. Knowing that for her he was the god.

He laughed. 'Only one of your English coppers getting very wet as he paced his beat.'

Helen made him tea and he sat by the gas fire which plopped and spluttered, cupping the drink in his hand.

'Your mother is asleep?'

'My mother would sleep through a deluge of ravens,' she said softly. 'Christoph has not woken since nine and I have finished trimming the hotel photograph. Did you have a good meeting?' Helen sat down on the worn carpet in front of the fire. The heat was comforting. She clutched her knees, seeing the dust lying on the mantelpiece, on the hearth.

'Yes, we are trying to find firms that will sponsor those that are going to have to leave Germany if it goes on and on. So far in America and to some extent here we have been fortunate. But there is a great deal to do and unemployment is a problem in both countries. I think the time we have and the dissidents have and the Jews have, is short.'

He put his mug down on the table and leaned back, his hands clasped behind his head.

'Oh God, it's the studio portrait tomorrow, Helen. I know I said I would do it but I can't. I have to be at the Embassy by ten. Darling, can you?'

Helen nodded, laying her head on her knees. Yes, she would do it, as she did so many others. She would have to tell her mother that Heine was out on another assignment again. It seemed easier to lie than to try and make her understand that some things were more important than making a profit. And they were, in this case they were, because people were being saved and Heine's eyes were no longer dark, his steps were no longer heavy. At last, he had told her in the spring, he felt as though he was doing something again, actually helping people threatened by Hitler's regime.

In September one of his Munich friends arrived at their flat with no money and few clothes but many bruises and cuts because storm troopers armed with revolvers and piping were roaming the German streets looking for Jews and Communists and liberals. He told them of a concentration camp which had been opened for these 'dissidents'.

'It is at Dachau,' he said.

Helen made up the bed for Isaac in the spare room and listened to his story and cried. That evening they ate a stew which she had padded out with vegetables and she told them that Christoph had said 'dada' and that Heine really did need to make sure he arrived at the art gallery promptly at ten tomorrow because they were leaving up the paintings until he arrived. They particularly wanted him because he had produced such fine work for the catalogue last year. She said nothing when he explained that he had other more important things to do; just nodded and smiled at Isaac and handed him more rice. She had overcooked it and it clung to the spoon in a lump; so white against the old stained table spoon.

That night in bed she told Heine that he must do tomorrow's assignment because she could not, she was already booked to cover the meeting at Whitechapel. Her voice was calm but high as she told him that they would have to earn more money if the bills were to be paid and there was Isaac to feed now. He became angry and told her that she was being trivial; there was a vast problem, or was she too much of a child to see? His voice was tight but low, because they were not alone in their flat, were they?

Headlights flashed across the ceiling and walls from the passing traffic and Helen watched as the brass picture frame over by the door glinted, caught by the lights of one car and then another.

Her voice remained calm as she answered but the effort made her hands clench. She breathed slowly.

'Is it childish to deal in reality?' she said. 'If we are to help your friends we need to work to pay for it or our child will suffer. You prefer reality. You told me.' She pointed to the glinting frame which held the photograph he had taken of London Bridge. 'You have used no soft focus there, Heine. There is no place for it in our lives at this moment. We need to eat, and in order to do that we need to work. We both need to work. You have responsibility to your family as well as your friends.'

That night she did not sleep but lay on her side, tense with anger and disappointment, aware that he was not asleep either; but she could not touch him, she could not bridge the distance between them because suddenly she was tired. So tired and the sun of their German honeymoon seemed too far away.

That morning they dressed without speaking and neither looked at the other's nakedness. Her tiredness hung heavily on her. In the kitchen she poured his tea, watching the tea leaves fill the strainer. Still they did not speak. She fed soldiers to Christoph, then watched as Heine went to the studio and returned with his cameras.

He stood in the doorway, leaning against the doorpost, his eyes watching Christoph as he dropped his toast on the floor and smeared butter all over his face. His shrieks and banging were the only noise between them.

Helen leaned back against the sink. It was cool across her back. She looked at the brown lino which was worn in the far corner, the strands of hemp showing through.

Heine spoke. 'You are right, my little wife. I'm sorry.' He blew her a kiss and she watched him as he left and thought, I am not a little wife, I am an adult.

In December 1934 Christoph was two. In 1935 conscription came into being in Germany, Hitler took possession of the Saar, and Helen's house became even more full of frightened, thin young men. Her mother no longer came to stay because it was not proper amongst so many foreigners and there never seemed to be the time to try and make her understand how necessary it was. How it would not last for ever because Hitler would fall. Surely he would fall?

But her mother should have known it was necessary, Heine told Helen. There wasn't time to make him understand that the distance between mother and daughter was still too wide to discuss such things.

There were camp beds in the sitting-room and the spare room and others were folded up ready for use if necessary in the studio. Heine was eager and young, his limp hardly noticeable. He talked until the early hours with the refugees until they left to go to jobs and countries Heine and his friends had organised. But always new ones came, occasionally bringing wives, sisters, children, and the sunshine of their honeymoon seemed never to have existed.

The refugees were 'placed' but sometimes it was difficult as the flood of those escaping thē swastikas and black boots increased and so some stayed on. Each night when she returned from carrying out commissions and Christoph was in bed, they talked over wine and sometimes remembered to speak in English until Helen left to work again or sleep, but she never slept soundly now and her dreams were bleak.

Full of the horrors she had listened to, steeped in loneliness, one night she dreamed of a lichen-covered bridge and hands which held her safe and she woke up crying.

At night Heine crept in beside her and sometimes he would hold her but he was tired, so tired, and so was she. Christoph was passed from one to another and did not know that his father was different to all these uncles.

At the beginning of May in 1935 they had only four staying and on Silver Jubilee Day she helped the neighbours set out trestle tables in the street while red, white and blue bunting hung across the road, and she asked Heine who was sitting at his desk to carry down some cakes and to come and join her and watch his son enjoy himself.

'I am so busy, my darling. I have letters to write.'

He had said that too often and Helen felt the anger come. It crept from every pore of her skin and she knew now that it had been there for months and months but it had not formed into words in her head until now. But why this moment? She did not know, except that she was English and this was an English celebration and she asked nothing of him but that he should join her, as she had for so long joined him. She turned to the window, where they were on a level with the bunting. She watched Mr Frazer who lived above the tobacco shop hauling on a line festooned with flags which stretched from his flat window to Mrs Briggs who lived opposite. Heine had never met them, he did not even know their names.

All she asked was a little of his time for the world which she and their son lived in and he would not give her even that. There were so many other people in their lives, so much that needed doing; but there should be time for happiness as there once was. She smoothed the curtain between her fingers, rubbing up and down, up and down. Then she turned, looking at Hans, Georg, Hermann, Ernst who had been with them for two months.

'You will all come to see how we in England celebrate, and you, Heine, you will come too.' And her voice was firm. She walked to the desk and covered the notepaper that he had pulled towards him. 'You will come because you are part of

40

England now. You will come because your English-German son needs you there.' The paper was cold and dead, the room was quiet.

Heine looked at her, his eyes puzzled, surprised.

'You will come because you are my husband and I need you there.' Her voice was calm but the anger sounded in her own ears and she wondered when the child inside her had gone and this woman had taken her place.

Helen turned then, walked past Hans standing awkwardly by the door, his face turned from her in embarrassment. She stooped and picked Christoph from his playpen, sitting him on her hip. She did not look back but walked from the door to the studio where she picked up her Leica, for she never went anywhere without it now.

'You will come,' she said as she walked down the stairs feeling so much older than twenty-two. The stairs needed painting. The pushchair had marked the walls and too many hands had felt their way up. Perhaps she would ask Hans and the others to help, and Heine too. But, of course, he would be too busy. As she reached the street the daylight hurt her eyes. The flags were thrashing on their poles in a burst of wind and she turned and looked up at the windows of their flat. Would he come?

He came with the cakes and the jelly and the hats she had cut from coloured paper, and Hans, Georg, Hermann and Ernst came too and they danced throughout the afternoon and evening and Heine bought wine for the street because Helen had worked on five studio portraits in two weeks and for once all the bills had been paid on time.

Helen laughed with Marian, the girl who was married to the greengrocer and gave Helen yesterday's vegetables without charge for the rabbit they both knew she did not have. She had a daughter of four and Helen had photographed her in return. Heine drank with her husband Rob and learned of this for the first time. He kissed his wife though she did not know why, and then sat Christoph on his shoulders and danced him up the street and back again along with the surging crowd. For the first time he met and spoke to their neighbours in the street.

That night he helped Helen to bath Christoph and he said he had not realised he had grown so much and bent over the cot to watch him fall asleep. He had not looked at him for so long; he

41

had not looked at his wife for so long. He must remember that they existed. He must remember that he loved them; that he was responsible for them.

Helen stood in the doorway, glad that at least this room was safe. Its ornaments of trains and dogs and bricks in place on the mantelpiece. This was family territory, to be kept secure for her son. There would be no sleeping bags here, no camp beds.

That night Heine made love to her, slowly, gently, and she wept and told him how much she loved him and he said that she would always be loved by him.

'Will I?' she asked against his shoulder. 'Will Christoph?' She dreamed of the dark cupboard that night.

Helen's photographs of the Silver Jubilee celebrations were bought by an American magazine and she celebrated with champagne. She and Heine had one glass only for there were three others with them, but what did it matter? Isaac's cousin Joseph laughed with them and Wilhelm and Günther too and it was good to see their eyes full of fun, their pain, which tore at Helen daily, gone for just a moment. But then Heine left to meet a contact. Helen watched him leave without surprise for what else had she come to expect? She pushed the bottle with one more glass in it towards the bruised, thin boys who were as young as she was and went to bed alone, for that also she had come to expect.

In 1936 during a January that was dank and cold George V was laid to rest and Helen and her mother lined the route. Christoph was warm in his knitted suit and coat and he wore a black arm band like the rest of the crowd. The mood was sombre. Helen was thoughtful as her mother pointed out King Edward VIII walking behind the gun carriage pulled by sailors because she had read in the letters which came from America of the liaison between Edward and Mrs Simpson. She brushed the hair from her eyes. So even the succession seemed as uncertain as the rest of the world, which darkened as Hitler and Mussolini growled and raged. Peace was never more fragile, Heine had said, and Helen feared that he was right and what would happen then to a German who lived in England?

Her mother held Christoph's hand as Helen lifted him high on to her shoulders.

'That's right, then he can see and tell his own children, poor

42

little mite,' her mother said, glaring at the man behind who clicked his teeth and moved so that he could also see.

'But he won't remember surely? He's only three,' Helen commented.

'You always said you remembered your father taking you to the stream at that age. He was on leave,' her mother said with an edge to her voice, a voice which had been more mellow since Helen had begun to take Christoph to see her every two months. Alone of course. Her mother was looking back at the procession now; it was almost past.

Helen looked up at the grey sky. She must go to the stream and take Christoph. She touched his knee briefly with her ungloved hand. The wind was sharp now and her fingers were becoming numb. She lifted her camera to her eye again and took more photographs because she did not want to think about why she had not thought of going to the stream with Heine.

'You'll get the backs of all these people,' her mother protested.

Helen smiled. 'I know, Mother,' she said as she took more and more, glad of her interruption. 'That's what I wanted to do, to somehow catch the bowed shoulders of the people, the hats being removed, the sadness against the pomp.'

'Oh really, Helen, you don't sound like a mother at all. What is this poor boy growing up into. All he'll know about is camera angles, public meetings, distant views. It's not right. And all those men cluttering up the house. It's just not decent, you know. I can't imagine what your neighbours think.'

Helen didn't know either because she did not ask them. She covered the lens with the cap and shrugged, lifting Christoph down, holding him close.

'We do all right, don't we, my darling? You have lots of uncles and I take you to the swings. And he has his books and toys and his own room when they smoke too much.' She did not add that these days she too stayed in her own room when the processing was finished for there seemed no place for her. But her work was becoming more popular and it enabled them to help more of those persecuted by that mad Austrian.

She lifted him into his pushchair, brushing the hair out of her eyes. 'Anyway, tonight there is no one there, not even Heine. He's taken three of them to Liverpool to board a ship.' Helen

43

pushed a way through the crowd for them both and did not see the smile on her mother's face. The pushchair caught on a lamppost and she heaved at it, pulling it clear.

That night they sat in front of the fire and Helen enjoyed the clean air, the sound of the gas spluttering and hissing, the click of her mother's knitting, and for the first time since last winter she too picked up wool and needles and began a jacket for Christoph. They did not talk but listened to the wireless and then they drank cocoa and said goodnight. Helen was glad that she had replaced the hair brushes, stacked away the camp beds and made the spare room her mother's, just for tonight. As she watched her close the door she realised that this evening she had not been lonely.

As she lay in bed she felt her limbs relax and grow heavy and again she wondered why she had not thought of taking Heine to Hemsham, to the stream. She watched the clouds gust between the moon and earth, blocking the light and releasing it, and faced now the separateness of their lives. She did not ask for Heine's company these days because, with a blown kiss, he would refuse. Too much to do. Too many important things to do, he would say. Some other time when it is over. But when would that ever be, Helen wondered, turning over and holding his pillow to her, pushing back despair, breathing in his scent.

A New York magazine bought Helen's pictures but addressed the letter to H. Weber, Esquire. Heine was pleased at the news and said the cheque would pay the telephone final demand and the extra food bill which was larger still this time.

By August 1936 unemployment was falling in Britain but Hitler's troops had entered the Rhineland and Mosley's Fascists were pinning up anti-Semitic posters in the East End. Helen left Christoph with Marian and went to photograph these and was hit across the face by one of the blackshirts and called a Jewish bitch. She told Heine as the pain throbbed through her face and he said that now she knew how his friends felt, but that their treatment was much worse, and he did not turn from the letter he was writing.

She looked at the back of his head and wanted to scream that she already knew how his friends felt, hadn't she listened to them and cried with them, cooked and washed for them, soothed their nightmares and not resented one moment? No, it was not that she resented but she said nothing, just turned from

44

him and bathed her face in cold water and then slept that night with her back turned to his still body.

The next day she took Marian and her daughter Emily and Christoph on the train to Eastbourne for Bank Holiday Monday. The sun was hot and soaked deep into her skin, reddening her arms and her legs where she had pulled up her skirts. The deckchair dug into the backs of her thighs but she watched Christoph hold his face to the sun and forgot the ache in her cheek. But the sun could not warm the coldness she felt deep inside.

They ate sandwiches curled at the edges and ice-creams which a man in a red and white-striped apron and cardboard top hat dug out of a round tin container with a scoop which he dipped into a jug of water first. Christoph smeared his across his face and up into his hair as well as his mouth but Emily licked hers carefully and her dress was not marked either. Helen took photographs of them both and of Marian and Marian took one of Christoph and Helen together and as the sun at last lost its heat they straggled back to the station.

They took an Underground train from the station and Helen waved goodbye to Marian before climbing the stairs to the flat. No one was there and in Christoph's room his small bed had gone and there were two camp beds. For a moment she felt as though the air had gushed from her body but then something deeper than rage gripped her, mobilised her.

She turned and walked through to her own bedroom and there was the small bed jammed tight next to theirs with his toys on top. She laid her child on their double bed and washed his face and hands, gently soaking his hair while he was asleep. She eased his loose limbs into his pyjamas, then draped the sheets and the two blankets around him, kissing him, smelling the sun still on his skin. And then she left the room.

She walked to the small bedroom and picked up the camp beds, the blankets folded on top, and threw them across the sitting-room, not looking where they fell, not hearing the crash of the vase they hit. She moved then to the darkroom, not able to spare the time to shout the anger that she felt, the outrage, the hurt.

She heaved at the hinged board which Heine had left on one end beneath the sealed window, saying that they had no need of it. But oh God, they had need of it now. Yes, they damn well had need of it now. She dragged it into the bathroom, sweeping Christoph's rubber duck on to the floor, wedging the board on top of the bath. She moved the developer into the bathroom, came back for the enlarger, the chemicals, everything she needed. Finally she dragged the cabinet across the frayed carpet, across the cracked lino in the passage-way into the bathroom too.

She took the chisel, hammer and nails from the cupboard under the sink and wrenched the hardboard from the dark-room windows, going back for the saw when she saw that it was too big for those in the bathroom. Leaning on the hinged top, she sawed the boards to the correct size, then, holding the nails in her mouth, she stood on the edge of the bath and hammered them in. Heine came in then. He stood in the doorway and said, 'What in God's name are you doing, Helen?'

She did not turn but said, 'Get out. Get out before I kill you.' She leaned her head on the wall. It was cold. 'Get out and only come back when I have finished.' There were others there. She could hear them and so he left because she knew he would not care to be embarrassed.

She had to keep the electrical equipment away from the water so she used an extension lead which could be plugged into the hall socket when power was needed. She hung a heavy opaque curtain from a rail above the doorframe. There was already a louvred vent above the door. She turned out the light to check that it was lightproof and it was.

She turned on the light again and ran her hands down her dress. She had not put on an apron and she was dirty but it did not matter. Sweat was running down her back but that did not matter either. She carried in the stool so that she could work at the hinged board comfortably. She lifted the board easily, peering into the bath, knowing that it would be adequate for the wet work, for the cascade system which she had made for herself. She set up the trays one above the other beneath the taps, then watched the water fall from one level to the next and realised that she was crying.

She put the board back and set up the portable red light then went to collect her camera. Using the changing bag, she loaded the film on to the tank reel inside the bag, then put the reel in the tank. Later, much later, she had developed, printed and enlarged the photograph that Marian had taken of her and

Christoph. It was lopsided but they were both smiling, holding hands, and it was full of love. She carried it to the bedroom and took from its frame her wedding photograph, throwing it on the bed. She then inserted the one of herself and her son and placed it on her bedside table. Then she took Christoph's mattress through to his old room, and dragged his bed after her. It caught on the door but she unscrewed the feet and there was room. She took the toys, the books and finally her son, carrying him close to her, whispering into his hair before placing him in his own bed, in his own room. She then sat in the sitting-room, which was also their dining-room, and waited.

Heine came in alone at two in the morning, his face white, his lips tight. His grey jacket was unbuttoned and he smelt of cigarette smoke and beer. He threw his hat on to the square table.

'How dare you?' he said. 'How dare you shame me before my friends? Are you a child that you behave like this?'

He stood before her, looming large, but she was not intimidated. The smell of beer was stronger now and she could hear his breathing, heavy but fast. His keys bulged in his trouser pocket.

'Sit down, Heine,' she said. Her voice was not hard or cold. It held nothing. 'Sit down.'

But he did not and so she stood, pushing herself up from the chair, feeling its wooden arm beneath her hand as she did so. 'I am not a child. Your child is in that room, in his bedroom where he will remain. Is that quite clear?'

Heine shook his head, shrugging his shoulders. 'What a fuss about nothing. Does it matter where a child sleeps?' He pointed to Christoph's room. 'In there, or in our room. What does it matter?'

'It matters to me. I am his mother, he is my responsibility.'

'I am his father, he is mine too. I love him.' Heine's voice was rising, his hand gripped her arm.

'Do you, do you really?' Helen was shouting now. 'So where were you today? Where have you been for the four years of his life? We love you but we don't know you any more.' She pulled from his grasp. 'We were going to fight the battles together.'

He grabbed at her, spun her round. 'You are a child, you see? It is only yourself you care about. Only yourself. Can't you see that we are just fragments in comparison to this great

47

tragedy? Just fragments.' His face was close to hers now and she could smell the cigarette smoke on his breath and the beer, stronger still.

She reached up and gripped his lapels, shaking him backwards and forwards. 'How dare you call my son a fragment? Or me. We are not fragments, we are people. We are your family. You will not ignore us, you will not watch me cooking for your friends, working for money to feed them and then call us fragments.' Her knuckles were white, her voice high, loud, insane. What was she saying, for God's sake? Whose mad voice was this coming from her mouth, shaking the man she loved? What had happened to them?

He slapped her then, breaking her hold on his jacket and she fell across the chair, and for a moment there was silence until Helen turned awkwardly, pushing herself up, aware that the grunting noises she heard came from her. That she was crying like an animal, that her mouth was open and mucus from her nose and eyes were running into it and past it. That she tasted blood in her mouth. She pushed him from her as he came to her, his face shocked.

'I love you, Heine.' Her voice was strange, she could not find the breath to end her words. 'I love you but I wonder whether you love me.'

Heine came towards her again, his arms outstretched, his own eyes full. 'I do love you. I love our son. I'm sorry, so sorry.'

'Don't touch me,' Helen said and backed towards the hall. He mustn't touch her until she had finished. She did not want hands on her, pushing her into cupboards, gripping her in anger. She was tired of it. No, she was not a child or a fragment but a person.

'I insist on becoming a partner. I produce more work than you. I earn more than you. I want it to be offered under my own name.' It was important to her now that she had something of her own, something that would keep her son safe for she could not trust her husband to do so. Somehow she feared that she could not trust him at all any more and it broke her heart because of the loneliness that the thought brought.

He came to her then, holding her, soothing her, stroking her hair which was damp with sweat. 'My love, my love. Forgive me. I love you, love you. Believe me, I love you.'

Helen nodded in his arms, wanting to be soothed, wanting their lives to go back to the sun-filled days when it was simple. But those times had gone, for now at least, and so she said again, 'I must be a partner. I can only rely on myself.'

CHAPTER 4

Helen watched Heine as he turned over the second page of his father's letter. It was a colourless November day in 1938 and her husband looked older, and very tired, but then they both did. His eyes met hers and he reached across for her hand which was already stretching to meet his. The new flat was smaller, the kitchen had damp walls but it had not known their bad years, the pain of a life too full for them to reach out and touch one another as they did so frequently now. It had not heard the blows of that night, the grunting despair of a woman she could not recognise as herself. It had only known Heine as a man who loved his wife and child, who held them as though they must never leave him. A man who had said as he had looked at his wife, sweating, bleeding on that dark night, that life was too short to wait for a time for themselves, that time must be carved out, no matter what else needed doing. That he had been a fool. That he would prove to her that she could trust him.

That night when her lip had split and blood had flowed on to the carpet he had held her, but she had fought. He had soothed her but she had shouted. He had promised her that it was over, that he would make room for her, for his son. That they would be loved as they should be loved but she had not believed him, seeing only the loneliness of the life she had led with her mother and then again with him. Each day, after that night, she had watched and listened as he spoke to her and Christoph. Each day she held herself upright, and had merely nodded when he brought the partnership papers to be signed. Each day throughout 1937 and into 1938 she had watched and waited until, with the coming of spring she had allowed herself to love again and be loved. To trust in this man.

Helen watched now as Heine put the letter on to the small

50

pine table they had brought from the other flat. They had moved from Alton Mews after Chamberlain landed at Heston Airport in September, two months before, waving his piece of paper, calling to the waiting press and photographers, 'Peace for our time'. Heine had taken no photographs but had driven without stopping, back to London.

He had rushed up the stairs, into the sitting-room, wrenching his coat off, calling out to her that they must now sell the flat as they had talked of doing. It was time to buy the cheaper flat near Stepney and send the balance of their capital to America with Claus, the refugee they were sheltering. He had held her as though he needed support, his hands cold, his face pinched. Chamberlain has not opposed Hitler, he had groaned into her neck before moving past her to the desk, picking Christoph up from the floor, holding him on his knee as he searched for the sale agreement in the large compartment. He had scattered papers on the floor as Helen watched.

We must do as we agreed, he had said, his hands shaking. Hitler will never believe that anyone will stop him. There will be war, but when?

Helen remembered nodding, feeling the chipped gloss paint of the door frame, watching, wondering how much longer peace would remain. Wondering whether England would allow the Weber family to remain in its midst once war was declared or would its people be like some of the neighbours they had danced with at the Jubilee – those who had no longer stopped to talk as the Munich crisis had deepened?

She had watched her husband as he scanned the papers he had prepared for partnership with Claus. There might not be war, she remembered saying. Russia has sided with no one yet, but Heine had not heard. She had run her hand up and down the paintwork again. She would sandpaper and paint and the smell would take thoughts of war away, for a moment at least.

Claus will take our money to America when he goes in April, Heine had said, turning his head, talking to her over his shoulder. He will establish the studio that will support us too. We will go to America if we have to; if war comes and Germans are really not welcome here. But only if you can bear to leave, my darling.

She watched now in her smaller kitchen as Heine put the letter from his father back into the envelope, his face set.

51

'Is it bad news?' she asked, coming to him, holding him against her, wondering when Claus would be back from the ticket office, when Joseph would wake. He had arrived from Germany only last night, carrying just the ten marks refugees were allowed to take but a firm in the city had been persuaded to sponsor him and so he had been allowed entry. He had cried for his Jewish parents who would not leave their house because it would be confiscated and they would be aliens with no pride, with nothing. He cried for his parents who thought the whirlwind would pass. Would it pass, she wondered. What would Russia do?

'When do you need to collect Christoph?' Heine asked. 'It's band after school today, is it not?'

'We have time. Tell me what is wrong.' Helen looked at the clock. She had one hour until four.

'Father has written, after all these years he has written. He would like us to go and see him before it becomes impossible. He would like to see his grandson and so would Mutti.'

'I'm so glad,' said Helen, speaking carefully because Heine's face was still set and she did not know whether he cared for his father at all. Whether he could forget that they stood on opposing sides. 'But is it safe?'

'Oh yes, it is safe enough because he has vouched for us with officials. He is a Nazi Party member, do you not remember?' But Heine's voice was not bitter as it usually was but quiet, thoughtful.

He pushed her back and looked into her face. 'I promised you after that night when you re-arranged the darkroom' – he grinned now and she did too – 'I promised you that you could always trust me to look after you. I have tried to do that, but now I have something to ask of you.' He took her hand. His cuffs were frayed and a thread of cotton drifted on to her green flowered overall.

He looked away now at the clock. Helen checked too. There was half an hour.

'You have done so much for me and my countrymen. I have to ask you to do one last thing. Father wants us to go, but he also wants us to take something to him that a man will bring, if we agree.'

Helen picked up the letter taking it from the envelope but it was in German.

'Something has happened to my father. He has changed but he has to be careful with his words.' Heine took her hands in his, crushing the letter as he did so. His voice was slow. 'He has, he says, realised the meaning of my words on our last visit. That he hopes my leg has healed as well as his sight and his hearing. He wants us to take a camera, my love. He doesn't say so but I know what he means, and I know which one he wants. It has a wide aperture lens which takes photographs indoors without flash. Ideal for working inside courtrooms, at meetings.'

'But won't we be stopped at the border? Photography is allowed only with a permit, isn't it?'

Heine did not answer and there was only the sound of the clock. They had fifteen minutes and then Helen realised what Herr Weber had meant and she sat down, her hands cold. The camera was for secret work. His sight was better and his hearing. Of course she knew what he meant.

'You see what I mean when I say I cannot promise to keep you safe – but I need you with me. You are English, they have to be more careful with foreigners. We are not yet at war.'

Helen picked the white cotton thread off her apron, curled it round and round her finger, watching her fingertip turn to purple. It was four o'clock.

'But most of all I need you because you will give me courage.'

She walked alone to the school and stood at the railings waiting for Christoph. The children called him Chris and thought his father was Dutch. He ran towards her, past the white-chalked hopscotch squares, his cap on the back of his head, his blond hair too long. His smile was wide and his eyes were her father's: dark brown.

'Did you bake the conkers today?' she shouted as he reached her but did not kiss her cheek because none of the other children did and, after all, he was nearly six. She laughed and nodded and they walked back through the park. Other children trailed in front and behind with their mothers. Helen held his sandwich tin which smelt of Marmite when she opened it. They stopped by the swings with their rusted chains. He ran to one and pushed off with both his feet.

'So you ate everything today then,' she called as he swung himself high, his socks down at his ankles, his knee black. One

53

dark woman pushed her son on the swing next to Helen and turned and smiled.

'Said I would if you baked 'em for me.' He was slowing now. 'Hey, I bashed a tenner today, so now mine's the king. It's got sixteen so far. Is Dad home? Did he get any good shots today? Did you?' But he wasn't listening, he was scraping his shoe along the ground as he slowed the swing, ready to jump from it before rushing to the roundabout.

'Chris, for goodness sake, don't do that and come on now. It's time to get home.'

'Man and boy, they're all alike,' the other woman said and laughed. Helen smiled, the tin was cold against her skin. She put out her hand to steady the swing after Chris ran off. The chain links stained her hand.

'Yes, man and boy,' she echoed and added silently, German and English too; we're all alike. She waved to the woman. 'See you again,' she called and hoped that she would.

They walked down the path which ran alongside beds which held no flowers now that summer was gone, just heaped dark earth. Chris kicked a stone, scratching his toe-cap but Helen said nothing, just breathed in the smoke from the bonfire that the greensman was fanning by the tennis courts. There were hardly any leaves left on the trees and the sun seemed to have been sucked from the face of the earth.

'How would you like Grandma to come and stay with you for a bit? Daddy and I have to go away, just for a while.'

There had been no decision to make really, she had known from the start she would go because a father's love was too important to let slip through your fingers, too important to waste. And besides, Heine had said he needed her.

Chris would not stay behind. He did not like his grandmother, he told Helen as she read to him that night. She was always too close, always wanting to take everyone away from him so that it was just the two of them. Helen listened but she already knew. That night in bed she told Heine that the three of them would go and that it would be all right. She dreamed of a sun-filled stream and she woke in the morning crying.

Four days before Christmas Helen sat next to Heine as he drove slowly up to the border posts, his eyes on the slush-covered road, his hand wiping the inside of the windscreen

54

where his breath had condensed and begun to freeze. Helen took out the leather from the glove pocket, leaned across and helped and then did her own. This time there were no birds singing, only snow which dragged down the branches of the trees. Neither of them spoke of the camera, of the search that must come when they stopped.

There was no 'Grüss Gott' from the young blond border guard dressed in his green jacket and black trousers with his high black boots. This time he stood erect and snapped 'Heil Hitler' while Helen smiled, her shoulders tense, willing Heine to reply in kind which he did, but only when he had climbed from the car, because she knew he did not want her to hear him say those words.

Chris eased himself up against the back of her seat, leaning his elbow along the top. There was a box of Christmas presents on the seat beside him and another box with the remains of their picnic beside that. They both watched Heine walk to the customs post and then climbed out at his gesture. Another guard came and searched the car, picking up and shaking the presents and opening some. Would he find the camera? But even if they did, they wouldn't hurt a child, would they? Helen felt her headache throb more deeply. It had clenched down one side of her neck and head since they had left Britain.

She took Chris's arm and pointed down the road. 'That's Germany, where Grandfather and Grandmother Weber live.' She must look natural, at ease. She must not appear afraid.

She looked at the Nazi flag which hung limp at the top of the pole, at the trees which had been cut back so that it would be clearly visible from a great distance. She looked at the scarlet background, the white circle and the hooked cross marked out in the deadness of black and her hatred of it gave her courage.

She smiled at her son and he took her hand. She could see his breath in the crisp cold air. Behind him the guard was looking at the picnic box, his face full of distaste at the apple cores, the banana peel, and he turned from it and nodded to the officer who waited with Heine. She smiled again at Chris and told him to stamp his feet to keep warm and knew that for now they were safe.

They drove without stopping through verges no longer full of poppies or brown-eyed Susans but heaped with snow stained by slush and dirt. They saw no blonde-haired maidens, just iced ponds. No window-boxes, just inches of snow on ledges and long daggers of ice hanging from pointed eaves. They stayed on the first night at a country inn and the second in a town, but in both they said little because the people might have been Nazis.

On the third day they drove through the flat beet fields and Helen told Chris of the boys his age who picked beet through the snow and ice. There were no commercial advertisements as they approached the outskirts of Hanover because the Nazis did not approve. They skirted around the city and as darkness fell they drove into Heine's village.

'Why wouldn't Grandmother come? She will have Christmas on her own now.' Chris's voice was sleep-filled, his lids heavy.

Helen shrugged. 'Older people get set in their ways,' she answered and was glad that her mother was not here because the older woman's eyes had been hard since Heine had come back to them.

She climbed out of the car and opened Chris's door, holding out her arms to him, breathing in his warm scent as he clung to her. The picnic basket was on the seat and Heine reached in past her and picked it up.

'Clever girl,' he said. 'I thought he was going to look in there for one moment.'

Helen laughed quietly, her headache gone now that they had arrived. 'Men don't like dirty nappies or mess, surely you haven't forgotten.'

He pulled a face and Helen remembered the woman in the park.

'Man and boy, you're all alike,' she murmured and as he kissed her the front door opened, flooding the garden with light, and she was glad they were spending Christmas in Germany.

They sat at the dining-room table eating by candlelight. Frau Weber had brought down from the attic two honey wax candles to celebrate their arrival, and their sweet Christmas aroma was everywhere, mingling with the pine of the Advent candles. Chris sat next to Helen, smiling because his Oma, his grandmother, had said that he could light the last Advent candle on Christmas Eve. They ate asparagus soup, as they had on their last visit, oh so long ago, Frau Weber said. Venison, chestnuts, sprouts and potato puffs followed decorated with sliced orange. The Bordeaux was thick and strong on Helen's tongue and she smiled when Heine's mother said she must call her Mutti.

Heine and his father spoke quietly when they spoke at all, but both seemed content to share the sight of the child and the women talking of St Nicholas and Christmas stockings. Chris leaned his head on his mother's arm when he had half eaten his venison. His lids were heavy and the talk spun around him. There were strange smells and sights and voices but the German was familiar and it made him remember the men who had come to his home, the men with thin faces and shaking hands who had been kind; who had sat him on their knees and seemed to drink in his laughter as though it was something they had never heard.

He turned to his mother. 'My uncles liked me to laugh, didn't they?'

She didn't hear and so he pulled at her sleeve. It was silk, so soft and smooth and he wanted to sleep. His mother turned and smiled. 'My uncles liked me to laugh, didn't they?'

Her face was close to his. 'Oh yes, my love. It was a sound that was very sweet to them.'

He saw her look across to his father but his chair was empty and he felt panic. Had he gone again? He had always been away, but not for months now. He turned again to his mother and she was there. She was always there and he leaned his head against her again. But then he felt strong arms around him and his father's rough chin against his cheek. His Oma rose and kissed him and then they left the warm honey-scented room and climbed the stairs, and his face was against his father's chest as he drifted in and out of sleep.

Helen went ahead, into the room which was to be Christoph's for the next two weeks. It was cold, so cold. There was ice frosted on the inside of the double windows and she scraped a finger from top to bottom, collecting frost beneath her nail.

She marched from his room into theirs. It was warm from the stove. She walked quickly to the top of the stairs, hissing at Heine to stop, pointing towards Chris's bedroom. 'There is no heating in there. It's freezing.'

Heine stopped. 'In Germany the children sleep in cold rooms.'

She turned. 'In my family, children sleep in warm rooms even if it means the adults go into the cold one.' Her hands were on her hips, anger in her voice.

Heine shifted his son's weight slightly and then laughed. 'My darling girl, do not prepare to do battle. I am too tired and too intelligent to risk my life fighting over something which is easily remedied.' He passed Chris to her, walking quietly into their room, riddling the stove as she stood behind him and watched, feeling the heat from the ash and red-hot coals as he drew out the pan. He moved ahead of her into the smaller bedroom and heaped them on to the kindling and coal already laid in the stove, leaning down to open the draught doors at the base, and she saw his long thin hands on the brass knob, his wrists against his good shirt cuffs, his eyelashes casting shadows on his cheeks in the dim overhead light. The Nazis seemed far away in this room. War seemed an impossibility.

When the room was dark and warm and Helen and Heine had kissed Chris goodnight, he watched as they left the room, then waited because he knew she would be back. She always was. The door opened again and his mother was there. 'Sleep tight, my darling boy,' she whispered and only then did he close his eyes.

Herr Weber's study was lit by a small table lamp which cast a circle of light that barely reached Heine and Helen as they sat in their armchairs. They watched in silence as the older man laid old shirts against the gap at the bottom of the door, pushing hard until it was plugged. They watched as he pulled the telephone plug from the wall but still did not speak because he had held his fingers to his lips. Only when he was completely satisfied did he sit near to the low fire, opposite them but close so that his whispers could be heard by them.

'You see, Hans has been with us for twenty years and Ilse too but we dare not trust them. The telephones can be tapped too. I am not suspected. Not yet. But now as I said in my letter I can see and hear all that Heine saw and heard. But it is too late really. I know it is too late.'

Heine laid his hand on his father's knee. 'Be careful, Father.'

'Oh I am most careful.' Herr Weber laughed softly. 'I carry

out my duty to my utmost ability. I am in and out of the courts. In and out of interrogation rooms and so I need your little present very badly.' He raised his eyebrows to Heine, who nodded at Helen.

She lifted her handbag and took the camera out. 'Please, do be careful. We see the refugees. We hear such stories.' The camera was cold in her hand as she passed it to him. His hand was thin, with veins which knotted and bulged. He had been a strong, fit man. He was that no longer.

They did not watch as he took it and moved behind them. He did not want them to know more than they had to and it would be elsewhere by tomorrow. He started to speak only when he had returned and again in a whisper.

'I have taken the post of *Blockwart*. I am now the leader of a local group of Party comrades. I am, my dear son, honoured to serve at the lowest level of the Nazi political system but I know what is going on. I can, with this camera you have brought me at such risk to yourselves, take photographs with a view to recording crimes and, as importantly, blackmail.'

Helen looked at this old man who had held legality above all else.

He laughed but there was no amusement in the sound. 'Yes, my dear. Legality loses its appeal when it is used to remove from society "vermin" such as gypsies, Jews and parsons. I use the Nazis' vernacular, of course.' He was still whispering. Helen looked at Heine, who took her hand, holding it tightly, and she saw in his face love and fear for this man.

Herr Weber leaned forward, his face sharply etched in the dull dim light, and started to speak, but Helen interrupted.

'Parsons. I didn't know. Why parsons?'

Herr Weber clasped his hands together. He was still leaning forward. 'Because according to our noble leader God was a Jew, and so one does not allow a faith which worships such as he. But also because Christians owe an allegiance to something apart from our dear and glorious Führer. We Germans, the master race, must ignore such superstition. We must follow the Nordic beliefs.' He lowered his head. 'I feel such disgust with myself. I did not protest soon enough. I looked at the promises he had fulfilled. The orderly streets, the employment, the national pride and then I saw Herr Weissen beaten to death and his small son too, on the street, and people laughed and I did nothing then. I was too frightened.'

His voice was so steady, Helen thought. So cold and steady, and her hands were steady too, because she and Heine had lived with the knowledge for years now. But always, inside, the anguish coiled and lashed.

'The Nazis had such a glorious party in November, my dear. It was far more spectacular than, what do you call it – ?' He paused. 'Ah yes, your Guy Fawkes Night. We called ours *Kristallnacht*. Such flames, such delightful bonfires, such sharp glass, such ruin. Such disgrace.' His voice became tight and hard. 'And now the officials are angry because the insurance companies have to buy imported glass with precious foreign currency to replace the damage the verminous Jews brought upon themselves.'

Helen could not listen to any more of the words which were pouring from this old man in the small dark room and she rose, but before she left the two men together she went to Herr Weber and said, '*Ich leide seelisch*,' and kissed him. Knowing that he also was 'sick in his soul'.

When Heine came to bed he held her and said that his father had saved some people already and would save others too with the camera, with his courage, and she asked him if he were not afraid for him.

'It is his gesture,' he said. 'What more can he do?'

When Helen rose in the morning snow was falling from the dark sky, big flakes which fell faster and faster, settling on the already white earth. The room was light, everything was quiet. A cart passed but it could not be heard as it ground through the soft clinging snow. She could see the horse's breath, its shaking head and then she heard Chris and took him out into the snow, dressed in his grandfather's fur hat and his father's old fur boots. Heine found a sledge and as the snow stopped falling he pulled his son along and there were deep fresh grooves carved in the cold whiteness.

Then Hans came and shovelled the path and so they helped, nodding and smiling, and wondering if, one day, he would betray Herr Weber. Ilse came with ashes, salt and sand and scattered them on the ice which had been beneath the snow and in moments it became soft and brown and ugly and Helen

60

turned from it, watching the sundial far out across the garden near the orchard. Children passed behind the hedge which looked foreshortened against the depth of the snow and Helen listened to their laughter and made herself ignore the ugliness of the path.

Later they drove to the forest on roads cleared of snow and chose the Christmas tree and took the toboggan down a thirty metre slope again and again. The snow clumped in Helen's hair and scarf and trickled down her neck but all she could feel and hear was the laughter of her husband as he watched, his leg too stiff to participate, and that of her son mingling with her own. On and on they went until the sky turned pink and the sun lost its weak warmth. She and Chris took the last run together. Chris in front, then Helen, and as the wind caught her cheeks and the toboggan jarred and flew, she held Chris tightly and did not want the slope to ever end because now, this minute, she had her family safe and close.

That night they watched a torchlit procession from the window and Chris thought it was pretty, like a moving Christmas tree but his father said that sometimes things were not as they seemed and then Chris saw that they were soldiers.

On Christmas Eve Chris went with Helen and Oma to the attic and she showed him the decorations, the electric candles, the crib and its figures, the provisions. They carried boxes down and decorated the tree so that it was ready for the evening, for it was tonight that they would have their presents, Helen told him. Frau Weber smiled and said that it was because it was the German way and, after all, he was half German.

Chris looked at her and then at Helen. 'I can't say that at school,' he said.

Helen looked away and then at Mutti who touched her shoulder. 'I know. I know,' was all she said.

That evening they opened their presents before they ate. They were set on low tables either side of the tree which shimmered with silver strips, baubles and electric candles. Set before the tree was the crib. Hans and Ilse came to receive their gifts and there was the sound of paper crackling and laughter until Hans turned on the radio for the Government's Christmas Eve broadcast and Helen heard in this room, so full of gifts and light, the voice which had changed so many lives.

61

She looked at the tree and counted the candles, she breathed deeply ten times and then counted the candles again because she wouldn't listen. No, she would never listen, not even to the sound since the words would escape her anyway. She looked at the Advent wreath of fir branches which was hung from plaited blue, green and red ribbons suspended from the ceiling in the dining-room. Christoph had lit it before they started to open the presents, his arm steady as he reached forward, held up by Heine, his face red from the cold of the day. She had kissed him when Heine lowered him and he said that she smelt of ginger. She laughed because she had baked ginger biscuits most of the morning, cutting him out a Hansel and Gretel for his stocking which she would put on his bed tonight because he was also half English.

Before dinner, before they left the tree, Herr Weber went to the piano which stood in the corner of the room and played carols for them and when he came to 'Silent Night' Helen sang it half in German half in English as her present to the Webers. Her voice was pure and strong and there was silence for a moment when she finished.

During dinner the smell of ginger and honey mixed with the cool white wine and took away the strong taste of the carp and horseradish which Helen had found strange and Chris could not eat. She smiled, doubting if he could have eaten even his favourite food, bacon and eggs, after the tea of toast and honey and the cakes, and she felt the flush in her own cheeks from the afternoon's tobogganing. Talk flowed gently and quietly and for now there was peace for each of them.

Herr Weber told Christoph of the Opera House in Hanover where Heine had been taken as a child to see the children's play. How the chandeliers had sparkled and the seats had pricked him so that he wriggled all the way through. How the gilt boxes full of officials and their families had glistened. He told him how his father had taken the toboggan out one day with his friends and come back so late that there were icicles on his mittens, his hat, even his nose. He laughed gently when Christoph said that today he had gone down on the sledge with his mother because his father was an old man with a stiff leg who could only watch.

Helen did not laugh at the words which dropped from

Chris's mouth, wondering if Heine felt the pain of them as she did, but he looked at her with his eyebrows raised.

'This is how you bring up your son is it, Frau Weber? To show such scant respect for his father?' He was laughing, his blue eyes clear and without hurt.

Helen laughed then and lifted her glass to him, to the man he now was, looking from him to their son. So like Heine except for those eyes and she looked up at the Advent candles. One, lit on the first Advent Sunday was burnt almost to a stub. The wax from today's was burning with a strong firm flame. She could smell the pine and the honey.

She could not remember a Christmas with her father. Would he have laughed? Would he have sat on a toboggan? She thought so. Would her mother? She knew she would not.

She thought of her mother on Christmas day when they walked through Hanover. She had left presents and cards with her but her mother had sent none out to Germany in the car.

Frau Weber had said this morning that she sent a card each year but never heard in return. As they walked in the air which was so cold it hurt her lungs, Helen felt the tension knot in her shoulders but pushed it away because it was Christmas and she was happy. She kicked at the ice which had chipped and protruded up into the road. Frau Weber took her arm.

'Come, Helen. Do not be left behind, they miss you.'

Helen looked up and waved as Heine and Chris called.

'Yes, I was just thinking,' she said, smiling at Frau Weber.

'There is much to think of these days,' Frau Weber said as they walked along down the alley into the centre. Heine and Chris carried the red ball which had been in his stocking from Father Christmas. It showed up clear and shining against the snow, the grey buildings with icicles hanging like witches' fingers from the eaves. Would her own mother have wanted to hurry to join with everyone else? She knew she would not. She would have tried to hold her back and would not forgive her when she pulled away. But that was all in the past. She could not hurt her ever again. This was Christmas and she was far from England.

As they reached the men, Helen smiled and looked at her mother-in-law; the daylight showed up the lines around the eyes, the hair which was almost white. She looked fragile, strained, her skin almost translucent. Did she know of Herr

63

Weber's activities? It never seemed safe to ask. There were many people in the city centre, walking, nodding, and Helen moved to look into the window of the toy shop where the shelves were now half empty. She turned to call to Chris and saw an old man slip and fall in amongst the milling crowd. She moved to help but Heine caught her arm.

'Leave him,' he said, pulling her round, back to the shop.

His hand was tight on her arm and she stared at him and then twisted round again. Chris was staring as the old man struggled on the unsanded ice near the road. He was still on the ground, his black coat and hat smudged with white. His earlocks too.

'Are you mad?' Helen said. 'Let me help him.'

Chris was looking across at her now, his face puzzled. Helen looked at Herr Weber, at his wife. They did not move to help but turned away as though they had not seen, but they had seen because Herr Weber's face was white. Those in the square did not help either but passed either side. Still the old man could not rise.

'He is a Jew. If we help him Father could be in danger. There is too much to lose, too much work yet to be done.'

Again Helen looked at the old man and then at Heine. She looked at Chris then and saw him move to help but he was only six and not strong enough.

'Let go of me, at once,' she said to Heine. 'I do not bring up my child to pass an old man who has fallen, or is he just a fragment?' Helen turned to Herr and Frau Weber who were standing with their backs to them, looking in the window. 'Move on, don't be seen with us. I shall try to protect you.' Her voice was quiet but firm.

She followed Chris, lengthening her stride, holding his arm, talking, and then Heine saw him nod and throw his mother the ball which she missed. He saw its redness against the black of the old man's coat, saw it land by his leg, saw Helen's hand reach for the ball, saw Chris stand on his other side, shouting for his ball. And then the man was up, walking away quickly. Too quickly for him or anyone else to have seen what had happened in the crush. The Webers had no need to fear.

Helen held her son's hand as they walked towards him but she could still feel the thin arm, the smell of poverty, the

64

cultured voice which had said, '*Danke*,' while she had said, 'I'm so sorry. So sorry.'

She stood before Heine now, her face gentle. 'I was the only one who could go. Chris and I were the only ones who could go and there was no possible way we could have walked on. It was our gesture. Do you understand?' She didn't touch, just stood there and waited, still feeling that thin arm.

'I love you,' Heine said and kissed her, turning from her only when Chris called.

'Catch,' and the ball hit his arm.

Heine had wanted to help too.

Her mother's telegram arrived the next day.

'Return immediately. Stop. I am unwell. Stop. Mother.'

CHAPTER 5

They arrived in the Avenue at midday on the 30 December having travelled almost without stopping. It was cold. A heavy mist coated the trees, the last few skeletal leaves hung like rags and the houses looked grey.

Her mother was sitting up in bed eating a lightly boiled egg, which, she said, a neighbour had kindly cooked just a moment ago. Helen just looked at her, at her pink cheeks bearing no trace of illness, at her permed hair tucked into a hairnet.

'Just a touch of flu, after all,' her mother said and her smile was the same as it had been when Helen came out from the cupboard.

Helen turned, and left the room, straightened the pictures on the stair wall, placing her feet carefully on each stair, concentrating on this, not on her anger which was so intense that she felt sick. She walked into the kitchen where Heine was lighting the gas under the kettle. There was a smell of sulphur from the match, a smell of gas from the front ring.

'Stay in here,' she said. 'Whatever you hear, stay in the warm.' She smiled at Heine, at Chris, but did not stop and explain.

She returned upstairs, made up the spare bed in that bleak room and then told her mother that she would stay for three days so that the neighbours did not have to boil eggs for her and watched the smile increase.

'Heine will stay with me and you will move to the spare room, as you felt Father should. There is no room for Heine unless we use your bed.'

The smile disappeared, the eyes were dark, and Helen was glad. She took her arm and led her without speaking, without listening to the harsh voice. She helped her into the bed and now she spoke again.

'Should I hang a damp blanket to contain the germs?' she asked. 'Would that be wise, Mother?'

She left her then with the anger hanging in the air between them.

In the front room on 31 December, she and Heine saw in the year of 1939 with mulled wine, praying that peace would endure, that somehow Hitler could be stopped without great carnage; that hostility would not blossom in England towards Germans and Italians. That in Germany, God was with Heine's parents.

As they drank quietly together Heine touched Helen's hand and said, 'Your mother is widowed and lonely. We have our lives before us and one another. We should be generous, my darling. Ask her to join us, please.'

She said nothing, just looked at the fire and the flames which lurched round logs and coal. She did not want her mother down, she did not want to see in the New Year with her in case, somehow, she tainted it with her presence.

'Please,' Heine said again. 'There is enough bitterness and pain throughout the world without continuing a feud within our own family.'

So Helen helped her mother down the stairs although she was not fragile enough to need help. She eased her into a chair, handed her a glass of warm wine, feeling the heat from her own as she sat and watched her mother smooth her satin dressing gown and sip with pursed mouth. Yes, all right, Mother, she thought as she sipped her own wine, tasting the warmth in her mouth. All right, I shall do as Heine says and be generous tonight and in the future, but I will never let you spoil any part of my life ever again.

In January the gas mask drills which had been desultory for the past year took on a new urgency in the schools, and in Germany Jews were banned from cinemas, theatres and concerts. They were banned from being vets, pharmacists and dentists and so the refugees continued to pass through Helen's flat.

In February her mother complained that she earned too much from Ernest's pensions to claim a free air raid shelter and Helen said that she was not in one of the priority target areas anyway, as she, Heine and Chris were.

67

Helen was glad when Heine began digging in early March when the soil was frost-free and easier to work. It helped to feel they were doing something as the tension in the press mounted, as people grew edgy and ignored the warm spring. She watched as he sliced the spade deep into the earth at the bottom of the narrow strip of garden behind the flat, heaving cold heavy sods on to the lawn. She was glad that her arms tugged at the shoulders when she and Chris put them into the rust-smeared wheelbarrow and then transferred them to the left side of the garden where the sun struck in the afternoons. She was glad to be working, to be doing something to protect themselves, glad too to be creating from that need a rockery which would thrive. For she wanted flowers to bloom; even if bombs fell from black-crossed aeroplanes she wanted flowers to bloom, then some sanity would remain.

She watched as Heine dug again and again, the sweat soaking his shirt, his hair. There was a smell of fresh earth; there were old pennies, pipes, bottles, tiles and Heine smiled each time they fell from his spade and then threw them up to Chris who would hold them, turn them, then put them to one side to take to school for the 'precious table'. Worms bored holes in the straight glossed sides of the pit as the weekend passed and Helen took them to the rockery which now held small, wide-spaced plants, and it seemed almost a game as the sky turned blue and the trees budded and blossom bloomed. Almost.

At three feet Heine stopped and helped Helen drag in the fourteen steel sheets which had been dropped off on the pavement by council lorries to each building in the street. Her hands tore through gloves and her shirt was ripped at the shoulder as they dragged them one by one through the narrow passage-way into the garden.

Sandbags had been left also and while Heine fixed the sheets in the late afternoon Helen and Chris doused the bags with creosote to stop them rotting and the smell sank into their skin and their hair and their lungs and although they slept with their windows wide that night they could still taste it in their mouths the next morning.

Helmut arrived that morning and so Heine was too busy to ease the sandbags against the shelter and Helen was taking photographs in the studio, but the next week, with Helmut helping, they pushed and carried and kicked the sandbags into place and Helen's back felt as though it would break. Chris threw earth on the roof of the shelter with the spade he had taken to Eastbourne and Helen did too, but with a large shovel. It would be added protection against blast and shrapnel. She called to their neighbours, the Simkins, who then did the same. She lifted Chris who would not be seven until December – but already weighed enough to be twenty, she whispered into his neck.

'Higher, Mummy, I can't reach,' he called.

She growled and he laughed but she lifted him higher still and then he threw the seeds – forget-me-nots, love-in-the-mist, marigolds – across the shelter roof, and for a moment Helen wondered whether they would be at war when the flowers bloomed.

They painted the inside walls white while Chris broke cork tiles into pieces with his fingers, leaning over, watching the pile of bits grow on the upturned dustbin lid. An ant ran over his shoe and then on into a crack. Some bark was caught under his fingernail and he dug it out, rolling it between his fingers. It was bouncy and warm.

'Smaller, Chris,' Heine called and so he worked for another hour and then he climbed down into the shelter and threw the cork at the wet paint, again and again until the cork stuck to the sides. And he nodded as his father said that the pieces would absorb the moisture and prevent condensation.

'It's going to be a good play-house, Dad,' he said.

They had to hang a blanket not a door, the inspector said when he called. 'Don't want to be shredded by splinters now, do we?' Helen looked from him to the rockery. Would the alpines take root and bloom, she wondered, not wanting to hear the words.

In the middle of March Hitler took over Prague and spring-cleaned the country, Heine said between thin lips. Czechoslovakian Jews now began to come and the flat was full again. Claus had written from America that he still had not established an agency for the partnership but was working for another firm to make some contacts. It would take at least two years, he said, and Helen had been glad because England was her country. Heine had been worried.

Helen smiled and kissed him. 'There is no war yet, there

might be no war. Look, the Russians still have signed no pact with anyone. Hitler needs that signature to neutralise Russia before he can bite into Poland. And in the street there has been no unkindness towards us, no anti-German feeling.'

'Do they know we are German?' Heine asked and Helen did not answer because she could only have said no.

In April conscription plans were endorsed after Britain and France pledged to defend Poland and that weekend Heine and Helen took Chris to the Avenue and dug her mother's shelter. They bolted, doused, heaved, while Helen's mother told her neighbour that Heine was too old to be called up and had an injured leg and later told Helen that perhaps they would think he was Dutch.

On Sunday evening before they returned to London, Heine and Helen took Chris to the stream and floated sticks, swearing that the winner was the one which Chris had thrown even though it was not. Helen watched as Heine lifted his son over the parapet, saw the strong hands, the fine blond hairs. Saw the green lichen which stained Chris's coat. Saw her father, quite clearly now, his face, his shoulders, his hands, and remembered the horror of that war and its legacy for the women who waited and the men who never returned. She prayed that another war would not come.

May was hot and the British Government declared again that it would side with Poland in the event of a German attack to the East but negotiations were still being conducted between Russia and Britain with a view to a pact and so hopes for peace remained. Helen watered her rockery and sewed Chris's initials on his shoe-bag and swung him in the park, talking to other mothers whose faces were strained as they listened to their children talk of the evacuation practice or the gas mask drill. She stood and watched as Chris played cowboys and Indians with the other boys, seeing him load his pistol with a roll of red caps, hearing the snap as he fought his battle, smelling the blackened roll when he gave it to her to carry home.

She was asked to photograph the trenches being dug in the parks, the builders reinforcing the basements, the brick surface shelters which were going up in many London streets. She did but she would not think of them afterwards.

In July a local boy won a big boxing match and Mr Simkins, their neighbour, drank until he passed out in the street. Heine carried him up to his flat above his tobacconist's shop which also ran beneath theirs. It was then that Mrs Simkins asked if they would be evacuating Chris. She clicked her tongue and said that she supposed the Government was right to want to remove anyone who would get in the way but it seemed very hard and would the bombs really come? Heine said he did not know.

That night he and Helen talked as they did every night about Chris, their love for him, their need to keep him with them, but they spoke also of his right to safety, to a billet in the country. But then they thought of him with a stranger, of his face as he woke, soft and full, his arms which hugged them. They thought of his fear of the dark. Would foster-parents understand? They drank him in as he came home each day, listening to his voice, his ideas, hearing his laughter, watching him grow, holding him when he fell, kissing him when he was asleep, and knew they could not bear to be parted, not even for a week, let alone for the years of his childhood, for who knew how long a war would last?

And then in the darkness of night they talked again of the bombs that had fallen in Spain, of the buildings which had crumbled and killed, of the shrapnel which had sliced, the blast which had destroyed, and knew that they could not bear any of this to touch their son.

They talked then of them all moving to the country but Heine said, 'How can we? We need to stay, to work for the nation as everyone else will do.'

'But he is our child,' she whispered, watching high clouds nudging in front of the moon.

'How can we run away?' he replied as he held her, his breath moving her hair. 'I've done too much of that. And we must earn a living, darling. As photographers we need to live in London, we have our contacts now. I can work as an air raid warden, earn my place in your society.'

On and on they talked, night after night, but neither spoke of the question to which there was no answer. What would happen to a German in this country if war was declared?

After a hot dry summer the children of the neighbourhood were tanned and Helen's arms were brown from weeding the rockery. In August negotiations between Russia and Britain collapsed and on 23 August, as Helen and Heine listened to the wireless on a hot still evening, it was announced that Germany and Russia had signed the Nazi–Soviet Pact. Helen cried while Heine held her but she did not feel safe, even with the feel of him so close because it meant war. She knew it meant war but what would that mean to them?

On 31 August Helen packed Chris's bag. They had bought an enamel cup, a knife, fork and spoon and the list of allowable clothes had been ticked and folded into the case because Christoph's school was to be evacuated tomorrow and Helen and Heine had decided that he must go. He must be safe, but they were numb with grief.

The next day they took him to school, walking past police cars which crawled the kerbs telling parents through tannoys to take their children to the schoolyard where they must assemble in front of their form teachers. Helen kissed her son at the gate, smoothing his hair with her hand, and somehow, she let him go. They joined the other parents outside the playground and watched through railings which held none of the summer heat. They saw the register being taken and the children being formed into columns two abreast. They saw him labelled by a teacher, saw him not look at them as they pressed with other parents against the school railings. Helen gripped the flaking metal, feeling the cold hardness, thinking of that, not of her heart which seemed to fill her chest and which was destroying her.

Helen did not hold Heine's hand, could not move hers from the railings until they marched from the playground and then she thrust them into her pockets where they were bunched into fists, trying to keep the pain clasped inside them.

The children marched with their gas masks banging against their sides, their cases in their hands, following the Headmaster who held a banner with the letter 'S' and the number '60' inked on. Along the streets they marched, with Heine and Helen and the other weeping or silent parents.

They crossed the road in waves as they had learned to do in the summer practices, the parents waiting as their children queued up along the pavement in lines two hundred yards long before turning to face the road and crossing quickly at a teacher's command. The traffic was held up by police for three seconds only.

So efficient, Helen thought. They are taking my child from me so efficiently. Old men and women stood outside their doorways watching the children followed by their despairing parents, and their eyes were full of the knowledge of what war really meant.

At the station the children marched past the barriers to the waiting area, where there were other schools milling or sitting on cases talking. The Stepney children stopped close to the entrance and Helen watched as Chris stood quite still, looking across at the group beneath the clock. His face had been still and quiet all morning and now she saw it close, saw his shoulders drop, his head turn but not before she heard, 'It's that bloody German.' It was a high voice and she turned and looked and there were the Alton Mews children from Highlands School, standing behind their banner, carrying the same gas masks as Chris, the same cases. But they were not the same; they were English and at the flash of fear on her son's face, she moved.

She felt Heine hold her arm but she heard the call being taken up as it had been in 1938 when faces grew ugly and words even uglier.

'It's that bloody Hun.'

'What you doing 'ere, boy? You should be over with that Hitler.'

The other children were turning now, staring first at the boys from Highlands, then over to Chris.

Around them women were looking, talking, pointing.

Helen moved again, pushing forward and this time Heine was with her. She passed the woman she had talked to in the park.

'Please let us through,' she said and the woman looked at her and then at Heine. Her own face was blotched with tears.

'Please let us through. I have to reach my son,' Helen said, clutching her arm.

The woman wrenched away. 'I didn't know you were one of them,' she said, her mouth twisted in her face. 'If it wasn't for you, our kids wouldn't have to go.'

Her words were taken up then and Helen was pushed and so was Heine but they got through, somehow they got through into the station, and saw Chris yards and yards away, standing with space between him and his friends who were no longer his friends. A teacher was there, his face cold, his hand on Chris's shoulder. A train was pulling in now and there was hissing steam and shrieking brakes and the harsh engine smell all around them.

A guard came towards them, his hat large, shouting at them to go back.

'You've made your decision. Stick by it.' His teeth were rotten and his breath smelt. Heine put his arm out and pushed on by. Chris was crying now, watching them but moving, always moving towards the train, the children still shouting, the teacher herding his column onwards.

A WVS woman in a hat intercepted them. 'Go back, please, behind the barrier. If we let you through they'll all come.' Her voice was loud but the shrieking brakes were louder and Helen pulled free of the hands which held her, dodging past the children as they turned to look for their parents one last time, and now there were tears from many children and they were on her face too.

Still she could hear the calls of 'German' 'Hun' 'Murderers', and she wanted to scream at them and at Heine because it was all his fault.

A boy with red hair shouted at her, 'Bloody Hun.'

'Stinking German.'

Christoph's column was moving now. His face was white and pinched but the tears were still there and they were too far away. He was getting on the train and suddenly she saw that he must not because now she knew what it was going to be like being German when England was at war.

A teacher was taking Chris's shoulder, pointing to the door, and she wasn't going to reach him, there were too many children, too many teachers, too many hands pulling at her but then she was through and Heine was with her. She reached Chris and he felt her hands on his arm, her voice.

'Chris, come home.'

He turned and pressed his face to hers. The boys were shouting at him because he wasn't Dutch as he had said, he was German. The teacher told her that there were many who would be kind, it was only a few and she knew that he was right but a few was too many and so the three of them went home to a city almost without children.

That night she whispered to Heine, 'I'm sorry, my darling,' because she couldn't forget that she had blamed him and part of her still did.

At eleven-fifteen a.m. on Sunday 3 September, Chamberlain announced over the wireless that Britain was at war with Germany, and fifteen minutes later Helen heard the air raid siren and stopped with a duster in her hand, fear making her mouth drop open, making her scream come as though she were a child in pain. Heine picked up the gas masks and turned her, pushing her towards the stairs, calling Chris, shouting at her to hold her son's hand, get him to the shelter, get him to safety, and then she moved, pulling her son, her head down, waiting for the whine of bombs, the crash and splinter of glass.

She ran down the garden, hearing nothing but the siren, hearing their neighbours rushing down their path, hearing Heine running behind. Her mouth was open and saliva ran down her chin. She felt a fear deeper than anything she had ever known. She looked up but could see no planes, no black crosses, no falling bombs, but they would come. She thrust aside the curtain and went down into the dark, the bloody dark which she could not bear, which her son could not bear. She took the masks from Heine, watching as Chris put his on, his chin in first and then the mask over his face, the straps wrenched over his head, and still the siren filled the air.

She pulled hers on; it was hot and smelly and pulled at her hair. She felt that she could not breathe, that she would die here and now in the noise and the fear. She held Chris to her, watching Heine who sat with them but then the mask clouded up with her breath and she could not see his face. They waited but no bombers came that day though the liner *Athenia* was sunk on the third and then the letters from German-haters began to drop through the letterbox, harsh, cruel and accusing.

Internment also began. Men were taken from their homes, locked away where they could do no harm to Britain. Their friends went, those who had come to escape the Nazis and who loved Britain. They went in police cars, handcuffed, interned without trial but no one came for Heine and they dared not think of it or even talk.

There was no school now because there were so few children, but Helen asked Dr Schultz who ran a small private school a

75

quarter of a mile away if he would have room, and because he knew of Heine's work and was Austrian he took Chris. He would only charge half the fees because Heine had been visited by the police and told he could no longer use a camera because he was an alien and they soon found that he could find no other work for the same reason. Dr Schultz offered to approach a bank manager he knew who might find essential work for him so that they could live once their savings had gone. They felt exposed, impotent and afraid.

Each morning Helen walked Chris to school past alley-ways where children who had not been evacuated and who did not now go to school waited. They never hurt them, just shouted and Helen told Chris to ignore their talk because they knew no better, but they made her tremble and see only greyness around her. Even the rockery had bloomed then faded.

In the afternoon Heine collected him and walked back to the swings but Chris did not want to stop where people could see him with his father because his father, Herr Weber, was German, wasn't he, and the British were fighting the Germans, weren't they? So Grandfather and Grandmother were their enemies and planes would come and blow them to bits and those planes were flown by Germans, by people like his father. So one day he went screaming from the park and when Heine ran after him he shouted, 'Leave me alone. Why can't you be English? I hate you. I hate you, you're a Hun.'

In November they heard that Heine had to appear before a tribunal which would decide whether he was to be imprisoned.

That night they did not sleep but then neither of them slept any more. Helen listened to their son crying and she could not do anything to help because nothing could be altered. Heine had cried too because he was the cause of all their tension and she had held him and said, 'Sshh, it doesn't matter. It will be all right. Everything will be all right.'

But she wondered how it could be because already he was not allowed to travel more than five miles from the house. Already they had swept up shattered glass from the stones hurled through their window. Already their son was weeping because he did not want his father to bring him home from school but neither did he want him to be kept from them in a prison camp.

In the morning there was a letter from the bank manager that Dr Schultz had spoken too. He offered Helen a job, not Heine. It would be deemed war work and keep her in London with her family. Heine had kissed her as she left for school with Chris holding her tight, looking at her face, the lines, the eyes, and loved her more than life itself and tried not to feel humiliated, just as she was trying too.

His son would not kiss him but pulled away and went from the house but then ran back and hugged him.

That night Heine was home again. He was not considered a danger to the country, he told Helen over a glass of wine, sitting Chris on his knee, explaining to him about Category A and Category B but how much could a child who was not yet seven understand? He looked back to Helen.

'I'm Category B, my love. I'm not dangerous enough to be interned immediately but unfortunately I didn't merit refugee status, Category C. I was not deprived of my occupation by my government or deprived of their protection. I merely ran away from them.' His laugh had no humour in it.

Helen gripped his hand. 'But they must know how hard you've worked to save people. They must know you won't do anything to hurt this country.'

Heine hugged Chris to him but the child pulled free and went across to Helen.

'I want to go to bed, Mummy. Will the German bombers come tonight?' He did not look at his father and Helen could not either because of the hurt she would see there.

Heine was not allowed to register at the Labour Exchange and so Helen earned for them while he washed their clothes, swept the flat and made sure their supplies were ready to take into the shelter if there was a raid. But there was no raid. There was no real war. Just hostility, just fear and pain. He was refused as a warden. He could only walk his son home and try not to feel that his life had no worth any more.

In the evenings the lights were dim, the voltage reduced as a wartime measure. The blackout was in force. Helen asked her mother to come and stay because she felt she should but Mrs Carstairs refused because Heine was at home all day and he was a German, wasn't he? She told Helen that she did not want to be whispered about, did not want a brick to be thrown at her.

Helen met Marian one day and smiled but she walked straight past, the collar of her coat drawn up, her gloved hand holding it together at her throat. Her brown shoes scuffed the leaves which lay on the path outside the park. Emily was with her because Marian had not been able to face the thought of evacuation either.

'Hello,' Chris said.

There was no answer because Marian dragged the child along too quickly. Helen didn't watch her go, but took her son into the park and watched him on the swing. It was so quiet with no children.

At the end of November her mother came to stay and Helen was surprised.

'It's Chris's birthday and he must have a party,' her mother said. 'For the children at that nice little school.' Helen looked at Heine and smiled and was touched at her mother's efforts.

Her work at the bank was not interesting but it kept her from the war factories outside London and earned them just enough for party food but not enough for a present for Chris. So each night she sewed in the dim light of the sitting-room lamp as her mother drew up plans for games and made hats out of cardboard with Heine, sticking the seams while he held them together.

Chris came out of his bedroom looking at his father as he drew coloured circles on the paper hats and then he walked over and leaned against his leg, taking up a pencil, colouring in the circles, and Helen turned away because she did not want him to see the tears which would not stop running down her face and into her mouth. It was the first time he had touched his father for weeks.

All that week she came home from work into a house full of secrets and excitement and voices which stopped when she entered the room. The first of December was a Friday and so the party was planned for Saturday.

In bed on the night when their son was seven, in a room guarded from the moonlight by the blackout, Heine held her, telling her that he wanted to give her something to show how much he loved her, how he would never, ever stop loving her. That tomorrow he would be away for the morning but would be back in time for the party and Helen said he must because it

78

would be the first one he had attended and they loved him so much. She stroked his smooth skin. His warmth and his lips were on her body and as the night wore on they loved one another as though there was no tomorrow.

Helen baked on the morning of the party, while her mother talked and her son played in the cowboy outfit Helen had sewn during the evenings while her eyes ached with the strain of wartime Britain. He drew his cap gun in and out of his holster, firing at Mrs Simkins in her garden and then at his grandmother. She would not play dead but Helen did, gurgling and groaning until he shrieked with laughter.

Before lunch her mother put on her coat and hat and said that she would walk for a while in the fresh air to build herself up for the next few hours. She had a slight headache. Helen laughed and watched her mother walk down the street, her gas mask in a tin box hanging from her arm. The war had pulled them together, she thought, watching through the windows which were criss-crossed with strips of sticky paper to protect against stones as well as bombs.

The children arrived at three o'clock and her mother's head had cleared. She was laughing and joking in a way which Helen had never known. There was a happiness in the older woman which warmed the daughter. Some of the children who came were English, but some were the children of refugees and it was good to hear laughter from other children, not hissed profanities. It was good to see Christoph's face loosen and hear his laugh too.

At four o'clock Heine had still not returned and Helen could not watch the children for more than a few minutes before going to the window and looking down the street. Dusk was falling, a chill mist was settling and soon the parents called to take their children home before dark. They were friendly and kind before they left and Helen wished that Heine could have been there to feel the warmth of friendship. She must talk to him, they must meet these people again, but where was he?

She walked again to the window, wiping her breath from it with her hand. Beads of moisture remained. Worry tore at her. She looked towards the High Street and then towards the Church but no one stirred. Chris stood by the window now, watching, crying, and her mother said, 'He'll be fine. He's just been held up I expect.'

79

'But where has he gone? Where would he have gone?'

Then Chris turned. 'Grandma knows. I heard her tell Daddy what you would like more than anything.'

Helen turned to him. He was rubbing the window where his breath too had condensed. She held his hand still and turned.

'Nonsense, Chris.' Her mother's voice was sharp as she carried plates from the table to the kitchen. 'Come now and help me carry these things.' Helen watched as she pointed to the hats which the children had discarded by their plates.

Chris walked across and picked them up, then looked at his mother.

'Daddy made nice hats,' he said. 'I wish he had been here.' It was dark in the room now. Helen pulled down the blackout blind, and then the curtains before putting on the light. She walked to the kitchen.

'Where has he gone, Mother?' she asked because fear made her cold.

'I don't want to spoil his surprise,' her mother said without turning.

'He said he would be back. He promised. It was important to him.' Helen knew she was shouting. She could tell from the look on Christoph's face. 'I'm sorry, my darling. I just want to know where Daddy is.'

'But Grandma knows,' Chris said, standing by the sink as his grandmother ran the tap, her flowered overall pulled tight across her breasts.

Helen turned again to her mother but then the knocking started on the door, started and did not stop, and Helen ran to it, seeing Chris behind her, seeing her mother turn.

It was the police. They had come to tell her that Heine had been arrested in possession of a camera in Hemsham. He would not be returning. He was in custody and would be interned, probably on the Isle of Man. He was considered Category A now, a danger to the country.

'The police had acted on information received,' one of the policemen told her because he was a friend of theirs and had drunk wine with them last month.

'But you can't just take him,' Helen said, holding Chris in front of her, keeping her voice calm. She must stay calm or she would not get Heine back and she could not go on without him.

'But you can't just take him. He's not dangerous. Bill, you

know he's not.' She wanted to reach out and touch Bill Rowbottom's arm but he looked different in a uniform.

'We can, I'm afraid, Mrs Weber. We don't need a judicial warrant for his arrest. We act under the Royal Prerogative. There is no charge necessary to imprison enemy aliens.' He paused. 'But, Helen, what was he doing outside the five-mile limit? And with a camera? He'll be interrogated. This is very serious.'

Helen just looked at him, at his eyes which were not unkind, at the badge on his collar, the helmet which he had not removed.

She gripped Chris tightly. An enemy alien. How could Heine be an enemy alien? And she wanted to shake this solid, kindly man but instead said, 'When will he be back?'

'I don't think he will be, my dear. Not until all this is over. Not until the bloody war is over.' He nodded at the other uniformed man who left to wait downstairs. Helen knew he was there because she had not heard the front door open.

'Now I need his passport and some clothes.'

His passport was in the top right-hand drawer, beneath the letters from his father. She packed pants, shirts, trousers, pyjamas, toothbrush, shaving kit, mirror, hairbrush, saying the words aloud. She carried the case back to Bill. It wasn't heavy, she told him. 'It really isn't heavy,' she said again and again, until he prised the case from her and left.

But she didn't see him go. All she could see was Heine's face, tired and drawn and full of love, all she could feel were his lips on her body and now they had taken him.

She stared ahead at the door and saw that it was dirty. There was jelly on it. There was red and green jelly on it, bloody jelly.

Her mother was there behind her, holding her arm, shaking her.

'It will be all right now, Helen. I am here. I can look after you. It will be all right. It will be just the three of us now.'

'There's jelly on the door, Mother,' Helen said, pulling herself free, sitting Chris in the chair, reaching for a cloth from the table, rubbing at the marks. How dare they take him? How dare they take Heine? He was good and kind. How could she cope without him? How could she face the stones, the hate? Oh my God. But what was he doing there and with a camera? How could he do it? He should have been at the party.

'What was he doing there?' she said, leaning her head on the door, crying now, shouting the words. 'What was he doing there?'

She turned, leaning her back against the wood, seeing the fire flickering low, the debris of the party, her son sitting curled against the dark red cushions of the chair, his eyes large and alone. She went to him and held him, stroking him, telling him it was all right and then he was crying and talking and his words came together into a sentence.

'Grandma told him to go and get a picture of the stream for you.'

Helen could not move her body but her mind became clear, rapid and cold, and she remembered Bill Rowbottom's words and now she looked at her mother. At the smile which was playing on her face, at her happiness this afternoon. At the words she had spoken – 'There will be just the three of us now' – and knew without a doubt where her mother's walk had taken her; knew who the informant was.

And then she screamed, 'Mother.'

And all the hate in her body was in that word.

CHAPTER 6

The plain-clothed police had been waiting for Heine when he stepped from the train. They grasped him by the elbows, pushing him over towards the waiting-room, pressing him up against the red-brick wall, his back flat to it. He felt the strap of his gas mask digging into his shoulder, saw the faces of passengers as they paused, looked, then hurried on. The train drew out, noisily with sparks flying from the wheels.

'Your registration card, sir?' the uniformed policeman said, stepping back, taking it from Heine's hand together with his ticket; looking, nodding to his companion who tightened his grip on Heine's arm. 'It's him.' They did not give him back his registration book.

'Your camera?' The policeman spoke again and this time there was no 'sir' and now Heine knew what Helen's mother had done. He knew that, for him, at this moment the war was over and he was filled with anguish because he could not bear to be parted from Helen, and fear because he knew that the bleakness of imprisonment was all that waited for him. There was no anger yet.

They took him to the local police station, locking him in a bare, cold cell with no blackout blinds because there were no windows. They removed his shoe laces and his belt and he walked backwards and forwards in stockinged feet because he could not stand the slopping of his shoes. He wouldn't kill himself, he wanted to shout. He had done nothing wrong. He had a wife and child. They brought him cocoa with grease floating in blobs and bread and margarine on a tin plate and then he tried to sleep but could not. He tried to think but could not. Nothing stayed still, there were just flashing images of party hats, rust-streaked wheelbarrows, toboggans which sped down slopes. He asked the policeman when he came to check

83

that he was still alive if he would tell Helen, and he said that he would ring his local police station because they needed his passport anyway. So his wife would know when they arrived, wouldn't they? His voice had been hard and his eyes too.

In the morning they returned his registration book and took him by car back to London, the handcuffs uncomfortable on his wrists. They had not charged him at the police station and they did not charge him now.

'No need,' the policeman said. 'There's a war on, mate.'

Heine knew they were right. He thought of the stream which he had not reached, he thought of the party he had missed. He looked out of the car window at the houses which crowded the roads more densely now; they were approaching London. He knew exactly where they were going but he would not think of anything except this moment; only the house they had just passed with the red roof, the sandbags at the windows of the Town Hall to the left. The churches into which people hurried and which were tolling their bells. For him? Yes, it should be for him.

His mouth was dry. It was hours since he had eaten because he had been unable to face breakfast. It was hours since he had spoken to another person as a free man and that weighed like a stone around his neck. Now he was an enemy, a man to be grunted at, to be ignored, to be treated as though he was nothing. But he was someone. He was Helen's husband, Christoph's father, but he could do nothing for them now and so, therefore, they were right. He was nothing, just an enemy alien. He belonged nowhere.

Heine clasped his hands together, feeling the cold of the handcuffs, wanting to stretch out his arms, roll his shoulders, but the policemen sat either side of him, and as they drove up to Olympia at last he wanted to break free of them, run through the streets, back to his home. Because what would they do without him? And what waited inside the sandbagged entrance for him? But he knew the answer to that question. There would be Nazis waiting for him at this huge building which was now the collecting centre for enemy aliens. He did not move from the car at the policeman's command because fear had taken his strength from him and all he could see were the brown shirts of Munich and feel again the pain of his leg.

'Get out of this bloody car before I make you,' the policeman still sitting at his side shouted, pushing him.

Heine moved then, side-stepping his way along the seat, stumbling from the car because his hands were latched together and he could not find any purchase. The soldiers with fixed bayonets standing in a line outside the building did not look as he passed through the entrance. They just stared ahead as if he did not exist. The hall was in semi-darkness, the light excluded by the blackout, and Heine remembered the decorations and the noise of curious crowds at the exhibitions before the war and it seemed as unreal as he now felt. There were people, but they were milling aimlessly beyond barriers which marked off the area nearest to the door. There was a low murmur, that was all.

The policemen pushed him forward towards a dimly lit table behind which two British Intelligence Officers sat, heads down, pens writing on paper. In shadow at the edge of the desk was an inkstand and two mugs which were coffee-stained and half empty. The badges on the officers' hats glinted on the chair at the left of the table.

They did not look up as Heine stood there, his shoulders aching from his immobility. The police stood too, sighing, coughing, until one of the men looked up, but not yet at Heine, only at his companions.

They nodded and the police left but the handcuffs were still on. Heine raised his arms and the Intelligence Officer nodded and called the men back, watching as the key was inserted and the metal fell from Heine's wrists and the police left again. Heine did not look round but he could hear the fading click of their shoes.

The Intelligence Officer did not ask him to sit and Heine rubbed his wrists where red marks hurt.

'I'll have your registration book, please.' The Intelligence Officer was not rude, just cold. His eyes were pale, expressionless and his hair was thinning on the crown. Heine wanted someone to speak to him as though he was a person.

He took the police registration book from his pocket and passed it across to the officer who didn't smile or speak while he examined it and then he looked up.

'Category B is a bit out of date, Mr Weber, isn't it?' he said, his lips barely moving as he spoke.

'I was only in Hemsham to take a photograph of a stream behind my mother-in-law's house. One that my wife is very fond of,' Heine explained but it sounded foolish, absurd.

The man just nodded. 'We'll discuss all that in a moment, shall we.' It was not a question but a statement and Heine felt totally helpless.

He was not carrying his passport and so the man nodded to his colleague who telephoned, speaking quietly into the mouthpiece before placing it carefully on the rest and returning to his work.

'Can I tell my wife, please?' Heine asked.

'I dare say someone will be telling her soon. We have to have your passport, don't we? Can't just go in and take it, can we?' His voice was crisp. 'Any more than we can just have people taking photographs, especially Category B aliens.'

Heine said nothing. He emptied his pockets when he was asked and watched as a list was made, but it was short because he only carried one handkerchief and some money. He was allowed to retain these and his watch. Then the questioning began and always the murmur of the other detainees ran like a river around him.

It was not until midnight that Heine was allowed to sleep. He was marched up to the gallery where three-tiered bunks were set up, row upon row. The guard pointed to one. There were no blankets and he did not know where to wash and so he lay down amongst the snores and mutters of a night which was dark and lonely.

In the morning the blond middle-aged man in the next bunk sat up, swung his naked legs to the floor and looked across at Heine.

'So, another joins us, eh?' He laughed and stood up in his underpants, snapping his heels together, raising his arm. 'Heil Hitler, my friend. I am Hauptmann Meiner.'

He wore a vest, his lips were full and his belly sagged. Heine turned from him but felt a hand on his shoulder, pulling him back. It was not Meiner but another man, blond and young with anger in his face. He wore blue-striped pyjamas and his hair was cut so short that Heine could see the pink of his scalp.

'You do not return our salute?' he said, his face close to Heine's. His night-time breath was stale.

Heine stood up now, pushing the hand from him.

'Surely, my dear Hauptmann Meiner, you are incorrectly dressed for saluting. You have no hat. You look ridiculous,' he said, his voice heavy with contempt.

He walked from them past bunks where men loitered, some half dressed, some fully dressed, some still asleep. It was as dark as it had been last night. No daylight came past the blackout. It was so large, so full of so many people. His head was aching and in the cloakroom a man was shaving, peering into a metal travelling mirror, pulling his face to one side as he ran his razor down his cheek. His voice was distorted as he said, 'Good morning.'

He was English surely, Heine thought, and replied, 'Good morning,' as he drenched his face and hair with water so cold it numbed his hands.

'So, you are not newly arrived from Germany?' the other man asked.

Heine shook his head. 'I've been here since 1930. Had a bit of trouble in Munich.' He smiled slightly and dried his face on the corner of a sodden towel hanging from a hook. The other man had his own. It was blue and thick, not like the one Heine held which was threadbare with a red stripe running down the centre.

'Ah, Munich.' The man sluiced the shaving soap from his face and Heine ran his hand over his own chin. It was rough but he had nothing with which to shave or clean his teeth.

'My name is Isaac Stein. I have been in England since 1919,' the man said, watching him carefully. 'I have a spare razor if you would care to borrow it.'

Heine looked at him, at his face which was narrowed and wary and recognised the look. It had been on the face of the fallen Jew in Hanover.

The door was opening as he said, 'Thank you, that would be most welcome.'

He reached across as Isaac handed it to him but a hand with thick hairs and raised veins gripped his wrist and as Heine turned he saw the young blond man and Meiner.

'Aryans do not use Jew-boys' razors.' It was the young man again, his hand gripping tighter still. Heine looked at Isaac who said nothing, just waited.

Heine at last felt angry, a deep fierce anger which slashed at Mrs Carstairs, at himself, at the world for tearing his family apart, at this blond young man who dared to touch him and speak such filth and he turned, lifting his knee into the German, bringing down his free hand against his neck, then sweeping his fist round to catch the side of his face and nose.

The grip on his wrist was gone and the German lay on the tiles, his nose bleeding, his mouth slippery with saliva, his throat heaving as he gasped for air, and there was no pity in Heine because it had all gone on for long enough. Meiner had been watching from the door.

'Hauptmann Meiner, I met your brownshirts in Munich. You taught me many things. Now your friend knows some of them too.'

Heine turned back to Isaac and kept his hand from shaking, though he did not know how, as he began to shave.

'Did you know that in Southern France and Northern Italy they call brown the colour of the beast?' Heine said, fighting to keep his voice level whilst Meiner pulled the German boy over to the sink, washing him, throwing water on him.

'You will pay for this,' Hauptmann Meiner said but Heine would not look at him. He washed the soap from his face, handed back the razor to Isaac and followed him from the room. He felt cold now but not frightened. He was tired of running. Just so damn tired of running, he told Isaac, and so angry.

Breakfast was bread and margarine and stewed tea which coated his teeth, but his hands shook so much that Isaac had to lift the cup to his lips. His hands were throbbing now and he kept seeing the blood and hearing the gurgling, and was angry that he shook so much. It was not through fear, it was just reaction. He looked at the men who ate around the table. They were quiet as Isaac told them what had happened and then one old man turned to say, 'It is good to hear such news.' His eyes were dark and his face drawn.

Heine was glad that for the first time he had fought back.

After breakfast he was interrogated again and it lasted until the evening when he moved his bunk to be nearer Isaac and the non-Nazis who had accumulated at the far end.

For the next two days he was questioned but on the fourth he was left in peace for a day.

By then the Nazis and Hauptmann Meiner had been transferred to another camp but there were other Nazis to take their place and they talked in loud voices of the victory that would soon be theirs: of the Dachaus they would build in

Britain when Hitler came. They sang the 'Horst Wessel' at night when the others wanted to sleep, they jeered the *challahs* which a new internee brought in for the Sabbath, telling them that the plaited bread was like the blonde hair of the Aryan maidens who were the women of the master race.

Heine talked quietly to men he met; those who had fled from the terror which was now Germany, Austria, Czechoslovakia, who moved away from the raucous noise and tried to understand why they were here, locked up with those whom they thought they had escaped. At night, only at night, Heine allowed himself to think of Helen and Christoph.

When the police had been to collect his passport they had brought back clothes and shaving kit, a mirror, a hairbrush, and it helped to know that Helen's hands had held them but he could hardly bear the loneliness which tore at him.

The questions stopped in the second week and the next morning his section of the gallery was told they would be moving, that they must gather their luggage together. They were taken in unheated lorries away from London, sitting quietly, huddled together for warmth. They were driven to the siding of a railway station, jerking past large heaps of coal until they stopped and were ordered out, jumping to the ground on numb feet, reaching up to help the old men down. They stood near discarded sleepers beside the track, letting the elderly sit on the stacked wood, turning their backs to the wind, collars up, hats pulled down with their gas masks hanging from their arms, their cases at their feet.

A train arrived after half an hour and the guards formed them into columns, marching them along the chippings. One old man stumbled and Heine caught him before he fell. They embarked from a deserted platform at the count of three and then they rumbled off to an unknown destination.

Isaac was not with him. He had not been transferred yet but there were other friends. There was Albrecht who had fled in 1938. There was Werner whose parents were in a concentration camp. There were Georg and Wilhelm who had lived in England since they were six and were now twenty. There were the Nazis too.

In the carriages they were forbidden to lift the blind or open the window. Neither could they move about. Drinking water was not available and though they travelled throughout the day they were not allowed to buy tea at any of the stations that the train eased into.

They arrived at four p.m. at an unnamed station, parched and no longer talking, but they knew it was near the sea. They could tell from the gulls and the smell in the air. They were marched through the town with the Nazis holding up their arms in salute. The crowd jeered and Heine wanted to explain, to tell them that all Germans were not like this but as the sounds of the 'Horst Wessel' drowned out the gulls he knew it was no use.

They marched out of the town and down a lane where leafless hawthorn grew and the December wind was chill. It was darker now but there was light enough to see the gates that Heine and his friends straggled towards though the Nazis still marched.

There were low white painted wooden huts set in neat rows behind flowerbeds containing hard pruned roses and an empty swimming pool with a solitary spring board. Lichen grew on the tiles and momentarily Heine saw Helen marking in the number six on the bridge parapet. The guards pointed towards one large single storey building.

'Down there,' they said. 'Assemble in there.'

Heine took Willi's arm, a boy of eighteen who had walked alongside him from the train. He had told Heine quietly, his voice hesitant, his eyes anxious, that his father was in Sachsenhausen concentration camp, where he too had been but had escaped. He was glad to be back in a camp, he told Heine, because the English guards would protect him when the Nazis came and Heine did not point out that there were already Nazis here. He just patted his arm and kept close to him, because he would want someone to take care of his own son.

The lounge they filed into was carpeted and there was no longer the sound of crisp Nazi boots marching and Heine was glad to see their militaristic fervour thwarted by a piece of worn Axminster. The settees were comfortable but everyone was still hungry and thirsty. They were not given anything yet but were called in groups of ten to see the doctor.

Heine was called with the boy, Willi. He was examined and interrogated but only for two or three hours this time. They were escorted in groups of eight to huts by two soldiers with

90

bayonets fixed who told them that they were at a bloody holiday camp.

'Comes to something,' one had said to the other, 'when you put these buggers into a bloody holiday camp.'

Heine said nothing because there was nothing to say.

They were pushed into a hut filled with four two-tiered bunks and no one moved as the door locked behind them. They still had not eaten or drunk. There was a mirror, a wardrobe and hot and cold running water and Heine felt proud of the British. Proud that they treated their prisoners as they did and he smiled at Willi and nodded.

Two hours later they were called back to a large hall where they were served tea, cheese and bread from two trolleys, each with an urn, one of which dripped on to a folded dishcloth. Nothing had ever tasted so good. Willi ate too, tearing at his bread, hiding some in his pockets until Heine told him that this was not a concentration camp, that the British would feed him again.

The Camp Commandant spoke to them when their meal was finished; explaining that they could only leave the fenced sleeping quarters under military guard. That they would only leave those quarters in order to eat in the dining-room.

'A camp leader must be chosen to be responsible for the performance of your obligations and your conduct as prisoners-of-war. He must be able to take the necessary measures to see that any orders I may give are complied with, and put any complaints or suggestions before the Commandant of the Camp. This leader must form a committee which will be responsible for the cooking arrangements, education, recreation, even hair-dressing.' He paused. 'One last point. Everybody who wishes to can appeal to the Home Office for release and Advisory Committees have been set up to examine cases.' His voice was crisp and professional.

Heine sat quite still, hope in him once more. There was more than a murmur of conversation. People were laughing, slapping one another's arms, and the Commandant smiled before he left.

The Commandant stopped at the door and called back, 'You have three-quarters of an hour to hold the election for your camp leader. You will then be escorted back to your quarters.'

There was a pause in the talk then and Heine ran his hand

along the wooden table. The grain was straight and smooth from the scrubbing of many years. He would appeal as soon as he could and be home. Perhaps by Christmas. He watched as a tall man stood up. He was not young, and his voice was loud as he called for quiet, moving towards the back of the room where he could be seen by everyone. He stood next to an urn that still steamed.

'I propose Captain Rettich for Camp Leader,' he said into the quiet which had wrapped itself around the room. 'We must show these British how efficient the Germans are. We must run the camp along clear lines for the short time we will be here. Our Führer will destroy these British before long. We all know that.'

He pointed to a man who sat smiling quietly. Another man stood up. 'I second Captain Rettich.'

Heine looked around at the nodding heads knowing by now that the vast majority in the room were Nazis, most of them prisoners-of-war whose ships had been sunk. They would win any election but they must not be unopposed. Oh no, they must not be unopposed again.

He looked down the table. The men with him were liberals, Jews, refugees, all were non-Nazis.

He said quietly, 'We must not just let them take control. They must know there is opposition; that their authority will be questioned. Someone should stand against them.'

Heine waited for an answer; there was none. He looked around the room. The Nazis were talking and laughing now. They must announce a nomination soon or it would be too late, there would not even be a vote.

Herr Thiene said, 'I have a wife, you see, and she is unwell. I want to be fit to argue my appeal. However, I will stand if no one else will.'

Others nodded, shrugging, talking, and at the next table it was the same. Willi said as he leaned back in his chair, 'I have seen the Nazis in the internment camp I started in. They beat a man to death who stood against them.'

There was silence and then a cheer was heard from across the room and Heine thought of his father in Hanover, his friend in Munich, but then he thought of Helen and the life he owed her, her grunting tears when he had hit her what seemed like years ago.

There was not much time now. The Nazis were beginning to raise their hands, their laughter was louder still.

Friedrich, who sat at the end of the table, leaned forward. 'We should not ask our friend, Herr Thiene, to challenge these people.'

Heine knew that this was true and as he heard the Nazis he spoke. 'Nominate me, Willi, second me, Herr Thiene.' He felt he could not breathe.

Willi looked at him. 'You know what you are doing, Heine? They could hurt you.'

Heine pushed him up. 'Quickly now, there is no time.'

He listened as Willi called out the nomination, listened as Herr Thiene seconded him, and knew that this would make him the spokesman against the Nazis. He listened hard to the words, watched closely the hands which voted for the Nazis, the fewer hands that voted for him. He pushed away the thought of Helen's face if she ever came to know what he had done.

He had not won the election but the wire fence around the huts did not suffocate him as it had previously done. The guards with their fixed bayonets meant nothing because he was fighting back. At last he was fighting back and he felt strong again.

The next day he bought camp notepaper which the inmates called eggshell paper and wrote to Helen restricting himself to the twenty-four lines they were allowed.

He told her that they were by the sea. That the gulls woke them in the morning. That he loved her. That he was going to appeal. That smoking was not allowed outside the dining-hall, that he would miss her and Chris at Christmas in five days time. That he worried about them and the hostility that they lived amongst in their street.

He did not tell her that he had been punched in the stomach as he left the dining-hall that morning and warned to keep away from his *Moishe* friends but that he had caught his assailant across his cheek as he turned to leave.

The next day was 21 December and the Nazis held a festival, for it was the day the Teutonic pagans celebrated the solstice. Timber was set ablaze for this occasion with the Commandant's permission, but Heine wondered whether the

93

man ever saw the Nazis' salute raised in the light from the bonfire.

On Christmas Eve Willi sang 'Silent Night' and Heine remembered Helen's voice soaring as they listened to her in the candlelight of his parents' home and that night he wept but so did many others.

In January the snow was heavy and it was cold, so cold, and Heine stood with Willi and watched the Nazis build snow swastikas and Herr Thiene said that when the thaw came they would melt as, in time, the Third Reich would.

'But when will that be?' Willi asked and no one answered.

The Camp Committee was set up in January under the direction of the Camp Leader and it was in charge of the food distribution as arranged. There seemed never to be enough for the non-Nazis. Heine lodged a complaint with the Camp Leader. It was ignored. He lodged a complaint for the Camp Commandant through the Camp Leader. It was not passed on.

He stopped the Camp Commandant one day and told him and knew that Nazi eyes were watching. The next day the food improved but he was beaten in the latrines. After that the non-Nazis stayed together, close together, and Heine's eyes and lips healed but they had kicked his leg and that still did not mend.

In late January he received his first letter from Helen.

My darling,
At last I know where you are. Your letter only arrived in the second week of January. We are well. Christoph continues to go to Dr Schultz and so far there has been no bombing.

I know it was my mother who caused all this. I cannot speak to her now, or see her. I am happier this way but miss you so much and long for you to be at home with us. How is your appeal going? Please write and tell me.

It is a relief to know that you are safe, away from the hostility which you would otherwise face. That comforts me each night.

I will write again soon, my love.
Helen.

*

In March Heine received leave to attend the Advisory Committee. Herr Thiene had already been released and Heine missed him and Wilhelm too. He stood at the window looking out at the snow as he pulled on gloves that Willi lent him and hugged the boy to him before he left. He had taught him English and mathematics and anything else that he could because he needed to feel useful as much as the boy needed the attention. But could he really be called a boy? Willi had seen too much to ever be young again.

The guards were knocking on the door now and Heine walked down the snow-cleared path, dirty with ash and sand and laughed at the shoes and slippers that were thrown at him by his friends for good luck. It was like being in Germany again, the Germany of his youth. He did not look at the huts where the Nazis lived and from which came the sound of jeers. He knew they were at the windows and he would not look at their faces.

He travelled by train under guard, and then by Underground to Piccadilly Circus and wanted to run to Helen, he was so close. They walked through to Burlington Street and his breath was visible in the cold. People passed them, hurrying, busy, free. There were posters on the newspaper stall and he saw the headlines: 'US peace mission fails.'

He wanted to stop and buy one, to see newspaper ink on his fingers again because they were not allowed the sight of one in the camp and lived on rumours. He looked again at the headlines. Britain would need the United States in order to survive. Would they ever join in?

As he sat before the panel of ten his feet and hands hurt with the warmth and he held Willi's gloves and told them where and when he was born. What his business had been, his present address.

'How often have you been abroad?' they asked and he replied with the truth.

'When was your last visit?'

Again he replied with the truth.

Here they stopped and the Chairman looked at the others, slowly. Again and again they took him back over that journey.

'Why did you go?'

'To see my parents.'

'Yes, but why then? War was so close. Wasn't it strange?'

Again and again they asked and he held the gloves tighter each time because he could not tell them why. To do so might injure his father. Word might get back. Oh God, Helen, he thought as he looked at the dark panelling, at the Chairman's face, so set, so dark. Oh God, I'm not going to come home now. I know I'm not. He pushed down the panic. Could he tell them of the camera? His knuckles were white as they held the gloves. He knew he couldn't. 'But you see, it was because war was so close that I went. I needed to see them again. Surely you can understand that?' He watched their faces. Would it be enough?

It was dark when they left and the guard held a torch whose slit of light barely picked out the path shovelled through the snow and Heine looked at him and wondered how far he would get if he pushed him to the ground and ran. But he didn't because it would be pointless. He would not be able to go home, for that is where they would look for him.

At the station the guard bought him tea and the steam rose into his face, blurring his eyes, warming his skin. He pushed his gloves into his pockets and held his hands more tightly round the cup. He sipped, knowing that Helen was not far away, that his son was there too. Knowing that his appeal would be rejected because he must not betray his father. They left to board the train but it was late into the station and the guard looked around. He was young and looked kind and Heine had told him about Germany, about Munich, about Helen.

'There's a phone over there, mate,' the soldier said. 'Give your wife a ring. I won't listen.' He handed money to Heine and walked behind him to the booth.

Heine lifted the receiver, dropped in the money, pushed the button and heard her voice and for seconds he could not speak. Then he said, 'Helen, it's me. I'm just about to get on the train. I've had my appeal hearing. I'm going back but it's breaking my heart, my darling.' He didn't know where the sobs were coming from in a grown man.

'Heine, I'll come. I can come. They've told me I can come and see you. Don't cry, darling. Don't cry. It will be all right.'

But on the train with its meshed windows, its black out blinds, the dim lights, he knew that it would not be all right because he had set himself up in opposition and now he was not going to escape the Nazis. Would he ever get home again?

CHAPTER 7

Helen sat on the wooden seat. The brass plaque which had been screwed into the wood was dull. What would Sir Reginald Potter think of that, she wondered, as she watched Chris swing high into the air, lifting her face to the spring sunshine of 1940, and who was he anyway to warrant a park bench as a memorial? It was Sunday, her day off, and there were other children here after a winter bare of young voices. The children were trickling back from the countryside because no bombs had fallen. Nothing seemed to be happening and people were kinder to her now that Heine had gone and no invasion had occurred.

Chris laughed at the boy on the swing next to him. He had grown since Christmas, he was tall for seven and mature and he smiled more now that the schools had opened in the mornings and the boys no longer had time to lie in wait for him en route to Dr Schultz. He was happy there, secure, and Dr Schultz had said that it would not be a good idea to move him back to the old school where hate might still lash out at him in snarls and punches.

Helen fingered the letter which had arrived from Heine yesterday telling her that visits could be made twice a week for two hours. He knew she could not come so frequently but if she obtained permission it would lighten his days and his nights.

She looked up at the sky again, where white clouds drifted against the blue, where no aeroplanes had yet roared, bucking and firing; bombing. Yes, she had obtained permission and would go soon to see him and the thought filled her with joy.

Shading her eyes, she watched the barrage balloon which was anchored by wires in a corner of the park. The airmen who were always there now, guarding, winding, checking, sat outside their metal hut smoking, occasionally talking,

97

sometimes laughing with the children who hovered near. Perhaps they were reminded of their own families, thought Helen. Did Heine ever speak to children?

The balloon's elastic sides heaved in the slight breeze; its floppy ears trembled. It was never still, always fighting to escape, to climb higher still. In February one had broken loose, its wires snapping as the wind had torn and snatched at the air-filled hulk above. It had floated off, its wires breaking tiles and chimney pots but it had not escaped. It had been shot, sinking airless and powerless to the ground, covering the road and the gardens. You should know you can't escape the war, Helen had said, and knew that she had spoken aloud because a man who was walking his dog paused and laughed.

Would these lumbering balloons really force aeroplanes up into the sky so that accurate bombing was impossible, so that strafing of civilians would be impracticable? 'We shall see,' Helen murmured, beckoning now to Chris because she felt sure the bombers would come. But when?

'Time for lunch.' She smiled as he shook his head. 'Come along, no arguments.'

He came then and they walked home past the Wardens' post where they too sat outside in the sun, their overalls unbuttoned at the neck, ARW embroidered in yellow. Mr Simkins from the flat next door was there, his tin helmet resting on one of the sandbags which lined the walls. There were more bags on the roof and a post with the number '51' stuck out from them. Mrs Simkins, who looked after Chris until Helen returned from work, said that a bit of power had turned her old man into a right little 'itler.

Helen nodded and waved and Ed Simkins smiled, flicking the ash from his cigarette on to the ground before throwing her a half salute. They had always been kind and helpful, and other neighbours were too now that Heine had gone. Helen lay awake at night and felt guilty at the relief his absence brought. She lay awake too because of the pain that absence also brought and could make no sense of anything any more.

Chris did not hold her hand now as they walked. He was too big, he had said, and Helen had been pleased at his confidence. They passed posters stuck on the wall showing them how to remove distributor heads and leads, how to empty petrol tanks or remove carburettors in the event of an invasion. They were torn now and discoloured, one hung by a corner only and folded over on itself. Chris swung his gas mask at the sandbags which were heaped at the foot of the lamppost outside their house.

'Careful, Chris. You might need that.'

He just grinned. 'It's good for putting my lead cowboys in, Mum. They fit in beside the mask. There hasn't been any gas, has there? No bombs either. Nothing's happening, is it?'

Helen turned the key in the lock. No, nothing was happening.

They sat quietly in the evening, either side of the small fire because, though the days were warm and blossom hung from the trees in the park, the heat vanished with the sun. Helen could smell the smoke which hung above the coal which she had wrapped individually in damp newspaper to make it last longer. Smoke drifted out into the room but she could not open the window wider because the blackout would be broken.

She knitted, her hands sore from digging up the lawn for vegetables as everyone else was doing. More things would be rationed soon and she would grow potatoes and cabbages.

Chris was making a balsa wood aeroplane and the sharp, clean smell of glue cut through the bitterness of the smoke. His lips were set together, a frown dug down between his eyebrows. He was eating well, though meals were dull and repetitive with only half the usual food being imported. At least now everyone had two ounces of butter, and in the grocer's yesterday afternoon one woman had said that she had never tasted it before in her life and that if this was what war did to you, it was a bloody good thing. She had laughed then, showing blackened teeth and gaps where there were none and Helen had smiled but felt angry that so many people who lived in this part of London were tasting butter for the first time and that it took a war to distribute food fairly.

She watched now as Chris took out the Oxo tin which he kept in the cupboard under the wireless. There was a concert playing quietly and he should really go to bed but it was good to have someone else in the room.

He took a cotton reel from the tin and cut notches in its high rims.

'What on earth are you doing?' she said, setting down her knitting, pushing back her hair. 'Be careful.'

99

Chris did not look up but said, 'I'm making a tank.'

Helen did not want him to be taken over by the war. 'What about your cowboys and Indians, the lead ones? A head came off, didn't it? Have you repaired it?'

'Of course, Mum, like you showed me. I stuck that match you gave me into its head and pushed it down into the body.'

Helen poked at the fire and flame flickered up, clearing the smoke, giving off heat. She looked at her son kneeling on the floor, his socks down by his ankles, his shoes off and under the table. She wished she had her camera but they had all been confiscated.

'But why a tank?'

'Because the other boys are making them, that's why.'

He was poking a hole in a stub of candle now, then making a slight groove along the top side. He pushed an elastic band through the hole and tried to keep it in place with a matchstick which lay in the groove. It would not stay and so Helen came and settled on to her knees too, holding it for him, hearing his breath as he concentrated. He threaded the band down through the reel, keeping the candle stub on the top, and pinned it fast to the bottom with a drawing pin.

She watched as he wound up the elastic band and laid the reel on its edge with the matchstick touching the small table. The frown was still there and so was the heavy breathing but slowly the tank began to move, unevenly but inexorably, and now he looked up at her and smiled. 'That's good, isn't it?'

'Very good,' she replied. 'Daddy would be proud of you.'

He just smiled and wound it up again.

The next week the warehouse behind the bank was filled with *papier mâché* coffins and the man who usually worked next to her was absent, arrested for filtering the red pool petrol through his gas mask filter and selling it on the black market for 6/6 a gallon.

On 9 April, the war which the Americans called phoney became real. German troops entered Denmark and moved into Norway, taking Oslo, Bergen, Trondheim and Narvik. The British newspapers claimed that the collapse of Norway was due largely to betrayal from within and Helen felt the tension knot in her back.

In May one Borough Council dismissed in the interests of

public safety seventeen enemy aliens who had been engaged in Air Raid Protection work for the previous five months. A stone was thrown at Helen's window but did not break it because of the gummed tape. She began to walk Christoph to school early, before work, because the boys were going later to school and waiting in the alleys again and her son grew drawn and tense and took a safety candle to bed each night, carrying the saucer it stood in, sheltering the flame with his hand as he walked, smiling to his mother, but the smile did not reach his eyes.

On 10 May Germany invaded Holland and Belgium and Chamberlain's government fell during a debate on the Norwegian campaign. Winston Churchill became Prime Minister. On 12 May, it was declared that in the interests of safety male Germans and Austrians over sixteen and under sixty who lived near the coast were to be interned. The newspapers called for more action against the fifth-columnists who were probably signalling to aircraft, who were making plans behind their blackout curtains to betray the British nation to Hitler.

Each day there were more calls against the aliens and Mrs Simkins looked worried, though she still looked after Christoph because Heine was already interned, wasn't he, dear, she had said, and could do no mischief. Helen had wanted to snatch her son from her but she needed her job and anyway would not be allowed to resign as it was necessary work.

Other aliens, from non-coastal areas, had to report daily to the police station in person and not use any motor vehicle, except public transport. They had to observe a curfew between eight in the evening and six in the morning. On 15 May, Helen had to appear before a tribunal because she was married to a German but was exonerated and that night she thought her head would burst with the pulsing pain and wondered who had written to the authorities. Who was trying to ruin her life?

Mrs Simkins heard in the greengrocer's that one of the mothers in the park had reported her for taking too much notice of the barrage balloons and Helen just nodded but did nothing, for what could she do?

Helen washed the curtains that night, and the carpet, the paintwork, wanting it clean and fresh and new, wanting an end to it all but it had not even begun. She knew that, as the rest of Britain knew, because the bombers were waiting, somewhere

101

they were waiting, and so were those in her area who hated the aliens. Despair was close.

She worked later now because there was so much to do and came home aching with tiredness, but Chris was crying in the night again and she told him that soon they would be able to go and see Daddy but he would not go. He didn't want to because it was his daddy who made him different, who made people throw stones, and shout and spit at him, he sobbed. Each night he cried and each night Helen held him, angry that her son was frightened and confused. Angry at these people – angry at Heine. And then, when Chris slept, her anger faded because she loved her husband and wanted him, but still the anger was there, and the pain, and the tiredness. And still there were no bombers.

She travelled to the internment camp on 25 May after receiving permission to enter a coastal area. At each change of train police stopped her and everyone else, checking their identity cards, their driving licences, before allowing them to proceed. She bought weak tea on the platform, sipping it, watching people waiting on platforms for trains. They were normal, fighting a war, an enemy they could see clearly, and she was envious because she remembered Heine's parents and friends and wished she did not know so many good Germans for then it would be so much easier.

Her tea was nearly finished and now she could hear the train. She talked to other passengers as they lurched and rattled away from the station. She did not tell them why she was travelling but talked instead of her son and an old woman asked, 'Will you evacuate him?'

'Perhaps.'

As the wheels rattled she looked out of the window but could see little through the mesh. Perhaps, she thought to herself, because evacuation had been in and out of her mind since 9 April, not because of the planes which still had not come, but because of the boys who shouted and attacked. But Chris could not go where he was known, he could not go where the other children had gone, so where? Joan who worked beside her at the bank had an aunt in Norfolk who was kind and tolerant and had said she would have him, but how could she let him go? He was only seven and she loved him, needed him. How could she let him go?

From the station she walked through the town, asking in a shop where the internment camp was, and ignored the stares and the hostility because she was used to it. She walked past the houses, the barbed wire which seemed to be everywhere, coiled in long rolls along the beach. Past the empty ice-cream stands, the rows of boarding houses, some shuttered, forlorn. Past the gardens which still held flowers. She heard the gulls which Heine had written of, smelt the sea breeze, saw the hawthorn in full leaf as she walked down the lane, heard the birds, full-throated, melodic.

There was a high wire fence at the bottom of the lane, and gates guarded by sentries. More barbed wire was rolled on top of the squat huts. It was like nothing that she had seen before and Heine was here, barricaded like a criminal. Helen showed her pass and was escorted to a hut by a soldier with a bayonet that glinted in the sun. It was two-thirty p.m. Behind that door would be her husband but she must not tell him of Chris crying, or of the boys, because he must think that they were safe.

He was there, sitting at a table, but then she saw that it was not one table, but two pushed together. He looked older, thinner and she went to him but was waved back by a guard.

'Sit there,' he ordered, pointing to a chair at the other side of the two tables. 'And you must not touch your husband.'

Helen walked towards the chair, looking at Heine, not at the two tables that had been pushed together so that she could not reach him, could not touch his thin hands, his tanned skin. Could not smell his skin or kiss him. She sat, clasping her hands together and they said nothing yet, just looked, and then he smiled.

'Hello, my darling.' His voice was the same.

They talked then and another prisoner brought coffee in a tin mug and she told him of the bank manager who dealt with all the munitions and war factory accounts and how she worked until late because records must be kept, details must be logged, or production would falter. She told him of the balloon in the recreation ground and how it had torn free. She told him of Mrs Simkins's kindness. All this he already knew from her letters but it did not matter because they were speaking words which reached over the distance between them.

She did not tell him of Chris.

Heine told her of the English he taught Willi. Of the hairdresser who had opened up in one of the huts. He told her of the concerts which were held every Tuesday. He did not tell her of the barbed wire which had pierced their roof, letting in the water when it rained. He did not tell her of the Nazi sailors who were picking flowers to make victory wreaths. He did not tell her that they sang in the evening of Jewish blood dripping from Nazi steel, shouting also that Hitler was very close. He did not tell her that he had been beaten again for taking the scissors from the hairdresser because he would not cut Jewish hair. Neither did he tell her that she was too thin and her eyes were sad.

'You are so beautiful, Helen. You are so very lovely.'

'And so are you, my darling. You will be careful. You will think of us, remember that you must come home to us.' Helen could see the bruise on his neck which he had not spoken of. But she would say no more because they both had their war to fight and when she left she didn't cry or look back until she was far along the lane and all the time she wondered if she could bear to come again, only to leave him so thin, so hurt.

On 28 May Belgium surrendered and the evacuation of the British Expeditionary Force from Dunkirk began. Small boats, big boats, ships; anything that could float took men from the beach and the sea and filled up the stations, the trains, the camps, the hospitals in Britain. Helen saw them in lorries being driven from Waterloo, dazed and defeated, and wondered what would happen now, and she was frightened, as everyone she met was frightened. Invasion could be only weeks away, the press said, and so did the girls she worked with and the passengers in the tram queue as they craned to see the illuminated number which had been moved from the front top to the side to avoid attracting enemy aircraft and Helen wanted to run home, snatch up Chris and hide. But where?

Then the newspapers began again. Act! Act! they screamed. Lock up all refugees from Austria, Germany and Czechoslovakia. Lock up those of British nationality who could be considered in sympathy with the enemy. And so they were locked up, including the British Fascists, and so too were German and Austrian women between sixteen and sixty. Many of those had escaped from the threat of concentration camps, from the terror of the Nazis, and Helen wondered whether she would be sent for again and could not sleep for the fear which ran through her because of what would happen to her child.

By June there was still no invasion though Italy declared war on Britain, German troops entered Paris, and on 23 June Britain stood alone.

'Got rid of those bloody frogs. Now we can get on with it,' Mrs Simkins said.

No one had called to take Helen away and she spoke to Bill Rowbottom because she could not bear it any more and he told her that she was safe. She was British, she had been cleared once and that was enough. She went home and weeded the garden, digging down into the earth for the dandelion roots but snapping one off in error, knowing that next year a dozen would come in its place. Would there be a next year? She threw them into Chris's small wheelbarrow, watching as he took them to the compost, putting her hand on her aching back and lifting her face to the breeze because at least she was free.

In the summer small-scale air raids occurred but not near them. Signposts came down. Road blocks were put up, ringing of church bells was banned and Heine's camp was to be moved but when? For weeks she heard nothing from him though the newspapers told of prisoners being evacuated and interned in Canada and she wondered if he would be exiled. But he wrote to say that he would not.

On 2 July the *Andorra Star* was sunk by a German torpedo. It had been carrying internees bound for Canada. Nearly six hundred were drowned and now, at long last, the newspapers said, 'What have we done to these friends of ours?' Overseas internment ceased and people began to think rationally, not with fear. Neighbours were chastened and left lettuce on the doorstep, not stones, and Helen showed the paper to Christoph who was glad it was not his daddy who had drowned and said to Helen that he loved his father and she held him close because he had not said these words for far too long.

Marian, from Alton Mews, came round and said she was sorry for everything she had not done. She came each week after that and sat with Helen in the evening and read stories to Christoph because Emily had now been evacuated to her

105

grandmother in case Germany started bombing, and without her child she could not sleep or eat.

In July the police drew up outside and Helen watched as they knocked, gripping the window ledge, wondering if they had come for her but they had not. They had come to tell her that her mother had been knocked down in the blackout and killed. She stood quite calmly while they told her, watching the clouds scudding through the sky as white as the gypsophila which she had picked from the edge of the garden that morning.

When they left she sat in the chair and thought of her mother; the tight curls, the smooth skin, the eyes which were hard so much of the time but which had softened when she saw her grandson; the hairbrushes on the dressing table; the young refugees whom she could not condone, and Helen wondered if she would have been able to at her age.

She thought of the evening they had had together when Heine had gone to Liverpool, the loneliness which had been assuaged for those few hours. Then there was the day of the Jubilee, the laughter, the talk and now regret crept in and guilt.

But then she thought of her father; the damp curtain, the bleak room. She thought of the telegram to Hanover, of the sight of her mother's smile when she arrived home from Germany, the same smile when Heine had not returned from Hemsham that day. That smile which had played across her mother's face each time she was released from the cupboard. That night she didn't sleep but sat up stirring weak tea, not knowing what to think or feel but knowing that there was a loss inside her. She heard the ticking of the clock on the mantelpiece, the twelve chimes of midnight from the church tower. Then one, two, three, four, five, six o'clock and still she did not know what she felt.

She arranged the funeral but did not take Christoph, and on a hot sunny day she buried her mother next to her father, standing with Mrs Jones and Mrs Sinclair while the vicar spoke, his voice calm and quiet as the bees nuzzled the flowers from the Avenue and her wreath. As she threw a handful of earth warmed by the beating sun on to the coffin, she cried, but not in grief for now she knew what she felt. She cried for what might have been; for the companionship they might have found together, echoes of which had reached them both but which had been destroyed.

106

She cried for the woman her mother must have once been; for the loneliness she must have experienced especially when Helen turned away from her finally but in the end she could feel no guilt because her mother had betrayed Heine. She turned from the grave as the vicar finished and now there was a sadness which bit deep and would be with her always.

In a dark cool office, sitting behind a dark cool desk, the solicitor read the will, his voice as dry as his lips, and Helen received the rocking horse her father had made for her before he died. The house and all other effects had been bequeathed to her mother's cousin.

She walked then from the office to the untarmacked lane where her father and Heine and her son had walked, down to the bridge where the stream barely flowed on this hot dry day. She leaned over remembering so much, wondering why the world had gone mad. She rubbed the lichen, dry and crumbling, and felt her father's hands around her waist, saw Heine's hands firm and strong throwing the stick, heard her son's laughter as he peered to see who had won the race, and then she turned and left the bridge. Would she ever come here again?

As the summer grew hotter the hospitals took pilots whose faces had been burnt beyond repair as they fought the Luftwaffe in the skies above the fields of south-eastern England. Still no sticks of bombs fell. Chris did not have to pass the boys because it was not term time and Marian or Mrs Simkins stayed with him while Helen worked.

She thought of evacuation as she walked to the tram, to the shops with her ration book. She thought of it in the evening but who would hold her hank of wool while she wound it into balls, she asked herself as she looked at her seven-year-old son, so big now with the fear gone from his eyes. Who would smile and warm her heart?

At the end of August bombers got through to London, but not over them. Lying in bed, her hands limp at her sides in the heat, Helen feared that the time was close for Chris to go because his safety must be everything, but how could she bear it? And so sleep would not come because she knew that she must cope, as so many other mothers were having to, and so many children.

*

On Saturday 7 September at five-fifteen Helen was peeling potatoes in the kitchen, watching Chris in the garden, kicking the ball up and down the ash path, missing the potatoes by inches but not the cabbages. She opened the window to shout and then she heard them, droning, rumbling, inexorably following the Thames and then there was the air raid siren, rising, falling, rising, falling and she knew that at last they were coming and her son was down there, playing on the path.

She dropped the knife into the bowl and water splashed up at her, cold, so cold and she could not shout as she saw Chris stop and look and turn to her and then back towards the sound which was everywhere. The siren and the unsynchronised beat of the bombers wrapped around her head but the sun was out; it was Saturday, people were shopping; how could they come? The noise grew louder, and now she moved, reaching for the gas masks, for the bottle of water she kept for the shelter as instructed and then she ran down the stairs, along the path, picking Chris up, her breath hard in her chest and then through the curtain of the Anderson, into the darkness, and still there was noise, nothing but noise and no one to hold her. Heine was not here. She must not moan and cry with the fear she was feeling because her child was frightened too. She must smile and say, 'It's fine. It's fine. We're in the shelter Daddy built. It's strong. It's fine, Chris. It's fine.'

On and on they came, hundreds, darkening the sky, thundering, and Chris began to cry and so Helen told him of the ravens, telling people to hide until the gods had gone by. But these were not gods, her mind screamed, these are black-crossed monsters and then the thunder of the aeroplanes was overhead and the thud of the ack-ack was louder. The noise was like nothing she had ever heard, pressing into her, tearing her mind from her. Now she pulled Chris's gas mask up over his chin, his nose, his hair, and then hers, the straps catching at her hair, suffocating her, and the bombs began to fall, screaming, crashing, shaking the ground, and her breath was clouding the mask so that she could not see Chris and she tore hers off so that he could hear her talk, hear her sing to him, as she held him on her knee, leaning over him in case they were hit.

The shelter moved with each juddering crash but at the end

108

of one hour they were unhurt and the planes were gone and no bombs had fallen near but the docks were ablaze. The all-clear wound on as Helen waved at Mrs Simkins who was crying. Smoke was rising above the docks and there was a smell of destruction in the air which was quite new to her and to her neighbour.

Helen forced herself to walk up the path, leading Chris, calling to Mrs Simkins to come too, because neither of them wished to be alone. It was good to be back in the flat, away from the rising palls of smoke, but inside the ceiling of the kitchen was cracked and plaster lay in the bowl of potato peelings. She picked the knife out of the water. The wooden handle was cold. Fire engines were driving past the flat and ambulances and lorries, then more fire engines, bells clanging, and while Chris watched and counted from the window, calling out to her when they reached ten, Helen tried to scrape the potatoes but her hands shook too much. She boiled them in their jackets and made Mrs Simkins eat with them because Ed was on Warden duty, though neither of them was hungry.

Helen sat watching Chris eating fast, eating theirs too, and Mrs Simkins spoke in bursts and so did Helen and what they said made little sense. The siren went again at seven and the bombers came in 'V' formation and they walked to the shelter because Mrs Simkins could not run.

'I don't want to die alone,' she whispered as she sat on the bench looking at Christoph picking at the cork, but not seeing him.

'We won't die,' Helen said against the wail of the siren.

She was right, they did not die, but others did in the two hours when the bombers flew and targeted and dropped their loads which screamed and crashed until darkness fell. When they pushed the curtain aside this time the sky was red and Helen could see the cabbages quite clearly in the light from the burning docks and the smell was everywhere.

The fire engines came again and the ambulances and the lorries for the bodies and they ran along the road towards the greengrocer's – which was no longer there, just rubble and dust that caught in their throats. Helen turned Chris away as Mr Taylor was dug out, dead, and fire roared up suddenly in what had been his home.

'So this is war,' she whispered.

The bombers came again that night, blasting and searing, and at three a.m. a bomb tore and whistled too close and the shelter shook and shrapnel banged on the roof as the ground lifted and dust choked them. The curtain billowed and they felt the blast. Mrs Simkins cried out that they should wear their gas masks but Helen could not bear to breathe in the smell of rubber and Chris screamed and kicked and would not have his put on his face. But Helen could not hear the scream only see the lips pulled back, the fear and rage, because the planes were circling now, their engines drumming, the bombs pounding, drowning out all other sound and she knew that the next one would hit them, but it did not.

Again and again the ground shook and fear became less sharp though it was just as deep because the bombs fell for hours. There was a sourness in Helen's mouth and her breath was shallow and remained so until the all-clear went at dawn.

They climbed up the steps of the shelter into a dawn which was dust-filled and like no other that Helen had known. There was the smell of burning still heavy on the air, the crackle of fire, the screams of people, but the drumming was gone. At least the drumming was gone, but for how long?

In one hour, while Chris slept on the settee and they waited for the siren yet again, Mr Simkins came to fetch his wife. He was drawn and white and covered in dust but people had used the shelters and that pleased him, he said, as he helped his wife down the stairs and then he stopped and turned, saying quietly, 'The Hopkins boy has been killed. A direct hit. He was eleven.'

Helen watched as Mrs Simkins seemed somehow much older in a matter of seconds. Her lips were quivering, her head wobbling, and Helen knew that now it was time for Chris to go to safety and she knelt by the settee and laid her head on his, not waiting to see if Mr Simkins and his wife had left.

CHAPTER 8

The train stopped and started throughout the November night and morning but Heine could see nothing of the country they jolted through because the blinds were pinned down but he heard the planes, drumming overhead, coming in waves. He looked at his cards, his matchsticks in a small pile on the cases they had piled up to make a table and smiled when Willi won, but there was little talk. They were listening for bombs to fall and split the train apart, to crash and tear into their bodies.

How many had fallen on Britain since September, Heine wondered. How many on London where Helen still struggled in to work over craters where roads had once been and water spouting from broken mains, round cordons, fire engines, ambulances? And he wished that she too could have moved to Norfolk as Christoph had done.

As the train stopped yet again he put his cards down, shaking his head at Willi and Leopold. The noise of the planes was too loud and Wolfgang threw his hand down too, his face intent as he eased the blind away from the window, levering it from the pins with his pen.

'They fly high still,' he said. There was relief in his voice.

They had become complacent, Heine thought, tucked up in their holiday camp by the sea. They had heard the bombers day after day, night after night, but always they were going somewhere else, weren't they? And now we too are going somewhere else, but we don't know where, and perhaps we shall feel the judder of the ground which we have only so far had to imagine as we listened to the wireless or read the newspapers or received letters which told us our families were dead.

Not mine yet though. Not mine.

They were travelling up through England to another camp,

the guard had said as they had embarked before daylight in alphabetical order. Leaving the train is forbidden even in the event of a raid, he had continued, so that when the first formation of planes overrode the rattling of the train on the rails, their hands had become too wet with sweat to deal, and Heine hoped that the Nazis who had cheered when Martin Stein had heard that his family had been killed in the first raids felt the same fear.

It was not until midday that they reached the covered station that their guard told them was Liverpool. So they must be bound for the Isle of Man, Heine thought. Their mouths were parched because the water had run out at eight in the morning but there was nothing to drink, just soldiers with bayonets pushing and shouting, herding them into columns, marching them from the train.

Heine fastened his grip on his case, printed with a 'P' for prisoner. He did not look at the passers-by who stopped, their faces tired and drawn, darkness dug deep beneath their eyes. He did not turn as they cursed the column; he looked ahead but then he could see the raised hands of the Nazis, their swagger nurtured by their months in safety by the sea, their chants of 'Heil Hitler, Heil Hitler, Heil Hitler' ringing out in rhythm to the march until the guards shouted and thrust their rifles at them.

Now there was just the sound of feet; the clanging of train wagons, the barked orders, the coughs as they reached the landing stage and the grey cold entered their lungs and the dampness from the riverside seeped into their clothes and their bodies. But at least the sky was above them and they could feel the wind in their faces. They marched in step until a floating stage was reached and then they were ordered to stand at ease. Heine looked at the small grey steamer tied to bollards with thick hawsers which dripped wet slime. The river was stained with fuel oil, rainbow splashed in the cold shrouded sunlight.

'It is the Isle of Man we go to now, so says the guard,' Willi said, turning to Heine.

'We will not all fit on that boat?' Wolfgang asked from behind.

'He says that there is another coming. They have already taken an earlier load,' Willi replied, not turning his head but looking towards the boat as the gangway was secured.

Heine was watching the gulls as they wheeled in the wind which licked at the river, and wished that Helen was here, travelling with him, away from the mainland, away from the bombs. He thought of the letter he had received from her and reached into his pocket, feeling it with his cold hands, feeling closer to her because of it, because her hands had also touched it.

He drew it out, reading it again as the wind snatched at it.

My darling,
I have just returned from the station where I saw Christoph leave for Norfolk. He has gone to Joan's aunt, Laura Manners who moved there to live with her husband many years ago. He is dead and she is lonely and Joan tells me she is kind. I wanted to go with him so much but Mr Aster would not allow me the two days away from work that I would need.

He was so very brave, so very small, and I could hardly bear it but at least he will be safe. Mrs Manners knows that he is partly German but to her it doesn't matter. She thinks it better though, not to tell the villagers because the vicar's wife is a 'patriot' and there may be others.

Oh, Heine, I miss you so. I miss our son. When will it ever end?

I love you,
Helen.

The siren began then, a penetrating sound which silenced the clamour of voices, the shuffling feet. On and on it went, striking into their shocked silence and then they heard the planes, drumming with that German beat, louder and louder, but they were not allowed to move towards shelter. Instead, as the sky darkened with wave after wave of wide-winged, heavy-bodied, black-crossed planes and the drumming seemed to press the air from Heine's body, the first of the men clambered up the gangway.

'Come on, get going. Move it along.' The guards were shouting but they could not be heard now against the bombs thudding, bursting, whistling. The ack-ack was stabbing up into the sky and Heine held Willi's arm, his own shoulders hunched as the stage shook, even though it was not part of the battered earth. He pushed the letter into his pocket, unable to believe the noise.

Soon no sound existed other than the crash of bombs, the crackle of the burning riverside, the explosions of warehouses, the clamour of fire engines and ambulances. No cold air filled their lungs now. It was hot from the flames and their fear.

The guards were waving the men forward, always forward, their mouths working, no words audible. Bombs dropped to either side, ceaselessly, the noise filling Heine's head, stretching it, hurting it. The heat was greater now and the birds were no longer wheeling but had gone. Gone where? Where was there to go?

Some men were crouching and shrapnel was flying through the dust-laden air. The soldiers wore tin hats and pulled at the men, then pushed them on to the gangway.

'You can't take shelter. There's nowhere to go. We must sail, go quickly, out to sea,' the sergeant mouthed at Heine and Wolfgang, rushing forward, hurrying those at the front.

Shrapnel clicked and slapped on to the floating stage, hot and jagged. It clicked and slapped into backs and arms and soon men were being dragged back on to the quay, blood staining the ground, no cries audible, just faces and twisted mouths.

They were at the steamer now, the gangway rope rough in Heine's hand as he pulled his way up, his case banging against his leg, his gas mask in the way and still the raid went on and on until at last the Manx steamer cast off and moved away from the noise, the destruction, the inferno. Sailing down the Mersey, away from the red flickering flames reflected in the river, away from the roaring heat to the open sea beyond the bar.

Heine took hold of Willi who was crying, throwing their cases against a bulkhead. He passed Martin Stein staring wordlessly back at the conflagration and took hold of him too; pushing and shoving through the jam of men until he reached the side, until they all reached the side. He looked each way and then he saw what he wanted. He dragged them both towards the lifeboat.

'Come on,' he said, again and again, as Martin turned to

look at the flames, which reddened the sky, at the planes which flew in 'V' formations, at the gaps which appeared as the ack-ack found their targets and a burning mass plummeted to the earth.

'Come on,' he said, forcing a way through until at last they were there, resting up against the lifeboat tackle, breathing heavily. At least they had a chance now if they were hit. Still Martin looked back and Heine did too, knowing now what Helen went through each day, each night, and he felt ashamed because he had been safe and would be again.

He looked at Martin, at the dead eyes which had seen nothing since the letter had come, at the lips which never smiled, and knew that now he had seen how his family had died. His father, a successful manufacturer, had left Germany with nothing. His mother, cultured and refined, had played the violin. They had died in an air raid pushing their vegetable barrow because they had been Jews in Hitler's Germany.

He put his hand on the young man's arm but there were no words. What words could help?

The Nazis came then, shouldering their way through, standing before them.

'No Jews allowed near lifeboats, *Moishe*,' one with broad shoulders and blue eyes said, standing with his hands on his hips.

Heine looked at him, moving forward, and words leapt from his mouth, burning as hot as the Mersey had done. He was shouting, his fists were coming up, and Nazis were laughing. But when he called them 'Pigs, not worthy to lick the boots of my friend' they did not laugh, but shouldered closer and Heine wanted them to. He wanted to crash his fists into their faces and their bodies and fight their bestiality.

''Ere. Break this up. There's enough bloody trouble back there!' The guard was pushing in with his rifle, moving Heine along and Willi too. Martin just stood but Heine reached for him, pushing past the guard.

'Why do you not move your real enemies along?' he shouted, pointing back at the Germans. 'Why do you not move those swine?'

The guard took his shoulder and turned him forward, pushing him from behind.

'Because there's too bloody many of them, chum, and just three of you. For God's sake, keep your nose clean.'

Willi had his arm then, pulling him along, through the men who patted him, told him not to fight. It was not worth it. It was pointless. Such a small thing.

A small thing? Heine thought as he turned and looked across the sea wanting cold air on his face; wanting his wife, wanting her love, wanting his son. Seeing the old Jew on the ground in Hanover. He closed his eyes for a moment and then leaned on the rail thinking back over the months of his captivity, the endless battles with these Nazis who shouted and laughed and waited for the invasion. He thought of the words, the fists which had struck at him in the dark because he fought back. He was tired of it, and frightened, but he would not stop. No, he would never stop. There was a war going on, wasn't there? A damn war.

He stood there until they drew into Douglas Bay. It was still light. Willi pointed to the white building standing in the middle of the promenade and the square dark one on the hill behind the town.

'Look, Heine, Martin. Look, it must be a church up there, see, it has a tower.'

Heine looked and nodded but Martin did not.

They berthed at the pier, straggled on to the firm ground, their legs uncertain, their heads heavy with tiredness, following the guard who marched them, slowly this time, along the promenade. They marched to the right of the tram lines which ran between the sea and the tall boarding houses. This time there were no passers-by, just other prisoners, other guards and barbed wire which was tangled on the beach to their left and strung tautly between posts on their right where it surrounded clumps of houses, converting them into camps.

They marched past three camps, each with great locked gates guarded by soldiers, but the fourth was theirs and as the gates opened and then swung shut Heine wanted to clasp his hands to his ears because he could not bear the sound.

He was allocated a house called Sea View, together with Martin and Willi. Wolfgang and Leopold were at The Croft. The House Leader met them at the door and showed them to their room. It overlooked the sea and he explained that this had been a choice room in the days before the war when these were all holiday hotels.

Heine looked out through the salt-stained windows. There

were only four strips of brown gummed paper forming large diagonals and through these he could see the gulls wheeling again and grass on the lawns which fronted roads blocked by the barbed wire which ringed their group of houses.

'The islanders wanted evacuees, not internees,' Johann the House Leader said as he showed them the wardrobe space. 'So they were paid extra to sweeten the pill. I will see you downstairs when you have unpacked. Bring your palliasses with you.' He nodded and left.

There were five single beds in the room, each with two blankets, a pillow and three with empty palliasses. A mirror was suspended above the basin in the corner of the room and a picture of Douglas Bay hung above the door. On the cupboards by two of the beds were photographs and books. The others were clear.

Heine unpacked, then helped Martin who just sat on the bare springs of his bed. He took his clothes, shook them, then put them on to hangers. He placed the Hebrew Bible, his yarmulka, the photograph of his parents on the bedside cupboard. Nodding at Willi to follow, he carried his palliasse downstairs making Martin do the same. They filled them with straw, coughing at the dust, pushing, smoothing, then struggling back upstairs, laughing as they felt the sharp stalks through the canvas, but Martin did not laugh.

A meal was served in the dining-room while Johann explained that all the houses had to work together as a whole to ensure the successful running of the camp. There were schools, lecture halls, even a sports area. Within each house the jobs were shared, each taking a turn to cook and clean.

He told them that goods could be sent in by relatives, and Heine wished that he had not said that because Martin's eyes had flickered then. There was no English money allowed in the camp, he went on. The authorities took it and exchanged it for camp currency which consisted of celluloid discs for anything under sixpence and the rest was paper. No more than ten shillings was allowed to be drawn per week from the camp bank.

Willi asked, 'But what can it be spent on?'

There were about forty men in the room and they laughed. One called out, 'There's the coffee shop. The tailor's. You might like a nice haircut. In fact, you should have a nice haircut, my boy.'

117

Willi laughed and ran his hands through his hair. It was long, too long, and Heine smiled.

'You might have noticed that big white building as the steamer came in?' Johann said. 'Well, that is the old cinema which is used as the depot for camp food. Bread, meat, fish and milk are supplied locally and the military authorities allow us the same rations as the soldiers. You are each allowed four ounces of sugar a week, half of which must go to the cook.'

He paused. 'Now, we have a great many prisoners-of-war here. German sailors from ships sunk by the Royal Navy, airmen and so on. Many of these are Nazis. We have none in this house but they *are* in the camp and we find that it is sensible for Jews and non-Nazis to keep their distance, though for some it is difficult. There are taunts, surreptitious attacks which sometimes cannot be ignored. Be sensible, that is all I say.'

That is what they had said in the other camp but sometimes it was too hard, Heine thought. Later after roll-call, Johann came up to their room, nodding to Heine to follow him out to the landing, asking him if it would be better for Martin to go to the camp hospital. But Martin, who was only twenty, would not go. He wanted to stay with his friends, Willi and Heine, and so he did on the understanding that Heine watched over him.

That night in bed Willi called softly to Heine, 'Can Britain ever win?'

Heine lay on his back. It was very dark though there was a bomber's moon on the other side of the blackout. The mainland would be hurting more than ever tonight. 'Not unless America comes in, and so far they don't want to.'

'So the Nazis will come and we will be lost,' Willi said, his voice still a whisper remembering the camp he had left in Germany.

'No, Willi. Finally they will come in. I'm sure of it.' But he wasn't.

Each day was full with food preparation, chores, lectures and long country walks along the cliffs where the wind hurled at them, pushing them backwards until they leaned into it and strode on. He was pushed as he walked to the lecture hall by the Nazis from the boat. Georg, the leader, kicked at his leg when he would not return the Nazi salute. Heine dodged the next

118

kick, elbowing him, taking the breath from his lungs before walking on. He talked with other non-Nazis and walked with them, Martin alongside and Willi too.

He wrote to Christoph on his birthday and wondered what it must be like to be eight in a strange house in a village you did not know, with your parents far away. He thought of his father in Germany. Was he well? Had he survived? Were the bombs falling on Hanover? Had the Nazis discovered him? He thought of Helen each day and each night and he wanted to hold her just once more. To stroke her skin, feel her lips open beneath his, her breath rapid against his mouth, her body moving, eager, but he could not write and tell her this because the censor in Liverpool read each word, and these words were for her ears alone.

She could not visit, she wrote, but had sent a parcel. Work was busy, travel too difficult. He must wait for the spring to come and the bombers to go. But each day she loved him more.

He gave a lecture in the large hall, talking of photography, of clear images, abstract images, telling them of his wife who preferred to use images to reflect her feelings and how that could be just as effective and, for a moment, he felt closer to her. He walked round the compound with Martin twice a day, talking, always talking. Asking, hoping for a reply, but there was none.

At the start of the second week in December he walked with Willi to the school hut and spent two hours explaining about film processing to a class of seventeen-year-olds. It was cold when he left, cold and brisk, and he walked along by the wire, looking out across the sea, watching the white foaming waves peak and trough, pulling his coat tightly across his chest. His hands were cold, almost numb but the air was fresh and no one else was there but then he heard the shouts, the laughter, and turned and there by the corner of Sea View was Martin.

He was being forced by Georg to kneel. Those large hands were gripping his collar, pulling it tight while five other men laughed. Heine ran, pounding across the ground, the breath was pumping in his chest when he stood close to the men and his leg was aching but that didn't matter.

'Put that boy down.' Because now Martin was being hauled up higher and higher, the collar wrenching tighter and tighter until his toes were almost off the ground. The slats of the

119

wooden fence behind him were broken and the shafts lay on the ground. Heine reached for one but was held from behind.

'Well, our little Nazi hater,' a big German said, 'you don't like the way Georg holds your friend?' He turned to the other men who were laughing still, their faces red in the cold, drips on their noses. 'Do you like the way Georg is holding this dirty little person?' He laughed as they nodded.

'Ja. Ja. Ja,' they said, clapping their hands and chanting.

Heine looked from them to Martin whose eyes were not blank any more, but filled with a fear which was not human. Saliva was running from the corner of his mouth and Heine could hear his breath gurgling in his throat as he struggled to suck in air. Georg pulled harder.

Heine struggled against the hands, there was no time. For God's sake, there was no time. 'Let him go, you animal. You God-forsaken animal. You bastard. You're worse than your bloody Führer.'

He wanted Georg angry, wanted him to drop Martin, to turn on him, but he didn't. Heine relaxed then, slumping into the arms which held him, and then he moved. Quickly, sharply away, pulling out, shouting, 'Johann, Wilhelm, help, help.' Leaping across at Georg and Martin, reaching for the whistle Johann had given Martin in case he ever needed help but he had never understood. He ripped at the boy's pocket, thrusting aside the man who came from the side at him. He had it, cold and shiny in his hand, then his mouth.

He blew but it was jerked from his mouth. Martin was choking now and Heine fought free of the hands again, ramming his head into Georg's side, belly, hearing the groan. He brought up his hand, smashing into his face, seeing Martin drop and fall limp to the ground as Georg sagged backwards.

The hands were on him again, but again he struggled free, using his feet, his head, his fists, reaching for Georg again as he in turn reached for Martin, bringing his fist up on to his jaw, feeling the pain shoot up his arm, and then they were on him, punching and kicking and gouging and for a while he fought back until a kick caught his leg and he screamed. But then the others came from the house, shouting, calling.

'Heine, where are you?'

'For God's sake, where are you?'

He could not call, his mouth was full of blood but then the

Nazis were gone, running before they could be seen, hauling Georg away, his feet dragging limply on the ground, turning to tell him that this was not the end. They would come for him again.

Johann found him and called the others, wiping the blood so that he could talk but all Heine did was to point at Martin. Back at the house Heine spat blood into a bowl while Johann bathed his broken nose, his split lip, the torn eyebrow, but he hardly noticed as he sat in a chair watching Martin rock and moan like a wounded dog. At midday a guard arrived and arrested Heine for fighting.

He was accused of assault on Martin Stein and taken to a cell, while his friends objected. He was frisked before the door was locked and bolted. There were brackets on the wall supporting three loose planks of wood which separated when he lay on them so he sat on two blankets on the floor and did not sleep that night. Not because of the pain but the despair.

When he came before the Commanding Officer at eight the next morning evidence was given by Georg's friend that he had witnessed the unprovoked attack. This was substantiated by three others. Martin could not give evidence. He had been taken under escort to the hospital where he was to be committed to an asylum for the insane. He was completely and utterly deranged, the Adjutant said. His Sea View friends could not give evidence because they were not witnesses to the attack.

Heine was sentenced to four days at Camp Easterley where the punishment block was based. It was a light sentence, the Commanding Officer said, because he was not convinced of the accuracy of the statements but had to accept them. The cell was six feet by three with a small ventilator, no window and a damp cobbled floor. There were eight cells, one of which was the lavatory and the smell permeated the block but Heine did not care. Nor did he care that he had to sit or stand until blankets and a palliasse were brought by another prisoner at ten a.m. All he cared about was that the Nazis had broken Martin's mind. Each day as the guard paced outside that was all he cared about.

Christoph had been eight for almost two weeks when Heine was released but he could not think of his son because he was too full of anger, too full of hate. Instead he watched the orthodox Jews walking and talking. He watched the non-Nazis

121

discussing the war. He read his letters from Helen and received a food parcel from her which had been held up at the administration office run by Hauptmann Rusch, a Nazi. The food was rotten and smelt and Heine sat and looked out of the window, thinking of Helen, bombed, frightened, sending food she could not spare to the Camp where provisions were more than adequate. Thinking of Hauptmann Rusch knowingly destroying her gesture.

He thought of her sending money each week. Money which she earned and he could not. His anger was so deep that he could no longer sleep or eat properly. The next day he walked through the country and ran in the sports field but still he could not rest. He thought of his father, so tired and old, so brave, and on 14 December he gave a lecture entitled 'Democracy versus Totalitarianism', in which he publicly castigated Nazism and everything it stood for.

That night a stone was thrown through his window wrapped in paper on which had been drawn a skull and cross-bones. Willi swept up the glass and the other men helped while Heine burnt the paper but knew that nothing could erase its message. The death sentence had been passed, one which the Nazis gave to those they considered arch traitors to the Fatherland.

CHAPTER 9

Christoph lay in bed listening to the silence. There were no bombs, no aeroplanes, no ack-ack, no cold damp shelter, just a warm bed, a stone hot-water bottle at his feet, and silence. Each night the quiet lay like a blanket around him in this room with the sloping roof, the dark beams, the fireplace which was boarded up. Each night Laura kissed him, pressing the sheets and blankets tightly round his neck to stop the draughts. Each night he lay straight and still and safe and could not sleep because his mother was not there.

The candle in the saucer flickered, shadows catching the dried flowers which hung from string wound around the nails driven deep and rusting into the overhead beam. Marian had given him a string bag full of vegetables when he left London. She had stood with his mother on the platform crying, but his mother had not wept. Her face had been still, her lips barely moving as she said goodbye, bending to kiss him, to hug him, pulling his arms from her shoulders when he clung, pushing him to the WVS lady who stood at the open door.

Other children were all around, crying. He had not cried but he had clung again because he could not bear to leave her. She had pushed him again and her eyes had grown red and full and her lips had trembled as though she were cold. He had gripped her coat and still she had pushed and said, 'Darling. I love you. You must be safe.'

Her lips had not moved around the words, they had just gone on trembling and her voice had been thick and he knew it was with love. He moved away then towards the door and the fat lady, climbing up the step, smelling the train, the soot, the steam. Sitting on a seat that itched, sitting too close to a boy whose gas mask dug into his side, watching as the WVS lady lifted his case on to the rack, looking at the children who sat opposite, wanting to rip off the linen labels which had been pinned on at the collecting post outside the Town Hall. He knew none of the children. They did not know him, did not know that he was German.

As he lay in the soft bed, Christoph pulled the sheet up around his ears. It was cold but warmer than the shelter where his mother would be. The light from the candle caught the flowers again and Christoph felt the string bag once more, full of vegetables and sandwiches, so heavy, cutting into his hand. He had not let go until they had been travelling for two hours because the pain had stopped his tears.

He had shared his sandwiches with the fat girl who only had two of her own. She had travelled on with him and four others by bus to this village and was nice, but she smelt. He didn't mind though because of her smile, and he would not let the others shout at her because Mary was his friend. She could throw stones that hit the targets and laughed when he pulled faces behind the teacher's back. She didn't ask questions about his parents or talk of her own like the others did all the time.

At six the next morning Laura called him, but he was already dressing, pulling on the grey socks with diamonds down the side that his mother sent for his birthday. He lifted the blackout hardboard from the window and saw hoar frost whitening the stunted apple trees in the bottom orchard, stiffening the grass into frozen clumps and knew that today his knees would be frozen again.

The stairs were narrow and dark but the smell of porridge was warm in the kitchen and so was the black-leaded stove which burnt with the logs he had helped Laura to bring in from the woodshed yesterday. She had said that it was good to have a man about the house and he had smiled, liking her grey hair which was wound round her head in a plait, her cheeks so red and full, her laugh which made her chin wobble. His mother would like her, he knew.

He did not stop at the table but walked on through and out of the door, laughing as she flicked at him with the tea cloth. The latch was stiff and Laura called, 'You can use the pot under the bed.'

But he didn't turn. He didn't want to talk about things like that with her. He was not a baby. He was eight now. He closed the door behind him. She had baked a cake and sung 'Happy Birthday' on the first and it had almost not mattered that his mother was not there.

He ran up the garden path, the cold air sharp in his nose and mouth, catching in his throat. He passed the outhouses, hearing first the pig in her sty, then seeing the sawdust outside the woodshed, hearing the hens in their shed. The latch on the door was frost-coated and his fingers stuck to it for a moment and he knew that the seat would be covered with ice again and shuddered. As he sat he could hear the hens calling, forever calling.

'Wait for a moment,' he called back. 'Just wait.'

Laura smiled and pointed to the sink as he returned, and he nodded, washing in cold water which felt warm to his frozen hands.

'Give 'em a good rub with this,' she said, passing him a rough towel. He wanted to sidle up and reach out towards the fire but she would not let him because it would give him chilblains. His mother had always told him that too, so Laura must be right.

He sat at the oilcloth-covered table, smoothing it with his hands, wishing it was white, not black, watching Laura as she ladled porridge into a bowl. She passed it to him, the steam rising, curling bits of hair which were too short for her plait.

He poured thick milk from the jug into the hole he had scooped in the middle and then she spooned honey on top with the same smile that she had used when he handed her the vegetables in the string bag. She had kissed him in front of the WVS lady who had brought him last of all to Laura's cottage. How kind, she had said. How very kind. And it was only later that he had seen the long back garden filled with sprouts and potatoes, swedes and parsnips but he did not feel foolish because Marian had given him the only things she had and Laura had been pleased.

He watched as she moved from the stove, carrying the kettle to the draining board, pouring boiling water on to the bran mash in the chipped enamel bowl, mixing it up with the old dented spoon. Her arms strained beneath her sleeves and her face grew red. She hummed. She always hummed, Chris thought as he took another mouthful of porridge and then stirred his spoon round and round until the honey and milk

125

were mixed completely. She was a happy widow, not like his grandmother.

'Are you a grandmother?' he asked, licking his spoon.

Laura did not turn from her mixture. 'No. I had no children, but your dear mother works with my niece, young Joan. She is almost the same as a daughter to me and no doubt I shall one day be a great-aunt. When I'm wrinkled like a walnut,' she laughed now, turning to him, her cheeks shiny from the mixing.

'You'll never be like a walnut,' Chris said, running his finger round the inside of the bowl. 'You're like a plum.' He wanted to lean against her, feel her arms around him because his mother wasn't here but he was too old for that.

'Look here, while we're chatting away, those hens are getting hungry.' She held out the bowl to him. 'And don't you be cleaning your porridge bowl like that. Your mother would have my guts for garters. Now be off with you.'

Chris took the bowl, feeling the heat of the mash through the sides. 'What about the potato peelings we roasted last night?'

'I'll bring those, but you put your coat on first. That's a bad frost out there.'

They fed the pig next, leaning over the pen door, watching the steam rise from the manure on the other side of the sty, watching the pig snuffle and breathe great belches of warm air. Laura pulled her jacket hood up round her head, tapping his shoulder. 'We'll clean Peggy out after lunch. Pigs are clean if you let them be. We'll get her down to the orchard. She likes a bit of exercise.'

Chris nodded. It was too early to go yet. He was meeting Mary down by the blacksmith. It was Saturday, no school.

'You meeting Mary, are you?' Laura said as they moved to the woodshed to fetch wood in for the fire.

'Yes, by the blacksmith. It's warm and we like the smell and if I'm not there she just wanders about on her own because her lady doesn't like her in the house, under her feet.'

He looked at the pig again. Would his mother let him stay with someone like that? He knew she wouldn't.

He did not see Laura frown as he bent to pick up the spliced logs, loading four into the crook of his arm, not bothering yet to brush off the sawdust and splinters, but breathing in the clean smell of the wood. He followed Laura in, heaping them by the stove, then walked into the sitting-room, lifted up the willow basket from the inglenook and eased it through the door and back out to the woodshed.

Laura was there already, bending and throwing logs into a bucket.

'How are you sleeping now, Chris?' she said, looking at him, rubbing her back with her hands.

'Better,' Chris said, leaning down now, throwing the logs into the basket as Laura moved away. Last night he had not lain awake as usual until the dawn came. Last night he remembered nothing after thinking of Mary laughing in the carriage which had no corridor as one boy had peed out of the window. He had not dreamt of the bombs either.

'You bring that Mary back for lunch. It's rabbit, and if the frost keeps up, we'll have ice-cream as well.'

He walked down the lane past Laura's neighbour Mr Reynolds, who tied his trousers with string at the knee and came after dark every day to empty the night soil from the earth closet and put it on the ash pit beyond the orchard. For the tomatoes in the summer, Laura had said when Chris had thought the neighbour was a spy who came each night because his father was German. When she told him what Mr Reynolds was doing he almost wished he had been a spy instead, and knew that he would eat no tomatoes in the summer.

He was glad it was Saturday but school was quite good. They were taught with the village children, not separately as most of the evacuees were. There were so few so far, Laura had said, and Chris hoped it would stay that way. It was nice and the village boys swapped baked conkers for spent bullets, flattened like mushrooms where they had hit the road. He had picked up pocketfuls in London and so had the other boys. Mary had shrapnel which his mother had not allowed him to bring because it could have sliced his skin. Mary had no mother or father and her sister did not care. He sometimes wished he had no father.

He passed the cottages which were built of grey stone. The women hanging out washing nodded and waved. Would they if they knew what he was? He waved back, then walked quickly on. Were people shouting at his mother, cursing her husband, his father? Was she safe, were bombers dropping their loads now as he walked along safely, as his father sat writing letters safely? Chris kicked at a stone, his feet cold in his boots. He dug his hands into his pockets, his gloves not keeping his hands warm. Laura said that they thought his dad was the same as the others, a British soldier.

He looked back at the women. Laura had also said there was no point in putting out washing today, it was too cold and there was no sun.

He stopped at a gap in the houses, leaning on the stile. The trees were wild and free not like the club-like ones which lined the London streets. The fields stretched into the distance gently rising into a sloping hill. White frost streaked the brown earth and the straw stubble which lay in furrowed lines. The beetfields were further from the village.

He kicked at the post and watched the ice in its cracks shatter and whiten. He kicked again then stood still. Ice covered the fence too and each head of dried cow parsley, each twig of the hedge, each blade of grass. The puddles in the road were thick with it.

'I hate you, Daddy,' he said and knew that he was speaking aloud because he could see his breath burst into the cold air. I hate you, Daddy, he said again, but to himself this time. I hate you for making me different, for making Mummy have to listen to people who shout. For making Mummy have to work in London while the bombs fall and you sit on an island and I stand here, safely. I hate you for making me lie, making me say you are a soldier, making me want the bombers to be hit by ack-ack but when they are I hate you again because I think of Grandpa and can't cheer. He dug at the puddles with his heel, again and again until the ice was crushed and shattered.

But I love you, too, he thought as he walked on and so he pushed the thought of his father away because it was too difficult, all just too difficult.

Mary was waiting by the forge, the hem of her smock dress hanging down at the back. Her mackintosh hem was down too and her cardigan sleeves hung below the cuffs. Her wrists were red from the cold and her gloves had holes in the fingers. She waved and beckoned but he couldn't run because it was too slippery.

They stood beneath the awning and watched as Ted the

128

smith talked to the carthorse. It was tethered to an iron ring in the wall. He nodded at Chris.

'Come to see us again have you?' he said as he reached down and lifted one large hoof between his knees, bending double, paring with the knife, his leather apron stained and burnt.

He grunted as Chris nodded.

'Got your postal order too, I reckon, my old boy,' he said, his head down, his voice muffled as he eased back.

Mary looked at Chris and then away but he caught her arm, pulling the postal order for sixpence from his pocket. 'We'll go to the shop afterwards. Mrs Briggs won't say the sweets are all gone. Laura went in and told her that they should come out from under the counter. Sweets weren't just for village children.'

He smiled at her and was glad his mother sent him this each week for his pocket money and that there was enough for Mary to share. 'And come to lunch. Laura said you must.'

The smith was pressing a red-hot shoe on to the hoof and they heard it sizzle and watched the sweat run off Ted's nose and down his face to his shirt. The heat from the fire reached them and warmed them. They moved closer. Ted lifted the shoe off and doused it in the water tank and the smell came up with the steam to mingle with that from the charred hoof.

They waited until all four were done and then Chris moved to the grindstone near the wall and wound the crank, sharpening his penknife, though he seldom used it.

They moved on then, to the bottom of the lane, shouting back at Tom and Joe who had moved down from London too. They waited for them, walking with them, sliding on the ice, passing the goat which was tethered by an iron ring to a thick stake in the middle of a field between Teel's Lane and the crossroads. Chris pushed his hands into his pockets. He wondered if Mrs Briggs would be cross after Laura's talk.

The Post Office was open and smelt of spices and tobacco. It was dark after the whiteness of the frost and the mahogany counters gleamed. Chris asked for a quarter of gobstoppers after he had cashed the order, knowing he would get six and some liquorice. It was Mr Briggs in the shop today so it was all right after all.

He passed the gobstoppers round and then they slid down Nag's Lane, balancing, waving their arms, wobbling on the stream of ice. They did not speak much and when they did they dribbled pink saliva and laughed. Joe told Chris how his foster-mother had rushed out last night to bring in the washing off the line in case a German bomber came and the whiteness guided him to her cottage.

They laughed again but then walked quietly for a while, round the back of the pub where sometimes a packet of crisps could be found, unopened. There was none today and so they leaned against the wall, still not talking but thinking, because they knew the bombs were dropping on their homes in London whilst here people knew nothing of the noise and the dust and the screams.

The village boys came then, kicking a football up the back lane and so they made up two teams and the village won 6–2, but it was five boys against four, Joe said, squaring up as Ted's grandson laughed. But then they squatted, while Joe pulled out a Woodbine packet, squashed and flattened from his coat pocket, lighting up and talking of his father in the Army, waiting to kill some of those German bastards.

'You shouldn't smoke. You're only ten,' Mary said, taking another gobstopper from Chris, pushing it into her mouth, wiping her hand across her lips. 'You only do it to look big.'

'You don't need to smoke to do that, do you?' Joe said, drawing on the cigarette, blowing the smoke up into the air while the others laughed.

Chris wanted to push him back so that he fell and pull his cigarette from his mouth, because Mary had flushed and dropped her head, and because Joe had called the Germans bastards. But he just pushed himself upright and walked away because Joe was much bigger and he was scared.

He took Mary back for lunch, eating the pie slowly at first, watching Mary looking at the pastry and the meat, then the knife and fork until Laura showed her how to eat.

'I only have chips at home and eat 'em with me fingers from the newspaper,' Mary said, her elbows wide, her hands awkward. 'My sister's too busy. She's got a job. It takes her out a lot, that and her boyfriend.'

'You must miss your mother,' Laura said.

Mary shrugged. 'I don't remember ever having one. She died when I was two. You can't miss what you don't know, can you?'

'What about your father?'

'I don't remember him either.'

After the pie Laura took them out into the garden, round to the north side to the rain butt where they watched as she scraped the ice and frost off the top. They brought it into the house where she showed them how to crush it, then mix it with milk, cornflour and honey from Mr Reynolds's hive. They ate it from dishes in front of the inglenook fireplace and Laura nodded when Chris asked if the slates were in place in the chimney ready for the evening. He and Mary were frightened that the firelight would beckon to bombers which might fly overhead.

They stayed in all afternoon, playing snap and dominoes, laughing at Laura who lost, watching as she fell asleep in front of the fire, whispering, not shouting, 'Snap'. And then they just sat sprawled in chairs, feeling the heat of the fire, listening to it crackle and Chris almost told her about his father because he didn't want to lie to Mary but he did not because neither did he want to lose her.

CHAPTER 10

Helen walked through the streets, glass crunching beneath her feet, shrapnel lying on the ground still warm from the afternoon raid. She thought of Chris's letter telling her of his conker swaps and was glad that normality existed somewhere.

She was tired, more tired than usual today. The warehouse behind the bank had been hit last night. The coffins had gone up in flames and the plate glass windows of the bank had shattered from the blast and the heat. Water had poured in from the fire hoses which had been used to stop the bank from burning. Helen had arrived in the morning to see Mr Leonard in boots and coat, his bow tie immaculate and his face red with fury, standing on a chair directing the staff as they brushed at the water, the glass, the dust which filled the banking hall.

He had handed a broom to Helen, pointing to his ground floor office which he felt she, as his secretary, should deal with but she had passed it back to him, telling him he should do that himself while she helped in the bucket chain which was bailing out the basement strongroom. She had not listened to his protests but had smiled as Joan and the others turned away to hide their laughs because Mr Leonard did not care to deal in practicalities. He had come in from another branch to take over the position of manager two months ago when Mr Aster, Dr Schultz's friend, had been killed during a raid. He always wore a bow tie and would not allow gloves during office hours, though he wore them himself. He hated Germans and Jews.

All day there had been no gas or electricity and daylight was kept out because the windows had been boarded up, the hammering piercing their headaches. They had been cold and wet and the dust had hung in their hair and throats but by eleven o'clock in the morning the bank was open for business, though Mr Leonard had complained that his hands were quite ruined.

'In spite of your gloves?' Helen had asked.

The accounting machines were out of operation and most of the typewriters were no longer serviceable. All entries had to be made by hand in the light of candles whose flickering was reflected in the pools of water which remained in some areas of the banking hall. All letters had to be handwritten and as they worked, the frost cut through the staff so that they felt sick with cold.

Helen had gone out to a café and arranged that jugs of coffee should be sent into the staff, sending one in to Mr Leonard who smiled until she told him that she had billed it to the bank. He did not protest, though, but insisted on Helen staying late to finish urgent correspondence. Tit for tat, she thought as she passed dark shops, walking in the middle of the pavement, feeling her way past sandbagged lampposts, Belisha beacons, and other pedestrians.

A lorry had given her a lift this far, the driver asking if she knew where he could find a Christmas tree for the second festive season of the war. Helen had shaken her head, not knowing. She did not want to know either because she would not be able to see Chris. Mr Leonard had refused her request for leave which was why she had thrust the broom at him. He knew, of course, that Heine was German but now she was fighting back.

Number eight Warden Post was on her right; she could see it quite clearly now that the wind had carried the clouds clear of the moon. It was bright and the clouds had almost gone. A bomber's moon, she thought, and then the air raid siren rose and fell and the man walking behind her increased his stride as she did, hurrying towards the Underground station which was just ahead. The planes could be heard beating in the air and she ran. Joining all the others who pushed into the entrance of the station and down the steps, but she wanted the District Line and so she turned, forcing her way through the people, taking the route she needed, then on down the corridor.

It was warm on the platform and camp beds were already set up for the night, row upon row with women guarding two or three until the family arrived. So few children, Helen thought, standing and watching. So few men out of uniform. She smiled as two women danced to an accordion player. They lifted their skirts, kicking their bare, mottled legs high as three sailors whistled and clapped.

Joan spent each night in her local station with her mother, she had told Helen. It was safer, more fun than on their own. More women were dancing now, their laughter ignoring the raid above them which was pulverising the city, perhaps their homes, but what else could they do? What else could anybody do? Helen watched as an old woman took out her Thermos flask and poured tea into a cup, tilting back her head and drinking. Helen watched as she placed it on the ground, taking her paper packet of sandwiches from a shopping bag on her camp bed, tearing the bread and scrape of butter into bits before eating them. She looked up at Helen and smiled, holding out a piece to her.

''Ere you are, dearie. Have some bread and butter.'

Helen smiled back, shaking her head. Knowing that the woman would need it for herself because she would not move from here until the morning.

She walked along, away from the blankets which hung from a wooden frame around the toilet buckets. The stench was still strong down at the other end of the platform and it was too warm, fetid. She undid her coat. A train came and although it was not hers the draught it caused was welcome and she wondered how these people could bear the airless stench once the trains stopped for the night.

She put her hands in her pockets and eased her feet in their boots and thought that anything was better than being crushed beneath the rubble of your home.

Her train came then and she could find no seat but did not expect to. She hung on the strap, feeling bodies close against her, hot and heavy, but when she reached her station and the fresh cold air she was sorry to leave the company of others.

The raid was over but the sky burned red as she knew it would. Rescue lorries ground past her as she walked on down deserted streets which had not been hit tonight. But there was still time. Yes, there was still plenty of time.

There were gaps in the terraces where houses had once been and through these she could see that the warehouses in Mill Street had been hit. She could see and hear the flames leaping high into the sky and then there was an explosion and she ducked instinctively, knowing it must be the spirits exploding. She held on to a lamppost, watching as more fire engines clanged and roared down the street towards the conflagration.

She saw more flames shoot into the air and the timber yard which stood close to the warehouse caught fire. Then there was a whoosh as the draught from the flames sent timbers up into the air to fall and set other areas alight. Over to the right a man ran past telling her the gas station was ablaze and that burning rats were running from the warehouse, and now Helen wanted to get home, to shut the door on all this, not to have to see and hear the destruction. And so she ran, knowing as she did so that there would be another raid, and another and another, and perhaps, next time, she would burn.

She ran until the breath pumped in her chest and hurt her throat. It was light now from the fires and she jumped over hoses which curled across the road and round people who came to stand and look. The road ahead was cordoned off and so she turned right, then left, but her way was blocked by an ARP rescue lorry which roared as it backed up to a pile of smouldering rubble. She turned again, crossing down a narrow footpath, then out into Kendle Street but she was walking now because her legs were weak and she wished that there was someone at home waiting for her.

She could not hear the sound of her footsteps against the noise of ambulances, rescue lorries, fire engines. She passed old women who pushed food from baskets into the mouths of rescue workers who could not stop to eat or drink. Further along a dead fireman lay on the pavement. Further along still a queue was forming at the Town Hall for missing relatives. She wanted to go up and shake them. Tell them to go away because there would be another raid and they would be dispersed and have to begin queuing all over again. But she did not because it happened every night and they all knew it did.

She looked at her watch. It was nine o'clock. She had left work at seven and not eaten since midday. Her mouth tasted sour and dry. She wanted to get home before it all began again. She started running once more down a street where no fires burned but it was darker because of this and so she slowed, moving out past a car slewed into the kerb, but a hand caught her arm and stopped her. She swung around, her hair in her eyes, her breath shallow. She pulled but could not break free.

'It's all right. It's all right. I'm a doctor.' The man's voice was calm and so Helen stood still. She could not see his face clearly because his back was to the burning sky.

'There's a man in there, down in the basement.' He was pointing to a house which no longer had a front, just floors which hung limp and wallpaper which was torn. 'He's not good but we can't get to him. We're too big.'

The doctor pointed again but this time two ARP wardens – one of them Mr Simkins – came over and guided her to the building over scattered rubble, glass and shrapnel, showing her a small gap at the base of the destruction.

'Can you get down there, Helen? Talk to him, see how he is? We can only hear noises.'

Helen stood there, the dust from the fallen masonry making her cough. I'm going home, she wanted to say. I want a drink. I want a hot cup of tea. I'm cold and I want to go home. And I don't like the dark. I don't like the dark.

'Be a good girl,' the doctor said, taking her arm again.

I'm not a girl, she wanted to say as he started to take her coat off, pulling it from her arms because there would not be room for her to pass through the gap while she still wore it. I'm not a girl, she repeated to herself, I'm a woman of twenty-seven but then women of that age shouldn't be frightened, should they?

'You'll need to go in head first. We'll hold your legs, drop you as far as possible. Call to him, see what it's like down there.'

Mr Simkins took her arm. 'It's Frank, the grocer,' he said.

She went, of course, head first down into the dark where the air was so full of dust she thought she would die, feeling the bricks scrape her legs and she cried out. 'My coat, put it under my legs.' She could feel them pushing it between her skin and the bricks, and the pain eased but it had made her cry.

Down into the dark and it was her mother's cupboard again, coming and closing itself around her and she cried, silently. It was dark, so dark.

'Call Frank,' the doctor said. 'Call him, see how he is.'

'How can I see? It's dark. Pitch dark, you bloody fool.' Helen shouted these words and anger drove the fears away. Along with the anger came surprise because she seldom swore. Ladies didn't, did they? 'Send down a torch, for God's sake.'

'Ssh, Helen,' Mr Simkins said. 'Don't disturb anything. We don't know how safe it is.' He paused and Helen felt the blood coming into her head. She closed her eyes. There was a scrabbling sound and then something cold brushed her face and she opened her eyes, seeing the beam of weak light catching the particles of dust, those same particles which caught in her eyes, her nose, her mouth. She gripped the torch, feeling the string round the handle.

'Don't take the string off. You might drop the torch,' M Simkins called.

She could hear grunts still and turned the torch towards them. There were just bricks and beams and one arm and one leg visible.

'Frank, Frank, it's me, Helen. How badly are you hurt?' There was no proper reply, just grunts and gurgles, but if they lowered her just a little more she could reach down and touch the hand and perhaps move the bricks.

'Drop me a little further,' she gasped, the dust thick in her mouth. Her ankles were breaking. 'Shall I move the bricks? All I can hear are grunts.' She started coughing now and her legs bucked as she did so and she dropped the torch, but it was still on its string so the doctor pulled it up and it was dark again.

She called 'Pull me up. Pull me up.' And now she was screaming because it was so dark and there was a man grunting, but he wasn't a man, he wasn't Frank any more. She had seen the blood as the torch swung, the bones and his head and knew why he grunted. They pulled her up but she couldn't stand, just sat with her head in her hands. And then she was sick and her mouth was sour as she told them again and again what she had seen.

The doctor wiped her face and held her head and told her he wanted her to go down again and give Frank an injection because no one should bear that sort of pain. But she couldn't. How could she go back down into the dark? How could her mother make her? How could this man make her? Where was Heine, why wasn't he here helping her? Keeping her safe. He had promised, hadn't he? She lifted her head. There was still the noise of the flames, the timber, the ambulances but up here at least there was some light.

It was dark down there. Didn't they know that? It was dark and there was a man with no face, grunting and gurgling, and she wanted to go home to her flat but there was no one there, was there? God damn it, there was no one there.

She was crying but it was inside and it was hurting her.

Mr Simkins helped her up, handed her the torch.

137

'Be a brave girl,' he said.

But Mrs Simkins wasn't brave, was she, Helen wanted to shout. She had left London, hadn't she? She had left and gone to live where bombs don't fall.

She took the syringe and listened as the doctor told her what to do when she got close enough to the arm. They held her legs again as she eased through the hole, her arms out before her, dropping down into the darkness, breathing the stifling air, the dust, hearing no crackling flames, just those grunts, and then the torch was lowered on the string. She caught it, using the light to guide herself back to the rubble, but she had to release it to move four bricks, slowly, carefully, hearing the creaking above her, feeling a sudden fall of dust, but nothing else moved. She groped her way forward. The torch swung round and round on its string, its light not reaching this far and so she felt over the jagged mortar, the splintered wood. She touched a hand. It was still warm and fingers closed around hers and the grunting stopped, just for a moment.

The crying inside her stopped too then, and so did her fear of the broken head and face and it was Frank who held her hand and for a moment they gave one another strength.

Then his groans began again and she talked through the dust in her throat. She talked of the shop and Christoph; the shrapnel he had swapped; Mary, the friend he had made. 'They're both outsiders you see,' she murmured gently as she plunged the needle into his arm, pressing the morphine into Frank.

Mr Simkins called, 'Shall we bring you up now?'

The blood was pounding in her head but it was not until the grip on her hand relaxed and the grunts ceased that she called, 'Yes, bring me up.'

The rescue team was there as she was dragged back through the hole and the doctor took the syringe from her, checking her carefully, making her sit, but this time she was not sick. This time she waited, breathing in the cold air, heavy still with the smell of burning and floating with ash fragments.

'Will someone be worrying at home?' the doctor asked. 'Shall I drop you off?' He turned as an ambulance stopped and a nurse called to him.

Helen shook her head. 'No. I shall be quite all right. You're needed again,' she said, clambering to her feet, moving out of the way. She waved to Mr Simkins as he answered a call across the street. 'Shall I wait?'

Mr Simkins turned. 'No, Helen, you get back. This'll take all night. Get your head down before the next wave comes.'

The flat was dark and cold but she did not light the fire. There was no point. There would be another raid soon. She lit the gas under the kettle, cut sandwiches, rinsed out the Thermos. Then she shook her coat out of the window, clearing it of brick dust, and did the same to her skirt. Her lisle stockings were torn and her legs grazed but before she stepped into the bath she poured water over the tea in the strainer. It had only been used once this morning and so was not too weak. She filled the Thermos and used what was left for a cup now, sipping hastily as she did so because the sirens might go and she must get clean today for the first time.

After her bath she put woollen stockings and socks on and then her boots. There was a candle in the upturned flowerpot in the Anderson from last night for warmth but she would need matches and so she put them in her pocket. She was talking aloud, listing her shelter provisions but that was better than the sound of nobody's voice. She had missed the nine o'clock news but the wireless was playing music and that was some sort of company. She did not put on the light in the sitting-room but instead eased back the blackout. Her hair was still wet from her bath and lay cold on her neck. She picked up a towel and rubbed it. Marian was coming tomorrow for lunch.

How was Frank? She paced to the kitchen, pouring more boiling water on to the tea leaves, drinking as she walked, frying rissoles in the pan. Listening, always listening for the siren, for the planes, and she was glad Christoph was not here but she missed him and paced again to push away the ache. She sat down and wrote to Heine by the light of the red sky and the moon, telling him of Chris swapping shrapnel for sixers, and for a moment she could smell the rotten conkers which they had found in the park beneath the tree. She told him of the bank because she hoped he would laugh, and of Marian coming tomorrow because it was Saturday and they had the day off. She told him she missed him and loved him, because she did, but she did not tell him that she wished he was British and that they were the same as everyone else. She told him she was so glad he wasn't here, that he was safe.

She did not tell him of Frank, of the dust and the darkness, because he blamed himself that he was not here and part of her did so too.

At eleven the bombers had not come back and she put on her coat because she wanted to see what had happened to Frank. She had walked as far as the corner of Ellesmere Road when the sirens went again and this time the bombers were close, roaring in, wave upon wave, and there was no time to go back to the shelter in the High Street, no time to go to her own. She pressed herself back against the wall of the gutted house behind her. It had been bombed in November.

The noise grew louder, spreading itself around her, trying to force her to the ground, and then the bombs came again, flashing, crushing and juddering. Helen crouched, knowing that the whimpering she heard was coming from her. She looked up at the black wide bodies, the bursting ack-ack, the two parachute mines floating down in the direction of the park.

She flung herself down, holding her fist to her mouth. She must not scream. She was not a child. She must not scream. Two long dull roars came and the barrage balloon stood out in relief against the blaze that came. Fire bombs were hurtling down now and white magnesium fires leapt up to turn red as buildings caught fire. The thuds of heavy oil bombs followed and now she could feel the heat. The bombs were getting closer.

She lay on the ground, rubble digging into her. She could hear glass shattering. More incendiaries fell; small, pretty. They did not blast, they just burned where they fell. A warden ran by, stopping, shouting at her as she lifted her head.

'Get into a bloody shelter.' His voice was harsh, impatient. Then he ran on.

But where was there a shelter? She scrambled up now, looking each way, then running to the corner, hearing the shrapnel falling all around. There was no safety anywhere. She ran blindly now, across the road, down a lane, but everywhere there was heat and falling walls, shouts and screams, and then she came to a crossroads and there on the opposite corner was St Bede's; dark, black and solid, and she ran in through the gate, past the gravestones, into the porch, panting. Gasping for breath. Holding her arms tightly round her body.

Was there ever a time when life was quiet, when nights were

for sleeping? It was madness. Absolute madness. She felt the ground juddering, heard the hiss of the falling bombs, and even here the shrapnel came and so she ran again, keeping close to the walls of the church whose windows had been boarded up when war was declared. She was stumbling now, tripping on the graves, falling on frozen grass until she came to the clump of lilac trees which bloomed each summer and there was a large door down some steps and Helen stopped. She turned, feeling her way down until she reached the bottom. There was someone else there, an old woman who caught hold of her, pulling her against the door.

'Bless you. Gave me a fright you did,' the old woman said, pulling her scarf tighter round her head.

Helen looked at her, at the camp stool she sat on, the knitting she was doing out here in the open air. On her hands she wore fingerless gloves. Helen pushed at the door. There was a crypt here. She remembered now because they had held the vicarage fête in the gardens before the war and the tables and chairs, the bunting, the stalls were carried in here afterwards. Heine had laughed because the vicar had been so busy directing everyone he had become jammed behind the benches and they had to move everything back again to release him.

The bombers were coming in another wave now, overhead. The noise was loud, the explosions close and over to their left. Shrapnel still fell, clattering down the steps, against the door. Helen ducked and pushed again.

'No good doing that, ducky. The vicar keeps it locked.' The old woman laughed but her voice trembled and Helen touched her shoulder.

'Why are you here?' she asked, crouching beside her, looking up at the sky, wincing as a bomb dropped nearby.

'Nowhere else nearby, is there, love? I ain't got no shelter, the station's too far and the brick one in Maine Street got hit last week.'

Helen ducked as the run of explosions drew closer still. The ack-ack thudded nearby.

'There's more poor souls out past the lilac bush. They got bombed out earlier. They've got nowhere else to go. They don't want to leave the area, see. It's their home.'

There were fires crackling and ash being blown across from the nearby streets. Helen eased herself up, pushing once more

141

at the door, and then again. It gave a little each time but not enough. She eased herself up the steps.

'Have you asked the vicar to unlock it for you?' She was shouting now against the noise.

'He's too busy, isn't he? Rushing around seeing all these dead people.'

Helen was up the steps now, running round to the back of the church and on towards the vicarage. She knocked but there was no reply. She ran round to the Anderson, too angry to fear the bombs. Too damned angry.

There was no one there. She ran back, wrenching at the upright garden fork stuck deep into the soil, dragging it along behind her so that it clattered on the path but that was just one more noise in the bedlam.

She dragged it past the lilac bush, shouting at the people there to come down; the crypt was going to be opened. She carried it down the steps, forcing it into the gap between the door and the frame, just below the handle, pushing on it. It gave further this time but still not enough. Helen threw her weight on it but still it did not open. She turned then as old gnarled hands added their weight and an old man nodded. Together they tried it and then the wood of the door splintered and the lock gave way. The door was open.

Helen turned. 'Get in here. Quick.' A bomb dropped outside the churchyard.

'Get in quick!' She was screaming now, grabbing at the old woman, who dropped her ball of wool and went back for it. Helen pulled her, running for the wool herself, pushing at two more people who came running down the steps from the graveyard where they had been sheltering. The wool caught in her fingers, she dropped it again, picked it up once more and this time held it to her, backing into the crypt, slamming the door shut.

'Everyone away from the door,' Helen said, her voice hoarse now, remembering the inspector who had insisted on a blanket for the shelter because of blast splinters.

It was pitch black. There was no light and almost no noise.

'Can't see to move,' the old man said.

Helen was fumbling in her pockets. She had her matches. She struck one, cupping it in her hand, moving forwards and then sideways to get out of the line of the door, hearing the shuffle of feet as they followed her, feeling a hand clinging to her coat for guidance.

There were benches piled high and a stuffy feel to the air but no shrapnel clicked and cut. One of the old women had a candle in the bag which held all that she now owned.

Helen lit it and with the old man who smiled a smile without teeth she left them in the dark on seats they had found while she moved amongst the vicarage fête material looking for more candles.

The old man found a new packet, long, thick white ones, which Ruth, the woman who had dropped her knitting, said they could not use because they were for the altar. Helen looked at her and at the others.

'I will speak to the vicar in the morning,' she said, burning the bottom of the candle so that the wax melted and then setting it down on the lid of a tin of old powder paint they had found. They sat or lay on the benches which Helen pulled round into a square until the all clear at four-thirty a.m. They had been cold but safe and Helen had not been alone.

She was tired and angry as she watched the others leave, walking out into the grey dawn. But then she called, 'Come back tonight. It will be open and there'll be hot tea. Bring some bread and butter and some tea if you can.' She went round to the vicarage again and knocked on the door, and when there was no reply she waited, sitting on the step until the vicar came up the path, his face grey with tiredness.

Helen stood up; she held out his garden fork. 'I broke into your crypt last night.'

He paused, his hand in his coat pocket, where he had been searching for his key. 'Why?' was all he said.

'Because we needed shelter,' she said, but what she meant was that she was tired of people locking doors in her face, dropping bombs, making her send her son away, making her feel anger at her husband.

'Come in, we need some breakfast.' He was an old man, bent and tired, his face thin. His tea was as weak as hers but his toast was warm and she was hungry in the cold green kitchen with its half empty meat safe on the windowsill.

She told him that she had people who would come back again tonight. That there was no other shelter and she would break the crypt open again if he barred it to them.

He smiled, stirring his tea and told her that she could use it. They needed a rest centre in the area as well as a shelter; a refuge for those bombed out, for those unable to endure loneliness any longer in this world which had once known peace.

'Do you understand what I mean?' he asked, his eyes heavy-lidded and dark. 'War is lonely as well as dangerous.'

Helen nodded, for she understood too well.

'We'll need toilets, primus stoves, cups, blankets,' Helen said, washing her cup in water poured from the simmering kettle.

He nodded as she continued, drawing up a verbal list because she had used the hours of the raid to channel her rage into this. There was no work at the bank on Saturday this week and she was glad because she had to go to the ironmonger's for rubber gloves and a hurricane lamp but the first one would not sell them to her because Heine was a German. Helen was too busy to speak to him as she would have done yesterday.

The second one smiled because Heine had taken his son's photograph shortly before he had been killed in a car crash. He sold Helen two hurricane lamps and filled them with paraffin though he would not sell her a can because of the risk of fire. She could come each day for more. He gave her the gloves because she had no more money on her.

She carried them back to the crypt, kicking away the rubble from the path in the churchyard, clearing the shrapnel from the steps with her boots. The vicar was there already, pushing back the benches, setting out tables. He had found two camp beds in his attic and had spoken to the Red Cross about chemical toilets.

Helen looked across at the bucket she had found last night and which was now full. She grimaced and the vicar moved towards it but she stopped him.

'Go and get some sleep,' she said, pulling her rubber gloves out from her pocket.

'But you must be tired too,' he objected.

'No, I'm not. I'm not at all.' And she wasn't. She carried the bucket to the door, walking behind him, watching him climb the steps.

'I should have done this before,' he said, turning. 'Somehow there wasn't the time to stop and think.'

Helen nodded. No, there was never any time to stop, never

any peace to think. She turned then, carrying the bucket down the side of the church to the back, pouring it down the drain, scrubbing with a brush while the smell made her retch but as she did it she thought of the letter she would write to Heine, telling him of the crypt, telling him of the people who now had shelter, of the buckets instead of toilets, of the altar candles which the vicar had laughed about, of the sign he was going inside to write, pointing people towards the new Rest Centre. But first he must speak to the authorities.

She would tell Marian of the work that needed to be done. The tea that needed to be brewed, the advice that needed to be given about lost ration books. Marian would help. It would stop her brooding over Emily. Over Rob, her husband, who had been posted to Scotland.

She scrubbed the bucket with disinfectant and stacked it beside the door which the vicar had said was to remain unlocked at all times. At midday she left because Marian was meeting her at the flat where they would heat thick soup and talk of their children and their husbands until the next siren went.

She picked her way through debris and chaos, turning left as a cordon blocked the street. The air was thick with smoke but then it always was. She came into the street and her flat was still standing but the one opposite was down and Mr Simkins stood waving pedestrians past.

'Did Frank survive?' she asked him and was not surprised when he shook his head. She remembered the clasp of that weak hand and was filled with the waste of it all.

She was tired now, and pushed at the front door which was singed by the heat from the bomb which had dropped so close. There were blisters on the paint. She eased it open, hearing Marian call as she came down the street, so she turned, her hand on the doorpost and saw the telegraph boy riding his bike, then stop by Mr Simkins and ask directions.

She saw her neighbour point to her, then stop the boy and take the telegram from him, carrying it himself, his overalls dirty, his yellow initials blackened by dust. She watched as he came, but slowly, oh so slowly. She watched as though from a distance as his ankle twisted sideways on a piece of brick. 'It's for you, Helen,' he said, his voice cracked and dry from the nighttime dust.

145

She knew it was for her. Of course it was for her, she had seen him pointing, hadn't she? But Heine was safe from the bombing, wasn't he? And so was Chris, wasn't he? So it was a mistake. She shook her head, pushing the envelope from her. She turned but Mr Simkins's hand pulled her round and pressed the telegram into her hand.

'It's a mistake, you see,' she said, still shaking her head. The paper was cold and limp in the frosty air. She could read her name, Mrs H. Weber. The type was black against the buff. She knew she must open it, she knew that she must lift the flap and read because Mr Simkins and Marian were standing there and it was cold and she mustn't keep them waiting. Mrs Tomkins hadn't kept Helen waiting when her telegram had come last month.

But it couldn't be news which would tear her heart from her body because both of them were safe. They weren't here as she was, living next to fire and death. No. Neither of them could die. They couldn't die. She wouldn't let them die.

Marian came to her side. 'It might not be bad news.' Her hand was on Helen's arm.

So Helen peeled the envelope open, lifted the telegram out and read, aloud, that Heine was dead.

Killed in a fall from rocks while on a walk. Stop.

CHAPTER 11

For over an hour Helen stood in the doorway, pushing Marian and Mr Simkins from her because they were not Heine and he was all she wanted but how could she tell them that when the only noise she could make was this moaning from deep within her? When the only sound she could hear was his voice? There was no cold piercing her coat, no war in front of her eyes. There was nothing but him; but he was gone and she couldn't bear it.

And then she said, 'How could he die like this? I don't understand how he could die like this?'

She turned and walked over trailing hoses, only now seeing the firemen on the top of ladders, hearing the coughing from all sides from the smoke which hung over the city, over them all. How could he die when he wasn't amongst all this? It was wrong. They must be wrong. She walked on towards the vicarage, towards the only phone that worked, because she had to tell them that they were wrong.

The telegram was damp in her hands and it still held the words which told her Heine was dead. It still, still held them but she was not going to cry because they were wrong. She picked her way round the brick wall which had run round the back of the grocer's but now spilled across the pavement. She listened to Marian who held her arm and talked of how bad the trains were and how she shouldn't think of going up for the funeral, she really shouldn't.

Helen cut through these words because they were wrong, weren't they? She said, 'I've opened the crypt. Why don't you come and help? It will need a committee to get things running smoothly.'

She eased between the cordon and the rescue truck. Its rear bumper was ripped from its nearside support, hanging suspended by only the right-hand screw. There was a jagged

147

hole in the bodywork. She crossed the road, passing the queue of people waiting for a new delivery of eggs. They all seemed so clear this afternoon, as though they were etched in glass.

Marian was shaking her arm now. 'Yes, I'll help. Of course I'll help. It's so lonely with Rob away.' And then she suddenly stopped talking.

Helen crossed the road to the vicarage. Yes, it will be lonely with Rob away, she wanted to say. But neither of them are dead, are they? She wanted to shout it, scream it so that it would reach the Isle of Man. She hurried because she must tell them quickly – but they were at the gate now. Soon they would reach the telephone.

She pushed at the gate, leaning her weight on it, looking again at the telegram in her hand, hating it, tearing it, again and again and again as she hurried forward, throwing it, watching the wind take it, piece by piece, fragment by fragment, because it was wrong. But why was there this terrible pain inside her when it was so wrong?

The vicar came when she knocked and now she was holding her arms around her body because she hurt so badly.

'They say Heine is dead but he can't be. I must ring them and tell them. I have some hurricane lamps but Mr Simkins has taken them for now.' It was important that he should know about the lamps.

The vicar looked at her, and led her to the kitchen but he wouldn't hurry. His voice was gentle and kind but why wasn't he hurrying? He made her sit while Marian boiled the kettle, lighting the ring which burnt blue. They said nothing while they listened to the kettle rattling on the stove, while they listened to the vicar talking on the telephone in the hall, for he was ringing for her.

'Yes, I understand.'

'Yes, I shall explain to Mrs Weber that it was a tragic accident – a fall from the rocks – into the sea.'

'I see. Yes, I'm sure she'll understand.'

But Helen did not. She did not understand when the vicar told her that the telegram was true. That Heine was dead, drowned before he could be rescued. His body had been recovered and he had been buried yesterday. That the delivery of the telegram must have been delayed due to the bombing. That she would never, ever see him again.

She walked up and down the kitchen, listening to the kettle, seeing Marian taking it from the stove with a tea towel round the handle. She watched the steam rise from the teapot before the lid was put on and then it escaped from the spout. She watched Marian's hands holding the pot, watched the vicar fetch cups from the cupboard.

And then she said, 'They've won,' her voice calm and cold. 'They've won. I thought when we took the camera through that we had won. But we hadn't. They have.' Because now she knew. Somehow she knew that they had killed him.

She turned and walked out of the house and down the path, and then she ran; hard, fast, past the Heavy Rescue Truck which was jagged and torn – jagged and torn – jagged and torn – like her life was now. Her legs were running in time to this until she was home, back in the flat, back in their bedroom and then she lay on the bed which would never feel his weight again.

Marian came and bathed Helen's face and the cloth was cold on her skin but it did not touch the pain inside. Marian left at four because the vicar wanted to prepare the crypt. Helen watched her leave the bedroom, heard the front door click. Her arms felt heavy, her legs too. Her mouth was dry and in the silence she thought of his arms, tanned and strong, that would never again hold her. His voice, slow and deep, which would never again speak to her. His skin which would never smell of the summer, never feel the sun. Skin which had been made wet and cold by the sea, and she thought she would die.

The light faded as the minutes passed. How many minutes, how many lifetimes? She had to move at last because there was banging on the door and it wouldn't stop. It pounded and pounded, and wouldn't leave her to die too. She pushed herself from the bed, feeling old and tired and still the banging continued. Didn't they know the bombers would come soon and then the pain might go because the bombs might find her? Her hands hung limp at her sides and her feet seemed too heavy to move towards the door but then there was the sound of a key in the lock.

'Heine,' she called, turning to the door.

It was Mr Simkins who held out her hurricane lamps and told her that she had things to do. He was kind but his voice was firm as he brought her coat, guiding her arms into the sleeves.

'You must not give up,' he told her. 'Heine would not want that. He was a good man. I liked him and I am so sorry he's dead. But the raids will begin soon and you have a son to live for.'

He took her to the crypt, walking in silence with her, and she was grateful for that because she was listening to Heine's voice inside her head. She could see his face, so tanned; his hair so fair.

The vicar and Marian were gentle when she arrived and she knew now that they had arranged for Mr Simkins to come for her. They asked where they should set up camp beds, benches, chairs, and somehow she knew, pointing to an area well away from the door. She reminded them that they must make definite aisles between the rows but to her own ears her voice sounded dead.

The vicar held her hand and asked, 'Would you rather just lie down, my dear?'

'No,' she said because then she would have time to think and then she might cry and her mother had taught her not to cry, hadn't she?

The vicar had brought down two old paraffin stoves which they lit to try to build up a bit of heat before the sirens began.

'We'll have to turn them out when the raid begins. How much paraffin is in them?' Helen's voice was quite level but slow, so slow. Her lips could hardly form the words but nobody seemed to notice and she wondered how the world could keep on as though nothing had happened. But what else was there to do?

'Not much, Helen. So it should all burn through by six. It would be a fire hazard.' The vicar heaved at a pile of blankets, walking down the rows of camp beds, dropping one on to each.

Helen nodded slowly. 'It would help if we had some old carpeting or something to stop the cold seeping up from the floor. And what about the chemical toilets?' She could still hear Heine's voice and she hugged him to her.

The vicar handed the blankets to Marian and stood looking towards Helen, his face thoughtful.

'Let's get back to the house. There are carpets and rugs up in the spare room at the top. Quick though. It's five-thirty.'

They passed people coming in through the door. Helen wondered how she could be quick, her legs were so heavy. She stopped near two women of her own age.

'Can you come and help?'

They did and two others joined them. They carried three carpets back and Helen asked Marian to organise a party of people to unroll and lay them before placing the camp stools and benches on them, watching herself work as though she were outside her body. Others came to help and soon there were carpets beneath some of the camp beds too. But there were no chemical toilets, the vicar said, because so far they were not a designated shelter.

As the siren started Helen slung the stage curtains used in the peacetime pantomimes over bamboo poles which she tied horizontally between two pillars. She tipped disinfectant into three buckets and lined them up behind the curtains listening to Heine.

'There'll be a bit of a bloody performance going on behind there soon,' cackled Ruth, the old woman from last night who had brought her knitting again.

'Just so long as there's not a round of applause every time,' Helen replied, smiling, and was surprised that words like these could come while she was listening so hard to him.

The vicar came and stood behind her. 'Helen . . . what about the men?'

'That's a point, ducky,' Ruth said, cackling again, her arms waving as her hands wielded needles and wool.

Helen sighed, then looked up at the vicar and smiled. 'Come on, you can help.' But she didn't want him to talk because then she would not hear Heine.

She bent and picked up the remaining two curtains from the floor, collecting up twine and another bamboo from the storage area. The vicar carried the ladder to the other end of the crypt, walking in front of her. She could hear his breathing, heavy and laboured and knew this man of sixty felt much older because of the sights he had seen over the last few months and remembered then that her grief was one amongst many, but somehow even that did not give her any relief.

The raids had begun now. They could all hear the bombs, feel the earth as it juddered, see and taste the plaster as it fell in narrow streams from the ceiling but the conversation continued as before. Or almost as before. There were moments of silence, of tension when some of the crumps were too close, too loud, too violent, and they had drowned Heine's voice for the moment and she couldn't bear it. Helen stopped, her hand to her mouth because she mustn't cry or she would go in the cupboard.

She must follow the vicar, she must reach forward to move that chair from his path and slowly it was all right again. She coughed as plaster dust fell on to her head, catching in her throat. It itched on her scalp but she had no hands free to scratch and it was important that she did. Why was it so damned important? Her husband was dead, wasn't he? Dead. And she wanted to scratch. Her head was aching now, throbbing, and her mouth was dry and again Heine had gone.

The vicar looked behind.

'Whereabouts, Helen?'

She pointed to the two pillars over in the corner and he opened the ladder as wide as the rope would allow then started to climb, but she shook her head.

'I'll do it. I know how to fix the pole.' His breathing was laboured. He was too tired.

He held the ladder while she climbed on legs which felt like lead but she tied the bamboo, then hung the curtains, listening while he told her that the Red Cross had been very pleasant but they would just have to manage for now.

Helen shook her head. 'Oh well, we'll see about that,' she said, anger surprising her, raging through her, cracking in her head, making her hands clasp the ladder, bringing sweat coursing down her back. 'We'll see about that.'

Marian walked down the centre aisle carrying one bucket which she had found by the bamboo poles. It would not be enough.

'There are more in the vicarage,' the vicar said.

Helen put her hand on his arm as he moved to the door. 'Let me,' she said, because in the vicarage she might hear Heine again and when she heard his voice it was as though he had not left her.

'But surely we've enough?' Marian asked. 'There's a raid going on. It's dangerous.'

Helen listened. It was drawing away. There had been no plaster trickling down for the last ten minutes. She looked at the people sitting and talking. At the two young children running up and down the aisles.

'No, it's not going to be enough,' she said. For her there

152

would be no danger, but there would be peace. The vicar put his hand on her arm.

'Wait until it is quite quiet,' he said and so she did. Sitting on a camp stool watching Ruth knit, finding comfort in the regularity of the needles. Counting the stitches because it filled her head with numbers, not his poor, lonely, cold, wet body which had begun to nudge at her mind.

Ruth handed her a red jumper and scissors. They were rusted but sharp and Helen picked away at the sewn seams until it was in sections and then she pulled the kinked wool, watching row after row unravel, winding it round and round her hand; red upon red. Had there been red on his face? Had he felt pain?

'It should be all right now, Helen,' the vicar called.

She rose then, smiling as Ruth smiled, but her face felt stiff and unreal. She nodded to the vicar and slowly edged in front of the curtain in the doorway, then opened the door, knowing that there would be no light showing. She could not run, there was no strength in her legs. She watched the searchlights stabbing the skies, saw the puffs of flak, and drowned in the noise of the aeroplanes, the bombs and shells away to the south. Had he been afraid as the water entered his lungs?

She heard the revving of the auxiliary fire engines from the yard behind the vicarage but then she was inside the house, feeling her way down the hall, into the kitchen where there was a sort of peace and she stood for a moment but his voice did not come back. But neither did the image of his body.

She dragged two pails from beneath the sink and then a third from the scullery, searching for him in her mind, feeling her way back into the darkness of the hall, hearing the bombs, not him. And then as she moved past the telephone table there was a hush, a silence, a moment of utter calm, and she called his name then but there was no answer, just a tearing endless sound that filled the space around her and the ceiling dropped, and great timbers crashed to the ground and Helen was swamped with a blackness which took all pain, all thought away.

It took the rescue party over two hours to pull her free and take her to the first aid point where nurses pulled splinters of glass from her hands and arms, for the wedged timbers had protected her. It was now that she cried and cried and thought that the whole world must hear over the sound of the bombs and shells and alarm bells. But it was not for the pain and the blood, but at last for Heine.

Her leg was not broken but badly cut and bruised and by the time it was dressed the all-clear had sounded and Marian helped her back to the flat where the vicar was waiting. His house was ruined and so Helen asked him to use her spare room and was grateful when he agreed because she did not want to be alone any more. Marian came too and used the studio because she could travel more easily from here and she too was lonely.

The vicar put a hot-water bottle in Helen's bed but she was not ready for sleep yet because there was something to be done. She walked steadily back down the stairs, pushing aside for now the pain in her leg, hugging close to her the thought of her husband.

'I could have died and I didn't. I thought I wanted to die but now I know I don't,' she told Marian who had tried to stop her. 'I felt fear when I had thought I would not feel anything but grief again. They mustn't think they've beaten him or me.'

At first the woman at the Red Cross was annoyed at Helen's interruption, at her dust-covered clothes, at her description of scrubbing out dirty buckets. Helen lifted her hands; the blood from her splinter wounds had seeped through the bandages.

'I want those chemical toilets. The vicar has been assured that we are to become an accredited shelter. I want those toilets and I want them now.' Her voice was still and slow. She stood in front of the desk; her leg was throbbing and her hands too.

'I will not leave until I have them.'

The woman came round the desk then, taking Helen's arm, drawing her to a chair, calling for a drink.

'My dear, you shall have them.' Her voice was kind and her face was too, and Helen's anger was gone again and only the despair was there, coming out in endless tears, and she wondered if grief was always like this, hard and fast, then ebbing for a moment leaving life to run on as usual until the next bout of tears. She cried on and off all that night in the crypt, lying on a camp bed while more than sixty people sat or slept around her.

Ruth came and held her. 'You 'ave a good cry, my dear. It

154

helps you know. My old Albert never came back from the last lot. My grandson's in this one. His dad's dead.'

Helen told her then that Heine was German and had not been a soldier but a prisoner because it seemed unfair to accept sympathy unless she was honest. Ruth just smiled.

'They're all young, poor little buggers. They all bleed just the same and we cry, just the same.'

Helen lay in the dark, feeling the pain of her hands and arms, of her leg, wanting the comfort of the only person who could not give it. Thinking of the bombers who flew over London, dropping their bombs, thinking of the bombers who flew over Germany, and wondered how she could tell Heine's parents that their son was dead.

The next morning she received a letter from Willi.

Dear Frau Weber,

I ask a friend of mine who is being today released to post this to you when he reach the mainland. I want you to have knowledge of how Heine is killed. He had stood against the Nazis you see, too loudly, too strong and in the end they hurt his friend. Martin now is insane. It is something which makes him want to fight them with more effort.

We walk near the sea on a cold rough day. He had been sent the death sentence but it not stop him from speaking out on that walk too. The guard was in front. I was behind Heine and was pushed to ground from behind. I saw these men come to Heine and push him hard, over edge, on to the rocks, into the sea. They had promised they would, Frau Weber, and I do not tell you this to pain you further but to tell of his courage.

I was with him the night before he died. Perhaps he had knowledge of it in his heart. He said, if he die, I must tell you that he make his gesture as you did in Hanover with the old man on the ground. That these years are just a fragment of time in the great age of the world and that they will pass. Tell her it will all pass, he said to me. And tell her that I love her.

Your husband was brave man, Frau Weber. We

155

shall miss him, miss his spirit. He was honoured amongst us. He was loved.

Your obedient servant,
Willi Weiss

Helen was late into work. She walked in the icy drizzle of that Monday before Christmas to the Red Cross and spoke to the woman who had brought her tea and kindness. She was able to assure Helen that a message could be conveyed through the Red Cross to Herr Weber informing him of his son's death in an internment camp on the Isle of Man. It was 23 December and Helen wondered whether there would be carp for the Christmas Eve dinner in Hanover or just bombs and tiredness as there was here. She wondered how long love lived when there was no one to accept that love.

She felt the drizzle turn to rain on her face and was glad she had sent presents for Christoph two weeks ago: a carved catapult for knocking targets off the wall as he had asked and books which she had bought from the stalls which still opened down many side streets. It seemed too much of an effort to think of Christmas now. Before Heine's death she had hoped to travel down for two days but the vicar had rung the rector in Greater Mannenham to tell him to pass a message on to Laura that the trains were too difficult. But it was not travelling that was too difficult, it was the knowledge of Heine's death which would be too hard to hide from her son and he should at least have peace this Christmas. It would be time enough in January to tell her son of his father's death. She stood still and looked at a smouldering ruin, pushing a brick with her foot. Who knew if there would ever be another Christmas free of Hitler's rule?

On Christmas Eve people still came to the shelter although raids had almost ceased for forty-eight hours. They had found companionship and safety down here beneath the church and had no wish to spend Christmas alone in houses, flats or Anderson shelters. Helen dragged out old bunting and everyone helped to hang it round the crypt. There was no midnight service in the church but beneath it they sang carols and Helen found that her voice was too uncertain to sing 'Silent Night'. The vicar said prayers for all those under attack; those in the provinces, those in Germany. Afterwards he pumped the

156

primus and as a light raid continued outside they made tea and soup, using goods that people had brought.

They ignored the crump crump of bombs and Helen pushed the pain of her leg and her hands from her as she listened to the groups talking softly. Sometimes they laughed and sometimes they cried because a father, a son, a husband had died and Helen did not feel alone in her suffering any more and there was some comfort in that but still each day and night seemed to last a lifetime.

On 29 December when there was due to be a tidal low-point in the Thames the Luftwaffe came again. The water mains were damaged at the start of the raid by high explosive parachute mines and then at least 10,000 fire bombs plummeted from the planes. In the crypt they could not feel the heat of the fires which raged unchecked until water was available again from more distant mains but in the morning they smelt and saw the devastation and that night there were more people who had been bombed out arriving to stay in the crypt. The next day, which was Monday, Helen was late in to work because she took them to the Town Hall to get coupons until their ration books could be replaced.

Mr Leonard could say nothing because so many were late, unable to force their way through the havoc which had once been London. Some never came because they had been killed.

That night the vicar explained as they all sat talking that a fire-watching rota was to be drawn up at the request of the authorities and those in the shelter were eager to put their names down. Helen decided that there should be soup available at one penny a cup and Marian volunteered to organise it. The old lady, Ruth, stood up and said that she thought there should be a knitting group to make socks and hats for the soldiers.

'All you need to do is pull out old jumpers,' she said, holding up a dark green one. 'Just pull it out and knit it up again.' And so a knitting group was formed, but Helen could not yet bear the thought of wool being drawn across her cut hands and so, instead, she formed a small choir at the back of the crypt and found solace in the music.

The days passed and December became January. Britain and Australia's attack on the Italians in the Western Desert

157

proceeded. Nits became a problem in the shelter and Helen bent her head over newspaper and combed out several lice. One of the women was a hairdresser and soon most of the women had bobbed hair and Helen looked at herself in the mirror and wondered how Heine would have liked it. She did not cry this time but put her arms round the young mother whose husband was missing in action and, instead, held her while she wept.

By 17 January Helen's hands and control were improved enough for her to leave London to see her son.

The train journey took six hours and was cold, so cold. Again and again the train was shunted into a siding to allow troops or goods wagons to pass but there was no raid as they travelled and little to see through the mesh of the windows. There were other mothers on the train, travelling to see their children. They were pale, tired. Their eyes sunken. No one talked very much but some slept, jerked awake with each stop only to fall asleep again within minutes. But Helen couldn't sleep.

She caught the bus from Thetford and dusk fell after twenty miles. The journey took one hour more, the slitted headlights picking up the white line painted at the side of the road but nothing of the flat countryside beyond. Helen eased her leg, flexed her hands, glad that her gloves covered the red scars. The bus stopped three times but each time another village was called out and Helen watched as the women she had travelled with on the train stepped down into the darkness. Would there ever be a time when they would see the welcome of lighted windows, she wondered.

At last the bus pulled up again and the driver called, 'Greater Mannenham.'

Helen rose, lifting her bag from the seat beside her. She had brought Christoph a knitted hat from Ruth and some more books and one change of clothes for herself because she could not stay more than a night. She thanked the driver and stepped carefully from the bus to the road; her leg was still stiff, still sore. For a moment she couldn't see Chris but then he was there, his arms around her, holding her, and she knew she must not cry but she did when she heard him say, 'Oh, Mum, I've missed you.'

She heard the bus move off, smelt the exhaust, and saw

Laura standing behind Chris, but all she felt was his arms around her, his head pressed into her body. She dropped her bag and held him, stroking his hair, bending to kiss him, wondering how she could have forgotten the sound of his voice but somehow it had indeed become lost.

They walked back through the centre of the village. It was cloudy so there was not even the light from the moon or stars to light their way. Laura held a torch covered with tissue paper and gripped Helen's arm, guiding her along the lane while Chris held her hand tightly, causing pain to stab right up into her arm but it didn't matter now that she was with her son.

There was a fire in the inglenook and Helen sat on the settee, keeping her gloves on, saying that she was cold. One of her cuts had begun to bleed and Chris must not see. But Laura saw and beckoned her out to the kitchen while Chris sat on the rug in front of the fire and looked through the books. She bathed and dressed the cut and all the time there was the smell of stew in the air and Helen realised she was hungry. She realised too that she had not felt hunger since his death. She looked at Laura and knew she should tell her about Heine but the words hurt too much in her throat.

Laura smiled at her, pointing to a chair, calling to Chris to come in and wash his hands. He ran through and Helen thought again how much he had grown, how strong and straight and tall he was. He ran the tap and it splashed up and over the sink but Laura just laughed and threw him a towel and Helen felt excluded.

This was her child but she did not even know where the towels were which dried his hands. She didn't wash them, or any of his clothes. She didn't serve up his meal, as Laura was now doing, heaping rabbit, carrots and potato on to his plate and then on to theirs and now jealousy surged into her throat and chest and she was appalled.

She looked down at her plate, not wanting to see familiarity between her son and this kind, plump woman.

'Chris talks of you every day. There is no one in his life but you,' Laura said.

Helen looked up and saw Laura looking at her and then at Chris and knew that after all she was lucky to have placed her son with this woman.

'He knows that it hurts you much more to let him stay here

than to take him back with you to London,' Laura continued, and Chris looked up at her and smiled.

'I think you're very brave, Mum. You have to stay there. I know you do because we need the money. Laura has explained it to me and Daddy told me too, in one of his letters.'

Helen picked up her knife and fork now, tasting the rabbit, the thick gravy, the potatoes, but there was no appetite again. Later she must tell him about Heine. Later.

She listened while she ate sparingly as Chris told her how he had pulled the carrots and stored them in sawdust. How he fed the chickens and the pig and how they had called one of the piglets Heine and one of them Helen. She listened as he told her of the fat girl called Mary who was his friend and who lived in a cottage where no one cared. She listened but he did not talk of his friends at school. He did not talk of the games they played and he lowered his head and told her about the butterfly net Laura had found in the attic and she thought she saw a darkening in his eyes when she asked about his school friends and he did not answer.

Later she asked Laura if the boys knew of Chris's German heritage but she said that they did not. How could they? Only she and the rector's wife knew. Helen looked closely at her son as they sat in front of the fire and could see no shadows now in those dark eyes so perhaps there had been none earlier?

They sat and talked in the quiet of the cottage and Helen was restless. There was no normality in the hissing of the fire, the voice on the radio reading out the nine o'clock news, the hoot of the owl. There was no normality to this quiet evening which came from the peacetime past.

She read to him in his room that night. A room warmed by logs burning in the grate, their light shielded from the sky by more slates, like the inglenook downstairs, Chris told her. She sat by his bed, holding his hand with her wounded one and she told him it was nothing and then asked him if everything was all right in the village. If the boys were his friends too, as well as Mary? He kissed her hand and held it to his cheek and told her she must be careful of the bombs because he loved her so much. He loved Laura too but more as a grandmother, not as he loved her.

Again Helen asked him if there was any trouble but this time he said, 'No, Mum. Everything's all right. Honestly it is.' And most of the time it was. Most of the time.

In the morning Helen fed the hens and the pig, watching the squealing piglets born too early.

Laura said, 'Too impatient, couldn't wait for the spring. It's because old Reynolds let his damned pig into the orchard.' Helen laughed then walked with Chris along the lane, watching him as he stamped on puddles. Laughing as he slid on frozen skid paths. Listening as he told her about the blacksmith at the forge.

He showed her the goat, their school and pointed to the copse in the distance to the left of a line of elms.

'That's where I'll go with the net. Mary said she'd come. I wrote to Dad about it.' He kicked at the frost-stiffened verge. 'Mr Reynolds says the Germans are buggers. They drop bombs on you, hurt our animals, kill our people. They've hurt your hands. They're buggers. That's what Mr Reynolds says anyway.'

Helen stood next to him, staring over at the copse, seeing the rooks' nests high in the bare branches, hearing his words drop into the still air. Her face was pinched and cold. She wet her lips, clenching her hands, wanting to feel the pain.

'It's war that's the bugger, Chris. Most of the people in it are like us. Doing things we don't want to do just because we have to. No, I don't hate the Germans but I do hate the Nazis and that's the difference that you and I must remember. The Nazis hurt other Germans too. They've somehow dragged everyone into the war.'

Chris turned to her. 'But it's easier to hate them all, isn't it? It makes us the same as everyone else here.'

Helen put her hand on his shoulder. His coat was getting too small. His sleeves were too far up his arms and his wrists would get sore from the cold wind soon. She must find him another.

'But it's not always best to take the easiest course, Chris, and we're not the same, are we, darling? Daddy was born in Germany.'

Helen gripped her son's shoulder hard because now, in the cold brisk air while the frost lay white on the ploughed fields, she must tell him. She turned him to her, holding his face in her hands.

'It's all so difficult, Mum,' Christoph said. 'I wish you were here.'

Helen nodded. 'Yes, Christoph. I wish I was too because we

are going to need one another more than ever now. Darling, listen to me; I have some terrible news.' She paused. 'Daddy died before Christmas.' Her voice was not level, it was full of tears and she stopped for a moment, watching the blankness of her son's eyes change to shock and then disbelief. He pulled away, snatching at her sleeve, breathing fast.

'What do you mean, died? What do you mean? How could he? There were no bombs there. I never had to worry about him, only about you. I never worried about him. Never, never.' He was shouting now, stepping away from her. She moved forward and grasped his shoulders.

'And why have you had your hair cut? You look silly. You look stupid.' He was hitting at her arms.

Helen would not let go of him; she hung on, feeling the blows on the splinter cuts but understanding his pain, his rage, because it was the same as hers. Perhaps they also shared the same guilt at resenting Heine's nationality.

She hung on and hung on until at last he was tired and then she showed him the letter and he knew that his father had been brave and honoured and they clung together and mourned him properly, here, in private, where the wind was now blowing cold and sharp.

They walked and remembered their lives together and Helen told her son of her anger at Heine when stones had been thrown, but she also spoke of her love. She hoped that Chris would talk to her but he didn't.

She stayed another night because her son needed her and the next and the next because she didn't care what Mr Leonard said – this was more important – but then she had to return because she must earn her money and there was no work down here, Laura said, shaking her head. The farm had all the workers they needed and there was nothing else.

The night she left Chris did not sleep. He lay looking up at the ceiling, seeing the beams in the glow from the ashes. He was glad his dad was dead. He was glad because now he could tell them at school that his father had been killed by the Nazis and maybe Joe would stop asking questions. So many questions. Would the stones start again if he knew?

He turned on his side, the pillow was wet. He couldn't stop crying because he wanted his dad. Wanted him to be here, to hold him, to be warm and alive; to hear his voice. He was brave, so brave, and what would he think of a son who said he was glad he was dead but who loved him so much that it hurt? Chris knew he would not sleep tonight because there was so much else in his head that was wicked and he could not tell his mother because she had the bombs and that was enough.

Winter turned to spring and in the evenings Helen took her turn at fire-watching and in the crypt she arranged further education classes for the regulars. She smiled when the old man offered to teach boxing and listened when he told her he was a southpaw and had fought in all the booths in the country during the depression. She watched as he shadow-boxed and was glad when others did too because his dignity returned during those nights and did not leave him.

The vicar arranged for a piano to be hauled from the church hall to the crypt and one of the young mothers taught Helen the tango and on Ruth's birthday they had a party and the vicar danced with Helen. The raids grew fewer but every night the crypt was open and the flat was seldom slept in. She wrote to Chris each week and slowly found that she could sleep now, though she still woke in the small hours and wept for Heine and wished that it had all been different. That they had been born in another time when war was not a consideration and they had been free to love.

In March Roosevelt signed the Lend-Lease Agreement with Britain and the crypt had another party and this time they did the hokey-cokey, with Ruth leading them. On 17 March Bevin announced the first steps in a massive mobilisation plan to release men for active service and Helen wondered if any of the farm workers in Greater Mannenham would be called up. She wrote to Laura and asked her to let her know because she knew that Chris would need her. Somehow she just knew.

In April Germany invaded Greece and the bombing of Britain continued in earnest again. Throughout the long nights they listened to the crump of bombs and sometimes Helen led the choir in a sing-song and everyone followed, but not every night because relatives were killed and people needed comfort.

On fire-watch duty Helen watched the flares being dropped and then the showers of incendiary bombs falling and knew that low level bombing runs would follow. Bert, the old boxer, was with her and said, as ack-ack hit one bomber which was flying in a straight line throughout his run, 'He was a brave one all right. Poor bugger.'

They both watched as the plane plummeted from the sky, a flaming mass to fall into the furnace of its own making. 'Poor bugger,' she echoed.

At the end of April the British were pushed out of Greece and Chris wrote to tell her that the piglets, Heine and Helen, were now his. Laura had given them to him. Laura wrote to her to say that he seemed to be sleeping better and was glad that Helen had left the letter from Willi with him. It was folded in his top bedside drawer and she knew that he read it every night.

On 11 May there was a brilliant bomber's moon and over 500 German planes dropped hundreds of high explosive bombs and incendiaries within a few hours. It was claimed to be a reprisal raid for the methodical bombing of the residential areas of German towns and Ruth said, 'The whole bloody world's gone mad. These are people in planes dropping bombs on other people. They're all dying. They're all somebody's sons and daughters. It's a crying shame. That 'itler needs to be strung up.'

Helen unpicked the jumper seam and pulled out wool, winding it around her healed hands. The hurricane lamps were dotted all over the crypt now; many had been brought by the people who sat around her and she was comforted by the smell, though the light was weak. As the hours passed she wrote a letter to Chris, telling him what Ruth had said and asking him to write to her because Laura had written that he was sleeping better, but was he really? Remember you can tell me anything, darling, she wrote.

In the morning they trooped up the steps of the crypt and wept at the devastation everywhere. Helen passed through a shattered city on her way to work and arrived three hours late and wanted to slap Mr Leonard because he was on time. Joan did not arrive until the afternoon because their house had been hit, but they had been in the Underground railway shelter.

There were cheers in the crypt on 28 May when the news came in that the *Bismarck* had been sunk the day before and Marian put a big notice on top of an old box.

SCRAP
Jam Jars, Iron, Bottles,
Paper, Rubber

Help to build planes and ships to
sink the enemy

The next day she and Marian brought aluminium pans from the flat and put them in the box because, as dawn had come, Helen had decided that it was her role to keep the Nazis and the Germans apart in her own mind and in her son's. The Nazis must indeed be sunk.

In the first week of June an exploding gas main ripped up the pavement outside the flat and they clambered through and into the hallway, but only to pick up the mail because they had to reach their offices. Laura had written to say that there was still no sign of the men leaving the farm but that Chris seemed to be fine and was looking forward to seeing his mother in the summer.

On 22 June the Nazis broke their pact and invaded Russia and that night Helen lay on her camp bed and thought of Heine; heard his voice saying, We'll be all right as long as Russia joins us.

She rolled over on her side, whispering aloud, 'Perhaps we'll make it now, Heine. But we still need America on our side.'

She cried though to think that he would not be here if they did survive and knew her grief, though dulled, still remained but it was mixed with anxiety for her son.

Part Two

CHAPTER 12

Chris sat on the old mac which Laura had handed him. He looked across at Mary and smiled; the egg sandwiches tasted good. The hens were laying well this week. They must have known it was spring. He looked up at the branches of the elm. He could see the blue sky through the leaf buds. There were bluebells in the copse, not many but enough to colour the ground.

'What did your mum say?' Mary asked, pushing a piece of crust into her mouth. 'Is she coming down yet? Did you say thank you to her for getting me out of old Ma Turnball's house and into Mrs Simpson's?'

Chris dug deep into his pocket, pulling out the letter he had received this morning. He read it to Mary.

London
May 1942

Darling Chris,
Well, though the bombs have tailed off I can't say that it is quiet here in London. As Mr Leonard grumbles, 'The Yanks are over-paid and over here.' We seem to have foreign soldiers everywhere now. Not just the Free French, the Poles but all these Americans. It is wonderful to see them. At last the end must be in sight, though of course it won't be as soon as we would like.

I was so pleased that it is working out better for Mary at Mrs Simpson's. Laura seemed to think that she was a kind person and believe me, the money I have to pay does not matter at all.

169

I am almost allowing myself to believe that I will be able to get to Norfolk soon. The Labour Exchange have said that it should be possible to exchange one form of war work for another but I need the permission of my employer and a replacement. They suggest that I apply for work in a sugar beet factory for the winter when even the permanent farm workers are laid off and then start work on Mr Jones's farm in the spring because I have his offer of a job in writing. If I apply to the Land Army I could be put to work anywhere and I can't be parted from you for very much longer. I will be able to get over to you every weekend once I start at the factory.

It seems a long time until the winter – another six months – but I have somehow to get Mr Leonard's agreement and you know how very difficult that will be. I will come though. I promise you that.

The vicar is still staying at the flat and is a constant support to everyone in the area and Marian is well and so too is Rob. He is stationed in Scotland still, in the Stores, and sometimes comes home on leave.

London is no longer the place you knew. In fact, I wonder if you can remember it. There are so many buildings destroyed. A bomb landed on the park and blew up the balloon and the horse-chestnut tree.

Write to me with your news when you can. Are you all right? Really all right?

All my love,
Mummy

Chris put it back in his pocket. She was coming. Not until the winter and then not to the village but he would see her every weekend.

'I'm glad she's coming,' Mary said, reaching forward and taking the last piece of bread. 'You need your mum. You'll have to tell her, you know.'

Chris crunched up the greaseproof paper, smaller and smaller but when he threw it to the ground it sprang out into a larger ball. 'Shut up', he said. 'Just shut up. She mustn't know. No one must know.'

He took a drink of water from the bottle, wiping the top before passing it to Mary. She took it and drank and now there were crumbs in the water but he didn't want any more anyway.

'She should know because they'll get you one day. They won't be satisfied with a postal order soon, you know.' She passed the bottle back and he pushed it down into the canvas bag which Laura had packed the picnic in.

'I don't want to talk about it,' Chris said, getting up. 'Come on, let's see how they're getting on.'

He didn't wait for Mary to catch up but picked up the canvas bag and walked to the edge of the trees, looking out towards the fields which had once grown wheat and barley but which were now churned up as men built huts at one end and hangars at another. The row of elms was still standing, though, hiding the airfield from the village. The runway markers stretched and stretched across three fields and Laura had said that they would never get it back as it used to be once the war was over. Chris looked back into the copse. Mary was coming, bringing the old butterfly net. It was too early but sometimes if the spring was really warm, Laura had said, you could be lucky.

He looked back again to the airfield and then to the village. There was no sign of Joe or the gang on the road. Maybe they wouldn't be waiting by the crossroads today, but he knew they would. They always were on a Saturday. He felt the postal order in his pocket. They would be there because today was the day he had to give them his pocket money or they would tell the whole village that his dad had been a German.

'My sister says the Yanks are good fun. They give her stockings and gum. Chewing gum, you know. And comics and cigarettes.' Mary stood next to him. 'When they come d'you think they'll give us gum? I've never 'ad it.'

Chris turned towards her. It was only two o'clock. Joe wouldn't be there until four and maybe today he'd be brave enough to stand up to him. Yes, maybe today he would but now he wanted to see the toad spawn. Yes, that's what he wanted to do. They walked round the edge of the copse to the pond and there, in long spotted strings were the spawn, stretched out in the water, crossing and recrossing one another.

'Blimey, I thought they was in one big blob like tapioca,' Mary said, and Chris laughed.

'So did I but Laura told me last night.'

They lay on their stomachs, their hands in the cold water. The moss on the stones was close to him, like a miniature forest. His breath blew up puffs of dry earth and there was a smell of spring in the ground. In the summer, Laura had said, fly agaric grew here, the red and white spotted toadstool which was poisonous for humans but which slugs loved.

'Maybe I should push one down Joe's throat,' he said to Mary and smiled when she laughed.

They walked over to the hollow which was where the badgers had a set. Where would they walk to now that the airfield had been built across their path? They looked for the long scratch marks on the other bank and there they were, made with the long digging claws.

'I never want to go back to London, do you?' Chris asked as they walked on down the deep rutted track where the cart-wheels had churned the earth.

'No, it's lovely, ain't it? Just so quiet and lovely, except when it's harvest time. Then it's too bloody busy. Like Piccadilly.' They had reached the larger pond now, where the old tin bath was still stuck, half submerged out in the middle. Chris crouched, and together they discussed whether they could get a rope out to it and bring it back and have another go this summer.

'Maybe it won't sink this time if we put a couple of empty drums either side,' Chris said.

Mary was breathing heavily next to him, sucking at a new blade of grass. 'How d'you fix the drum, clever clogs?'

Chris shrugged. 'Well, how about a plank going across the top and tie everything to the plank?' It sounded good to him and she smiled.

'All right, but how do we get it back? I'm not going in after it.' Mary was scrambling to her feet, dusting off her dress which hung from her shoulders like a sack.

Chris pushed himself up too, taking the butterfly net from her, heaving the canvas bag on to his shoulder. He didn't want to go in either and feel the sticky mud under his toes again, the soft wriggling which could have been anything.

'Oh well, we'll think about it,' he said, walking on.

They didn't take any eggs from the nests today. Laura had said they must only take one or two otherwise there would be no birds for the mothers to hatch. Somehow they had not thought of the eggs turning into birds before and now they did not want to take any at all.

Chris felt the jam jar filled with diced laurel leaves in his pocket and wondered if he would really be able to catch a butterfly if he saw one and ease it into the jar with the bitter almond smell, leaving it to die. He remembered Mr Reynolds's butterflies pinned into position with their wings fixed so that they were beautiful. But were they really? Weren't they only beautiful in flight or resting on a plant with the sun on their wings? Would he ever be able to bring his net down and capture them, kill them, mount them? He didn't know but saying that he would gave him a reason to come out into the woods, to leave behind the games of Germans and British convoys, not cowboys and Indians. It gave him a chance to keep away from Joe and his gang.

It was four o'clock now, they could hear the chiming of the church clock from here and Mary had to be home for tea. They walked towards the village. There were fresh young nettles growing on the verges and Joe was there, in the distance, down by the crossroads. Mary had seen them too.

'Tell your mother, Chris, or Laura, or someone. There's too many of them to fight, you know.'

But he couldn't tell anyone because Joe had said he would tell the village and Chris couldn't bear the thought of the stones again and the shouting. Not here, not in this countryside that he loved.

He shook his head. They were closer now. He could see Joe swiping at the verge with his stick, and Chris stopped, staring at Joe and then he slowly and deliberately bent and gripped the nettle by the side tightly, jerking his hand upwards, knowing that this way it would not sting you. He pulled it from the earth, holding it up so that Joe could see.

He watched as the other boy laughed and did the same but he pulled it downwards, touching the top of the leaves, stinging his hand and his fingers.

'Blimey, that was a good one,' Mary said.

Chris nodded, looking with satisfaction at Joe's red face, at his hand which he clutched between his arm and body and it didn't matter so much when the boys came and grabbed him, digging in his pocket for the sixpence, but not Joe. Joe was holding his hand and swearing.

In August the sun was hot, so very hot. Chris had sat up with Laura last night, making another butterfly net from a forked oak branch and thin hoops of hazel which they threaded through the hem of an old net curtain sewn to the correct shape. He had then twisted old fuse wire round the hazel and the oak, fixing it into place with wire. Chris did not tell Laura that since the nettles Joe had been waiting for him more often. He had beaten him twice and then broken his butterfly net, but his father had suffered too, hadn't he, in the internment camp, and so he must be as brave.

'Are you going out to the copse with Mary today?' Laura asked, frowning when he said no.

'But why? You're spending too much time on your own. You're only nine. You need friends.'

Chris took up the canvas bag. 'She's a girl,' he said. 'She can't keep up.' But that wasn't the reason. It was because she cried when she saw them waiting for him and it made his eyes water too.

He walked through the long grass of the two meadows leading to the copse. The cornflowers and red poppies hung limp in the hot sun and the Common Blues rose in front of him. He stopped, waiting for them to settle again and they did, with closed wings, the undersides of which were a medley of orange and black spots and rings on a grey background. The female was dark brown touched with blue, edged with orange rings and she lifted up into the air and then settled. Chris didn't catch them. He never did. Laura knew it, he knew it, but nothing was ever said.

The copse was cool and dark and nightingales used to sing when he and Laura walked in the evenings but that was before the bombers came, two weeks ago. They had thundered over in wave after wave, coming in low over the village and the evacuees had thrown themselves on the ground, some scream-ing, while the village children laughed. But they had never been bombed had they, the teacher had said, his face white with anger at the village children's laughter.

Where had the nightingales gone, Chris had asked Laura but she didn't know. He looked around. The fly agaric were bright against the greens and browns and he wondered if Mary came

174

to the copse at all. He walked to the larger pond. The tin bath was still half sunken. He missed her. Really missed her.

It was dark, too dark here, he felt suddenly. He wanted the sun on his face, pushing the shadows back, away from him. He ran through the wood, leaping over gnarled roots, skidding round trees, going faster because there could be Indians. Faster and faster. Quick, the arrows could be coming. Thwack, thwack into the trees, but missing him, always missing him. He was out into the daylight now, the breath was heaving in his chest but he felt better. He walked towards the airfield, seeing the great dark shapes of the planes behind the elms.

The planes were so huge and dark and, at dawn each morning, seemed to claw through the air, climbing higher and higher, but so slowly and heavily, pushing their noise down on to the earth, the village, the cottage, his bed, until the buildings shook. This morning he had watched from the window and seen the planes turn at last into silver specks in the clear blue sky.

He walked up to the perimeter fence, seeing the heavy equipment and vehicles running more easily over the heavy clay ground now that the summer was here. A jeep roared along the edge of the tarmacked runway, skidding to a halt beside a towering B-17. Nissen huts clustered together and there were Quonset huts too with flat roofs and straight sides.

He had cycled up to the wire with Laura and Mary when they were building the airfield. They had watched as the curved corrugated iron plates of the Nissen huts were buckled together and Laura had said they would hold twenty or thirty men. Chris had listened to the shouts, the laughter of the men, seen their mouths endlessly chewing the gum, some of which they had thrown through the wire for them, though Laura had forbidden them to pick it up.

It was a disgusting habit, she had said, but Mary had slipped it into her pocket when Laura blushed and turned away as the men whistled at her.

They had watched all morning as they heaved the panels up and locked them together and he remembered how his father had built the Anderson shelter and he had cried, standing there at the wire he had cried, then ridden home when Laura had seen. He had cried all night and she had stayed with him but did not know that it was more than grief, it was because he was

175

still too afraid to let the village know about his father and he was ashamed.

Chris felt the sun on the back of his head, his back. On his hand which held the butterfly net. He was thirsty and moved off, down the road waiting for two jeeps to pass before crossing. The horse manure had been squashed flat and dry by so many trucks and he smiled. Each morning he had to collect the cow pats from the field behind their cottage to put on the vegetable garden and on dry days it was easier. Today had been a dry day.

He sat on the edge of the copse again, watching the air base. They were only training, the publican had told Laura. The Americans came into his pub each evening and on the first night they had drunk him dry.

The water in Chris's bottle was warm but he drank it, taking deep long gulps, watching the rolling walk of the airmen in the distance as they strolled about the airfield. They didn't march like the English. They had rubber soles which were quiet and they rolled their feet. He stood up, rolling his, slipping his hands into his pockets, chewing his sandwich as though it was gum. He didn't hear the man until he laughed.

'Well, I guess that's a pretty good imitation,' he said, and Chris turned, whipping his hands from his pockets, standing silent, fearful, watching the flyer who stood in his uniform, his back to the trees, the sun on his face.

'Hey, ease up, fella. I was just out taking in some of the countryside. It's different. You know. Kind of different.' The man turned and looked out over the flat fields to the low undulating hills in the distance. He had his hands in his pockets and his leather jacket was unbuttoned, his cap was slipped back on his head. He turned back to Chris who was chewing his sandwich, trying to make it small enough to swallow.

'You like candy?'

Chris shrugged. He didn't know what candy was.

The man laughed again. He had dark eyes like Chris with deep lines running down from them, like Chris's father. But he had a moustache too; it was brown like his hair.

'Well, I guess I mean, would you like a sweet?' The man rounded his mouth and said again. 'Would you care for a sweet?' He almost sounded English.

Chris watched as he brought out boiled sweets, a bag full, from his pocket. He hadn't tasted sweets for over a year because Joe had taken his pocket money for that long.

Chris took one but the man said, 'No, take the pack. There's plenty more on base.' He pushed them at Chris, nodding to him. 'Thank you,' Chris said, reaching out, feeling the bag heavy in his hand. 'Would you like one of my sandwiches? They're egg. Straight from the hen this morning.'

The man laughed again. 'Is that so? Sure. That'd be great.'

He looked round sizing up the ground, then sat next to the canvas bag, picking at the long grass while Chris took out the sandwiches. He unfolded the greaseproof paper and offered them.

'Have two if you like,' he said. The man's hands were brown and strong and his nails were short and square. He wore a heavy wrist-watch which glinted in the sun.

'One'll be more than plenty. I guess I was just coming out for a stroll and here I am, eating homegrown hen's eggs. My name's Ed. What's yours?'

Chris was chewing the sweet, swallowing its sweetness. He wiped his hand across his mouth before replying.

'Chris,' he said. 'Chris Weber.'

The man tipped his hat even further back on his head. 'Well, Chris Weber, you must be mighty proud of where you live. This is a nice little corner.' He waved his hand across the view. 'You born here?'

Chris was drinking from the bottle again and now he hesitated, wiping the neck with his sleeve, looking at the man. Then he passed it to him. Ed took it, looked at him and grinned, and then drank. Chris smiled, taking it back, burrowing it back in the canvas bag out of the sun. He brought out a stick of rhubarb and a twist of sugar saying as he did so, 'No, I wasn't born here. I lived in London but when the bombing started I was evacuated here. I like it.'

He broke the rhubarb in two and handed a piece to Ed. Then he spread out the paper. 'Dig the end in the sugar and then eat it.'

Ed did and Chris laughed at his face, at the strings of rhubarb which hung from his mouth.

'Jeez, what the hell's this?' Ed said, his face screwed up.

'It's a bit sour, makes your teeth feel funny doesn't it? But it's

177

nice when there's nothing sweet left to eat.' Chris was smiling and now Ed was too. Chewing but asking for more water.

'I forget that there's rationing over here. You must excuse us if we tread on your toes. We don't mean to but little England sure takes some getting used to.'

'My mum says we're very lucky Mr Roosevelt decided to come in after all, even if it took Pearl Harbor to do it. She says we can't win without you.'

Ed threw the remains of his rhubarb right across the field and Chris watched. He threw the remains of his too but it fell far short of the man's.

'Your mom is here with you, is she?' Ed asked, stretching out his arms, flexing his shoulders.

'No, she's in London. How do you throw that far?' Chris said, kneeling now, looking out across the field, trying to see where the rhubarb had landed.

'I was a pitcher back home in college. You know, baseball. You call it rounders.'

Now Chris did know but the boys at school called it a girls' game and sniggered at the American comics which showed pictures of the game. But this man wasn't girlish.

'I'll show you one day. How about it?' Ed leaned forward, pulling up another grass shoot, chewing it. He turned and looked at Chris who was nodding, his blond hair bleached almost white by the sun.

'So we're both away from home then, Chris Weber? Get's kind of lonesome, doesn't it?'

Chris nodded, packing up the sugar carefully, to take home and use again tomorrow. 'I'd like to learn to throw,' he said.

'Well, we got a deal then. You don't bring me any more rhubarb and I'll teach you to pitch.' Ed stuck out his hand and his teeth were strong and white when he smiled.

Chris shook his hand. It was big and warm and it felt good to be touched by a grown man again. It reminded him of his father.

'Where you going now then, Chris?' Ed was standing up, wiping his forehead with the back of his hand, lifting up his cap then brushing off his trousers.

A formation of bombers was coming in to land and Chris could not talk against the noise so they both stood and watched.

'I was just going to look for some butterflies. You can come if you like.'

They walked slowly through the meadows and Chris asked Ed if he flew.

'Yeah, I fly one of the Fortresses.' Ed stopped as a Nymph rose from the wheat. 'Say, is that one of those things that fly into the lampshade at night, banging itself to bits? Can't stand the things.'

'No, it's a Nymph, a butterfly. You can tell them from moths because butterflies' antennae have knobs on the end. Moths tend to hold their wings horizontally when they're at rest too.'

'You know a lot about this then? Do you collect 'em?'

Chris shrugged. 'No. I don't like the idea of killing.'

Ed nodded and started to walk again. 'I guess most of us are like that.' He wasn't smiling now but then a Red Admiral flew up before them and Chris held out his hand to stop the man.

'Isn't that beautiful?' Chris said. 'I mean, it's just so beautiful.' They stood quietly for a moment watching as the butterfly wove its way over the wheat.

'They get drunk on the rotten apples in the orchard, you know,' Chris said, talking to this man as though he had known him all his life. He was so easy. Not like the English grown-ups. Were all Americans like this?

Ed's laugh was loud.

'Do you get butterflies where you live?' Chris asked, moving the bag on his shoulder, then feeling it lifted from him as Ed took it.

'Not much. We live in Montana, ranch country. Down in the valley they come but not up near the sage brush. We keep horses, cattle, sheep. Herd them, and there's some hay too. It's kind of beautiful there. Mountains all around with deep snow in the winter and hot sun in the summer.'

Chris stopped. 'Do you ever brand them to stop the rustlers? And are there Indians?'

They were on the old cart track now and Ed sat on the oak which had been felled by lightning four years ago.

'Sure we brand them, but we don't have a big herd and it grazes behind fences now but in the days of rustlers there was a real need for branding. You ever seen it done?'

Chris shook his head.

'Well let me tell you something you can tell your friends.

Come the spring the cowboys would bring in all the cattle on the ranges, sort them out into the different owner herds. Then they'd brand the calves with a red-hot iron. Say, you got a blacksmith here?'

Chris nodded.

'Well, the iron has to get that hot, then you press it against its hide and the smell and the sizzle is just something.' Ed took a packet of Lucky Strikes from his pocket, tapping the cigarette on his fingernail, then striking the match on it too. Chris breathed the scent of sulphur pretending it was the smell of burning hide.

'Now, there are all sorts of brands, put on with a stamp iron. Usually no more than four inches long, not more than seven inches in any direction but they grow with the animal you see. Now a brand's made up like this. If it's the Lazy M Bar you would lay an "M" on its side with a line underneath. Kind of neat eh?'

He flicked the ash off on to the ground. 'But, oh my, did those cowboys know what they were doing, kid. They would have to drive a mile-long herd you know. They'd keep the stronger cattle forward and out of the way so they didn't trample the weaker ones. They'd call that keeping up the corners. The cowboys would keep the herd together, signalling by hand, using Plains Indian sign language.' He paused. 'Hey, should you be back at home by now? It's past four o'clock.'

'No, go on.' He could tell Mary and the others, but not Joe or his gang.

'Now did I tell you about a running iron for branding? That's what those darned rustlers would use. A straight poker drawn like a pencil to make any brand.'

'But what about the cowboys. Did they shoot the rustlers?'

'Yeah, they sure did. They were taking something which wasn't rightly theirs, you see. And the West didn't have the kind of laws you Britishers have. You've been here so darned long.' He laughed.

'What about stampedes? Have you ever been in a stampede when you've been moving your cattle?'

'Not moving our own but I have when I worked one summer down in the south. You have to churn them around to the right when they're spooked, always to the right and you have to have a good horse, one that ain't going to run out on you. You just got to squeeze that circle smaller and smaller until the herd becomes compact and stops. It's kind of spooky, I'm telling you. And there're no Indians any more near us but there were some on the plains. They got real mad when the white man came but who can blame them?'

He lit another cigarette. 'It all seems very far away now.'

'Is flying as exciting as being a cowboy?'

Ed smiled. 'Exciting isn't the right word. We go up into the sky and try to find the assembly ship which is shooting off flares so that we can see it. This can take an hour, Chris, and then we fly in formation at high altitude, hoping our bomb aimers are going to do their job properly. And we won't know whether any of us are going to turn out right until we actually try it and who knows when that will be. No. It's not exciting. It's tiring, it's worrying. Ships collide, crash. It's not exciting.' His voice was flat now and he stood up.

'I guess maybe being a cowboy is better. But I reckon I'd better be getting back now. I'll see you again, Chris, teach you how to pitch, eh?' He passed back the bag and punched Chris on the arm. 'Nice meeting you, kid. You take care now.'

Chris watched him go, his rolling walk, his cap on the back of his head and turned, his hand at his belt, wishing he still had his cap gun. He formed his hand into a gun and shot into the hedges that he passed. The shadows were longer now, the sun not so hot and his watch said it was five o'clock.

Joe was waiting at the edge of the village, beyond the grey stone wall where no one could see. Chris had forgotten him. How could he have done that? How could he have forgotten? He tightened his grip on the butterfly net and kept his hand as a gun. It gave him courage.

Joe lounged out into the lane, kicking a stone.

'I want to talk to you, you German swine,' he said, using a drawl he had copied since the Americans arrived.

'I don't want to talk to you,' Chris said, pushing past because it was not the postal order day. The gang came out from behind the wall then and they had nettles in their gloved hands. They grabbed Chris and he fought but Joe hissed, 'Keep still, or I tell the whole bloody village.'

He kept still while they rubbed the freshly picked nettles over his face, arms and legs as far as his shorts would allow. They then broke his butterfly net, again.

That week Laura wrote to Helen to come because Chris would not tell her what was going on, but something was because his limbs were covered in nettle rash and she was sure he hadn't fallen, as he was insisting.

Ed walked on back to base. No, he thought, it was not exciting. He had not expected it to be somehow, maybe because he was older than most of the kids who volunteered or were drafted. For Christ's sake he was thirty, so why the hell was he here? To get away from the ranch, from his father, his mother who loved him too much? Out of a sense of duty maybe? Who knew, who cared? He was here, wasn't he?

He looked over the meadows. England was so green, that was what had struck him when they finally landed at Liverpool and travelled out from the bombed city. It was so damn green. But Liverpool hadn't been green, neither had the run through bomb alley off Greenland on the transport ship because he'd travelled over by ship, not flown one of the Fortresses like some of the others. It had been cold and grey at sea and cold and grey in Liverpool.

Barrage balloons were moored to barges in the river the guys called the Mersey. There was a freighter with a torpedo hole, women with scarves round their heads. There were little trains with hooters, not whistles. Red tram cars but hardly any cars. Red Cross girls with doughnuts and coffee at stalls on the station. On the train there were closed blackout curtains, on the trucks which wound through these tiny little lanes there was just a wooden rail to hang on to.

At the air base there were only showers with cold water which shot up from the centre of a wide concrete dish and you washed yourself in the downfall. It was crazy. What a way to run a war; but as he walked he knew that he was thinking of these things rather than the daylight bombing runs they were training for.

Why daylight? He knew why. So that the Air Force could become a service in its own right, separate from the Army. They wanted to bomb accurately in daylight and win the war in a few months. Ed shrugged. But he wasn't being fair. After all, the Allies did need to put the pressure on day and night but they'd forgotten there was no proper long-range fighter cover. They had forgotten there were a lot of enemy planes up there, a lot of anti-aircraft guns. They'd forgotten that the people flying these damned Fortresses were skin and bone.

He thought of the boy, the butterflies, the pitching. Yes, he'd show him how to throw. He was a nice kid. It was better to think of that than assembling at altitude, flying in formation, dropping bombs, spotting Messerschmitts, hearing the stuttering of guns, feeling the shudder of bullets hitting the fuselage. He was thinking in time to his footsteps and now he stopped, his hands in his pockets, breathing deeply, wishing there were just a few mountains around, making himself stop thinking of aeroplanes and battles.

Making himself think of the Red Admiral getting drunk on apples, tasting again the rhubarb. Crazy people, these Britishers, but kind of nice.

Helen came down when she received Laura's letter. The trip was quicker now that the bombing was almost non-existent. The bus drove quickly down the lanes in the long evenings made longer still by double summer time.

She talked with Laura in the kitchen and with Mary too who would not say what was happening but only that one boy and his friends were ganging up. Helen fed the hens with Chris while Laura prepared salad and after they had eaten she walked with him, letting him take her towards the base, walking along the tarmacked road which was slippery with melted tar from the hot afternoon sun. They walked on the grass verge and stopped as Chris pointed out the hangars, the aeroplanes, the baseball pitch which had been marked out off to the left.

She listened as he told her of Captain Ed McDonald who was showing him how to pitch in the meadow near the pond; of Mary who came and watched. He talked of the butterflies he still watched and led her over the fields to the pond where they still had not recovered the tin bath. But he told her nothing of his fears, though she hugged him and said that she knew there was something wrong. He would not tell her about Joe though. No. His father had told no one of his battle so he mustn't either.

Helen stood at the edge of the pond watching her son flick his hair from his face. The shadows were there in his eyes and they had been there for too long.

'Right,' she said, walking over to him. 'Listen to me. I can't

183

make you tell me but I am going to teach you what an old boxer taught some of the lads in the shelter because you must fight back, Chris. Whatever is going on, you must fight back.'

She turned him round. 'Now watch me. You hold your hands like this, see?' She stood with her right hand forward and her left in close to her chin. 'You lead with your right and then hit hard with your left. Now, you've got to keep your feet moving. Don't stand still. You mustn't stand still or they'll be able to hit you.'

She stopped. 'Do you understand?' She was panting.

Chris nodded.

'Good, now put your hands up and try and hit me.' Her fists were up again and her feet were moving.

Chris just stood. 'Come on, Chris, hit me.'

He put his hands up too but it felt awkward. He moved his feet but he couldn't hit his own mother and so she hit him on the cheek and it hurt. He still couldn't hit her and she hit him again, on the ribs, and now he circled her and jabbed at her, hitting her on the chin.

Helen stopped, her eyes blinking. It had hurt. It had really hurt. She smiled. 'That's right. That's absolutely right. Come on. Again.' They circled and jabbed for the next hour and both walked home with red faces but they were laughing and when Ed drove by in the jeep and hooted, Chris said to his mother, 'That's my friend.'

That night Chris slept because his mother had come and looked so funny trying to help.

CHAPTER 13

It was September, a month after Chris had first met Ed and each Saturday when the American was not flying they met out on the grass patch near the big pond to practise pitching. The tin bath was now up on the bank but neither Mary nor Chris had clambered in to drag it out. Ed had brought it in.

Chris had stood on the bank with Mary while the American threw out a four-pronged hook attached to a line. It had landed in the bath with a muffled clang and they pulled the line gently, hearing the hook scrape against the sides but it had caught on the rim and they were able to drag the bath back.

It had smelt and Ed had swirled water in it, then called them to help him tip it up and left it to dry. Chris had a plank now and Ed had brought along two empty drums from the Airbase and, after pitching practice this afternoon, Chris was going to lash it all together and see if it would float properly this time.

'Come on then, Chris, let's get going,' Ed called from his position ten yards in front of him. 'Now remember what I said last week. The pitcher's got to deceive the batter, right. He's got to produce pitches which are fast or will swerve or dip because the whole aim is to get that man out. Now I want you to throw me a fast ball, OK? Mary, you get ready too, because I'll be sending one to you soon.'

Chris looked at Mary. She had begun to come with him again because he had told her that he could fight now and one day he would and she was not to cry when she saw him with Joe. So far, though, he hadn't fought. But the sun was too hot to think of all that now and Ed was waiting.

He was wearing a pitcher's glove which Ed had given him. It was padded leather with a webbed pocket to help to catch the ball.

'Remember to keep that foot in contact with the back plate

185

when you throw.' Ed called and Chris nodded, checking that his right foot was on the square that Ed had marked out with a stone earlier. He held the cowhide ball with his thumb underneath and his first two fingers on top, and close together. The ball was warm and smooth.

'Blimey, it'll be time to go to bed before he gets going,' Mary called and Ed laughed.

Chris threw the ball then and Ed scooped it out of the air, curving his body, moving his legs.

'That was great, really great. Real quick. Try catching this.'

As he threw it Chris saw the twist of his wrist and the ball came at him from right to left and dipped at the last minute but he caught it, hearing Ed's shout of praise and Mary's cheer.

Ed came over and stood next to Chris. 'Right, Mary, you get ready to catch the next one. Let's see if boy wonder can throw a curveball like that.' He checked Chris's grip. 'OK, the grip's the same as the fastball but the fingers are parallel to the seam. That's right. Now get that twist right. Like this, see?'

Chris watched as again and again Ed twisted his wrist but did not throw the ball. The American had tossed his jacket over on the grass when he arrived and rolled his sleeves up above his elbows. He had left base for two hours only today because there was a briefing at 14.00 hours.

'OK. Now try that.' He ran back, standing towards Chris. 'Move in a little, Mary. Ready to go when you are, Chris.'

He threw then; the grip was right and the twist. They both missed it and the ball rolled to a halt yards behind, near to the trees.

'You're going great,' Ed said, picking up the ball, showing Mary how to hold it and now Chris leaned forward, ready to catch. Again and again they did it until the sweat was rolling down Chris's back and his shirt clung to him. Ed was hot too and Mary had flopped down on the grass in the shade.

Laura had made them ginger beer and they sat in the shade at the edge of the copse, hearing the bees in the grass, drinking it from enamel mugs which Chris had brought. Laura had told Chris to ask his American if he would like to come home for tea.

'That's kind of you all but I have to get back to base and I reckon maybe I won't be back out again this evening.' He reached across and dug into his jacket pocket. 'Have a cookie.'

186

'Why?' Mary said, taking one of the biscuits, and then another. 'Why won't you be back out?'

The American shrugged.

Chris looked at him and asked, 'Is the training over? Are you really going to fly properly now?'

'Well, I guess maybe that's what's about to happen soon.' Ed grinned but the smile didn't touch his eyes and Chris looked away towards the pond.

He knew that look. It was how he felt when he saw Joe at the end of the lane and suddenly he didn't want this man to go up in those big dark planes, dropping bombs, being shot at. He didn't want the training to finish.

'Maybe they'll think you're not ready,' he said, looking down into his ginger beer. It was warm and not very nice. 'Maybe the war will be over by tonight. Will it be tonight you fly?'

Ed drank back the last of his ginger beer, holding the mug in his large hand, not using the handle. Chris copied.

'No,' his voice was short, clipped. 'Not tonight. We only fly in the daylight and as you say, Chris, maybe the war'll be over by tonight.' He grinned at the boy and reached out, flicking his hair. 'But somehow I don't reckon it will be. Sometimes you just got to get on with things.'

They sat watching the heat shimmering across the freshly harvested fields in the distance, seeing the wind brushing at the reeds near the pond, rippling the surface. A fly came and settled on Ed's empty mug and a Red Admiral danced in and out of the cowslip until they could no longer see it.

When would they start the real thing, Ed wondered. He had just sent a V-mail letter back to his folks telling them that it was great over here. That he flew and trained, drank in the pub and taught baseball to an English kid. He asked them again to look after his mare because he wanted her fit when he got back. When he got back, when he got back. If he got back. He picked up a stone from the grass beside him and threw it from hand to hand.

'No,' he repeated. 'Somehow I don't think this war is going to be over by tonight.'

Chris swatted at the fly, holding out the bottle to Ed and shaking his head. 'I guess not.' He liked speaking the way the American did.

Ed looked at Chris. 'So when's your mom coming back down then?'

Chris shrugged. 'I don't know. When she can, I suppose. He laughed and looked at Mary who was giggling.

Ed asked, 'So what's funny then?'

Chris was laughing still so Mary told him that Helen had shown him how to box last time she was down.

'Your mom? But why not your pop?'

Chris stopped laughing then and turned away. The wind was brisker now and there were ripples on the top of the pond and the reeds were shaking. There were clouds coming up from the east.

'My dad's dead,' Chris said, still looking away, but then he turned and faced the man who was running the rim of the cup over his lips, backwards and forwards. 'He was German. He was in a camp. They killed him. He was brave.' The words were high-pitched, clipped, but they were out, for the first time they were out and what would Ed do? Would he move away from him, pick up his ball, his jacket and go?

Ed touched his shoulder. 'That's tough, real tough.' That was all. He didn't move, he didn't shout. His voice had been kind. Chris looked across at Mary and she smiled. He pushed his hand into his pocket and took out Willi's letter which he always carried now. It had seemed too dead somehow, in the top drawer.

He pushed it into Ed's hand and then got up and walked to the tin bath, rubbing at the dried mud with a stick, clearing it off the sides, watching it drop as fine as sand into the bottom. He rubbed and rubbed and tipped the bath upside down, banging the base and then he rolled it over again. It was clean.

He picked up the plank and straddled it across and then he heard Ed walking towards him and Mary was there too. He didn't look round but took the letter and shoved it in his pocket.

'I thought I'd tie the drums on, then we can see if it floats,' Chris said, still not looking round.

They worked on the raft, tying, knotting, securing, and nothing was said until it floated out across the pond, tethered by the frayed rope which they had kept hidden in an old wooden box in the reeds.

Chris stood with his hands in his pockets, grinning at Mary and then up at Ed, who smiled back. 'That's going to be great,' he said, putting his hand on Chris's shoulder.

Mary took the rope from Chris. 'I told 'im,' she said. 'I told him about Joe. He wants to see what your mum taught you.'

Chris bit back his anger. How could she tell? It was their secret. Ed mustn't know he was afraid. How could she tell? He snatched the rope back.

'You should shut up,' he hissed at her. It was cooler now. There were goose pimples on her arms. He hoped she was cold.

'No, she shouldn't shut up.' Ed's voice was firm. 'She should have told someone a lot sooner. You need to give this Joe guy a good lesson, one he won't forget. Like your pop gave those Nazis, like your grandpa is trying to do out there in Germany.' He nodded at Chris's surprise.

'Yeah, Mary told me that too. But you need the tools to do the job, kid. You need to know what you're doing or how can you fight back? No one can expect you to. Britain couldn't do it. It needed all this stuff from the States. How can I fly without a plane? How can you fight back against this kid without knowing how? You're just like the rest of us. Brave enough but scared too. It's crazy not to be scared. It keeps you alive sometimes.'

Chris felt the American's hands on his shoulders. They were gripping too tightly and he remembered the look in Ed's face earlier. He was frightened too. That's why he was digging his fingers in like he was. Ed was frightened, and if a big man like that was, it didn't matter so much that Chris Weber was scared too.

So he showed Ed his right hand out in front, his left hand close in to his chin and the position of his feet but he still didn't feel comfortable. He stood up and shook his head when Ed asked if he was a southpaw. 'You know, left-handed.'

He shook his head and Ed smiled. 'Well,' he said. 'Your mom is some sort of special lady but she's learned from a southpaw. You need to put your left hand forward like this.' Ed's eyes had lines at the corners when he smiled and the sky was blue above. The trees from the copse were throwing shadows far out across the grass and Chris felt happy right down to his fingertips to be here by the pond with him.

Pitching was forgotten for the next half-hour while Ed taught Chris and Mary too, because she did not want to be left out.

It didn't matter hitting Ed. He was big and strong, not like

189

his mother and so his shoulders loosened and his head came down and he pretended Ed was Joe and landed punches, getting through Ed's guard.

He was stronger now from the pitching. He could feel it and he was quicker too. But it was something else as well. This man knew that he was half German and it didn't matter to him. Gee, he had said. Some Americans are Germans and Italians. How d'you think they feel fighting their own people? And should we hate them because they're Germans or Italians? It's what they are that's important, isn't it? It's the ideas we're fighting against, isn't it?

Chris punched harder, rhythmically in time to that last sentence, It's the ideas we're fighting against, isn't it, isn't it? until Ed called to him to stop, yelling at Mary too who was shadow-boxing just two feet away. He showed them then how to use judo throws because boxing sometimes wasn't enough, but it was getting late. Before he left, though, he kicked Chris's feet out from beneath him, quickly, neatly and the grass was close to his face and smelt fresh and clean. Ants were running in amongst the stems.

'Remember that one,' Ed said, breathing heavily as he bent to pick up his jacket, looking at his watch, then breaking into a jog. He had reached the copse, ready to run through it out on to the fields and then down the road to the base but stopped and turned. 'Hey,' he called. 'When's the next drop for the postal order?'

Chris sat up and cupped his hands round his mouth. 'Next Saturday; ten hundred hours.'

Ed waved. 'Keep practising and watch out for Mary. She swings a mean punch.' He turned and was gone and Chris realised he hadn't wished him luck.

All that week it was overcast, the cloud hung low over England and Europe.

'The summer's finally over,' Laura said as she ironed before the kitchen stove on Thursday afternoon.

Chris could smell the fresh hot linen and was glad of the cloud because it meant the bombers were not flying; that the training had not turned into something more dangerous. It meant Ed was safe.

He practised all that week, sparring against Mary near the

pond but he couldn't bring himself to hit her. She hit him though, and once he got angry and stalked off through the flattened grass, hearing her laugh, and he wished that Joe would walk round the corner that very minute so he could knock his block off while he was still angry.

He had to meet Joe in the woods because the crossroads was too busy with American jeeps and on Thursday he felt tired and taut because there were only two days now before he must stand up to him. He had decided that he could not wait any longer because his father had been brave and there were men out there in bombers with the same feeling in their stomachs and they went, so he must. On Friday he felt sick and his head hurt but there was only one day and night left.

Mary came round and she dodged and weaved in the garden and made him angry again but it didn't last. It was only the fear that was left as darkness fell and he climbed the stairs to bed on legs that felt too tired to carry him. He wrote to his mother that night in the candlelight of his bedroom, bending low over the paper, his hand tight on his pencil. He liked the flickering light, it gave off heat and a waxy smell which was comforting.

He told her that tomorrow, Saturday, he was going to face the boys. That his friend Ed had shown him how to do some judo throws. He did not tell her that she had taught him as a southpaw, because 'she was some kind of a special mom' and he loved her so much. I miss you, Mum, he wrote. I miss you.

The next morning was cold and dull and as he ate an egg which tasted strange and the toast which was too hard, he looked out of the window and hoped that the cloud cover was thick and deep again today and that Ed was kept safely on the ground.

He had not seen him since last weekend. The Americans had been confined to the air base all week but that didn't matter. It only mattered that the aeroplanes had not roared off from the runway at dawn, flown by men with frightened eyes.

'Eat up then,' Laura urged him, coming round the table, looking into his face, her flowered apron stiff from the ironing. 'Are you all right? You don't look too good.'

Chris nodded. 'Yes, I'm fine.'

He heard the postman come and walked to the door, picking up his mother's letter. He opened it and took out the postal order, putting it on the hall table but pushing the letter deep down into his pocket. He took his coat from the hook and left the cottage without saying goodbye, without seeing the geraniums along the path. There was no time.

He walked down the lane. The mist was thick and damp all around and the leaves lay sodden on the road through the village and smoke rose straight up from the chimneys because there was no wind. Jeeps came up and down the road, steering round him, clipping the verges so that grass became mud. Mary was waiting for him outside her cottage. He did not want her to come. He didn't want her to see his eyes, or to see him beaten.

'Stay here, Mary,' he said, heaving his collar up round his neck but she wouldn't. She trailed along after him and he was glad really because he liked her round face, her smile, her voice. His arms ached and he loosened his shoulders as Ed had told him to do. They were on the track now and it was muddy but he hadn't worn boots because he wanted to be able to move fast. He stepped from the mud of the track to the grass which was firmer but water splashed up the back of his legs and he wished he was old enough to wear long trousers. He stopped and pulled up his socks. Mary stopped too.

'It's so damp, ain't it?' she said, pulling her coat round her.

In the copse it was quiet and they didn't talk but edged along the path through the tangled undergrowth. Water dripped from the branches and leaves fell slowly, damply to the ground. The leaves were catching in his shoes and he ducked down, pulling out an oak leaf which had caught beneath his arch. His fingers were trembling and his arms still ached. He was angry with himself and with his fear. He stood up suddenly, hurrying now.

Mary followed and he whispered, 'Stay here. For heaven's sake. Stay here. It's my fight.'

'Oh no it ain't. He's a little snot and he deserves a bloody good hiding.' She grinned and came along beside him now.

The clearing was just beyond the holly tree and they moved slowly forward but there was no one there. Chris stood, his fists clenched, ready but unsure now. He looked at Mary and then all around.

'They're late,' Mary said. 'They got lost in the mist or had another slice of toast for breakfast, greedy pigs.' She walked over to the sawn logs which were piled near the edge of the clearing; brushed at some sawdust and some damp leaves and then sat, her chin in her hands.

Chris stood motionless. His head was still aching. He flexed his arms, then took off his coat, throwing it towards Mary. It didn't reach her and he started to walk across but then they came, bursting from the woods, swinging glowing cans round and round their heads, holding on to the wire and Chris knew that inside the cans were sticks doused in paraffin because he had seen them do it before, but never near another boy. Round and round they whirred, burning brighter and brighter as the air entered the holes which Joe and the gang had pierced in the sides. They were surrounding him now and one boy rushed forward and Chris had to dodge the can, leaping back, fear high in his throat.

Mary was calling out, trying to get through but Len dropped out of the circle and grabbed her, his can hanging limp as he coiled the wire up round his hand.

Chris turned this way, that way, seeing the brightness of the cans, one coming close, and then another. One nearly hit him and he scrambled back but lost his footing and fell. There was laughter now. Loud mouths and the burning cans were all around and over his head and it was like the torches in Germany that he had watched with his father.

'Daddy,' he whispered and then he heard Joe call.

'Don't think we don't know you took lessons from your Yank. We saw you, didn't we? Been on your boat yet? No, because we've sunk it, haven't we? Sunk it proper this time. You didn't know, did you?'

Chris pushed himself up, crouching because the cans were still above him, still too close. If they hit him, the lid would fly open and the wood would burst out and he would burn.

He was dribbling, he knew he was dribbling because it was running down his chin but he wasn't crying. They wouldn't make him cry but he could hear Mary. She was. She was crying and shouting and he tried to crawl beneath the whirling cans to her but then the boys were spreading out and he was up again. He could smell the paraffin in the air, see the trail of black smoke and then there gripping two of the boys was Ed, his face set and calm, his eyes hard and angry.

Chris spun round. There were two other Americans holding

a boy each, gripping them by the collars so that their feet almost left the ground. They were chewing gum and smiled at Chris but their eyes were angry too. The cans lay on the ground, the leaves steaming from their heat. They would not burn now that the wind was not tearing through them. The boy who was holding Mary ran off into the darkness of the wood.

Joe was the only one left and he stood uncertainly between Ed and Chris.

Chris wiped his chin.

'You OK, Chris Weber?' Ed asked.

Chris nodded, waving Mary away.

'I'm OK,' he said. 'I'll fight you, Joe. I'll beat you and then you leave me alone.'

They fought then but Joe used his head to butt and his teeth to bite. Chris did not. He punched and then he flicked Joe's feet from under him but Joe caught at his ankles and brought him down too, punching his ribs, his legs, biting his arm, butting his face. There was blood in his mouth but he could see Ed standing there, holding the two boys, watching closely, never speaking. Just watching.

Mary spoke though. He could hear her shouts, her groans, her cries.

'Kill 'im.'

'Oh Chris.'

'That's not fair.'

'Stop it, Ed. Stop it.'

But Ed didn't stop it. He watched as Chris fought, blood staining his cheek and he wanted to grab Joe and slap him because he was a bully and he was hurting the kid, like he'd been hurt when he'd broken his first horse in. His father hadn't stopped that and afterwards Ed had been glad.

He watched as Chris tried the uppercut but from the ground. He made contact, and again, and then he was on top, his knees resting on Joe's shoulders. Keeping his body on the ground, twisting his hair until the boy cried and told him to stop.

Ed let the others go then and didn't watch as they ran through the woods. He nodded to Earl and Mario who loosened their grip on the other boys, letting them push away, and follow the others.

He walked to Chris, helping him up, letting Mary come and grip Chris's arm, lead him to the logs. Then Ed dragged the other boy up, checked him over and led him from the clearing, right through to the edge of the copse. He told him that if there was any more trouble of any sort it wouldn't be Chris who dealt with it next time. It would be somebody much bigger. Did he get the picture? He watched as Joe ran back down the track to the village. He'd not be back.

Chris was sitting on the logs. His head hung down. It was still aching, banging and banging inside his skull. His hands felt swollen and his mouth was sore but he looked up when Ed came and stood in front of him.

'You did real good, Chris. Your pop would have been proud of you. And your mom too.' He held out his hand and Chris shook it, standing, feeling his legs trembling but he smiled. He felt so good inside.

'It doesn't matter if he tells the village,' Chris said, though it hurt to talk and spit had filled his mouth. He swallowed it.

'He won't. Don't you worry about that. You tell them when you're ready.' Ed was passing his cigarettes to Earl and Mario, then lit one himself. 'I guess it was lucky we were passing but I figure you could have dealt with it anyway.'

He smiled at Chris and they both knew the truth.

'You'd better get along home now. Get that face cleaned up, spend that money. Give Laura a heart attack.' Ed laughed. 'You can make it can you?'

'Sure the kid can make it, Captain,' Earl said, helping Chris to his feet. 'Someone who's as tough as this can manage just about anything.' He bent down and picked up Chris's coat, letting Ed help him on with it.

'By the way, this is Earl whose family came from Hamburg, and this other guy is from some strange hot place where they eat a lot of pasta.' Ed winked at Chris.

Chris pulled his coat around him, but he was hot, really hot. He looked at the men.

'Thanks,' said Chris. 'You know, thanks.' His voice was fractured now and small.

'I know,' said Ed, punching him lightly on the arm. 'Be seeing you then.'

He turned and walked back with the other two men and this time Chris remembered to call.

'Good luck.'

*

195

The next day Laura called the doctor who said that the headache was not schoolboy tension or the result of a scrap but rheumatic fever and an ambulance came. But Chris knew nothing of that, he just knew pain and illness.

He lay in the hospital bed, his legs aching too much to keep still even though the woman in the white apron told him he must not move so the nurses came and put iron bars across his calves and his forearms and the pressure of their weight hurt him even more. He cried and Laura held his hand but her hand was too heavy on his flesh. He was so hot and the screens around the bed were too bright. He wanted it dark, no light, nothing to blind his eyes.

The nurse came again, forcing his lips apart but they were cut. Couldn't she see they were cut and the medicine was bitter and scoured his throat. He was so hot.

'Mum. Daddy.'

He was so hot. The screens were still there. They were like Laura's knickers on the washing line, all gathered, but they weren't blowing. They were just white, glaring white. His legs hurt. Why wouldn't they take these bars away, these screens?

'Mum. Daddy.'

He was crying. He knew he was crying because he was shaking but it hurt his head. Where was his mummy? She'd been away for so long. Where was she?

Helen came on the first train. She took the bus to the hospital and ran in. The nurse at the desk called the doctor who took her into the side office, calling for a cup of tea for Mrs Weber.

'He has rheumatic fever and is holding his own, Mrs Weber. He has been delirious for two days and we have attached him to a heart monitor. Unfortunately we have had to restrain his limbs to prevent any unnecessary strain on the heart. This of course is the danger with rheumatic fever. It can affect the heart you see.'

He turned as the door opened and the nurse came in with a cup of tea. He was a small man, with lines of tiredness running from his nose to his mouth but then, Helen thought, the nurse had them just as deep.

And yes, she did know that rheumatic fever affected the heart but it must not affect Chris's. She loved him too much. She mustn't lose him, not after sending him away. Not after

196

leaving him here without her. No, she mustn't lose him; she had lost too much of his life already.

She said, 'Yes, I see. What can be done?' But she couldn't drink her tea because she was gripping the cup and the saucer too tightly.

'The remedy is rest and aspirins in fluid, twice daily. A tablespoon at a time.' He smiled. 'Try not to worry, Mrs Weber. It is usually most effective.' He took her then to see Chris. He lay behind screens and seemed so alone in the large room, but then she saw Laura and Helen was glad that she was there.

Helen smiled as the doctor moved back the screen, lifting it so that there was no noise. She touched Laura on the shoulder, then sat in the chair that the doctor indicated.

Chris was so small, so fevered. His face was red and beaded with sweat and the iron bars were there, pinioning his limbs.

'He's doing very well,' the sister murmured, taking the place of the doctor.

Helen touched her son's hand, slipping hers beneath his, folding her fingers over lightly.

He opened his eyes. 'Mum,' he said and smiled. 'Where's Daddy?'

He drifted in and out of delirium for one week and Mary looked in through the window, anxious, unsmiling. Laura stayed some of the time but Helen stayed every day and every night wondering if the flight of planes each morning and evening disturbed him. At the end of the week his fever broke but his limbs still hurt and one moment he was sweating and the next he was cold but now Mary could come in too.

She sat with Helen and talked to him of the boat which Ed had fished for and found. Chris smiled.

Helen left for two hours when Laura came. She walked into the town where the hospital was situated and bought blackout material which was not rationed. She sat and sewed each day and night, sitting at his bedside telling him of the crypt, of the vicar, of Marian. Telling him that it looked as though there would be victory in the Western Desert. Unable to talk of his village and his life but determined that soon she would be able to.

She brought her old lace blouse into the room and cut and hemmed a collar from it and cuffs for the dress which was to be for Mary and listened while Laura talked of the hens and the pigs and Mr Reynolds who had to gather in the cow dung now.

On the tenth day Helen was helping the sister to ease another pillow behind her son and watching as they removed the iron bars because there was no more delirium, no more asking for his father. She lifted the cup with a spout like a teapot to his lips, not allowing him to move at all because the doctor was still concerned about any strain to his heart.

'There is a murmur, you see, Mrs Weber,' he said as he watched her wiping Chris's mouth. 'A weakness. It is imperative that he rests.'

His words were over-hung with the roar from the aeroplanes as they returned from a flight. Helen looked not at the doctor but out of the window.

'Yes, I see,' she said. 'I will make sure he rests.' She looked at the temperature chart hooked on the bottom of the bed; the thin red line was more even now. She smiled at her son but he wasn't looking at her, he was looking at the door which had opened.

'Hi, Ed,' he said and there was such pleasure in his eyes.

Helen turned and saw the man, so big in his uniform, his hat slipped back on his head, his grin wide.

'Hi, Chris Weber. So, got yourself a bit of trouble, hey?' He walked over, his shoes silent on the waxed floor, his left hand in his pocket.

He walked to the bed, tossing some candies on the blanket. 'You'd better get out of here soon, that boat's going to get pretty rusty out there and the pitching's going to go downhill.'

Helen walked to the door with the doctor then turned and watched this big man talking to her son, his hands strong and kind. He picked at some fluff on Chris's sleeve, rolling it into a ball and flicking it into the dish on the beside table and Chris smiled.

'Well, that's the kind of aim you get when you've pitched as much as I have.' Only then did he turn to Helen, only when Chris was tired and his lids were drooping and for that she already liked him.

He rose and walked with that ambling stride to the end of the bed where she was now standing.

'I guess you must be Mrs Weber. That's a fine boy you have there.' His handshake was firm and his smile broad but there were the same lines of tiredness on his face that there were on everyone's.

'I think I have much to thank you for, Captain McDonald,' Helen said, because Laura and Mary had told her everything.

'Not a lot, most of it he did himself. Look I can't stop long, I've got to get back to base. We should be training tomorrow.' He paused. 'I wanted to get over much sooner but we've been kind of busy.' His smile was wry.

'It's enough that you came. He's been waiting for you,' Helen said, hearing him rattle the change in his pocket, hearing the hoot of the car outside the window. He moved across and looked out.

'There's my lift. I got to go. I'll come again, if I may?' He was looking towards Chris and she saw the fine cheekbones, the flickering left eyelid.

'Please do. Chris would be very grateful and so would I.'

He nodded and smiled at her. The jeep hooted again and he turned towards the door, waving as he went.

Helen watched him and then as she moved towards Chris again she saw the material lying folded on the back of the chair, the lace collar draped across it, and she went running out after him, down the corridor, calling, 'Captain McDonald, Captain McDonald.'

He stopped and turned.

Helen blushed. 'I'm making something rather special for somebody but I can't get any elastic and I've heard the Americans have everything.'

She laughed when he spread his arms wide. 'Well, I guess that's as good a war aim as any, Ma'am. Leave it with me.'

He came back every other day for the next three weeks and they sat by the bedside as Chris woke and talked, or slept.

He brought the elastic on his second visit and Helen sewed it around the waist of the dress she was making, listening as he told her of the farm in Montana, of the mountains which looked pretty much like Chris's earlier temperature chart, of the mare he was hoping to breed from. He told her that his mother loved him too much and Helen knew what he meant and so she told him of her own mother but then he said, 'Oh no, Mom's nothing like that.'

Mary came the next time, driven by Ed in his jeep. Helen

gave her the dress and she held it up against her and then turned to Chris, who smiled at her and then at his mother.

'It's got a waist. I've always wanted a waist but my sister said I was too fat. How did you know I wanted a waist, Mrs Weber?' Mary's face was eager.

'Every woman wants a dress with a waist, my dear Mary,' Helen said. 'And you have been such a true friend to Christoph. It is so little.'

She sat back then and listened as Ed told the children of the heat a cattle herd would build up, of the cowboys' fear of storms because they spooked the cattle and he asked Chris how a stampede could be halted. Chris told them and Ed laughed and called him a clever kid for remembering.

Then Chris told Ed the German story of the raven coming ahead, warning by thunder and lightning that the gods were coming and everyone should hide and Helen was glad to hear her son talking of his heritage so naturally.

The next time they talked of the Flying Fortresses because Ed's hands were shaking but he didn't say why. But when Chris was asleep he told her of the punishment a ship could take, his face pale, his uniform dark against the white walls.

'The rounds of gunfire, the blasting of an engine and still the old bus will get us home, or some of us.'

They talked or rather Helen listened as he told her that already there were not enough spare parts, not enough spare crews.

He told her how the planes were pouring from the Detroit plants but they would soon be pouring from the skies too, over Germany. That the crews were so young, too young to be killed, too young to kill. That though they would fly high they would fly in daylight and they would not have fighter escort the whole way. That they had twenty-five missions to accomplish before they could go home. He had flown in a British bomber as an observer last week, and now he knew what they would be facing when the training was finished. The next time he came he brought her candies because he had talked too much, but she didn't think he had.

It was October before Chris was able to sit up, and Helen left him for two days to travel to London and when she returned she told him that she would not be going back. She had spoken to Mr Leonard and insisted on him releasing her because

Laura knew someone at the beet factory and they would take her now.

She did not tell him that she had threatened to tell Mr Leonard's wife that he took flowers each Friday to a lady who lived in Harrow but she told Ed, who laughed and said that he reckoned that even if she did box like a southpaw she was a dangerous dame to meet on a dark night.

Helen did not understand but she laughed with him. When Ed left, Chris woke and picked at the crisp starched sheet with thin fingers, his striped pyjamas caught up above his elbows.

'Mum, I've got to tell the village you know.'

Helen took his hand. 'No, darling. I must tell them. I'm going to be living here too, permanently soon. I shall tell them, but when the time is right. Now, shall we finish this puzzle?'

She carried over the tray and put all the blue pieces to one side. There were planes coming over again.

'Mum.'

'Yes, Chris?'

'Ed's great, isn't he?'

'Ed's a very kind man.' Helen said.

'But he's more than that, isn't he?'

Twelve planes had flown over now.

'Yes, he's more than just a kind man,' she said but he couldn't be more than that for her, because she couldn't live with the threat of another loss and she still loved Heine.

CHAPTER 14

Helen signed an official contract to work in the laboratory of the sugar-beet factory on Friday 30 October. She had dropped her cases in the small room at the top of the boarding house on the main street of the town. She had stuffed newspaper in the rattling window frame and beneath the door which had been cut to ride over a now non-existent carpet and then left to spend the days of the weekend at the hospital with Chris and her nights at the cottage. She talked to him of the new Commander in North Africa, General Montgomery, who was beginning a big offensive along the coast at El Alamein, of the Russians who were hanging on grimly in Stalingrad, of the American Marines who had made a successful landing on the Solomon Islands.

She fed him ice-cream which Ed had brought and left earlier in a big container filled with ice. There was too much for him and so the nurses took the remainder for the other patients. Helen had not seen Ed, she had arrived too late and Chris asked why.

She told him of the boarding house, the rattles and draughts. The girls who had been smoking in the small kitchen and stubbing their cigarettes out on a tin lid and who had wanted to talk. So she had not been able to arrive any earlier, had she? She didn't tell him that she did not want to see the big smiling American who made her feel things that she thought had died with Heine.

  She arrived back at her digs on Sunday evening carrying the dungarees that she would need for tomorrow. She had heard the planes straggling back as she travelled on the bus and counted, knowing Ed was flying his first mission, knowing that if he didn't return Chris would tell her, somehow he would tell her.

She climbed the stairs and slept from ten until five without waking. She was satisfactorily full because Laura had brought a picnic lunch into the hospital; chicken and bacon pie and eggs from the hens. The bacon had been a surprise but Laura had said little, only smiled slightly and said that the government allowed the killing of people not pigs in the war but after all, wasn't it strange how one animal could go missing and turn up in separate joints in villagers' houses? Helen had felt uncomfortable for a moment but then hunger had triumphed.

She walked to work through cold, wet, dark streets, stepping over mud spun off the wheels of the incessant beet lorries. Overhanging everything was the heavy smell of beet pulp which the boarding housekeeper had told her belched out from the chimneys twenty-four hours a day during the beet campaign. Others were walking with her now but nobody spoke, they were too tired.

She arrived at six a.m. and walked from the cold into a barrage of heat and noise. Within seconds she was too hot and she shrugged herself out of the heavy greatcoat, holding it as she knocked on the forewoman's door. It was opened but the woman could only nod, the noise was too great to hear any words. Her hair was wound up inside a headscarf and her breath was nicotine-heavy as she came up close and shouted, 'Follow me.'

The smell of beet pulp was thicker inside the building, too thick to breathe but somehow Helen did, following the woman who did not look behind her once. They passed machinery which roared and rocked and women who smiled before turning back, sweat running from their bandana-wrapped hair and from their faces and arms to drip on to the floor. They climbed up an iron stairway, slippery from the dripping overhead pipes and now there were men who wore no shirts and whose backs were beaded with sweat. One turned and whistled. Helen saw his lips but heard nothing but the clang and the clatter. Her short-sleeved shirt was sticking to her now and she held her coat away from her body.

How could these people work like this, how could they bear the noise, the smell? How could she? The woman was walking more quickly now, lengthening her stride, checking her watch, walking down half a flight of stairs, turning left. Helen caught up, taking shallow breaths, looking at the small grey office they were approaching. There were white stencilled letters on the door and she saw that they said 'LABORATORY'.

The supervisor walked in and Helen followed, shutting the door, reducing the noise by a fraction, but even that was welcome. The woman was beckoning to her, talking to a small man in a paisley tie and starched collar, soiled now where it rubbed against his neck. When Helen approached she shouted into her face again.

'This is Mr French. He is in overall charge of the laboratory. You will take your directions from him.' Her fingers, which she ran through her damp hair, were nicotine-stained but her grin made Helen smile. 'I'll see you down in the canteen for lunch. Half an hour, that's all we get.'

Helen stood watching as Mr French tucked his pen behind his ear and pointed to her coat and then the rack on the wall. He smiled as she walked back, having heaped her coat on top of two others.

'Tea break of ten minutes at nine o'clock. You'll need that on the first day.'

Helen nodded, looking round. Three other girls were working in dungarees and short-sleeved shirts, their heads down, their hair lank and wet.

Mr French tapped one of them on the shoulder and when she turned he said, 'Take Mrs Weber through the procedures please, Marjorie, I have to get on.' He smiled. 'Marjorie's our charge-hand.'

Marjorie rose then and stuck her hands into her pockets, leaning back against the bench she had been working on. She grinned.

'Right, they'll already have told you how long you have to put up with this bedlam. We knock off at two p.m. sharp and leave prompt for our breaks. That way maybe we stay sane. They'll also have told you that there are three shifts. We do two weeks on each. The graveyard shift is ten p.m. to six a.m. but I'm not going to tell you about it, I'll let you wait and enjoy its delights at first hand.' She laughed but it was sucked away by the noise as Mr French opened the door and left the room.

Marjorie jerked her head in his direction. 'He's OK. Pinches a few bums from time to time but he's never tried mine. Fancies them blonde and giggly.' Helen smiled and watched as Marjorie waved her hands along the benches.

'We're supposed to check that there is the correct standard of sugar in the beet and not too much going out into the waste products. Each result you get should be within just a few degrees of the standard.'

One of the girls rose from her bench and left and again there was an increase in noise as the door opened. Helen's head already felt as though it were bursting.

'Frances has gone to collect the samples. We have to take turns; it gets to be quite an art arriving back not dripping with the damn stuff. Once we get them here the waters are filtered and polarised, the beet pulp is dried out and weighed, then we record the results in the book. Sweet water and diffusion juice are brought up every couple of hours and five diffusion juices in bottles once every shift.'

Marjorie crossed her arms and nodded towards the other girls. 'That's Penny and Joan. Frances will be back soon and then I'll show you what to do.'

It was twenty minutes before Frances appeared. The waters and juices were thick; cloudy and dark grey. Like the weather, Helen thought, but thank heavens the East Anglian clouds didn't smell like this mixture. She watched as Marjorie added lead and distilled water to the samples, leaving them to filter, after which the liquid came through quite clear.

She wrote it all down on a notepad, her pencil slipping in her sweaty hand. It was HB and smudged black across the paper.

'Don't worry too much,' Marjorie said. 'It all seems strange at first but you'll soon get used to it.'

Helen thought she never would. She looked round at these people she didn't know and missed London, the crypt, her friends, the routine of the bank. The noise drilled through her head, the strangeness made her feel like a new girl at school. For now she had no home, just a room with newspaper stuffed in the cracks but her son was close, his heart murmur was improving and that was all that mattered.

She watched now, pushing her discomfort from her, making herself pay close attention as Marjorie poured the samples which had given a low reading into a polarimeter through a long tube with a funnel at the end. Those samples which had given a high reading were poured down a shorter tube with a funnel in the middle. She wrote this down. Then Marjorie took a reading by looking through an eyepiece which was like a telescope and turned a screw on the polarimeter until no shadow was in evidence on the screen. She copied out the reading from the scale at the top.

Marjorie made her do it too and then it was nine o'clock and time for the break. They rushed down through the factory without coats and out into the air where the cold and the quiet was like another world. They ran down the alley to the canteen where there was only time to take a cup of tea, already poured, from the trolley and sit and drink. Marjorie smoked, exhaling through her nostrils and mouth, talking, wafting it across the table, telling Helen that she would soon get the hang of the work, that she worked on a farm during the summer, though she was from Manchester and hadn't known one end of a cow from the other at first. Then she looked at her watch and they ran back because their ten minutes was up. Up the steps and into the factory where the heat, the smell, the noise hit Helen again like a bulldozer, sucking her breath from her.

'Come on,' Marjorie said, pulling her arm as she paused. 'Come on, we'll be late.' They hurried back past the women, the men, under pipes which dripped hot juice on to their bare arms and hair and Marjorie told her that later they would collect some of the sugar which had formed and she could take some back on her day off.

That night in bed she wrote to Chris, telling him of the sugar, Mr French, Marjorie, the canteen; asking him how he was. And then she slept and dreamt of Heine taking photographs of the beet girls near Hanover, saying he would look after her and make sure she never had to work with beet and he held her with arms that were strong and his skin smelt of the summer. His face was kind when she told him about Ed and how she wondered what his arms would feel like. He smiled but his hold loosened and he drifted from her, fading, and leaving her on the windswept beet fields even though she had called him again and again. She woke up crying.

Mr French told her that the heat in the laboratory was seventy-five degrees but the next day a belt came off one of the machines and because it stopped so too did the fans, as they often did. They all thought they would die and were evacuated down to the nearest windows, breathing in the cold damp air until the maintenance crew arrived. This too Helen wrote to Chris, and the next day told him that she had been the sample carrier, climbing up almost vertical stairs, walking along catwalks between hot sticky pipes to the tank.

She told him how she had been covered from head to foot in hot juice and how she had dropped one sample. When she visited him on Saturday night she explained how, that morning before she left, she had to set an automatic graph way up on the top floor and refill it with purple ink.

She showed him a piece of the sugar, collected by her for the girls' tea at its point of production. It was a yellowish grey colour, but sweet, gloriously sweet. Helen and Laura put some into their drinks at the cottage, sitting in front of a fire which burnt logs collected from the surrounding countryside and for a moment it was almost as though there were not a war on, as though there were luxurious food and warmth, as though men were not dying. At dawn, though, she was woken by the aeroplanes lifting off at thirty-second intervals and wondered if there would ever be something as simple as a dawn chorus of birds again.

After the second week she moved to the two p.m. to ten p.m. shift with Marjorie and was thinner, but then they were all thin and it wasn't just the rationing, it was the sweating, but Chris was even better and was allowed to sit up and hold his own cup, his own knife and fork, to turn the pages of his books. Ed came to see him more often because he was not flying at the moment. His Fortress had sustained a hole in the wing and an engine was shattered and there were no replacements yet, he had told Chris, but not Helen because somehow she did not arrive at the hospital until he had left.

On 15 November Helen was sitting with Chris when they heard the church bells ringing out in the town and Helen clutched at the white sheet, wondering if the German invasion had happened at last but a nurse came in and told them that it was in celebration of Montgomery's victory at El Alamein. At the end of November when the Americans were celebrating Thanksgiving the Russians began to turn the tide against the Germans but Helen sat in her room with the draught blowing past the newspaper and under the door, and read Claus's letter from America before she began her two p.m. shift.

My dear Helen,

I am still unable to fight because of my chest but I have established at last our business. So soon, perhaps, Heine's capital can begin to make your life a little more comfortable. I know it is what he would wish.

I am glad in many ways that he is dead because journalist friends of mine tell me from Geneva that the Nazis are systematically murdering Jews, Slavs and dissidents throughout Europe. Not thousands but millions. Can any of this be true? It would be more than he could bear, more than you can bear.

I shall write again, dear Helen.

My love to you and Christoph.

Claus

Helen worked all that day in the heat of the factory, glad that her head hurt, glad that her hair hung lank, that she was tired all the time, and that night she did not sleep because she remembered so much of her life with Heine, so much of the world outside work, rationing and bombing.

The ten p.m. to six a.m. shift was hard. She could not sleep in the day for more than a few hours and when she did she dreamt that she was searching for Heine but he could not be found and so she cried in her dreams and still heard the sound of his voice in those few first moments between sleep and waking. But at last she knew that Chris was going home to the cottage. The doctor told her that the murmur was so faint that there was no danger as long as Chris continued to rest. He could leave for Greater Mannenham on his birthday. Helen was going to book a taxi but Ed waited outside the hospital ward on 30 November to tell her that he had hired one and would collect her first from the boarding house at ten a.m. tomorrow which should give her a chance of a few hours' sleep.

It was pointless for her to protest, he said, because he and Chris had decided between them and apart from anything else, where else could he spend all this goddamn money?

He came at ten a.m. and Helen wore her best dress and coloured her legs with stain because she had no stockings. There was no snow but a white frost and her feet were cold in her shoes, and red. She sat next to him, listening as he described the Thanksgiving dinner at the base, but watching the back of the taxi driver's head and not Ed's hands which were strong and still. Watching the roads which were still muddy from the lorries, hearing the buzz of the windscreen wipers as they cleaned and smeared, cleaned and smeared the glass. She looked ahead but could still see those hands resting on his thighs. He was so good and strong, so kind, but Heine had faded from her dreams and she couldn't bear him to leave her for ever.

The ride back was full of laughter because Chris sat between them and she did not have to feel the American's thigh against hers and was safe. He opened the present that Ed had brought; it was a baseball mitt and two balls. Ed told him there was a bat waiting at the cottage.

Helen had bought an old cap pistol from Marjorie's brother because there were no longer any new toys in the shops. He had given her two boxes of pre-war caps too and Chris held the pistol with the mitt and rested his head on his mother's shoulder and she felt that he was all she needed.

The suburbs turned to fields and Helen saw partridges sheltering in the stubble and bombs stacked high on the near perimeter of an air base but she also saw Ed's face tighten as he saw them too. So she turned and looked instead at the walled churchyard on the other side, telling the American that the yews had provided the wood for longbows in olden times; that the berries and bark were poisonous and that in the old days the churchyard was the one place where cows had no access. She saw his face relax again.

They talked then about the cattle his family ran on the ranch in Montana, the miles of sage scrub on the foothills, the miles of riding range, the wild hay in the valley, and how his flying crew had laughed when they came to Greater Mannenham because they wondered how Little Mannenham could be any smaller.

'But it is,' Helen laughed.

'It sure is.' Ed leaned forward and helped Chris, who had stirred and woken as they pulled in to let an Army transport lorry pass. He fed the end of the cap spool through the hammer of the gun and Helen watched his hands again.

'Do you miss America?' Chris asked, clicking the hammer down gently, not firing yet; waiting until they reached the

209

cottage when he could pounce on Laura as she opened the door.

'Sure I miss it, Chris, but I guess there are compensations.'

'The flying you mean?' Chris asked.

'No, that's not what I mean.' He looked across at Helen but she was staring back at the yew trees, pretending that those words had not been said.

Before Chris went to bed that night he asked his mother if she had told the village yet about his father.

'No, darling, not yet. Joe has gone so you mustn't worry.'

Chris looked down at the mitt which he had brought up to bed with him. 'But we should tell them. Daddy was brave, wasn't he? We should tell them, Mum.'

But she didn't, not then and not on the following Sunday when she was working in the village hall with Laura after Morning Service, knotting camouflage netting with the other women of the village. Hemp was thick in the air but at least there was no smell of beet, no damp heat. No heat at all in fact. Her fingers were clumsy with cold and Laura passed her some fingerless gloves which helped.

Helen pushed her hand through her hair and pulled a face as Laura whispered, 'The vicar's wife was not pleased that you didn't wear a hat.'

Helen said quietly, 'Well, her very own archbishop has just revoked the rule that insists upon hats. It's all part of the war effort. Perhaps I should tell her that.'

Laura laughed. 'Perhaps you shouldn't, you'll get turned to a pillar of salt with that evil eye turned on you.'

'It's all so silly. There are so many problems and she worries about a hat. Anyway, it's stuck in the hole above the skirting board in my digs, stopping a draught. Perhaps I should tell her that instead.' There was an edge to her voice now. She was too tired, too damn tired. There was too much going round her head, too many thoughts, too many doubts, too many fears. When would it ever end?

Laura laughed again. 'You're right, and next week I shall not wear mine and you can use it to plug a few more holes.'

The woman sitting on the right of Helen turned to her. 'I shall be pleased to do the same,' she said.

Mrs Williams was an elderly woman who lived in a small cottage at the far end of the village. She had lived in India for many years, Laura told Helen as they walked home, and was gracious and kind and had taken two evacuees while the vicar's wife had taken only one even though she had three extra bedrooms. She also told Helen that Joe had overheard the vicar's wife telling her husband about Heine. That was how he had known.

The following week, as they strung the twine together in the village hall again, Helen listened to Mrs Williams talking about the hot sun, the plains which stretched shimmering into the distance, the hill stations where it was cool and beautiful and when hemp dried their throats she fetched tea from the hatch for the three of them, passing the vicar's wife who lifted her voice and said, 'Of course, these Germans are barbarians. They are wicked through and through, all of them. It is no good to say it is just Nazis, look at Kaiser Bill. He wasn't a Nazi, he was a German.'

Helen paused, spilling the tea into the saucers but Laura called to her, 'Don't let it get cold, Helen.' Her voice was loud and determined and so Helen walked on but all that afternoon she knew that she had run away again so she dug out Laura's Christmas tree from the bottom of the garden, thrusting her fork into the frozen ground, picking out the earth little by little, using up her anger with herself, her shame. As she dug she wished there were spare hours in which to think, to clear her head, but at the same time she was grateful that there weren't for what would her thoughts be? She carried the tree into the house, looking at her watch, knowing she had time to decorate it before she left for the bus.

She hung old decorations to Chris's directions and new ones that he and Mary had made, and then Ed came, bringing ginger biscuits which he had always hung on his Christmas tree as a child. He helped Chris light the second Advent candle.

'This is an American custom,' he said to Helen, looking at the Advent candle.

'It's a German one too,' she said. 'Heine's mother introduced us to it. It's part of Heine, that's why we have it. We love him.'

Ed looked at her quietly. 'I know. He was a good man. You were lucky to have him. He was lucky to have you.' He paused, smiled at Chris, then walked out to the kitchen where Laura was sitting at the table, peeling potatoes.

'I'm going to take Helen back now. It's too damn cold for buses,' Helen heard him say as she followed him. He turned. 'Get your coat then.'

They drove in silence all the way but Helen felt calmer now because she had told him that she loved Heine and he had accepted it and so perhaps now the image of her husband would come back to her at night and she would stop crying when she woke.

As she pulled at the handle of the car and stepped out into the cold, waving to one of the girls who was also returning, calling to her to leave the door on the latch, she turned.

'Thank you, Ed.' She smiled.

'That's OK, Helen.' He leaned across, holding the door open with his hand. 'But remember, you can't hide behind your grief for ever, some time you've got to go forward.'

That night she did not sleep but neither did she cry.

During the week Helen received a letter from Chris saying that Mrs Williams and Laura were arranging a party for the villagers and the Americans in the village hall and would she help?

She was on the early morning shift and so arrived in the village on Saturday during the early evening and together the three women talked of the arrangements while Chris lay on the settee and dozed. Ed was practice-flying again he told her when she arrived but not until next week, though he had to stay on duty all this weekend. Helen was glad she would not see him because she needed to push her confusion about him to one side in order to deal with something that had already been too long delayed.

They knotted the netting as usual after church but before they all rose to leave Helen stood up. Her legs were shaking but she could not wait any longer to speak as she knew she must. She felt Laura's hand pat her arm and Mrs Williams murmur, 'It will be all right.'

'I wonder if I could have your attention for a moment, ladies?' Helen began. She looked around, and saw the vicar's wife look up, her face red with irritation.

'As Mrs Vane, the vicar's wife, in her position of billeting officer for the area knows, I am the widow of a German.' She didn't look at the women who turned their heads to one another or listen to the murmuring which broke out, she just looked ahead at the clock which had stopped at ten to one.

'In London we knew great kindness and great prejudice and we survived. My son was the victim of blackmail from a small group of boys when he first arrived here but that has now been solved. Now I see that we must confront the problem again.'

There was silence now and her throat was dry and the hemp made her cough. Mrs Williams passed her a glass of water and she sipped, grateful for its coolness.

'All Germans are not Nazis.' She looked now at Mrs Vane. 'All Germans are not wicked. They are much as we are. They did not protest soon enough. I have not protested soon enough.' Helen reached into her handbag, drawing out Willi's letter.

'I would like to read you this letter.'

Her voice didn't falter as she read the words she knew by heart but she felt the thickening in her throat when she put it back into her handbag, heard the click of the clasp in the silence which still hung amongst the hemp. She walked through the door back to the cottage but did not mention it to Chris because she did not know what would happen.

During the week she received a letter from Chris and Laura explaining the details for the party. Ed had arranged for Earl to sing and a group from the base would be playing but the letter said nothing of Mrs Vane. The village women were providing some food and the men and children were decorating the hall. It was to be held on Thursday, Christmas Eve.

The noise of the factory was a relief all that week because it made her head ache so much that she couldn't think, not of Mrs Vane, not of Ed, not of Heine, and at night she dreamt but the images were confused, vivid and made no sense and she awoke each day tired and anxious.

She arrived in the village in the late afternoon on Thursday. She was to be home for two days and went picking holly and ivy for the hall with Mary who wanted her to climb up for mistletoe but Helen said the Americans wouldn't need it if the street corners in town were anything to go by.

But Mary pleaded and so Helen did and was whistled at by passing jeeps and had to stretch out across a thin branch which whipped up and down beneath her weight. She snatched a small clump from the top of the tree, dropping it down to Mary

213

who cheered. Helen laughed and it was the first time she had done that for weeks.

They dropped it into the village hall and people smiled and nodded at her and so her shoulders relaxed but the vicar's wife was not amongst them. That evening she tied Mary's hair into small curls with pipe cleaners, sitting her by a roaring fire to dry it in time. She wet Chris's hair where it quiffed up, then tied an old stocking of Laura's on to it but he hid in the bedroom until it was dry.

She painted her own legs and Chris told her the seam wobbled and so she licked her finger and rubbed it off and Mary took the pencil and did it for her while Laura laughed. Mary wore her blackout dress and her hair was a mass of curls.

Planes had straggled back in as they walked from the village hall back to the cottage but Helen had made herself not count and besides no one they knew was flying today. So they laughed as they all stood in the hall, looking in the mirror.

Laura and Mary carried the party cakes made with powdered eggs while Helen carried a cardboard box full of bottles of home-made elderberry wine. Chris walked beside them, carrying nothing because he was still too weak but smiling because his hair had stuck down on the top of his head.

There were no lights visible through the blackout of the village hall but they could hear the music tuning up and Helen looked up and down the road. There were olive green bikes slung around the hall and three jeeps parked with more arriving.

Inside the hall it was warm and the decorations glittered. The table was heaped with hamburgers and hot dogs, Boston cream pie and pumpkin pie. There was coke to drink. It was a gift to the villagers from the GIs.

'Pails of ice-cream are coming along later ma'am,' a sergeant told them and Helen and Laura couldn't say thank you because it was inadequate.

The band was playing now and Laura drifted off to talk to Mrs Williams. Helen looked around but Chris said it for her.

'Ed isn't here, Mum.'

'Maybe he will be later,' she answered, wondering why she felt tired suddenly, and irritated with the music, the food, the decorations.

Chris and Mary sat on the chairs spaced out along the walls

while Helen and Laura poured wine into glasses but still he did not come. Mrs Vane did, though, with her husband. They didn't stop and speak but walked down to the stage, through the GIs who stood in groups talking to girls, laughing, flirting, smoking, drinking. Helen watched as they mounted the stage to stand in front of the band. The vicar tapped the microphone; it clicked. He coughed and the hall grew silent. He coughed again, his black suit looking austere against the paper decorations, his clerical collar stark white.

'I would like to welcome our guests tonight. Some sort of a reception was long overdue, and for that we must apologise, but somehow there has been rather a lot to think about during the past year. We are enormously grateful too for the wonderful refreshments. It is as though Father Christmas has come just a few hours early.' He laughed and so did those in the hall.

'Before we begin, though, I have something I wish to say. Mrs Weber spoke to the ladies of our village hall last Sunday and reminded us that we are all human beings, that we all suffer in this war and I am grateful to her for her words.'

Mrs Vane said nothing, just smiled with tight lips.

The vicar continued, looking towards the back of the hall at Helen. 'My wife and I and the other villagers welcome you and your son to our village.'

Helen felt the heat in her face and looked at Chris. He smiled at her; the shadows had gone.

She looked back again at Mrs Vane and knew that there would always be people like her and that nothing on God's earth could change them, but perhaps they could be isolated and contained as she hoped this woman had been.

There was dancing now, gentle, cheek to cheek dancing and Helen sat with Laura watching. Still Ed had not come but Chris was laughing with the boys who gathered round and was not unhappy so it didn't matter, did it?

Earl hadn't come either and so there was no singing yet, just music and the vicar came and talked to Laura who nodded and asked Helen to come down to the stage, telling her quietly as they went:

'The vicar has asked if you will sing. There is a problem.'

Helen stopped. A GI took her arm and said, 'Come and dance, honey.'

'No thank you,' she said and he passed on. 'What do you mean? I've never sung in front of people.'

Laura took her arm. 'Nonsense, Helen, you've sung in the crypt. What about the choir? Now come on, we've worked so hard to make this a success, you can't let us down.'

'But what about Earl? He'll be along.'

Laura stopped. 'No, he won't, not now, not ever. He was on a mission today, taking the place of a sick gunner. He's dead.' Her voice shook.

Helen looked at her, not speaking, not seeing the couples dancing, not seeing the band playing. Earl was too young to die. He was far too young and too nice. He had helped Chris. He was too nice.

She sang then, for fifty minutes without a break, drifting into 'A Nightingale Sang in Berkeley Square', reading the words of 'Boogie Woogie Bugle Boy' before repeating it three times for the GIs who whistled and stamped; but all the time there was a pain in her chest for the young German American. And all the time she sang for him. Ed came in when she was singing 'White Christmas'. She saw him enter, saw him stand and watch, but didn't wave. She just looked and knew that he also grieved and that there was no time in this war to turn aside from love.

Ed watched her on the stage. She was thinner but still beautiful. He watched her and loved her and drank deeply from the glass he had been given. He listened to the words and thought of the snow falling in Montana, clear and white, not like the fog of this morning. Fog which had cleared to visibility of about a mile and so Earl had smiled and gone. Ed took another drink, nodding to Laura but not seeing her, seeing instead the B-17s leaving, one after another, but it had not been clear enough for accurate bombing, or so James Roten had said in his debriefing. Only Earl's ship had made a hit. God damn it, that damn Norden bombsight could drop a bomb into a barrel from Californian skies but how the hell could the bomb-aimer penetrate this damn European mist? What would it be like when the bombing runs really got underway? He drank more wine. He recognised it as Laura's and looked around, finding her, nodding and grinning, but the smile didn't reach his eyes and Helen saw that as she wove her way towards him, standing in front of him, letting him take her in his arms, hold her with those strong hands as they danced.

He talked, his breath soft on her neck. He told of the men in the Nissen hut who had thrown lighter fuel on the meagre coal in the centre stove and how the chimney had got so hot it had kept them warm all night. He did not talk about Earl whom he could not get out of his head.

She talked about the vicar's wife and how she hoped it was all over but not about Heine who she had loved but who, she had now accepted, was dead.

He talked of the interminable mud on the airfield. She talked of the smell of sugar beet which clung to her, although he said it did not.

She asked how Earl had died but instead of telling her of the burning plane which had plummeted, ripped in half, from the sky, emptying the crew into the factories they had just bombed, he told her how strong the Fortresses were, how they were called the battleships of the air, how you could land on one engine. While he said this and held her warm body against his he remembered Earl's grin in the copse with Joe and Chris and held Helen tighter because now his friend would never write his name in candle grease on the ceiling of the pub when he had finished his twenty-five missions.

Helen was called back to the stage during the refreshments and sang 'The White Cliffs of Dover' and 'We'll Meet Again'. Chris came up to the front of the stage then and asked her to sing 'Silent Night' and stood there while she sang the first verse in English and the second in German, his eyes on hers, their thoughts on Heine and Grandpa and Oma.

She left the stage again after that, taking Ed's glass from him, leading him out on to the dance floor, holding him to her, leaning her face against his neck, talking of the pain she saw in his eyes and he spoke now of Earl and how it hurt to know he was gone. Helen knew now that there could be a great love between them, if the war gave them enough time.

CHAPTER 15

In January and February of 1943 Ed flew only training missions and those were only possible when the weather permitted. Dawn take-offs were abandoned and he was still a million years from the twenty-five missions he needed for his ticket home but he didn't want to go home, he told Helen. He wanted to stay with her.

He would drive her from the boarding house to the village on Saturday evenings. Always they stopped halfway at a pub with oak settles. She would only drink a little and so would he, sipping at the weak beer he had bought, his sprinkled with salt to give at least a little flavour, hers without. They would sit together, his shoulder touching hers.

He would kiss her when they returned to the car and his lips were tangy with salt and beer and his hand would stroke her face and then they would drive home to Chris who was now allowed to go to school and into the playground where they played convoys, lining up, waiting for the submarine attack from behind the bike sheds, the toilets, the dustbins.

In February the campaign at the beet factory was over and in March 1943 Helen prepared to begin work at the farm five miles from the village. At the same time Ed was promoted to Major and given the post of Air Executive which meant that, for now, he stayed on the ground.

Laura cooked omelette that night with real eggs to build Helen up for the morning and to celebrate Ed's safety, she said, smiling at them while Mary nudged Chris and winked.

The next morning Helen lay awake, listening to the pre-dawn warm-up at the air base but there was not the familiar knotting in her stomach or the tension in her back because at least now, for a while, she could be sure he was not flying. She stretched, running her hands down her body, wondering what

218

it would be like to feel him close to her, touching her, and suddenly she allowed herself to feel like a girl again, eager and young, because she knew he would not die today, tomorrow or the next day and what came after that was 'the future' and the blitz had taught her not to think of that.

At five-thirty she dressed and sat at the low window, looking out on to the rear garden, seeing the grass of the orchard fresh and pale green in the thin light of the dawn. Mist drifted over the grey meadow beyond. There had been no frost so would that mean deep mud on the farm? But that didn't matter because the air would be fresh, there was no machinery to clang and grind and pipes to drip into her hair, her son was better and the man she loved was close.

She stopped by Chris's door, opening it, seeing his hair, still so blond, and she smiled, walking down the stairs in her woollen airmen's socks which Ed had given her to wear inside her boots. She put the kettle on the stove before feeding the pigs and the hens, feeling the cold on her hands, seeing the layer of heavy dew thick on the cabbage, the grass, the shed, undisturbed yet by the rising of the sun. But later her bike marked a long thin line across the ground as she took it to the road.

She rode to the farm, her dungarees clipped at the ankles, her old jacket buttoned tight against the wind. The farmer had told her last week where to leave her bike, pointing to the old barn.

As she approached the farmyard she dismounted and pushed at the gate, hauling the bike through mud, pushing it to the higher concrete where it was almost clear, then propped it inside the barn against an old mangle. The air was thick with the scent of hay. Already she was tired and it was only seven-thirty but maybe she would see Ed tonight and so what did it matter?

She stood in the entrance looking out on to the yard and then walked through the mud, hearing it squelch beneath her feet and splatter up her legs. There was a smell of manure and steam rose from a heap beyond the yard. Laura would love that for her garden. John met her then, coming round the edge of the long cow-shed which he had built just before the war, he told her as he led the way inside. It was limewashed and bright and he pointed to a Friesian which stood tethered to the manger.

'Just get on and milk that one will you, me old girl, but wash your hands over in that basin first.'

The water was cold and the towel rough and full of holes. John stood watching, his face lined and weatherbeaten, his shoulders hunched from his thirty years on the farm. He had been born here, he had told her, and helped his old dad as long as he could remember.

'Now you come on over and let's get this old girl finished.'

Helen nodded and sat on the stool, waiting for him to leave, but he didn't. The cow's udders were milk-swollen. She closed her eyes and tried to remember what he had told her last week, then took hold of the two front teats, pulling gently together. Nothing happened. She pulled one at a time. Nothing, and John was still standing there, his shadow falling on her hands, his breathing audible.

This is ridiculous, Helen thought. For God's sake, I'm a woman of thirty and I can't even milk a cow. She leaned her head against the animal, feeling its quivering flank against her forehead.

'That's better,' John said. 'You get right in next to her, she likes to get the feel of a person, our Daisy does. You're more than just a pair of hands to her, you know. She's got to like you.'

Helen tried again but still nothing, she pushed her head deeper into the cow's side. Like me, you stupid cow, just like me.

John moved then, bending down and yanking at the teats. 'Naughty old girl's holding back, give her a good pull like that. Don't you go pussyfooting around.'

Helen watched the jets of milk flooding into the pail and then took the warm teats in her hands again and at last some milk shot out, but not much.

'I'll go and start in the other shed then, now you've got the hang of it.'

The evening seemed a long way away as Helen tried again. She had not got the hang of it. She pulled and squeezed, banging her head against the cow, feeling her hand cramping.

'You damned old cow,' she swore. 'Holding back, how could you on my first day? How could you?' She looked into the bucket. There was still very little.

John came back in thirty minutes. He had finished two cows. He laughed and took her place and she watched and listened to the squirting jets, seeing the frothing milk, hating Daisy, hating the farm. All her fingers were red and sore.

She was sent out to help the men chopping out the sugar beets on the four-acre field. It was a long walk before she even reached the field and the hoe was hard against her shoulders and now she knew why John and the others wore folded sacks on their shoulders.

They did not look up as she arrived, but one shouted, 'That row, six inches apart, then single by hand.'

He was pointing and so Helen nodded, ramming the hoe in as they were doing, again and again, hearing it click against stones, feeling her hands growing hot and sore. Row after row was hoed, and lunch was taken at the edge of the field, quietly eating sandwiches which were squashed from being in her dungaree pockets, drinking tea which was lukewarm from the flask which had been banging against her leg all morning. After half an hour they were up again, finishing the hoeing, just doing the last ten rows, and then it was singling the clumps which they had left by hand – a hand which was blistered on the palms by now.

They knelt when their backs felt as though they would break, and then the mud oozed up into her knees and they also became sore, and Helen wondered if this was any bloody way to win the bloody war. She didn't just think it, she said it, again and again, her fingers cold and muddy from picking and then she heard the laughter from the man in the next row and looking up she saw his gap-toothed grin.

'Well, my old girl, I reckon as how it has to be the bloody way to win the bloody war, and soon the blisters will go. You'll toughen up.'

Helen laughed and looked at her hands. She'd bring gloves tomorrow, there was no way she wanted farmworker's hands for the rest of her life. She continued swearing but in her head this time.

John had told her to return at four and so she levered herself up and walked back, feeling the blisters on her heels now, waving to the men, still swearing in her head.

She had to fetch the cows from the pasture.

'Just call, they'll come,' he said.

She did call but they didn't come. She walked up behind and waved her hands but still they continued chewing the cud and now she was angry. Her feet hurt, her hands hurt, her knees hurt and Marian would never believe her when she wrote about this. She walked up to Daisy and shouted at her but she just slapped her tail against her sides and continued chewing without haste. Helen thought she looked like Mrs Vane and so she slapped her across the backside and now she moved and the others followed, walking sedately in single file and Helen shook her head at the feeling of success which coursed through her.

Dear God, she thought, a cow moves and it's as though I've been given the crown jewels.

She had to try and milk Daisy again but it wasn't until a week later that she achieved a frothing pail, stripping the udder, getting all the old milk out and milking slowly enough to draw out the fresh that Daisy was making at that moment. That evening she went home, her blisters drying and healing, and slept as though peace had been declared.

In April the Middle White sow had piglets and she brought Ed and the children up to see their short snouts. They stroked their floppy ears and soft skin, so unlike the mother's. Chris asked when his pig, Helen, would have piglets and Helen laughed and said it depended when Mr Reynolds's boar escaped into the orchard again. In April, the bombing missions began in earnest but Ed was safe. Grounded and safe but the shadows were in his eyes again.

In May he came to the farm and watched while she fed the calves in the small yard. They rushed up to her, pushing, mooing, and by now it seemed as though she had never done anything else but hoe, milk, weed, dig, feed calves. She put beet pulp and crushed oats into the trough, walking in deep straw, pumping up their water. She turned and pushed back her hair which was still curly but longer than it used to be and laughed. She was happy doing this work, loving this man, and she had not thought the war could ever bring anything but torment.

Helen forked hay into the racks, seeing some fall on the calves' heads as they milled about, and then there was just the rustling as they ate. She walked back to Ed who was leaning on the wall, his arms crossed, his cap back, a piece of grass hanging from his smiling mouth and she kissed him, smelling the sun on his skin, feeling strong and fit. He pulled the grass

222

from his mouth and kissed her again and again and she wanted him as she had done for weeks but could never tell him.

That evening he pushed her bike back along the road, his arm around her, pointing out the Nymph and the Tortoiseshell and she was impressed with his knowledge of English nature until he told her that Chris had educated him, last year. She laughed then and he leaned down and kissed her open mouth and the laughter died in her throat and she clung to him.

Ed held her chin in his hand and looked into her face and she knew that her eyes said the same as his and there was no shame or restraint in her. He kissed her gently this time before pushing the bike through a gap in the hedge into the hayfield where cornflowers, daisies and poppies grew, and they lay on the warm grass and kissed, their mouths opening and then they loved, slowly, deeply, and without memories intruding. Afterwards Helen lay and watched the scudding clouds, and smelt the rich hay which had been crushed beneath their bodies. It had been strange to be touched by someone who was not Heine but it had been beautiful. It was as though they had known one another since the beginning of time.

That night as Helen undressed, grass fell to the floor and she thought of his hands, so firm on her body; of his chest, so smooth, so tanned. She remembered the power of him, the pleasure of him, the words which had come from his mouth and from hers. I love you, they had said as they kissed.

He came as often as he could and the summer was warm. They grew to know one another's bodies and to love so much. In the long summer evenings Helen laughed as Chris and Ed pitched and batted in the garden and then let her and Mary try. One day the girls beat the boys and they sulked until Laura brought out the cricket bat and said that they would have to play with this next time if there were any more bad losers.

In June the hay was harvested and Ed brought some men from the base to help with the carting and the raking because, he told John, they needed to be reminded that something existed other than high-altitude bombing, ack-ack, fighters who ripped bullets into their planes, their bodies.

Helen and the farm workers had cut and turned the hay in the early part of the week and now she and Ed and Mario led the carts, each holding four GIs and the farm workers. They moved from the farm across a field of beet and down the long

223

lane leading to the hayfields where Helen had first lain with Ed, and she wondered if he remembered.

Above the clopping of the hoofs she heard him call, 'It sure is a shame to see that grass go. I got kinda fond of it.'

Helen flushed and turned, shaking her head at his grin but laughing back. Rocket was slapping his tail at the flies and nodding his head, and Helen tightened her grip on his harness, leaning back into his shoulder.

'Steady, old man,' she breathed and hoped that Chris and Mary would be able to get out here after school.

They turned sharp left, calling 'Here now' to the horses as Helen had instructed and they were safely into the field, but Mario had to back Satin up and try again and on the third attempt he made it and his crew cheered, yelling that they hoped he was a better flyer than a cart driver, for Christ's sake.

All morning they tossed hay up into the carts with forks while Helen stood in one cart, Mario and John in the others. She loaded from the outside first so that it would not overbalance when she took it back. Ed tossed hay up to her, his bare back glistening in the sun, his shoulders reddening. Her arms were bare and she felt the sun on them, on her head. There was a hay seed in her eye and he leaped up into the cart, pulling her lid down, easing the seed out with his handkerchief. She felt his breath on her face and his lips were so close but they did not need to kiss. They just smiled and he jumped down again and continued to pitch up the hay.

They carted their loads back at lunchtime but brought the wagons straight out again, eating a picnic the Americans brought from the base; chicken legs, hard-boiled eggs, cakes and beer, and John winked at her and said, 'I'm glad you came to us, my old girl. Nice to have this manpower around, not forgetting the chicken legs.'

Helen laughed as the men cheered but she knew that on many farms the Americans were helping, glad to work on the land, glad to be free of the war for a moment. She watched as the GIs eased themselves up from the ground, throwing a baseball to and fro, leaping and falling to catch it. There was laughter and shouting and they were like children but of course they were men, young men who could die tomorrow.

She lay down, her arm under her head, hearing the bees in the hedgerows behind them. The sun was bright on her lids, there was the smell of hay all around and she thought how much she loved England, its beauty, its smallness, its sameness, because she couldn't bear to think of the war.

They worked all that day and the next but there was a different crew this time because the others had gone out on a dawn flight. She had heard them leave but knew each morning that it would not be Ed because the CO had kept his grounding official.

When the hay harvest was finished she limewashed the old cow-shed, now stained green and brown. She scrubbed the walls and then John gave her a bag of dry limewash and pails. She carried a small spray under her arm and mixed the lime with water. It puffed up into her eyes and caught in her throat and as she sprayed one wall her arm felt as though it was on fire from the pumping. But then Ed came and took over and they were both covered in lime, and Chris too when he came with Mary. He only sprayed half the wall because he was still not absolutely strong, and Helen watched him work and smiled.

In August they began the oat harvest and the wheat but Mario was not with them because he had not returned from a mission in July. The men laughed as before but there were deeper lines because the daylight raids were still not escorted deep into Germany and now there were so many and the losses were too great. 'Too damn great,' Ed said as they toiled home from the fields, their faces flecked with chaff.

In late August they went to Cambridge when he had a forty-eight-hour pass. Helen had asked Chris if he would mind but he had shaken his head and laughed.

They stayed in an old inn, climbing up twisting stairs, Ed having to lower his head beneath the beams. Their room had an old marble wash-stand with a rose-painted bowl and jug. There were floral curtains and a big bed and Helen was nervous because this was the first time she had been in a bedroom with Ed.

She watched as he unpacked, hanging his trousers in the wardrobe, his shirts too. She had always put Heine's in the drawer. Helen walked to the window, peering out on to the narrow street. She mustn't think of Heine, not here, not now. Heine had gone.

'What about you, Helen? Are you going to unpack your grip now?'

She turned. It seemed too intimate somehow, to take her clothes out in front of him, to put them into drawers while he watched.

'In a minute,' she said, turning back to the window. She heard him move across the floor, the boards creaking beneath his weight. He put his arms around her from behind.

'It feels kind of strange, doesn't it?' he said. 'I had a girl in college, you know. We lived together for a year. I just thought of her then because she would never take her clothes out in front of me, or undress either.' He kissed her hair. 'I guess maybe you're thinking of Heine.'

She turned and put her arms around him. 'I'm sorry,' she said. 'I was but I'm not now.' It was true, she wasn't, because Ed understood and she smiled as he lifted her up and carried her to the bed.

Later they walked by the river in the cool of late afternoon, talking of Chris and how much fitter he was, of Mary who spent more time at Laura's cottage than in her own billet. Of her sister who never came any more because she had an American GI and so she did not have time.

Ed hired a boat and they punted down the river, under bridges, laughing when he was almost too late dragging up the pole. She trailed her hand in the water, looking up at him as he pushed and pulled, lifting the pole from the water, hearing the water dripping back into the river. His arms were so strong, his body so lithe, his face so tired. The water was cold but she did not feel it, she only felt his arms as he had held her in that small room, his warm lips, and she smiled.

They ate at the hotel and the meal was frugal but it did not matter because they were impatient now, and that night Helen did undress in front of him. Her body was fit from the farm and her hands were not hard because she wore gloves and so she stroked his body and kissed his chest, his arms, his legs and held him to her.

In the morning they looked around the town and Ed took photographs of the colleges, but then handed his camera to Helen because she knew the angles to take. He wanted the sharpness of the shadows on the ground, the age of the buildings etched against the sky. She told him then of Claus and the business in New York and he nodded but said nothing.

They had lunch in a pub and as they walked in the afternoon

226

along the river they watched other punters, other lovers, but none could love as much as they did, Helen thought, her hand in his. They walked in and out of the shadows, dragging their hands along the weeping willows, not seeing anyone else, only one another, and for a while the world stood still. But then they heard the straggling bombers return over to the east of the town and Ed grew quiet and that night he told her of his guilt at remaining on the ground but he did not tell her of his fear of being sent back into the air because they all had that.

Sunday was overcast but not cold and they walked again but Ed was quiet today and Helen too because tomorrow the war began again. They ate in a small café, watching the people going into the church, some women with hats and very few men, and that afternoon they sat on the bank while a mallard dived in the turgid water. A woman walked past, pushing a young man in a wheelchair. They were pale and thin.

Helen talked as they heard the wheels receding on the path but Ed's answers were short and his shoulders were tense and he counted the planes which flew back over at four, not looking at her, and she felt a distance grow between them. As the last roared over he pulled her to her feet, hugging her, but his mind was not with her. She lifted her face for his kiss but he turned from her, walking to the bank, throwing a pebble and watching it bounce three times. Helen felt cold for the first time that summer and tried to push aside the hurt of his rejection, but could not and walked in silence to the car.

It was a silence which was not broken until they approached Greater Mannenham as the day was drawing to its end. Ed pulled in to the verge by the hayfield and took her hand and asked her to marry him, come back with him to Montana when all this was over. After all, she already had a business set up over there.

Helen sat looking up at him, into his eyes which were still dark. She looked beyond him to the field with the cut grass; she saw the leaves turning on the trees, the clouds thick and full of rain. She looked at him again, his brown eyes, the deep lines. She loved him, so much, so very much, but there had never been thought of a future, the present was enough. Hadn't he learned that yet? The future was too dangerous. She did not dare to challenge the gods, to ask for more than she had. Couldn't he see that?

She looked ahead. There was drizzle on the windscreen now blanking out the road. That is what the future was.

She turned to him then, pointing to the glass.

'That's the future. We have enough. Darling, we have enough.'

She gripped his hand. 'Let's keep what we have, we don't need to talk of tomorrow.' She held his hand to her face. 'Don't ask for too much.'

He pulled his hand away then, looking at her strangely. His eyelid was twitching. He looked so tired, so scared, and she reached for him again but he brushed away her hand, staring out to the fields at the side, talking in their direction, not hers. His voice was tense, taut. 'It's too much, is it? All you want is today, is it? I thought we felt more than that. I thought we loved one another.'

She looked at her hand. 'That's not what I meant. For God's sake, Ed. That's not how I meant it. You know that. Surely you know that. I love you. I love you so much.'

He turned and looked at her now but she couldn't see any feeling in his eyes. She put her hand out to him, smiling because she couldn't understand what was happening; where all this had come from. But he shook her off and reached for the ignition, starting the car, grinding it into gear, skidding the car off the verge on to the road.

'I need you. I need to know you'll always be there,' he said.

Helen caught at his arm. 'I will always be here for you. You know I will, but marriage is different.' How could she tell him she was frightened she would kill him. Heine had died, hadn't he? 'I love you,' she said but he shrugged off her arm.

'Forget it, Helen. Just forget I said anything. Just for Christ's sake forget what I said. Just think of the two nights you've had with a guy with cash in his pocket.'

The car was speeding down the road, swerving past a cyclist, hooting at a jeep and Helen clung to her seat, feeling as though she had been hit. How could this have happened?

'You goddamn Limeys,' he shouted, his hand hard down on the horn as another cyclist came out of a turning, but Helen knew he was shouting at her, not the old man and now she was angry because all this had taken the sun from the weekend and smashed it into darkness.

Helen watched the fields as they drove home, she didn't

228

watch him, couldn't watch him, because it had all been too quick, all too sudden. Didn't he understand that in the war you lived just for now because you never knew when another bomb would fall, when a telegram would come? Why didn't he understand?

Chris didn't understand either when she told him later that Ed would not be coming to see them again because they had quarrelled.

'But he needs you, Mum.'

She knew that, but one husband had already died. Wasn't that enough? But she didn't say that to her son.

She said instead, 'But it would mean living in a strange country.'

Chris said. 'Dad did.' His face was fierce and he wouldn't look at her.

Helen replied, 'I know.' She didn't say, 'And look what happened to him,' but that night in bed she tossed in the darkness of the blackout and again the next night and the next until two weeks had passed, filled with endless hours, minutes, seconds, and as dawn broke in mid September she knew that she was wrong. That she loved him and had let him down and would marry him rather than live without him or let him be alone. Other people married and did not die. He would not die.

That morning as she listened to the planes taking off, she thought of the war. She thought of the GIs who were working their way up Italy, of the Nazis, who were being beaten in Russia, of Hamburg, which had been flattened, of the Jews who had been taken from Warsaw, the British who were winning the battle of the U-boats. She hurried from her bedroom and cycled quickly to the farm. She must see him, he would come, he had always come on Wednesdays. They had shouted but he would come, he hadn't last Wednesday, but he had been angry. Today she would tell him that she was wrong. That he was right, time could be short and they must take what they could.

But he didn't come. All day he didn't come. The next day he sent comics as usual for Chris but there was nothing for her, no message, nothing. She cried in her room, pacing up and down, but he never came.

The next day she herded the cows, scrubbed the cow-shed floor, always looking and listening for him. That evening she put on nylons that he had given her but they laddered on her chapped hands and so she painted her legs instead and walked down to the village pub because he might be there. He was not.

But Scoot Wheeler was, standing outside leaning on the wall, talking to the landlord's daughter.

'Hi, Helen, how're you doing?'

Helen smiled but she was impatient. Where was he, she wanted to shout, but instead asked, 'Have you seen Ed?'

'He's back on base. He's flying tomorrow.'

'Flying? But he's grounded.'

Scoot laughed and eased himself from the wall, taking a swallow of watered beer and pulling a face. 'I guess he was, Helen, but he ain't now. There was the most humdinger of a row and in the end the CO said OK, he could go. Guess the Major never did like being down here when his boys were up there. Do you want a drink?'

Helen shook her head. No she didn't want a drink, she wanted to see Ed. She started walking then to the base, but she had no pass and the guard wouldn't let her through the wire gate, so she walked back working out the words she would write to him, telling him, begging him to forgive her.

She passed Mrs Vane with the vicar near the church carrying dahlias and chrysanthemums for the altar.

Mrs Vane caught her arm and smiled. 'My dear, I had no idea your little liaison had finished. I'm so sorry.'

Helen stopped and stared. The red dahlias clashed with the purple chrysanths, didn't the woman know that? 'It hasn't,' she said trying to walk on. 'It was all a mistake. A stupid mistake.'

Mrs Vane smiled again, stroking the petals. 'If you say so, my dear, but I've just seen your Major McDonald driving towards the town with Madge Wilcox. They seemed so close you know.'

Helen looked at the woman's face and saw her mother and felt the cupboard, the darkness of the cupboard, and she said nothing, just ran home and up to her room. She did not speak for the next two days, just worked all day and cried throughout the night, and then she came down and told Chris and Laura that she would not try to see Ed again. But the darkness of the cupboard was still there and the scent of chrysanthemums was all around.

230

*

The controls of the *Emma B* were heavy but honest, Ed thought as he operated the four throttles with palms upwards. She had been cussed to begin with but he had pretty soon got into it again. For God's sake, he hadn't been away for that long, he had said to his co-pilot on that mission back in late August, when Helen had told him she didn't love him enough; or as good as said that anyway. He looked over to the tower, waiting for the green flare. Damn the woman, damn the Limeys, expecting us to come over and win their damn wars for them. Didn't she know he needed her?

Joe, his co-pilot was tapping his knees. Ed ignored him. They were both tense, they were all tense. He had watched the film of the target area last night at the briefing, it was near the ball bearing factory they had got last time, but what they really wanted now were the rest of the factories, the CO said, and then the group navigator had taken over, smoothing back his hair which was grey now, though it had been brown at Christmas. He had explained the route that would be flown before calling on the weather expert who had said the weather would be thick fog in East Anglia, but then it was almost the middle of October. At 2000 feet they could expect to break out of it and it would be clear over Europe.

But not clear of Messerschmitts, Joe had murmured, and Ed had nodded. When would they get long-range fighter cover? It was crazy, the losses were getting close to twenty-five per cent for God's sake. Ed shook his head. He shouldn't think of that now but if he didn't he thought of her. He eased his helmet. He had tried other women but it hadn't worked. He couldn't sleep, he couldn't eat but at least now he was flying he had the fear which stopped him thinking of her every minute of every day – but still, every minute of every night, she was there.

Joe was still drumming his fingers and Ed wished to God he wouldn't. He checked his watch, five-thirty a.m. It had been cold when they had crammed into their jeeps, four in one, the rest of the crew in the other and driven out to the *Emma B* as the dawn was rising over the airfield. He had stood by as they climbed in, checking they were OK, laughing at Patrick who wanted to pee but then he always did.

The engines had spluttered into life all around them, coughing, roaring, until all the propellers were turning except for the *Emma B*'s. He and Joe clambered into the cockpit, hearing the leather seat creak with his weight as his saddle in Montana did. They checked the levers, the dials, compasses, light switches and control yokes. There was a smell of paint and gasoline because the *Emma B* was new.

Still there was no green flare. Ed inched round and checked Joe again. He was still drumming his fingers. He looked back out across the countryside. She had never come to find him, never written and he wished that he no longer loved her as he did.

'There it goes, skip.'

Ed swung back, the flare was hanging in the air and they waited their turn, taxi-ing, lifting off thirty seconds behind the *Mary Rose*, climbing to the assembly point, then flying in formation with more than four hundred bombers from other bases.

Ed spoke into the intercom. 'OK, you guys, keep your eyes on the skies. You don't get a second bite at this cherry. Sam, you keep your eyes swivelling good, OK?'

He knew Sam, his tail gunner, would. His was the most important defensive position in the whole plane. He couldn't afford to foul up; he knew that, everyone knew that.

'Marco, you make sure you've got a fix for getting back,' Ed called and Marco replied, 'Sure, skip.'

The boys would be cold, Ed knew that. It was OK here in the cockpit but Sam's sinuses would give him hell again tonight. He checked with the gunners on the intercom. Steve in the top turret was fine, so too was Ross in the nose. Those in the waist section would be getting back the feel of their guns, bumping into each other, talking of last night's crap game.

They were out over the sea now with the Dutch coast in sight. The P-47s had picked them up now but they were only short-range protection. Ed sighed, easing his back. They would be in the air eight hours at least, and his feet would get cold, his back would ache, and he would get tired, but maybe he would get them back alive and he was hardly thinking of Helen any more.

He looked to either side. The flak was coming up over the coast but they stayed in tight formation because those crapheads at the top of the heap thought that formation was all the real defence that was needed. Ed would have liked one in

232

the pilot's seat now, assing on about having a thousand miles of coastline to choose from so casualties should not be so goddamn high. Try telling that to the men, Ed grunted, looking always to left and right, up and down.

The enemy planes would come, but when? Probably when their short-range fighter cover had run for home. He felt bulky, the bomber jacket, flying helmet, flak vest, Mae West and the oxygen masks were like some pantomime. The radio operator was flicking switches with a gloved hand. They drummed on for hours and Joe talked to Ed of his girl back home and his girl in the town but all the time they looked and suddenly the enemy was there, to the left.

Sam called, 'Hey, skip, we got friends visiting.'

'How many?' Ed's voice was sharp and the sweat of fear burst on his forehead. Jesus Christ.

'Four I think.'

'More up here,' from the top turret.

'Jeeze there's six here.'

The intercom was alive with shouts and Ed said, 'Cut it out. Keep calm, keep looking.' And to himself he said, Keep calm, keep calm. But knots of fear and panic screwed up in his body. He looked ahead, above, to the sides. Where the goddamn hell were they?

The *Emma B*'s guns were firing now and Ed kept on going, drawing up tighter, knowing that if he fell out of formation he'd be picked off sooner. Again and again they came but they'd been in the air nearly four hours, they had to be close to the target. His head was aching from the noise, the flashes, the fear which was still sour in his mouth, and he thought of Chris's raven but then pushed it away because it was black and death was black.

There was a burst of light in front and he jerked his head back, holding the *Emma B* on course as the *Mary Rose* burst into flames in front of them and dropped from the sky and Ed thought of nothing but drawing up into her place; keeping up, for Christ's sake keep up. Push the *Mary Rose* out of your goddamn head, push the flames away and the screams he could not hear, but he couldn't. He could only push it to one side but it kept creeping back and he could see Don's face in the bar last night. Was he screaming now?

The firing and the babbling went on and on and now he spoke, feeling the vibration of the ship beneath his hands.

'Give me a fix, navigator.' His voice was calm. How could it be?

'Five minutes to target. We're at 25,000 feet.'

'We OK for gas, Ed?' Joe asked.

'Look for yourself for Christ's sake. That's your job.' Steady, steady. Don't let it show. Don't let the fear show.

The firing was still going on and now the first of the Fortresses were making their run and Ed wished he had not shouted. He was always shouting now. What the hell was the matter with him?

'OK, you guys, we're going in, then we're going home.'

Ed kept his eyes on his instruments, listening to Marco, the navigator, listening to the gunners, still firing, knowing that their guns would be hot, knowing that so far, none had been hit because he recognised all their voices.

He looked across at Joe and winked and saw him smile in spite of his fear before turning to the front again.

'Keep it up, kid, we're almost there.' Then he heard the crack and the shattered windscreen blew into his lap and across his hands but he held on and saw the fighter go down in flames, hit by shells from the waist gunners, but it was too late for Joe whose blood was splashed all over what remained of his Mae West, all over Ed. It was sticky on his face. Christ, wet and sticky and Joe's, but the bombardier was aiming again so he must keep steady. He held on to the controls, seeing the glass in his gloves, feeling it in his hands.

The bombardier called, 'The beauties have gone, let's get out of here, skip.'

They did but it wasn't over. The ME109s were still waiting for them and stabbed and fired and sent Fortresses spinning from the group, down to the ground in flames, but not them yet, not them, but the blood was still all over his face, and the poor little kid was dead.

'Marco, you make sure you get us home,' Ed said, and laughed when Marco said, 'You're such an old spoilsport, skip. I thought we could drop in on Hitler for a decent glass of beer.'

Ed didn't look at Joe, at the blood which had run from the corner of his mouth, the blood which had spurted from his gaping chest. He mustn't look or he would crack. He knew he would crack, because he had never flown with a dead man before, a man whose blood was on his face, drying on his skin and lips in the wind from the broken screen. But he mustn't think of it, must he? He had to get the boys back so he pushed Joe to the side of his mind with the *Mary Rose* but he too kept sliding back.

They had two hours to go still and his arms ached and his hands hurt but the 109s had gone for now. He spoke into the intercom, checking with them all, but Eric in the waist section had been hurt.

'And he's hurt bad, skip. Got shell fragments in his shoulder but it's too cold to bleed much.'

'Get some pressure on it, Mart, when we finish the run and come in to land. He'll bleed then. And keep a grip of yourself too. Keep your eyes open, we're not home yet.'

The wind was icy in the cabin, streaming in through the broken windscreen, and his face was numb with cold. His hands were bleeding from the glass which had penetrated his gloves. He could feel them sticky against the leather but they didn't hurt now. He rubbed his face on his shoulder, wanting to scrape off Joe's dried blood but he couldn't. Push it back, just push it back.

He spoke into the intercom again. 'How's it going, Martin? Is Eric hanging on?'

'He's still with us, skip.'

The 109s came again then.

'Six above,' called Steve but then his voice choked and stopped and there was no firing from his gun. Ed held the plane steady, sweat on his face in spite of the cold.

'Jesus, where are the escorts?' he murmured. 'Where are the damned escorts?'

He craned his head round, seeing the 109 come down at them, guns firing, before turning away from the waist gunners' fire and then there was another and another and he did not know how the *Emma B* could survive. The men's ammunition was low and their top gunner was out.

He crept up tighter into formation, gripping the controls, holding her steady, hearing the waist guns firing again but then they were hit and the starboard outer engine sparked and flames belched. Christ! Feather, for God's sake feather it, he shouted to himself and his hands shook as he did so. Now there were three engines and his speed dropped and his mind cleared, ice cool in the blasting wind.

235

He could still get the *Emma B* home if she was a good kind lady but he was dropping back from the formation which was half the size it had been at the start of the mission. He talked to his ship, not listening to the battle which was raging, telling her that it was only one hour, one snitch of an hour she had to hang in, she had to stay up with the others. But she couldn't and he knew she couldn't and that they were as good as dead. The formation was out of sight.

But then the P-47s came and the 109s peeled away with the American fighters firing and hounding and he kept his voice level as he spoke to the crew.

'This is one kind of a cute lady, fellas, she'll get us back.'

They laughed but there was still the flak and he pulled on the controls, weaving, dodging, unable to gain height to rise above it, and they still had the sea to cross.

Ed looked down as the coast eased away. He could see the white foam of the waves but still the *Emma B* held up. His arms were so tired now. His eyes were raw from the cold wind. They churned on until they reached the Norfolk coast and then they were over neat hedged fields and another group of Fortresses was with them now.

'Eric's not looking too good, skip.'

'OK, we're nearly back.'

Marco called, 'Five minutes, skip.'

But Ed knew because he could see the runway lights, gleaming through the mist, and he peeled off from the new group, putting his own lights on, ordering the red flare to be set off to indicate that they had injured on board. He turned in and landed, seeing the ambulance roaring up and heard Marco saying, 'Let's get him to the meat wagon.'

But Joe wouldn't need one, ever again, and neither, they discovered, would Steve.

Ed taxied on to the hard stand when he had counted his men out. He left her with the maintenance crew who would work all night under tarpaulins to get the ship ready again after they had hosed down the top turret and the cockpit.

He debriefed and his voice was level when he told of Joe's death although he had been only twenty-two and he had shouted at him. It was level even when he described the *Mary Rose* which had been piloted by his friend Don from Milwaukee who was thirty with three children. His voice was level when he told them that it was murder to send out bombers without long-range escorts. It was just plain murder.

He had his hands dressed in the infirmary and he didn't shake or moan.

He walked back to his room and took the Scotch bottle down from the locker and tipped back his head, drinking down the harsh liquid because he wanted to go to Helen and feel her arms around him while he cried for his friends but there was no place for him there. She no longer loved him. So instead he drank, and then went to the pub with his crew and laughed and sang as though they didn't care, but they did. Oh yes, they did.

Only half the planes had returned today and more than fifty of their friends had died and it could not go on, for God's sake. They had to have protection or this daylight bombing was just a pointless massacre.

CHAPTER 16

The farm kept Helen on through the winter and so she did no have to sweat beneath the smell of beet but instead milked the cows, leaning her head against their warmth, feeling the twitching of their skin, seeing the steam rise from the bucket because 1944 came in hard and cold.

She wore extra socks inside her boots because the airmen's had worn through and, of course, there would be no more. Chilblains came and in the evening she rubbed on wintergreen, pressing it hard into her swollen toes, preferring the pain to the itching. With Chris each morning she fed Laura's chickens and Helen and Heine, then threw a few logs into the basket before cycling along lanes shiny with ice but happiness had gone with the hot summer days. She did not look up as the planes flew from the base but she ached for him.

In January British and American troops landed at Anzio and the bombing of Berlin and Germany by the Allies continued. They were cold in the village but reserved their fuel for the kitchen only, as the rest of the British were doing as shortages increased. In January the Russians broke through the siege line at Leningrad, and in February the Americans launched the Pacific assault and Claus sent through a parcel of warm clothing for Chris and tins of ham and so they shared their meals with Mrs Williams and Mr Reynolds. In March British troops entered Burma by glider power and the British began to dare to hope that soon it would be over.

But then Germany entered Hungary and Helen knew that Hitler would never give up until the Allies were at Berlin's door, nor the Japanese until Tokyo was reached and the slaughter would continue. In that early spring Mr Reynolds's son died in the Chin Hills and Mrs Williams's nephew was missing in Italy and prayers were said in the church for those in pain.

In April, as the sun broke through and warmed the budding trees, all coastal areas in Britain were banned to visitors, and large military exercises were mounted throughout southern England. Planes flew more often from the Greater Mannenham base and from all those around and Helen rode to work beneath the thunder of their passage and the shadow of their wings.

She worked in fields which had been ploughed, planting cabbages, sowing beetroots, smelling the rich soil, seeing the seagulls whirling in the air, counting the rows she worked, listening to the men, but nothing helped because each minute of each day she ached for the feel of his lips, the strength of his body, the heat of her own response, the words of love, the knowledge of his safety. But he never came.

After Easter they set the potatoes, stooping, pressing in the sprouting tubers, stepping forward, stooping, pressing. Stepping forward, stooping, pressing, and hair straggled beneath her scarf into her eyes, her mouth. The sun was out and it was warm today, warm and clear. Good bombers' weather. Was he flying? Was he safe? She straightened up, pushing back her shoulders, easing her back.

'Nearly time for lunch then, me old girl,' called Ernest and Helen nodded. They finished the rows they were working on, then squatted, eating their sandwiches, drinking their tea, saying little. She looked out across the fields, sprouting and green. Ed had said that England had so many different greens in just one square mile and he was right. Montana would have been beautiful in its way, but it was too late for that.

They worked on throughout the day and in the evening she pitched the ball to Chris, twisting her wrist as he had shown her but it was not the same as Ed. Mary took over and Helen walked into the kitchen. Laura sat by the stove, knitting.

'Sit down, Helen. You should rest while you can. You're getting too thin again. Much too thin.'

But Helen couldn't rest. The evenings were too long, the nights longer still, because then she lay and thought of him stroking someone else's body, moving in rhythm, his mouth on other lips, words of love, words of comfort which had been hers, and she was always glad when the dawn came again.

She walked back into the garden, pruning back the roses, remembering their scent from last year. She touched the tulips, the cool waxy leaves. She pulled couch grass from the soil, picking the earth from its roots, carrying it to the compost, and as dusk fell they heard the noise, the stuttering engines, the tearing, grinding sound and knew that a plane had come down, over to the west, quite close. They heard too the jeeps and the ambulances from the base and looked into the sky, but there was no thick black smoke as there sometimes was and so they knew there was no fire.

Helen took up the ball again and threw hard and fast until the garden sank beneath the night because she had no right to know whether it was Ed.

The next morning the sun was bright but cool as she rode to the farm, the wind flicking at her hair which was too long but what did it matter? Her gloves had holes and she felt the cold of the handlebars through them. The lane was rougher after the frosts of winter and she jolted and weaved then cycled into the yard, but was stopped by John.

'Let's be getting across to Top Field. Those damn spuds you sowed yesterday is in all sorts of a mess.' His face was red as he strode past her. 'Bring Rocket. Elsie's already there.'

Helen leaned her bike against the wall, watching him as he walked, calling to him. 'Why?'

Her breath caught in her throat and she coughed.

'And I hope you're not getting that damn flu. It's enough that one of them damn Yanks puts his plane down in me spuds. Just when they've been sown. It's a bloody liberty.'

He stopped and said, 'For God's sake go and get that damn horse hitched to the cart. I wants them bits out of my old spuds.'

Helen watched as he hurried down the lane, calling, 'Was anybody hurt?'

'Only the pilot and he's not dead.' John stopped and turned. 'Don't you worry, me old girl. It wasn't your Ed.'

Helen looked again at his bowed back as he continued down the lane, his stick swinging out before him, kicking sideways at stones, at young thistles. John had never said anything to her about Ed before, he had just been kind, talking of the years she had in front of her and how many fish there were in the sea and now she wanted to follow him, take his hand in hers and thank him. Instead she walked back to the yard and harnessed Rocket, pulling herself up on to the seat and taking him out of the yard, down the lane and up into the top field, tying his reins round the brake, leaping down and standing with John and the men as they looked.

The Fortress had crashed through the elm trees and there was freshly splintered wood and bark across the field, bright against the dull metal. There were great furrows gouged into the ground.

'Damn old boys baled out safe, but the pilot was taken away last night. Broke his poor old back,' John said, leaning with both hands on his stick, nodding towards West Field. 'The engines and wings are over there, on the other side of the hedge.'

Helen walked forwards, towards the broken wreck. It was so big and helpless, all its power had fled. She stood looking up at the spines which showed through the jagged fuselage, at the picture of a blonde with the words 'Sarah Jane' written beneath. It made it seem too painful. She turned to John.

'We can't move this,' she said. 'It's too big and they don't like us touching the ones that come down.'

'I know that, but we can move some of these bits.' He waved his stick at the jagged metal scattered all over the field. 'They've never brought one down on me spuds before and I'm not having it.'

Alf was already moving Elsie across nearer the elms. Rooks were cawing in the sky, raven black. Helen moved away, out of the shadow of the plane, picking up twisted metal as she walked back to Rocket, throwing it into the cart, coaxing him closer. He shook his head up and down and backed but she calmed him, crooning softly until he stood steady again. She and John scooped up more, sharing the weight of one bit which looked like part of a door, there was a scarf beneath it, stiff with blood. They tipped the door into the cart and then Helen returned for the scarf, putting it near the front, not in with the wreckage because it had once belonged to one of *Sarah Jane's* crew; somebody's son.

They worked for thirty minutes before the jeep from the base came roaring up the field, lights flashing and horns blazing. Helen ran for Rocket who jerked backwards, snorting. She grabbed for his bridle, gripping it by the bit, talking to him, soothing him but the Americans had leaped from the jeep and were shouting at John.

She shouted to John, 'Tell them to be quiet, Rocket will bolt.'

She hung on to the horse, talking, soothing, hearing John shouting at the men climbing from the jeep who took no notice.

'Leave that plane alone, bud.'

'That's US property. It's not to be moved by anyone but us,' the Colonel shouted.

Helen was using both hands now, pulling Rocket's head down. Another jeep came up the field but she was straining to hold him as he tossed and shook. He was too startled, though, too heavy for her and he knocked her back with his head, smashing into her face. She groaned with pain but the horse was slipping now, his legs kicking and struggling, and she reached out for him again but he went right down in the shafts and she moved forwards as he thrashed, hearing the clink of harness and chains. She caught his mane, and then his head. Her nose was bleeding down on to her dungarees and she cried with the pain but the big horse was snorting with terror and he could break his leg. She threw herself on top of his head, crying out to John, to the men who were running over to her now, knowing that she must press his head down to try and keep him still.

She could hear the shouts, the boots running through the ploughed soil and then she felt hands round her waist, lifting her, but she shouted as blood ran into her mouth, 'No, let me go. He's got to be kept still.'

'Helen, it's OK. Let go.' It was Ed, his voice, his hands and so she let him lift her clear but those hands now stroked another woman and so she pushed herself from him, wiping her face, mixing the tears with the blood.

'Someone must keep him still,' she said looking only at Rocket, but John was there now, pressing himself across the horse's head and Ed moved back to the horse, kneeling in the damp soil, his trousers soaking up the wetness and as he spoke and stroked the horse's muzzle, neck and chest, the thrashing slowed and gradually stopped but his legs were tangled in the straps.

She heard him say, 'Get those cutters from the jeep.'

The Colonel turned, signalling to the driver, who jumped

out, ran to the tool box and brought them across and she watched Ed's hands as he cut through the leather harness and unclipped the chains. Her nose was still bleeding and she undid her scarf which had slipped to her neck and held it against her face, waiting as John shouted at the others to back the cart away from the horse. Now Ed stood back, telling everyone to stand still. They all watched as Rocket scrambled to his feet, waiting as Ed came up, rubbing his hand gently under his chin, holding the bridle, leading the horse from the field.

The Colonel spoke. 'Hey, Ed. What about this mess with the plane?'

Ed didn't turn, he just called 'You can sort that out, sir. This horse needs a bit of peace.' He continued walking and the Colonel shook his head. 'Damn Air Execs, they're all the same. This one reckons he's back in Montana soft-talking his stock, not fighting a goddamn war.' But he was smiling. 'He sure is some kind of guy with a horse, isn't he?'

Helen's scarf was soaked through with blood and her face hurt. Her lip was swelling and she touched it with her tongue. She didn't look at Ed as he left the field with his rolling gait, his strong shoulders, but at John and the Colonel, but now her boss said, 'You get on back to the farm too, lass. Get that nose sorted out. Don't want you frightening any more horses, do we?'

Helen shook her head. 'I'm fine,' she said.

'Do as you're told, me old girl. Get on back.' John's voice was firm now and so she turned and followed on behind Ed, walking slowly so that she did not catch up, so that she would not have to talk to him, see those lips which were kissing someone else.

'And get a move on,' John shouted and so she was forced to quicken her stride, but only until she was out of the field and then she turned towards the farm but Ed was just to the left of the gate, holding Rocket still, waiting for her, leaning into his shoulder as she had so often done.

'You handled him pretty good,' he said, not smiling. His face was even more deeply lined, his eyes sunken with tiredness. 'I guess you'd do pretty good in Montana.'

Helen didn't stop. She bunched her scarf to her face and

243

hurried on, but he just brought the horse along quicker, rolling his feet, stretching out his legs.

'How're you doing, Helen? You look pretty good.'

She didn't turn.

'Plenty of colour on your cheeks today.'

She stopped, waiting for him to pass, but he didn't, he just leaned back into Rocket's shoulder, pulling on his bit, saying softly, 'Whoa.'

'Leave me alone,' Helen said, hating him for looking so beautiful, tearing apart inside because she loved him so much. She wanted to laugh because he was funny, wanted to cry because, though his words were light, his hands were trembling and so were hers.

Ed narrowed his eyes. 'I dropped in to the cottage this morning because I reckoned maybe you got hurt yesterday when the *Sarah Jane* came down.'

'Well, I didn't. I just got hurt when a crowd of Yanks rushed my horse.'

She walked on, wanting to lean into him, to feel him against her, to hear him say that he loved her, but he never would again.

'I love you, Helen,' Ed said, walking Rocket on again. She heard the stones clicking against the horse's hoofs, heard them slip beneath him, heard the soft snorting of his breath. A finch darted out from the hedge, and Rocket twitched.

She still did not stop; dared not stop.

'I said I love you.' His voice was louder now and he caught at her arm but she shrugged him off.

'No you don't. You love someone else. I've heard. Madge talks about you all the time.' And she did. About the way his moustache tickled when he kissed, about his eagerness in bed, the scar on his left shoulder.

Ed caught her again, his fingers digging into her arm.

'That was over a long time ago. I was hurt and frightened. I love you, you love me. I know you do. Marry me.'

Helen looked into his face now, searching for the truth and saw it in his eyes that were so brown, the face that was thinner, the lines that were etched as though with a chisel, but wondered if it was only there because she wanted it so much. She turned away, and then saw again the scarf as it had lain on the ground. She looked at him.

'Do you love me?' she said, her voice muffled by her scarf.

'Enough to stay over here if you won't come back with me,' he said.

She knew then that his love was as great as hers. She looked at the fields either side of the lane and the finch which was back in the hedge. She drank in the Englishness which surrounded her, the freshness, the smallness, and loved it but loved him more.

'I love you. I love you,' she murmured. He kissed her hand and then her neck, and walked back with his arm around her, knowing that he could not bear life without her again, thinking how glad he was that Mary and Chris had phoned him at the base to see if he was safe and then to tell him that Helen loved him more than ever.

The Colonel had to call at Laura's cottage to go through the formalities of ensuring that Helen was of a good enough character to qualify as an American Serviceman's wife. They drank elderberry wine and laughed to cover their embarrassment and he told them that Ed was the best Air Exec. that he had ever had and that the Major was giving him an easier ride now that they had long-range fighter cover. They laughed again but when he left Helen leaned against the door because Ed would be flying again in five weeks' time unless the war ended; but it wouldn't, it was endless.

They called the banns at the church where the vicar had said that he would be pleased to marry them. Madge looked the other way when Helen passed and Mrs Vane was too angry to be able to speak with civility. Ed completed affidavits confirming that he was in a position to support her financially but Helen had no intention of being dependent. She had her job and her agency in America. They were to be married on 1 May and Helen thought of one day at a time, because tomorrow and the day after were the future.

Helen stood with Ed inside the Parish Church, in a suit made of damaged parachute silk. Chris watched with Laura and Marian on the bride's side which was filled with villagers – but not Madge – whilst the Americans filled the right. Mary was the bridesmaid, also in parachute silk, and Chris found her lovely. She was not so fat and her hair was curled again with pipe cleaners and now she was looking round and smiling at him. He wondered how he could leave England without her because she was his friend, but also somehow more than that.

He listened to his mother as she spoke her words in a voice which was clear and true. He listened to Ed as he promised to love and to cherish, till death do us part, and hoped that his new father would never have to fly the Purple Heart Corner as Earl had done. That bottom rear corner was the most vulnerable position and won too many wounded-in-action medals for the crews that flew in it. Later they walked from the church to the lounge bar of the Royal Oak and talked to the guests, who ate and drank refreshments provided by the base and as the knife sank into the cake which the Master-Sergeant cook had sent, he whispered to Mary, 'Will you come to America too?'

She didn't answer, just looked at him, and then turned back to Helen and Ed as they kissed, then threw homemade confetti as they left, laughing as Mrs Vane caught the bouquet.

Helen and Ed took a taxi to Norwich. They sat close and he felt warm against her. His hands clasped hers and they did not speak. They climbed the stairs of the inn past peeling paper and beneath dimmed lights, but did not notice. The bedroom was warm, a fire burned and Ed said that this was his CO's present to them. His voice was low and he didn't smile as he took her coat from her shoulders and dropped it to the floor. He didn't smile as he slipped her clothes from her body and then his own. Helen didn't speak, just stood as he held her, kissed her, ran his hands down her body and now she trembled and lifted her arms to him, pulling his head down to hers, kissing his mouth, saying his name again and again because he was so beautiful and she was so full of love.

They did not sleep that night but lay together on the bed, feeling the heat from the fire, seeing the flickering shadows which licked at the ceiling. They clung together and then away, loose and easy and full. Tonight there was no war, no world outside this room. They talked of their love, their passion, their fears, and then they kissed again and felt the weight of one another and breathed in the scent. They talked of the blossom on the trees, the skies which were starlit tonight and then they merged again, lying together as the dawn rose, pink and clear and fine. They did not speak of the future because there might not be one for them both.

Ed flew the day after they returned and Helen counted the planes as she hoed the beet in the fields. Only seventeen Fortresses returned; twenty had flown out. Chris counted in Laura's kitchen and waited for the phone to ring but it did not and Ed came back that night to the cottage, tired and trembling but safe. Again and again he came back until, at the beginning of June, no more leave was granted. Helen lay in bed that night alone, missing him, wanting him, and full of fear because there were no Americans in the villages, in the towns. Something was happening in England.

As the fifth of June became the sixth the village and the country did not sleep because, wing-tip to wing-tip, British and American planes roared, circled and assembled: Mustangs, Thunderbolts, Flying Fortresses, twin-engined Marauders, Dakotas with wings swept back, Mosquitoes, Spitfires and Hurricanes, Halifaxes and Stirlings. In the cottage Chris and Laura wondered if now, at last, Hitler would stop fighting, but Helen knew he wouldn't because she had seen his image in the eyes of the black-booted torch-carrying soldiers.

All that long night preceding the sixth dawn in June the weather was not good, a strong north-westerly blew offshore from Europe but the German batteries were pounded along the French coast as night turned to day. At five a.m. while battleships pounded the German defences, a seaborne force of Allied soldiers landed on the coast of Normandy. British and Canadian troops took Gold, Juno and Sword beaches. American troops took Utah and Omaha. Omaha was steeper and there were many German soldiers behind quick-firing guns. Too many died.

At eight p.m. that night, while Ed was at the air base, safe, thank God, safe for now, Helen listened to the King calling for his people's prayers 'as the great crusade sets forth'.

She sat before the fire with Laura, Chris and Mary and listened as they talked of peace, and the children said they could not remember what that was like and she cried.

The next week the Allied advance continued and there was hope and satisfaction in the faces of the people she met. The next week Marian rang the air base. Their friend Roger, the

247

vicar of St Bede's and the crypt, was ill, and Ed was given a thirty-six-hour pass to accompany Helen to London because his station was being stood down now that the initial invasion force was working its way inland. He drove her to the station and travelled in a crowded train to London, walking to the Underground, then passing through a capital which was bare of troops though there were children. Again there were children but Helen watched them as they played and looked up to the skies. They walked to her flat through streets broken like rotten teeth. Rosebay grew in the bomb craters and over the ruins and all the time Ed looked around but said nothing.

The flat was untouched and the vicar pale.

'You've been overdoing it, my dear,' Helen said, sitting in the room holding his hand, looking round and remembering the telegram and her despair but she no longer had to remember Heine because he was always with her.

'Dear Roger, you really have been overdoing it,' she said, leaning over and kissing his thin forehead.

They had brought ham from the base and eggs from Laura's hens and together with Marian she cooked in her own kitchen again, looking out on the shelter, talking of the crypt members who, Marian had told her, still met each night but only because they wanted to.

As the afternoon drew on Helen watched Ed, who stood at the sitting-room window, looking, just looking. Then he reached for his hat.

'Guess I'll take a walk, honey, just a walk.'

His eyes were shadowed and his hands trembled and so she grabbed her jacket and went after him, walking down the street, holding his hand, which was warm and strong, hearing her shoes but not his, because of his rubber soles.

He looked at the streets, the buildings, the fronts of stores which had no backs, the wooden crosses which were hammered into rubble where a daughter, a son, a husband, a wife had died. There were flowers on some, wilted and sad.

That night he did not make love as they slept in the spare room but he held her all night, feeling not her soft flesh but the vibrations of the *Emma B* as he delivered her bombs. But buildings had no shape from 25,000 feet when flak was all around and fighters were diving. No human was ever visible beneath the falling bombs. No screams were audible, only those of his gunners as they bled for a second before their blood froze. He must think of them, not of the people beneath the ruins, the families he destroyed. He must not think of them because it was not his job to think. His job was to help to win the war. He knew that, it was what he told his nineteen-year-olds when they flew their first mission. It was what he told them when they were sick in the latrines after they landed.

He tightened his grip on Helen. But did the Germans put wooden crosses in their ruins too?

He wished that he had not come today. He wished there had never been a war.

He travelled back the next day but Helen stayed for two more days and it was while she was there that the doodlebugs hit London. Droning, revving, the searchlights tracing the streaking tail and the shells bursting to either side but without effect. On they came, buzzing, until, suddenly, there was silence and it was then that they fell to the ground and exploded. Helen insisted that Roger should move to the crypt and they took him in the afternoon, returning for tea and provisions and it was in the evening as they returned to the church that one came buzzing through the air and cut out. She and Marian threw themselves to the ground screaming, both of them screaming, because they had been through this too many times before.

The explosion rocked the street, showering dust, so much dust, and then they heard the roar and saw the flames but turned away, hurrying to the crypt, because the ambulances were already coming and they were not needed. Hurrying away from the shrieks and the groans, knowing that this pilotless plane which catapulted from the Continent in the direction of southern England was going to wreak every last inch of havoc that Hitler could manage.

Helen ran down the steps of the crypt, checking that Roger was all right, listening as Ruth knitted and cursed 'itler for not knowing when he was beaten. She drank tea already strained twice through a sieve and felt as though she was running away as she took the train back to the village.

Helen drove the cart out to the field for the hay harvest and this time there was no help from the young American boys, most of whom were now dead, but neither was there help from the new intake because they were too busy in the skies, too busy trying not to die.

She heaved at the hay, smiling at John as he told her to work harder and build up those muscles because the war would be over soon and Montana would want to know what little British girls were made of. They carted loads back and then forked again. They raked the next day and Chris came, drinking cold tea at lunchtime, picking up the grass beneath the hedge and tying it into knots before throwing it up to the wind and watching it as it fell.

'Will the war be over soon, Mum?'

'I don't know, I really don't know,' she said but she did know that it wouldn't. But John nodded because the Allies were advancing across France and the Americans were attacking Japanese strongholds in the Marianas Islands.

Hitler did not give up and bombed England with more doodlebugs and the crypt was busy every night. In July children who had returned to London were evacuated again and so too were those in the bomb alley in Sussex, Surrey and Kent because Hitler's doodlebugs were intensifying. Mrs Vane now glared at Helen but Mrs Williams patted her and told her not to take 'the merest bit of notice'.

Ed flew only when there were no other crews because he was too busy on base, but each night when he could he came for a few hours and laughed as Helen dropped grass on the bedroom floor and held her tight as she slept, knowing that when he was with her he was safe from the fear of dying, safe from the knowledge of his destructive load, though he did not tell her that. But Helen knew, each night she knew, because she did not really sleep and heard his whispered words which he spoke aloud to himself.

In August Russia captured Bucharest and its oil, and Nazi death camps were found in Poland, at Maidenek where one and a half million people of every race and creed had been murdered with great efficiency. Helen cried that night and was glad that Heine was dead. She cried too for his parents because they might still be alive. And still Hitler did not give up.

As they harvested the wheat, Chris asked if the war would be over by Christmas and Helen said again that she didn't know; but she did because the Allies had not reached Berlin yet and that madman would claw and bite every drop of blood from

250

everybody before he laid down his arms, and so would the Japanese.

In September the British and American attack on Arnhem failed and now other people also knew that there would not be an early peace. Now also the V2 rockets fell on England.

In October MacArthur landed in the Philippines and Helen harvested the beet, driving Rocket forward for the men to heave and empty their baskets up into the cart, then changing over so that John led the horse while she picked up beet, working in a steady rhythm, so much stronger than when she had arrived from the beet factory with the smell still in her hair.

There were prisoners-of-war to help now: Germans and Italians. And the villagers gave them fruit from their stores and knew that they did not suck blood from small children, but drew out photographs of their own, showing them and smiling, their faces gaunt from the war and memories which only they knew.

There were not as many missions from the airbase now. The Allies were gaining air superiority as the German bases in occupied countries were overrun and industries fell into the hands of the advancing Allies.

'Soon,' Ed said as he drank warm cocoa in front of the small fire in the sitting-room that they had lit for Chris's birthday on 1 December, 'soon we shall not need to go up at all.'

Helen did not reply because the Allies had not yet reached Berlin, though the Home Guard had been 'stood down' and Mr Reynolds had let his boar into the orchard because he was so angry.

But, she thought again, Berlin had not been reached and so the war had months to run.

That night Chris lay in bed, thinking of Mary because he had asked her again if she would come to America when the war was over, and again she had said she didn't know.

In the morning he asked Helen if they could take his friend when they moved to Montana and she nodded, pulling on her boots, wrapping her long woollen socks over the top, and her scarf around her neck because snow had fallen in the night and the cold almost crackled in the air. 'Only if she wants to and then we would have to sort something out with her sister. Mark

251

you, darling, if we adopted her she would be your sister, had you thought of that? You could never be anything else.'

She opened the door, just a crack before saying again, 'You must think of that.'

Chris flushed, he felt the heat in his face. 'Oh Mum, don't be so stupid.'

But Helen thought about it all the way to the farm because Chris was twelve now and he and Mary fitted like a hand in a glove.

On 19 December, on a day of fog and cloud when Ed had been due to fly, the Germans attacked the Allied front in Belgium, following the same route through the Ardennes that they had used in 1940. England reeled from the shock because they had thought Hitler was finished, but Helen had not. The Germans held up the Allied advance in Belgium and the casualty lists of the Battle of the Bulge grew longer as the days passed. The skies stayed cloudy and no aerial help could be given. Ed's nails were chewed by Friday and two of his crew had learned that their brothers were dead. The skies didn't clear until the last week in December but it was still snowing on the twenty-third when Ed climbed the tree which was slippery with ice and nearly fell reaching for the mistletoe and as Mary shrieked, Helen called, 'You bomber pilots! You can't even cope fifteen feet from the ground!'

He threw the mistletoe down on her and clambered to the ground, chasing her, calling to Chris to bring the sledge, scooping up snow and throwing it so that it sank down beneath her collar and on to her neck, laughing as he heard her scream. She ran faster, feeling the snow crunch beneath her feet but he caught her, swinging her off the ground and kissing her. Chris threw a snowball and it hit their faces and the snow found their mouths and they tasted it together.

They roasted chestnuts on an old shovel that night, seeing the skins crack and grow black, smelling the sweetness in the air, and they talked of the midnight service on Christmas Eve when they would be allowed to show light from the stained glass windows for the first time since war began.

'So it really will be over soon,' Chris said as he sorted the straight pieces of the puzzle which he had done three times before but Mary hadn't.

'I guess it might,' Ed said, smiling at Helen who said

nothing, just looked into the fire as she reknitted a pulled out sweater. Ed picked out a chestnut, throwing it from hand to hand and blowing on it but in the end he flicked it back on to the shovel while the others laughed.

'Don't be so impatient,' Laura said.

Ed nodded, rubbing his hands together and grimacing, watching as Helen knitted, the needles clicking softly.

'It's kind of nice to see you doing that. In the States they don't, or in Little Fork they don't anyway, not much. My mom has some pins somewhere.'

Chris looked at Mary. 'Will you come with us?' he asked her.

Helen looked up at Ed and they both listened as Mary said, 'I don't know. I think Laura will be lonely and I've got me sister too. I don't know what to do.'

Helen said softly. 'What's happened with Irene's GI then, Mary, do you know? Has she heard?'

Mary shook her head. 'No, he's never written, not after she told him she was having the baby.'

Ed took the shovel off the logs. It had burnt black from the smoke.

'Maybe the guy just got busy. He'll get in touch, Mary.'

Mary shrugged. 'I like it here so much,' she murmured and Chris looked up at Helen who smiled gently, and that night, as she said goodnight, she told him that he must let Mary make up her own mind because Laura had said she could live with her and come across to America in the holidays.

'I like England too,' Chris said, 'but I want to go to America.'

'I know, darling, but it's different for us. We love Ed so much.'

She walked down the stairs, running her hands down the vertical beams, hearing the creak of the cottage which had been home for so long and which she loved as much as she loved the fields and the towns of England. But she loved Ed more, she knew that now.

She told him as he left that night, called back to the base early by the Colonel, and she watched as the jeep drove away. Its lights were still dimmed but they would not be for much longer if the rumour was correct, but Helen knew that this did not mean that the war was almost over.

She looked down the road, following the path of the jeep,

253

knowing that the recall meant he.was flying and that night she
lay and cursed the clearing skies.

CHAPTER 17

The Sergeant woke Ed with a 04.00 call. He had slept and dreamt of Helen laughing up at him from the snow and he swallowed hot coffee quickly before walking through to the briefing room. He wouldn't think of Chris lighting the Advent candle tonight, he wouldn't think of the stockings on the bottom of his bed because there was a whole goddamn day to get through first and many miles to fly.

The Colonel told them that the weather had at last improved enough for air support in the Ardennes. That there was to be a combined attack on enemy airfields along the Rhine and other targets in support of the troops being pounded and pressed by von Rundstedt's offensive. They were given their route and the weather report and Ed lounged back as the others were doing because losses were light now and they should act relaxed.

He drove with two other officers on to the airfield, the wheels spinning on the hard packed snow of the verge.

'For Christ's sake, driver, let's get to the ships at least before we take a fall,' Bob Tucker said, chewing gum, rubbing his fingers together as he always did before a mission.

Ed grinned. 'Take it easy, Bob, you might end up with a sprained wrist and have the day on base.'

Bob laughed, throwing his head back and slapping his leg. He was over-reacting, too nervous, but then weren't they all? It helped them stay alive.

Ed was dropped at the *Emma Lou*. He felt the sweat start on his hands as he walked beneath her wing. The *Emma B* had blown up over Hanover with a new crew. The pilot of the *Emma Lou* had completed his twenty-five missions and, except for Marco from the *Emma B* who had been grounded for months, this was a new crew fresh from the States he was taking up, poor buggers. Poor damn buggers, Ed thought as he smiled at them, tipping his hand to his cap, thinking how alike they looked in their heavy cumbersome sheepskin jackets with gum rolling from one cheek to the other, helmets dangling from their hands. He wouldn't tell them until they were airborne that they had been assigned the Purple Heart Corner.

He handed out their packets of money, maps, survival rations. Joking, chatting, not remarking on the shaking hands which took them from him, hoping that his own weren't trembling. He took a look around the airfield, the ground crew in coveralls and fatigue caps were hanging around; the sky was pink where the sun was rising. Helen would be up by now, stirring meal and potato peelings for the hens.

He looked at the other bombers lined up, enormous, powerful, and then up at the sky again. Just get these kids back, he ground out to the Fortress, then grinned at his men. `

'OK. Let's get in.'

Ed checked the instruments with Barney, his co-pilot, then used his hands palm up on the throttles. This old lady was heavy like the *Emma B*, but balanced. Yeah, she was pretty well balanced. The sound was deafening as the engines turned over then caught and held, and he saw the ground crew clutch their caps as winds swept across the deck. He tipped his fingers to them through the cockpit window knowing that as the *Emma Lou* took off these men would drift back to the Nissen huts whose walls were covered with pictures of half naked women. Here they would play cards and shoot crap with only half their minds because the other half would be up here with the *Emma Lou* until she came back – or didn't.

The flare had gone up and they were taxi-ing now. He adjusted his helmet, the throat speaker and earphones, taking off half a minute after *Juliet*; tucking in behind and climbing as she did, following in position to the assembly point, then on to rendezvous with the squadrons from other fields until turning back on themselves in tight formation, safe in their own airspace for now, then out and over the Channel.

'Let's keep looking, guys.' Ed spoke over the intercom. 'The Mustangs are with us so that's a help but we need your eyes, always, every minute. I want to get you home to your hearths, remember, and I'm kinda old myself and need my pipe and slippers at the end of the day, not a dose of cold hard snow.'

He listened to the laughter, then checked the tail turret, and young Eriksson who looked as though he should still be in high school. The waist gunners checked out well, they were running through their guns. Ted in the top turret was fine and the nose too.

'You OK, Marco?' He smiled to hear the familiar voice reply, 'Great, skip. Fancy a little outing today but get us back, this is my twenty-fifth.'

Ed heard groans from the others and laughed, always looking to left and right but he'd picked up the escorts now, Mustangs who could fly at 440 mph and make Berlin and back. He did not think of the men who would still be here if they'd only had those little beauties earlier.

'OK, you guys, you'll get there one day,' he laughed into the intercom but knew that the life expectancy of a bomber was only twenty-one missions, so where did that put its crew? Maybe the war would be over by then. Maybe. His hands were steady on the controls and he could feel the vibration, smell the leather, the gasoline. The formation hadn't lifted to a higher altitude over the coast because there was no flak any more now that it was in Allied hands.

Ed relaxed his shoulders and glanced at Barney who said, 'Kinda quiet, eh, skip?'

Ed smiled. 'Sure is.' He wouldn't tell the kids the position they were flying in. What was the point?

He said again into the throat speaker, 'Just keep your eyes busy. Remember that.'

The formation was rising now, up to 25,000 feet, out of range of enemy guns because they were getting pretty close to the drop zone, Ed reckoned. It would be cold for the guys in the rest of the ship.

'Get your oxygen masks on,' he ordered. 'We're going up. Give me a post, Marco.'

'I reckon on another thirty minutes to target, skip.'

They flew on and he knew the crew would be huddled into their jackets and flexing their hands in gloves which made their fingers clumsy but stopped frost-bite. Did they know that if they were hit their blood would freeze as it hit the air? But Ed jerked his head, concentrating on the sky, the instruments, anything rather than staying inside his head because he was being crazy. They had been told losses would be light, hadn't they?

257

'So how many more missions have you got to do?' Barney asked, his eyes to the left and right, up and down. His voice was high with tension.

Ed shrugged. 'A few.'

'Yeah, but how many?'

'This guy's done thirty-two.' Marco's voice came in over the earphones.

Barney turned and stared. 'Thirty-two, but you could be home.' There was disbelief in his voice.

'Couldn't bear to leave us could you, skip?' Marco called.

'Something like that. Now keep on looking.'

It had been Helen he hadn't been able to leave, but she would never know he had volunteered for a second tour.

'Give us a post then, Marco.'

'Five minutes to target, skip.' Marco's voice was sharper now.

'Bombardier, you with us?' Ed's voice was crisp. He followed the squadron in tight formation.

'Right there, skip. Hold her steady.' But there was gunfire now from the ground and the ship lurched as a shell exploded nearby.

'Jesus,' Eriksson shouted. 'Jesus.' He was frightened, Ed could hear it in his voice.

He held on to the controls, feeling the sweat break out as it always did.

'OK, Eriksson. It's OK. Just keep looking.'

He was over the target, dropping the bombs, and there had been no air attack and the ground fire had been light. So far, no Focke-Wulfs swarming, no ME109s.

He pulled out and away, keeping in tight. 'OK, guys, we're on our way home. I guess maybe this is going to turn into a milk-run.' He was still looking and listening, up, down, left, right because they could still come, and they did, ten minutes later, roaring down on them, breaking away so close Ed could see the German in the cockpit.

The Mustangs were fighting too, but the Germans were getting through, again and again stabbing at his corner.

'Jesus, skip. I got one.' Eriksson was screaming. 'I got one.'

Ed cut in sharply. 'Keep looking, Eriksson. There'll be others.'

The Focke-Wulfs kept coming in on a pursuit curve, but this

time Ted in the top turret sent one spinning down in flames but still they kept coming from three thousand feet ahead and one thousand above, coming in fast before rolling and firing.

One passed, streaming thick dark smoke. Was he hit or was it just the synthetic fuel made out of coal and God knows what that the Germans were using? Ed didn't know, didn't have time to think because the guns were started up from below and he was falling back from formation.

'Come on, you bitch,' he ground out, pushing at the throttles, the controls, pulling up again and so far she wasn't hit but Eriksson was screaming, always screaming, and it wasn't because he had scored a hit, it was because he had just screamed that his arm had been torn off, for Christ's sake.

Ed shook his head. For God's sake, how could you think? He had a plane to get back but there was the screaming and the black smoke to fly through, the fighters to avoid and the fear to push away.

He hauled on the controls as another 109 flashed across in front, firing, and he felt the *Emma Lou* judder. She was hit but would she burn?

Barney called out. 'Number one engine's been hit, Ed.'

Christ! 'It's OK. I got her,' Ed said, still hearing Eriksson's screams, but there was no fire.

'Where are the Mustangs for Pete's sake?' Marco called out.

But they were there, fighting, turning, firing, but there were so many Germans. Didn't they know they'd lost the goddamn war? Now Eriksson was no longer screaming but voices were babbling and shouting and Ed called, 'Get off the intercom.' He must hear the orders coming through from the group. An ME109 was coming straight in, his nose cone pointing straight at him, his guns firing and the *Emma Lou* juddered again and now number two engine was windmilling and burning.

'Feather it,' Ed snapped to Barney and he did.

The *Emma Lou* was heavy now and he was fighting to hold her even, fighting to close the gap between him and the Shark in front but he was losing speed and altitude.

Frank, the radio operator called through. 'I got Ted here, upper turret empty now, he's hurt but not bad, the blood's frozen.'

'OK. Throw a spare jacket over him.' Ed's voice was firm, though his hands were trembling, and all he could see and hear were ravens coming, again and again, but they weren't ravens, they were planes, so for Christ's sake, snap out of it.

He did. Barney was swearing, long streams of words which he repeated again and again. There was an explosion amidships and the *Emma Lou* hesitated, shuddered, hit by cannon fire, but then carried on. The waist gunners were still firing, he could feel their vibration, see the tracers spitting into fighters but it was not enough, and now bits of his wing had been shot away and the ship was careening from side to side as another fighter streaked past.

'Give me a post, Marco. Give me a post,' Ed shouted.

There was no answer.

'For Christ's sake give me a post.'

Marco spoke then, his voice was weak. 'Four minutes to the sea, skip.' He gave him the course.

'You OK?'

Marco laughed but it was faint. 'That shell got a bit familiar, the bitch.'

Ed gripped the throttle. 'Hang on, kid. I'm getting you back. It's your last one. Trust me.'

Number three engine was spluttering and the *Emma Lou* was fighting him, swaying, but he held her firm, talking to her as though she were a mare, and now they were over the sea at last and the Focke-Wulfs and the ME109s were gone but the Mustangs stayed with them, waggling their wings to indicate that they would stay with *Emma Lou* until she made it, or didn't. She was losing height and her speed was still decreasing.

But land was in sight and Barney did a count of dead and injured and Ed listened on the intercom. Maybe Eriksson was dead, there was no answer. Marco, Frank injured.

The *Emma Lou* was lower now and he didn't know if he could get her back. Some of them must be saved at least.

'You guys that can, bale out.' He nodded at Barney. 'You too. Get out. Now.'

He didn't look as Barney left, but fought to keep the ship up because he still had Marco and Frank. Maybe he could do it but the fighters were still with them and they were indicating that he had no undercarriage and he waved as they flew past, not showing what he felt. He was cool and calm because he had to be. For Christ's sake, he had to be. Number three engine was struggling but the prop was still turning. The ship was yawing and he corrected her, just. Swearing, he kept her on course, checking the compass, seeing the fields too close, too goddamn low. He eased her up, feeling the drag pulling the wing round, but he fought back, careful not to stall. The airfield was ahead now.

The bombers were all down, all on their hard standing but the crews would not be debriefing, they would be there, waiting, watching, but he didn't think he was going to make it and he hoped to God there was no fuel left because he didn't want to burn.

The Mustangs were above him now.

'You OK, Marco, Frank?'

'Just fine and dandy, boss,' Marco said but his voice was very faint.

'We've no undercarriage. Just hang on, and I'll bring you in safe.' But would he? He was so tired and his arms were shaking. His mouth was dry, so dry.

The ship was yawing again and he had to bring her straight. She was low and slow, the engine still spluttering, and now he could see the ambulances hurtling from behind the tower, out to the end of the runway but he couldn't hear the siren because of the wind in the plane, the cracking of the fuselage, the spluttering of number three engine. She was lurching in over the tree tops, and he reached to put down the landing gear, but then stopped, because there was none there.

He brought her down on the runway then and he felt the drag on that goddamn wing, saw it tip then right itself, and then tip again, catching, tearing. He heard such noise, such noise as he had never thought existed, and then the plane flipped over and he saw the ground come up to crush the cockpit and for a moment he felt the pain, but only for a moment.

Helen was home, standing by the sink unable to work because she was so cold, suddenly so cold. She put the potatoes back into the water, then turned and stood quite still. She stood like that, just looking at the Advent candles, the tree which stood surrounded by presents, watching as Laura and Chris laid the table and looked at her, their eyes masked, uncertain. Then the jeep came.

They all heard the knocking at the door but Helen insisted

on answering because she knew who it would be and in a quiet voice the Colonel told her that the *Emma Lou* had crash-landed, that Marco and Frank were injured but that Ed had been hurt too, so badly hurt that the medics did not know how long he would survive.

Helen reached for her coat and looked at Laura, telling her to stay with Chris, and then she left, out into the starlit night. She felt the air harsh in her lungs and breathed it in and out, in and out, but then it changed into the thick leather warmth of the car. She sat back and breathed and counted and looked up at the stars and the moon and knew that she and Ed should not have thought of the future.

She didn't cry, she couldn't cry because he wasn't going to die. He was her husband and he couldn't die. But he might if she cried.

She sat, holding one hand with the other, squeezing, hurting, but not allowing the tears to come, or the hoarse voice to be heard. It must stay inside to tear jagged into her mind but it must not escape because the raven of the gods might hear, and lead them to him. No she must not cry or call because then he might be found.

They drove up to the largest Nissen hut at the field hospital at Little Odbury air base. The roadways were filled with jeeps, command cars, ambulances, MPs and a plane flew in low overhead to land. Men were rushing but not running and Helen wondered if she was going mad.

The Colonel pushed his way through the men and soldiers who stood in lines or wandered about, looking shocked, tired. He spoke to a corpsman who pointed to the far door, giving directions. They hurried from one hut to another but could not find him. In and out, from darkness to light, from cold to warmth and he could be dead while they walked like this.

'He could be dead,' she shouted at another corpsman who had shaken his head when McDonald was mentioned, pointing to yet another hut.

The Colonel took her arm. 'It's going to be OK. He's in the next one, I'll bet you.' But he wasn't and neither could they find Marco or Frank.

They pushed back to the clerk behind the main desk who told them that all three had been transferred to the Winton Hospital near Norwich.

They drove for what seemed like hours, picking out the white line along the side of the road when it existed and now the darkness inside her head was lifting and just despair remained. They passed through a village and saw the lighted church, the stained glass windows illuminated for the first time since war began but it meant nothing to her, not now.

It was two a.m. before they arrived and then they followed the nurse down a long ward, hearing her shoes squeaking on the waxed floor and the groans and breathing of the shapes behind the white screens which surrounded each bed. A nurse came out from one and a doctor from another and others were busy too. Ed was in the end bed, near the double doors and the sister's desk so that he was never beyond her hearing.

Helen stopped and looked as the nurse eased back the screens and she was counting again, breathing in and out; one, two, three, four. His head and body were bandaged but his hands were the same, lying still, so still on the sheets. She sat on the chair, holding his fingers.

'Falling from more trees, my darling,' she said and though her voice was steady tears were coursing down her face. His fingers squeezed hers but his eyes did not open.

She stayed all night and the next day and the next, refusing to be moved until the X-rays showed no broken spine but two cracked vertebrae and a broken leg. And head injuries.

She didn't know for another week whether he was going to be brain damaged, blind or crippled and so she could only sit by his bed, holding his hand, talking of Greater Mannenham, of the snow which was deep and cold, of the hoar frosts, and all the time she did not know if he heard her. She didn't think of the gods they had challenged, or the man in the wheelchair by the Cambridge river. She thought of Ed tossing hay, playing baseball, and gripped the sheet but not his hands. These she stroked calmly and never cried when she sat with him.

The doctor came to her as she left the room at the end of the first week in January, taking her into the office, sitting down behind the desk, steepling his hands as he smiled and told her that there would be no lasting physical damage but perhaps there would be trauma, though war had a habit of producing that anyway.

Helen went to the room she had taken in the local inn, climbed the stairs and sat by the window, not drawing the

263

curtains across because she wanted to see the snow, so clean and white like his bandages were. She wanted to feel the cold air and opened the window. Her breath puffed out in the crisp night. He was not going to die. She wanted to shout it out for the world to hear because this time the man she loved was not going to die.

On 9 January the Battle of the Bulge was over and the Germans were being squeezed out of their Ardennes salient and Helen had to sit by his bed, holding his hand tightly, and tell him that Marco had died of his injuries.

He cried and she stayed until he slept but then had to return home because she had to be up as usual at five-thirty to begin work at the farm.

Ed lay in the dark when she had gone, still unable to feel his feet or move them, but it was of Marco he thought, killed on his twenty-fifth mission and that night he had a dream of blood on his face, dried blood which would not scrape off even though he rubbed it against his shoulder. The nurse came and soothed him, asking who Joe was. He had almost forgotten but he dreamt the same dream the next night and this time the blood was all over him and it wasn't Joe's blood, it was all those people who had been beneath his bombs and the nurse came again, but he only wanted Helen and she came when the hospital called her.

In February he was transferred to a recuperation hospital in Scotland and was able to write to his father that at last he had seen the country where their ancestors came from and it was very like the valley in Montana where they lived.

From 13 to 15 February Dresden was bombed by the Allies when it was full of refugees. Hundreds of thousands died and Ed lay listening to the news of the raid, glad that he was lying here with pain coursing through his body because at least that particular guilt was not added to the load he already bore and which was heavier than anything else had ever been.

Helen wrote every day to Ed before cycling to work through a winter which was harder than any she remembered. Her hands were numb before she had left the village, her breath was frozen in the scarf which she wound round her nose and mouth. In March the Allies crossed the Rhine and now, when Chris asked if the war was nearly over she said, 'Yes, my darling.'

In the middle of March Ed was shipped back to the United States to convalesce and she travelled to Liverpool to catch a glimpse before he sailed, but the train was held up for troop movements and so she missed him and had to stand, watching the stern of the ship and its wake, feeling the cold, remembering Heine who had left from here too. She was alone again.

CHAPTER 18

The trip back on the troop ship would take ten long days, Ed had been told as he hauled himself up the gangway, a corpsman following close behind, but he would not go on a stretcher. He was going to walk out of England as he had walked into it.

He looked over his shoulder all the time but she didn't come. Helen didn't come. He eased himself down into the bowels of the ship, feeling the heat, the stench of illness and lay on a bunk in a converted hospital ward filled with bunks. Men lay groaning, swearing or were silent and Ed looked up at the base of the bunk above him. She hadn't come.

He felt the heave of the ship as they met open water and the pain in his back from his cracked vertebrae grew worse and his leg throbbed though it was out of plaster. A corpsman came round to each bunk checking pulse and blood pressure and it was good to feel fingers on his wrist and a voice saying, 'You're doing just fine, Major. Be home real soon.'

But he didn't want to go Stateside. He wanted to be with her.

Doctors were on call all day and all night and as the pain grew worse and the throbbing of his leg drowned out the vibration of the engines and the roll of the dice as three men shot crap, they gave him morphine.

'But not much, Major. Just enough. Don't want you getting too fixed on this.' The doctor smiled, holding the syringe to the lights, easing up the plunger, expelling the air.

'I seemed to be getting better, Doc,' Ed said, his voice tight from pain. 'So what the hell is happening?'

The doctor swabbed his arm, inserting the needle. 'Everything's going just swell, Major. It's those roads you had to use to get to the docks in Liverpool.' He grinned, pressing in the plunger. 'Got themselves a few pot-holes I guess, knocked everything about a bit. It'll settle, don't you worry.'

'Hey, Doc, there's a man here bleeding from his goddamn nose.' The voice was urgent, frightened, and the doctor moved quickly, dropping the empty syringe into the enamel kidney bowl the corpsman held. Ed heard voices, murmurs and always the groans, and then there was nothing.

When he woke the pain was better even though the ship was lurching and bucking and as the days passed he was able to ease himself from the bunk and, with a Captain who had lost a hand flying a bitch of a Fortress, he inched along the deck, feeling the lash of the wind, watching the other ships steaming with them, noting the zig-zag course.

The Captain handed him a Lucky Strike and put one in his own mouth but Ed lit the match because Captain John Bryan still held the pack and he only had one goddamn hand, hadn't he? It was good to be with a flyer, to ease into chairs and look out on to big seas which broke and sprayed the deck; to look out and see no planes, no wind socks, no bombed houses, to hear no dawn roar of departing planes.

He sucked on his cigarette, drawing the nicotine deep into his lungs, feeling its heat. He expelled his breath, seeing it whipped away. There was no reason for them to talk much because they had both felt the same fear and pain as their Fortresses were hit. They both remembered the judder and the stagger and understood the darkness in one another's eyes.

They ate a plateful of food in the canteen which would fill six stomachs in the villages they had flown over and John told him of the girl he had met but would not marry because his high school sweetheart was waiting in Arizona.

Ed told him of Helen, whom he had married. He cut up John's steak, grinning when his buddy said they would make a good team.

'I'll be your legs, cling on to that mare back in Montana, you can hold the reins,' John said, eating relish on its own. 'Gee, it's going to be good to get back.'

Ed shook salt on his meat, seeing the blood ooze from the rare steak. 'But do you reckon they'll understand?'

It was hours later that John replied. They were sitting in on a poker game, the two of them playing one hand; John holding the cards, Ed slapping them down.

'I guess Ruby won't know what the last two years have been

267

like. I've changed. I don't know if we'll make it. Maybe I should have brought my village girl back, she knows what it's all about I guess,' John said.

He said nothing more and the smoke was heavy in the room off the end of the ward. It stung Ed's eyes and he narrowed them, checking the cards, raising the stakes until they lost and then they walked around the deck, slowly because he was still limited in his movement.

They knew there were clouds above them because they could see no stars and there was only darkness around them because the blackout was still in force on this sea crossing.

John lifted his head, pushing back his hair with his stump. 'You see, I get these dreams. Ruby won't know why.'

Ed flicked his cigarette over the side, leaning on the rail, feeling it digging into his flesh. The Captain had told them they would be passing the Statue of Liberty at 07.00 hours but he didn't want to arrive and be in a country where no one would know how he felt, how John felt, how the thousands of draftees were going to feel.

But he did arrive and was flown by transport plane which rattled and bucked, bouncing into the nearest airfield in a way that Ed would never have allowed from any of his young flyers. And his pop was there, grey and strong, his stetson pulled down, his eyes the same clear blue. But his mom had been crying, her face was puffed and her lips swollen. They hadn't changed, but he had. Jesus Christ, he had. He wanted Helen, he thought, as he felt his mother's arms around his neck.

They drove through the dry cold air of late March. He sat near the window of the pick-up looking out across the space which England did not possess. Seeing the mountains which were his home but not really his home because Helen wasn't here. He looked up at the peaks and missed the flatness which was East Anglia. He didn't speak because he didn't know what to say to these people who were his parents but whom he hadn't seen for three years, three long strange years. They drove into Little Fork, driving past the wood-fronted stores which looked like something from the cowboy westerns which Chris sat and watched at the cinema. He missed the boy, he missed his wife.

Ma Benson was on the corner of the drug store, Ma Benson who had bounced him on her knee and who was now waving the Stars and Stripes as the pick-up approached. His pop slowed, then stopped and Ed wound down the window.

'Gee, it's great to have you home, boy,' Ma Benson said, kissing his cheek. She still smelt of lavender water. Some things never change and now Ed smiled.

'It's kind of good to be back, Ma,' he said.

The ranch was the same, just the same, and Ed lay in bed, looking at his curtains which still had the ink mark he had splashed across when he was sixteen and trying out his new pen.

The stars were bright and the moon too, throwing its light down on to the snow which Helen would not be able to believe was so deep, so hard, so cold. His leg and his back were hurting and it kept him awake all night and he was glad because he did not want to sleep.

That week he received her letter.

Greater Mannenham

My darling Ed,

I missed you. I travelled all the way but I missed you. The journey back was so bleak without a last look at your face, a last feel of your hand in mine.

It won't be long before I come. Let's just see this war out first. You will be home and in your own bed by now with your own people around you. I hope that you are feeling better and that you can relax but I fear there will be a gulf between you all, at least for a while. Be patient. You've come from a strange war world and you go back to something which has not been touched like Europe. Remember, though, that they will have had their changes. Boys will have gone, hearts will have been broken, even if buildings are not crushed and rations reduced as ours have been.

Get well, my love. That is all that is important. And try to forget all that has passed.

I love you, I love you.

Helen.

For the first two weeks Ed sat in a chair in his bedroom,

wanting the small room around him because it made him feel safe but now at last he was sleeping at night though his dreams woke his mom. He knew that they did because she came in and sat with him, but he wanted Helen because she knew where he had been.

In the third week he walked downstairs and sat by the lounge stove, listening to the crackle of the wood and the sound of the wind. The generator was cranking up, his father said on Friday evening, and Ed nodded but what did it matter? It always cranked up.

By the middle of April the pain was easing enough to push to one side and he walked around the ranch, but he was still so goddamn stiff, he murmured to his mother.

'I know, Ed. It's a plain nuisance and you must be plumb tired out. Shall I get you something from Doc Mathers for the dreams?'

He looked at her as she walked along the path to the creamery. There was mud everywhere, it had come with the spring thaw as it did every year. Did nothing change over here?

'There's nothing he can give me that would help. It was different over there, Mother, you see. We killed people, not cattle. People.' His voice was hard. 'And they tried to kill us.'

Her eyes were shocked and she moved ahead and he was sorry and caught at her hand. 'I'm sorry, Mom. I guess I can't quite get used to being back. It'll take a bit of time.'

'I know. I try to understand,' she said, taking some butter from the wooden ledge inside the damp building which his father had built when Ed was only ten.

'Business could be a whole lot bigger, you know, boy,' His father said as they ate turkey in the well heated kitchen that night. 'It's shipment that's the problem. That train takes so damn long, winding through the country, changing at Chicago. Anyone would think we hadn't got a living to make.'

There was half a turkey left on the platter and bacon too. It was too much, too damned much. Ed looked at the stove and there was too much damned heat. He looked out of the window at the buildings which were the same as the ones he had left before the war. There were no smouldering ruins, no wrecked Fortresses or Spitfires in the fields.

Ed couldn't eat any more. 'Some people over in England

aren't concerned with making a living, they just have a lot of dying to do. Don't you folks ever think of that?'

He got up, knocking his chair to one side. His back was painful tonight. He pushed from the room, climbing the stairs. He stood by his bedroom window, looking up to the mountains. It would be peaceful up there. Helen would like it. He gripped the curtains, the ink mark was dark against his hand and he wished he was sixteen again and not the old man he now was. He gripped the material so tightly that it ripped and he didn't care, he tore again and again, shredding it, wanting to wipe out the months and the years which had made him old and frightened.

His father knocked on the door but he didn't answer, just leaned his head against the window, feeling the cold, seeing the strips of curtain in his hands.

His father knocked again and came in and stood next to his son and now Ed turned to him and saw the face which had always been good and kind, the body which had always been bigger than his and still was and he moved and pressed his head against his pop's shoulder and cried as he had not done since he was twelve years old.

His father held him, rocking him backwards and forwards as he had done years ago, stroking the back of his son's neck which was still the same as that young child's and he didn't let him see the tears in his own eyes for the boy who would never be the same again.

They sat and talked into the night because Pop had heard the screams and had lain awake alongside his wife, holding her hand until the morning, grieving but impotent. Arthur McDonald told Ed how grey paint had been painted over the gold leaf dome of the Massachusetts State House on Beacon Hill in Boston three months after Pearl Harbor so that it was less conspicuous in the event of enemy bombardment. He told him how black paint was painted over the gold leaf roof of the Federal Building so it would not gleam beneath the moon and attract enemy submarines in American waters and they both laughed, gently.

He put his hand on his son's shoulder as they sat side by side on the bed, filling the ashtray with half smoked stubs, drinking Scotch from the flask which Arthur had filled and brought up with him.

271

'So forgive us for not understanding. We are trying,' he said.

He went on to say how German U-boats had prowled up and down the East Coast from Canada to the Gulf of Mexico and the Caribbean sinking tankers and freighters sailing for Britain with guns, tanks and planes. Many were sunk. Ma Benson's neighbour's son was drowned that way. There was no longer a star in her window.

Ed nodded, knowing that his mother had removed the one which had been in theirs when he returned home.

'The war has touched us in that way and in others. We have interned the Japanese. Their houses have been vandalised or sold for a pittance but we have allowed their sons to be drafted to die and fight for America.'

Arthur stubbed out his cigarette, grinding it down until the remaining shreds of tobacco stood out stark against the black.

'You see, Ed. War does strange things to people. On the one hand it gives them opportunities. Gee. Just think of the women who have been taking over the factory jobs, working alongside men, showing their worth. On the other hand war also brings despair. Think of the Little Fork families whose boys died on D-Day on Omaha. It does touch us but not as it has touched you. We feel for you. We love you but we cannot understand because your fear hasn't been ours.'

He rose then, leaving the flask with his son, hoping that tonight he would sleep. But he didn't, he lay away loving his father, his mother too, but it wasn't just fear. It was guilt, and how could they understand that, because they had never had to kill.

He was in town when the latest draftees left Little Fork. He stood on the sidewalk watching the crowd gathering outside the hotel where the kids ate breakfast – their last small town breakfast. He leaned on his stick watching the High School band falling into position and then the colour guard from the American Legion. As the boys, for that is what they were, he thought bitterly, came out of the hotel they lined up and the head of the draft board called, 'Forward march.'

Ed stood still as the kids marched down the street heading for the railroad station where the crowd gathered again. Ed walked along now, stiffly and silently, watching the parents forming tightly round their sons. Hugs were given, long strong hugs, and then the train came in and as they boarded the band played the Marine Hymn, as though it was a game, for God's sake.

Ed walked back to the pick-up, forgetting the stores his mom had asked him to buy from the grocery store, thinking only of the kids leaving, so young and fresh. Some would die, some would survive and not be scarred. Some would survive and have to fight to try to come to terms with the things they had done and seen. Would they make it? Would he?

He wrote to Helen that night, knowing that it would be a long wait until she came because he had heard from John in Arizona that he was going to marry this English girl instead and there would be no official ships until months after the war had finished and who knew when that would be? It was now March 1945 and even if there was victory in Europe, what about Japan? Would he have to fight again in the Pacific?

He put his pen down and reached for the flask he had filled in Little Fork and longed for Helen and for peace.

CHAPTER 19

Helen was planting beet when Hitler shot himself in a bunker at the end of April as the Allies swept through Berlin. The Germans in Italy had surrendered the day before. She sat in the garden that evening, seeing the hedge in bud and the apple trees in the orchard, watching her son and Mary practising pitching and batting, hearing the thud of the ball on the bat, their shrieks. They were slim – everyone was slim – because food had not been plentiful for the last six years but what there was had been equally shared and that was good.

She turned as Laura came out, wiping her hands on her apron.

'I shall miss you so, when you go, my dear,' Laura said.

'I can't imagine what it is going to be like to leave and so I just think of today,' Helen replied, looking out over the fields at the back.

'It'll be great,' Chris tossed back at them over his shoulder. 'It'll be just great.'

Mary pulled a face. 'Huh, when I come out to see you you'll be all American and sit there chewing gum.'

'Over my dead body,' Helen called and they laughed and so, for another day, Helen pushed the thought of leaving from her head though she could hardly bear to live without Ed for much longer.

The next week they heard of Belsen and Buchenwald and the millions of dead and the village was loud in its hatred of Germany again and Helen was quiet but wondered where Frau and Herr Weber were but Chris did not want to talk of them, or think of them now, he said, or ever again. Helen spoke to him, saying he was half German, saying that not all Germans had done this but he turned to her.

'I'm going to be American. I'm Ed's son.'

Helen knew that one day, she would have to bring Heine's son back to him but for the moment she did not know how.

On 1 May she received a letter from Montana.

My darling,
You would be pleased if you could see me. I'm getting about great. My folks send the enclosed affidavit saying that they are prepared to take financial responsibility for you if necessary. I guess I can see your face getting red and sassy but don't let it, this is just to support your application. I know you have my own affidavit and your money over here, and they do too, but I don't want anything going wrong at the last minute.

I'm getting real impatient to see you but it's not over yet and there's Japan still. I guess too that you'll have to wait for a while for passage. We were all shocked when Roosevelt died. It seemed wrong somehow for him not to see the end of this great mess and not even to know that Hitler killed himself. I long for you, so much. I need you. You just don't know how much I need you.

Ed.

On 8 May an announcement was given out on the wireless that on VE-Day all work would cease for two days and a party was held in the village when people danced and wept and could not believe that it was over.

There had been no blackout since April and at the air base searchlights swept the sky and fireworks soared up into the air as they stood on the green and watched. GIs then came into the village, screaming their jeeps to a halt, whirling the women off their feet and kissing them.

The Colonel shared his brandy with Helen, sitting on the benches which had been put up that afternoon, laughing and joking until she asked about Japan and then he said, nodding at the young Americans, 'They are happy tonight but they're scared they'll be sent to the Pacific. I hope your Ed will be spared that.'

Helen, Chris and Laura didn't leave the party until dawn was breaking and then they strolled back, streamers hanging round their necks, and as Helen fell into bed she thought of Ed, of Heine, of Roger the vicar who had died in March, of Marian whose Rob was home, and it all seemed much longer than six years.

On 6 and 9 August atomic bombs were dropped on Hiroshima and Nagasaki. On 14 August Japan surrendered and Helen knew that Ed would never have to fight again but she also knew that those who had survived would never be the same as they were before.

It was not until 1 March 1946 that she received notification from the United States Army that she would need to produce a British passport, two copies of her birth certificate, two copies of any police record, her original marriage certificate, three photographs on thin paper with light background, evidence showing that on arrival in the United States she would have a railroad ticket or enough money to buy one and finally two pounds or ten dollars to cover her visa fee. It told her that she would be notified any day now of her passage to the United States and would be expected to proceed to a collecting camp at Tidworth because the hotel in Bournemouth where mothers with older children normally stayed was full.

Helen went with Laura and Chris to Norwich, thinking only of today, not thinking of the collecting camp at Tidworth, not thinking of the North Atlantic or the land it led to. She bunched her fists and blinked at the flashlight, knowing the photographer had the lighting set up badly. She withdrew ten pounds cash for America and transferred her bank account to the one Claus used in America. On the train home she looked out at England and could hardly bear it, but Ed was over there and she loved him.

In the middle of March she and Chris received luggage labels for their ship and were asked to proceed to Tidworth for processing on 18 March. They were allowed to take one small suitcase each and one trunk which could be sent separately. She fingered the paper, folding it again and again while Chris whooped and ran down the road to tell Mary.

All that day Helen packed, her head down, folding, wrapping, not stopping to eat because she was not hungry.

276

She sat on the bed when she had finished, looking out of the window, and she cried for the country she was leaving, for Laura, for the years that had gone. She cried for Heine and for her mother, for the things that might have been, and slept then, until dawn.

On 18 March they travelled to London to meet a special train at Waterloo which would take them to Tidworth. As the train drew out of Norwich they leaned from the window and waved and waved until they could no longer see Laura and Mary and then she held Chris because he was thirteen now and felt he shouldn't cry but he couldn't help it and neither could he stop. Helen talked to him of the life they would have, of Mary who would come and of Laura, and at last he was silent and together they watched the countryside pass and Helen felt her heart breaking.

Lorries took the women and what children there were to the Wiltshire camp; it was late evening by the time they arrived. They were shown into huts which slept four to a room though Chris went to the service personnel barracks. He took his baseball mitt and ball and waved to Helen, then hid his face from her because he was crying again.

He looked round at the trees surrounding the camp, hemming him in, and dragged his sleeve across his eyes. The wool was coarse and scratched his skin. He wanted to stay with his mother but he was almost a man.

A GI showed him his bed and locker and asked about his girlfriend. He winked when Chris told him of Mary, pretending that he had kissed her, and now he put his shoulders back and rolled his feet like Ed as the Corporal took him back to the mess hut where a meal of pot roast and noodles was being served by German prisoners-of-war.

His mother waved and beckoned to the seat next to hers and they talked to the women either side, one of whom was trying to spoon-feed a toddler who pushed the food on to the floor. The mother cried and Chris watched as his mother took the spoon from her, gently pushing it into the child's mouth while a Red Cross helper led the woman from the room.

Talking and crying filled the hut, together with the scrape of cutlery on plates as people ate food they had forgotten existed because they were under the jurisdiction of the United States.

There were too many people here, Chris thought, that he di
not know, and Germans, those damned Germans, brushing hi
shoulder as they reached past him with food. Outside wer
great sweeps of chalk hills and he missed his home.

All night, in Helen's room, the babies cried in the cots whicl
had been constructed out of steel filing cabinet drawers, bu
she would not have slept anyway because her journey hac
begun and now there was no going back. Two of the womer
cried throughout the night and in the morning one left to gc
home to her mother.

All day Helen was interrogated along with everyone elsε
after she had surrendered her identity card, her ration book
and her clothing coupons and she felt that they were taking the
last of her country from her. She filled in a form nearly two feet
long and wanted to tear it up as she was required to answer
questions no one had any right to ask. Against the one asking
whether she intended to overthrow 'by force or violence' the
Government of the United States she nearly replied yes.

She was given a medical and had to stand in line with other
girls, waiting until it was her turn to have a torch shone
between her legs to check for venereal disease. Like the other
women she tried to ignore the American Army officers who
were standing along the walls watching and laughing.

Anger coursed through her but she said nothing because all
this was for Ed. She was given a smallpox vaccination and the
corpsman said that Chris would be given one too. She was
finger-printed in another room, as were the others, and the
smell of petrol was strong as the ink was wiped off with cotton
wool pads. She was leaving with Susan, another bride who was
married to a Naval Officer, when she was called back.

'Please return to the interrogation room, Mrs McDonald.'

Helen walked across the fresh spring grass, seeing the
moisture on her shoes, keeping her mind clear, knowing what
would be said.

'We would like to ask you some questions about your first
husband. It appears he was in prison over here.'

The officer's face was bland but his eyes were hard and
Helen sat down again, not letting him see the tension she felt,
but fearing that it was all going to start again and wondering if
there would ever be any peace.

For two days she was questioned and enquiries were made.

278

Those in her hut embarked on their ships on the fourth day, but she and Chris did not and she was told that there could be no guarantee that she would ever be allowed entry to the United States.

Helen insisted on an interview, and sat and talked reasonably for one hour to the bland-faced man but still he would not make any commitment and his voice was terse and dismissive when he spoke to her. It was then that she grew angry, standing up, banging the desk.

'My husband flew too many bloody missions. He is in Montana injured. I have a business in the States, pouring money into your Government's coffers. Heine Weber did nothing that was dishonourable and I was cleared by the tribunal. How dare you! How bloody dare you!'

He sat and looked at her, the colour rising in his cheeks. 'I suggest you calm yourself down, lady.'

'I suggest you pull your damn finger out. I didn't sit in a crypt while bombs fell or pull tops off beet to sit here while you shine your backside on that chair. Get on that telephone and sort it out.'

She stormed from the room, out into the March sun, then across to the recreation hut where the Red Cross were teaching seventeen-year-old mothers how to cope with babies they had not been alone with before. For the next three days she talked to the girls, helping them to change and feed, babysitting while they went to the movie house, listening while they talked of the men they had married and of whom they really knew nothing. She bought chocolate for Chris from the PX and he ate too much and was sick.

She didn't sleep because each day her clearance did not come. She hadn't told Chris because he hated the Germans too much already. She talked to the prisoners-of-war, hearing the guttural tongue, listening to the voices of worry and defeat from these draftees who were not Nazis. No news had reached them either from that broken, devastated land.

On Thursday when the sun was hot and long shadows sliced across the grass where Chris was playing baseball, a letter arrived from Ed, forwarded by Laura, and it was good to see his handwriting, to feel him close as she read his words.

February 1946

My dearest Helen,

The winter will be over by the time you get this. Our spring is so quick you would miss it if you blinked. But you will be here for the summer, thank God. It is so hot here, you won't believe it after little England. I had forgotten myself. It's so dry you see. You Britishers are going to have a shock when you finally come. I've been sorting the room and I hope you like it, honey. Maybe next year the new house will be finished.

Say, I've been hearing of this 'flying windmill' that's been developed over here. It's called a helicopter and looks quite something.

Mom tells me we had a bit of rationing Stateside, but I guess it's a tiny pimple, though not to her. She's been a mite short of sugar and you'd think the world had come to an end.

I do miss you so, your laughter, your anger, your Englishness, your soft skin. I'd better get on to something else quick, hey? How about a bit of American news? Did you know that we nearly lost our chewing gum in the war? Would we have won if we had, do you think?

Apparently the Wrigley guy had to put forward a case that chewing gum was essential to win the war if he wanted to continue in production, and he did, saying that it relieved the tension. So he was allowed to get his chicle from South American trees and ship it back on a war effort ticket. So, what do you think of that, Chris?

I just hope and pray you're here soon but you must be so sad at leaving, Helen. I love you for doing it. I need you. You don't know how much. I'm better but there are still bad times.

Ed.

Chris laughed when she read him the letter and so did Helen but inside she was knotted, and a headache never left the left-hand side of her forehead. Would clearance ever come through and were his dreams still bad or was it just his injuries? If so, it didn't matter so much because those would mend.

Helen's clearance came through quite suddenly. The bland-faced man wouldn't look at her as he gave it, just threw the paper on to the desk. She didn't say thank you because she hadn't survived a war to be grateful to people like him.

They boarded the ship in Southampton in the evening of 27 March hearing the gulls wheeling above them and all they could smell was engine oil, not salt. Helen and Chris carried a case each and took bags for the mothers with babies. They inched up the gangplank, seeing the oily water beneath them, setting their feet above the raised slat which was placed just too far to be taken in one stride and Helen did not look back because she was afraid that if she did she would leave the ship.

The chaplain waited on deck shaking each hand, and his smile was warm, his American accent familiar, and suddenly Helen wanted Ed, the slow smile, the arm about her. She wanted him to stand on the rail and help her leave England but there were others behind her and more in front and there was no time to think, only time to put one foot in front of the other, feeling her case dragging at her arm as she followed the other women who also did not look back.

The *Queen Elizabeth* was berthed alongside, large and splendid, casting shade across their smaller liner. A steward took Chris to the men's quarters and Helen followed a smiling Red Cross helper down the companionway into a room with thirty bunks, three high, and all were taken except for two on the top. The room was dense with the sound of nervous laughter, and stilted conversation as she unpacked, smiling at the girls around her, joining in with the ebb and flow of awkward sentences, pausing in the silences until she was shown the showers; semi-private stalls with the toilets further along the passageway. She returned in time to hear the message on the loudspeakers asking all brides to meet on the upper deck where dinner would be provided and informing them that they would sail at seven a.m. the next morning. She felt too old to be called a bride at thirty-three.

Chris was waiting by the door, talking of the steward who knew the knuckleball throw and was going to coach him and another boy, Tom, was going to Arizona. He was only twelve, and may he sit with him? And he was off before Helen could say yes or no. She laughed, looking at a woman who was in her room and whose eyes were red from crying; her blonde hair was swept back in a bun and her fragile face was beautiful.

They walked into the dining-room together, Helen grasped at anything to talk about while the other woman swallowed and fought her tears. She looked up at the painted ceilings evoking memories of past peacetime voyages and spoke of the history of the ship which she had read on the distributed printed sheet. She told Yvonne that when the *Nicholas* was a peacetime liner the passenger capacity was one hundred; when it was a troop ship it carried 2,200 and now it transported 530 brides and children.

Yvonne smiled and queued with her but neither was able to speak when they were handed a plate full of roast pork, mashed potatoes and succotash. They carried it to a table and ate the food too quickly because it was so good and there was so much. Frozen blackberries and cake made with sugar and fat followed. It was a luxury after rationing and their stomachs would only allow them a little. Helen hoped that Chris would remember the chocolate and be cautious. She looked around but he had already gone. Then there was bread and butter, jam, mustard, pickle, strong tea or coffee or cocoa.

Helen looked at the dark brown liquid, thinking of Laura straining the tea again and again and suddenly her tears came and now Yvonne talked to her, telling her that the trip should only take ten days or so an officer had said because the Captain would be following the shortest route. And so it went on all the night in the large room with thirty bunks full of women who doubted and wept but determined that they would go on.

In the morning the women lined the rails to see the ship leave, but Yvonne and Helen could not watch as England faded out of sight. Instead they stood with their faces into the wind, letting their hair whip back from their eyes, at last breathing in the fresh sea air as the ship steamed towards America.

At nine-thirty the brides were invited to a talk in the lounge about the ship and the voyage. They sat in chairs which were bolted to the floor in case of bad weather and here too the ceilings were ornate and there were gaps where chandeliers had once hung. The years of the war had soiled the walls and

282

Helen thought of the passengers who must have sat over cocktails, listening to music, playing cards, thinking their tomorrows would be the same forever. Where were they now? Were they the parents of the troops who had sailed across throughout the war? Where were those boys?

Seated later in the dining-room, looking through salt-streaked windows which showed a blue and balmy sea, they ate a lunch which Helen had dreamt of during the long years of rationing, and she wanted to be able to send some back to the village. Chris came running up to her afterwards, showing her the ball held between the thumb and first two joints of two fingers, telling her that it would not spin but turn, and that Ed would have to be sharp to hit that and then he was off again, his face red from the sun and the wind, his eyes bright.

Yvonne talked then of her husband who had been injured in the Ardennes offensive and was now at home in the Bronx. He had told her he lived in a mansion and Helen said nothing but later heard an officer telling her friend where the Bronx was. There were no mansions.

They were out into the Channel now and the feel of the sea was different; it moved the ship. Helen walked around the deck, unused to leisure, missing the feel of the ploughed earth beneath her feet, missing the sound of the birds and the snort of Rocket and the pony she and Chris had learned to ride in the past year in preparation for Montana.

She leaned on the rail, rising and falling with the ship, changing her weight from one foot to another, watching the sea running up against the sides and down. The waves chopped and broke, white froth breaking from their peaks. She looked up at the sky, feeling the weak March sun through the breeze, missing Ed, wanting him, wondering if the darkness inside his head was gone.

That evening they watched a film in the lounge after an early supper and then they slept for some of the night but girls were ill, clinging to their bunks though the sea was not rough, calling for their mothers because some were no more than seventeen and eighteen. Helen and Yvonne padded up and down, soothing, talking, bathing foreheads but the girls were still ill the next day. Sick call was extended and they were told to suck lemons. It didn't work, and Helen alternated between the girls and the deck, and Yvonne did too. They soothed the sick and then walked, then sat in deckchairs, talking of the blitz, the rationing, their families, but not yet of the future.

The girls in the bunks had no spare clothes left and so in the afternoon Helen washed and ironed and laughed with Yvonne over the thought that maybe it was better to be seasick. That afternoon the Red Cross gave out long-sleeved sweaters to supplement the meagre clothes that rationing and one suitcase had allowed them all, including the girls who lay on the bunks and who only wanted to die.

Helen wore slacks which Laura had made and pitched balls at Chris and Tom, the twelve-year-old and that night the clocks were put back one hour and they had 2,636 miles to go.

The next day the ship was rolling and the waves were fifteen feet high and no one was allowed on the open decks. The ship stopped for an hour for some repairs and they were told over the loudspeakers that they would be on the water for about twelve days, two more than expected. Helen groaned and so did Yvonne and soon they too were on their bunks wondering why they had ever come as the ship pitched and tossed. The lemons did not work for them either.

The storm eased in the night and the sun shone the next day, bouncing off the water into their eyes. They tap-danced in the lounge that afternoon in a class arranged by the Red Cross and Helen realised she hadn't laughed as she was doing for a very long time. She sang in the shower which was hot every night and a luxury she had forgotten existed and brewed tea for their room because they were allowed to do so now, after a general complaint that it was too long to last from five-thirty p.m. to seven a.m. without a drink. Bedtime was still eight-thirty, however, and surprisingly they slept.

On Sunday there was a church service in the lounge and there was turkey, asparagus and ice-cream for dinner but that afternoon there was another storm and the waves were eighteen feet high and grew worse during the night so that Yvonne was thrown from her bunk and landed on the floor, torn between laughing and crying. The clocks were put back again one hour and they now had 1,636 miles to go.

There was an orientation talk on food and clothing the next day and an emergency fire and lifeboat drill in the afternoon and one girl appeared in her towel straight from the shower and she danced in time to the slow hand clap.

On Monday fresh water was rationed because the journey was taking so long and purified water introduced. It tasted strange and Helen found it difficult to swallow.

They tap-danced again and now it was easier, though their next session and the movie had to be cancelled while the crew bored a hole through the lounge wall so that they could pump oil from one part of the ship to another because they were short of fuel due to the delays. They took the hose through the lounge and momentarily Helen saw the fire hoses again and heard the screams beneath the rubble, smelt the smoke and the darkness of the cellar beneath the shop, the arm into which she plunged the painkiller, the dark cupboard in her mother's house. She wanted Ed and went to her bunk so that she could lie in peace and remember him.

That evening it was announced the ship would travel at half speed to try and eke out the fuel or they would need to put in to Nova Scotia which would delay them even more. As it was, the arrival date was put back another day but there were only another 784 miles remaining. Now the girls were all up and some were visiting the hairdresser, pressing their good suits and dresses as the excitement rose.

Helen and Yvonne performed in a concert the next night, tap-dancing in the back row because they had only had two lessons. Helen did not sing but laughed and listened, eating mince pies after the show.

The next day there were only 523 miles to go and now Yvonne was quieter, twisting her ring and she spoke in a low voice to Helen of the lies Danny must have told, looking out on to the sea which was grey today, reflecting the sky and their mood.

At lunchtime the Red Cross gave out khaki towels for the showers because the women had only been able to pack one in the hand luggage they were allowed. There was a birthday party in the lounge for a bride who was twenty-one. Afterwards Helen sat in a deckchair listening to Chris talking of his friend, his batting action and Mary. She lay her head back and wondered what she would find in Montana, who she would find. Would it be the Ed she knew?

By Saturday there were only 200 miles to go and they were

all given a medical examination and the names of others going
to their states. Helen and Chris were the only ones travelling to
Montana. Excitement grew even higher on board. Women
with babies carried them around the decks, hugging them
tightly, talking into their necks, telling them of their daddies
their grandmothers. Helen listened and watched as joy, ther
anxiety, crossed their faces as they hugged their children to
them. She found Yvonne crying in her bunk, looking at the
photograph of her husband; so young, so handsome, and held
her but could offer no words of comfort because what could she
say? She felt so old suddenly, and when Yvonne slept she
walked the deck herself, calling in on Chris in his berth, staying
with him, watching his face, his hands, listening to his laugh
She reached across and touched his cheek and he did not draw
away but leaned his head against her hand looking at her, and
in his eyes too was joy and then anxiety. It was the same in
hers.

That night they went to bed, knowing that they were due to
pass the Statue of Liberty at six the next morning. The girls
whose husbands were meeting them at New York would leave
the ship first and Yvonne was quiet and said nothing, not even
to Helen.

At twelve-thirty that night it was announced over the
loudspeaker that they would be in sight of the Statue of Liberty
in half an hour. It woke no one because that night their
thoughts were too active to allow sleep. They threw on clothing
and rushed up on deck, seeing the lights in the distance, the
cars going along the road on Long Island. The Statue of
Liberty was floodlit and it seemed strange to Helen to see so
much light. The water was calm and oily black in the darkness
and all she could feel was the vibration of the ship and her own
uncertainty.

At four-thirty names were given out over the loudspeakers of
those whose husbands were waiting for them at New York and
although everybody had returned to their bunks they were not
disturbed because sleep had never been so far away. Those
leaving in the morning had red labels given to them and
Yvonne looked at hers, turning it again and again in her hand
and hardly ate her breakfast. Helen touched her hand but she
didn't look up and so she went on to the deck and stood at the
rails, watching the tugs coming to tow them in, staying there as

they berthed. She could see the Empire State Building immediately ahead and young men waiting behind a cordon, cheering and waving and she wondered which was Danny, with the smiling face and the black heart.

Chris joined her at the rail.

'It's all so big,' he said. 'I hadn't thought it would be so big.'

Helen nodded. 'It's a different world,' she replied, her voice quiet, still looking for Danny, but the faces were too indistinct, too far away. The clothes were a shock; no uniforms, just vivid shirts, warm jackets and trousers.

Only those who were being met in New York were allowed off the ship, the others had to stay until train reservations had been made but a tour of New York was organised for the next day. Helen nodded as Mrs Senton of the Red Cross told them this, but she was looking past her, at Yvonne who was waving to her from the head of the gangplank, her face white.

Helen ran through the other women and held her friend, pressing her address into her hand, telling her to come to her, to write if she needed help, and then she watched her walk down the gangplank, seeing her look over to the men and hesitate, try to turn, but another girl pushed her on. Helen watched as the other girls ran towards the cordon. There was only one woman walking and that was Yvonne and now Helen could see nothing more because her eyes were blurring and it was more than she could bear. And so she turned away, back to Mrs Senton. At least all the brides were entitled to a free return ticket.

It was quiet on board that night and she sat watching the movie flicker in the lounge, hearing the click of the projector and the laughter of the audience, but she was wondering how the Bronx would feel on a hot summer night with a man you had thought was someone else. Would Ed be someone else?

The next day they left the dockside in a coach to see the sights and drove through streets towering with skyscrapers which seemed to block out the light and would trap the heat. They drove round Radio City and wherever they went, Helen felt she had been there before, knowing that it was because of the movies she had watched on the ship.

They stopped outside a diner and she saw a road worker in unbuttoned shirt sitting next to a man in a business suit eating salami on rye, and knew that this mingling would not happen

287

in Britain and it was good to see it. Trucks hooted, whistles were blowing and buildings were being knocked down. There were police sirens, yellow cabs and cars, so many cars in the wide multi-laned streets and through the windows of the bus came the smell of gasoline, cigars, steam and restaurants. Helen leaned her chin on her hand, seeing people running down subways or clambering on to buses, so many people, so many different races and colours. She felt homesick for small streets, short buildings, trees and felt angry that here there were no gaps in the streets like rotten teeth. How could these people she had come to live amongst understand those who had survived? She wiped away her condensed breath from the window. How were Ed's parents understanding him?

When the coach returned to the ship, Claus, dear Claus, was there, flashing his press badge, coming on board, taking photographs, hugging her, hugging Chris who stood stiff because this man was a German.

'So, how are you?' Claus said, looking at Helen. He touched his nose when she asked how he had known, saying that the press had access to all sorts of information.

'A bit older,' she said, wanting to cry because he was from her past and he was here, the first person to meet her in her future land. He knew Heine, he knew her mother, her flat, so much that had made her. But he did not know Ed, or did he?

They talked of him and he had remembered the picture she had drawn in her letters.

'The dreams?' he asked. 'What about the dreams?'

But she didn't know and then he held her hand and told her that this is what must be solved, and she knew from his deep-set eyes that his mind had its darkness too because the shadows were there. His dark face was as thin as always, as handsome as always.

He told her of the business, which was thriving, of his wife, who was having a baby, of his parents, whom he had not heard from, but who he thought had been in Buchenwald. She asked of Herr and Frau Weber but he shook his head.

'There is no news,' he said, and for a moment they were both quiet and she knew that he had not yet solved his own darkness, his own dreams.

Chris moved from them, over to the rail, looking out towards New York.

Claus raised an eyebrow at Helen, his dark hair grey now. 'So like his father.'

Helen shook her head. 'He would deny that, my dear Claus. He doesn't like the Germans.'

Claus nodded, his face sad. 'But one day he will have to face that he is partly of that race.' He eased himself down into a deckchair, beckoning her to do the same. 'One day, my dear, he will have to be made to face it, be proud of it.'

Helen nodded, looking at her son who was so torn again.

'And now, the future for you?' Claus asked, looking through his camera, sizing up an angle.

'Who knows? Getting used to peace, I suppose, getting used to all this.' She watched Claus as he focused.

'Will you stay in Montana or can I persuade you back to photography? We need you. They remember you over here.'

Helen smiled, surprised. 'Really?' She leaned forward, her arms on her knees, seeing the wind lifting Chris's hair, the brides walking past talking quietly. 'It's tempting but Ed's home is in Montana. It's what he needs. At least, I think it's what he needs.'

She held her hands loosely together, enjoying his familiar voice, talking of little things, brushing against the larger ones, reaching out and bringing England close, Germany close, and now the future did not seem so vast. Then he left, called away by the First Officer because his time was up but before he went he left his camera with her, laughing at her face.

'Yes, why not, my dear? You own half the business. Who knows, you might decide to take on a project in those mountains. I could sell your work, you know.' He bent to kiss her. 'It might be something to hang on to, Helen, if the darkness comes between Ed and his life, as it did once with me. Call me, if you ever need me. I loved Heine, he saved my life. You saved my life too.'

He shook hands with Chris, his face solemn.

'You must not deny your roots. You are from good Germans. Remember that.'

Chris turned and ran off along the deck and Helen did not go after him but watched Claus walk down the gangplank waving, waving until she could no longer see him.

The next morning they ate a breakfast that was too large or was it just that none of the women were hungry? Names were called over the loudspeakers, requesting that the following brides report to the Immigration Officer in the lounge and have their landing cards stamped before proceeding to the library for their luggage tags. Chris sat with Helen, waiting, but so far they had only reached the Ds. Neither mentioned Claus and there was a barrier between them; it was slight but it was there and Helen wanted to push it aside but did not know how.

At noon they heard McDonald and joined the queue for Immigration and then for luggage tags. Helen told Chris to fetch his case while she collected hers from her berth. She tied the tags on, knowing that in a moment she would be starting on the final stage of the journey which would take her to Ed. They had also been given identity labels which they had to pin to their coats but Helen refused because she had not come all this way to be labelled. No one insisted when they saw her face.

Together with thirty other brides they were bused through the Holland Tunnel to New Jersey accompanied by two Red Cross personnel and there they boarded a Pullman which was larger than any train in Britain. The station was so large, the train too, and the suitcase was heavy in Chris's hand and cut into his fingers. He thought of the string bag he had taken from London to Greater Mannenham but he pushed that from him, because now he was going to a new life and, therefore, he had no use for his old.

He looked at his mother. Couldn't she understand that all he wanted to do was forget? That he could not bear to be from the same people who had made the village hate the Germans again because they had murdered so many people in camps? He couldn't bear always to be on the outside because of who he was. It was easier just to push it away.

They travelled for forty-eight hours, sleeping in bunks, then sitting for hours, and the rattle of the train drummed through their heads as they lurched through cities and great open spaces. They walked in the corridors, stretching cramped limbs, and Helen wondered how long she could stand it, but there were other brides and so they could still laugh together, and listen to familiar English accents.

When they reached Chicago she and Chris were met by the Red Cross, driven to another station and put on to another

290

train, this time alone. The conductor was told that he must hand Chris and Helen over to relatives or take them on to the next town where the sheriff must take custody of them. They must not be allowed free access to the country in case they became a drain on the economy. Helen listened to the poignant hoot of the train as it drew out of the vast town and she knew now how Heine must have felt, arriving as an alien in a strange land.

They travelled for another twenty-four hours and all the time her head was throbbing in time with the rattle of the train over the sleepers. The last four hours were covered in darkness. Chris and she had talked as the country unfolded, staring at the space, the mountains, the plains, the valleys, the rivers which seemed endless. They had talked of Ed, of the food, of the language, of Mary and Laura, but not of Heine because Helen knew that she must be careful or lose her son.

They drew up at last into Little Fork station which was small, like so many others they had passed through, but Helen could not see Ed as she peered through the window, holding her hand to her face to shield it from the light. The conductor came through, taking them to the door, helping them down on to the platform.

The Red Cross had sent a telegram informing Ed of her arrival. He should be here. She looked, then took Chris's hand and he let her because he was uncertain too. They walked through the booking hall with the conductor, then out on to the yard where cars and trucks were drawn up but he was not there and the sky was so vast, this land was too large and she was frightened of being adrift in it.

She turned back, walking towards the train and Chris but then she heard feet running behind her, his hands turning her, holding her, his breath gasping in his chest.

'You're early, for Christ's sake, you're early, darling.' He was kissing her, holding her and pulling Chris to him, clutching them both and he felt the same. Just the same as Helen leaned into him, so tired, so glad to be with him, so glad that, for a moment, it almost felt as though she were coming home. But only for a moment.

CHAPTER 20

Helen lay in bed that first night, feeling Ed beside her, his arms round her and neither of them slept and they did not speak, just touched and kissed, and as dawn rose she looked out through the window at the leaning jackpines on the ridges which seemed to surround the valley, holding them gently within the mountain range. The journey was at an end.

She stretched, counting the roses which climbed the wallpaper trellis, seeing their colour picked up in the new curtains. The chest of drawers was rough pine, made from the trees she could see from the window. A mirror stood on the top and Ed's hairbrush was there, silver backed; his graduation present. His photographs were on the wall, his face smiling down as a young man without lines, without fear.

She could hear the sound of pans in the kitchen and smell cooking and as Ed looked at her through lids half open she bent to kiss him, wanting to stay within the scent of his skin all day.

'I love you, I love you,' he said, reaching for her and as she sank beneath his kiss she thought of Yvonne and wondered how her mornings were.

She dressed at last, knocking on Chris's door but he was up, and as she ran down the stairs she heard him talking in the kitchen to the woman who had welcomed them to Little Fork last night; the woman who had taken her in her arms and held her close, saying that her son loved her and she did too. Ed's father had kissed her cheek and smiled, then picked up his pipe again and puffed before looking at Chris and saying that he needed a few more vittals inside him and then he'd pretty soon lick the hired hands into shape.

Mom, as she insisted on being called, cooked waffles and passed them thick corn syrup, followed by steak for breakfast and Chris looked at his mother and then ate until it was finished, drinking coffee while Ed laughed.

The black stove threw out heat though the spring morning was not cold, but fresh, the frost and snow all gone as April drew towards its end.

'So,' Ed's mother said, sitting down with them, pouring more coffee, her plump face pink from the heat of the stove, her grey hair caught up in a bun. Ed's eyes were the same as his mother's, Helen thought, looking from one to another and she felt good to be here amongst his people, but so far, it was not her home.

'So, there's no work for you today, Ed, your pop says. You're to look after this little family of yours, and look after them good.' She was shaking her finger at her son who dodged and grinned at Chris.

'We're going into town,' he said, levering himself up from his chair stiffly since his back and his left thigh were still not fully mobile. 'Thought I'd show Helen the place, get a few clothes for them both because there's this hotpot supper at the house behind the drug store on Friday.' He smiled at Helen. 'It's kind of a welcome shower.'

Helen looked up as she stacked the plates. 'A shower?'

'That great kid of mine means a party I guess you'd call it. It's just that a few folks said they'd like to meet "this girl from England" and I thought it would get it all over and done with and then you can get on with your life.' His mother wiped her hands on her apron smiling at Helen. 'That's what you all need, you, Ed and Chris. Just to be allowed to get on with your lives the best you can.' She turned and walked to the sink with the dishes, waving Helen away and calling to Ed.

'Just get your new wife downtown to the store to pick up some books for her to read when she's feeling kind of lonesome for England and then on to Joanie's for some clothes. But before that, maybe you should show her the house.'

Ed put his hands around Helen's waist, pulling her down on to his lap. His laugh was the same and his body too. His lips as he touched her neck were gentle and she smiled at Chris who was lifting his eyes to the ceiling and drumming his fingers on the table.

'Shall we get into town first, Ed?' he said. 'And then, when we get back can you show me the horse you said I could have?

Mum and I have been learning to ride on John's old mare for the last year you know.'

'Is that so? Well, you kept that kind of quiet in your letters, didn't you, Mrs McDonald?'

He laughed and kissed her forehead and Helen remembered the falls she had taken as old Betsy had trotted up and down, up and down, and how she thought the world had taken a tumble when she had been lurched into her first canter.

Ed squeezed Helen and let her rise, holding her hand as they walked to the door, slapping Chris on the shoulder.

'Come on, cowboy.'

They drove down the narrow road which ran alongside the creek edged by muddy banks and interrupted by clumps of willow. Helen looked out either side of the truck towards the mountains. Those to the west had snow on them which, Ed told her, remained throughout the year. Those to the east had been whipped into towers and turrets by the winds which swirled around the range day after day without respite.

'We get our ravens here too,' he told Chris. 'Some real mean storms blow in but towards the end of the summer I guess.'

There was mud on the road and tracks leading to fields where hay was beginning to grow and he looked at Helen as they passed and both were remembering the first time they discovered one another's bodies. Ed told Helen that the roads were always like this in the spring because there was so much snow.

'When it thaws it makes one hell of a mess,' he said. 'And it makes it kind of slippy to drive. Now, you must remember that when I teach you because you'll need to learn out here. It's not like England with buses and trams.'

He drove on, showing them where he had skidded off the road when the first snows had come after he had just learned to drive. He pulled in to show them where his pop said his great-grandfather had first pitched his tent, down on the bank of the creek.

'My great-grandfather settled here because it looked so like his home. He had come from the lowlands of Scotland and ran sheep here because it was all he knew about. He kind of bought up the other homesteads.'

They sat quietly for a moment and Helen thought of these people coming so far and staying to build a farm and a family and felt less alone.

He started the engine again, slipping it into gear, showing her what he was doing and it was not so very different to the old van which John had insisted she drove round with the hay in the hard winter of forty-five.

In the town he drew up and pointed to the railroad shipping pens to the left of the station where they would bring the sheep in the autumn.

'Who was here before the settlers?' Chris asked, peering through the window at the swallows' nests which hung beneath the eaves of the few stores in the street.

Ed drew into the side of the road, checking his mirrors, pulling the steering wheel over before stopping. 'The Crow Indians. They hunted across here in the early days. There was wild turkey, all manner of things then, or so pop says.'

'Where did they go?' Helen asked climbing down from the truck behind Chris, looking up and down the street, wondering if this really was all there was to Little Fork.

'Across to the long-grass prairies over the Missouri River,' Ed replied, touching his hat to the two old men who had chairs at the open hotel door. 'Hi, Jack, Tim. This is my wife straight out from England. And her boy, Chris.'

'Hello,' Helen said and smiled. The men nodded and sucked on their pipes, their faces wrinkled and their hands gnarled.

'Couldn't find no nice clean girl over here then, Ed?' Jack said and Helen felt cold and turned, walking on, hearing Chris come up behind and then Ed who took her arm, his lips thin. 'Ignore 'em, honey. They are the only two likely to be sour. Nothing's ever right for them.'

But it had been said and Heine had had to live with that all the time, hadn't he? Even the dress which Ed bought her with a long zip instead of buttons which she had never seen before and the shirt and thick trousers for riding could not brush the words aside. She watched him walk ahead of her into the grocery store, leading her to the books beyond the shelves which were stocked to bursting in a way that Helen had not seen for so long. She longed to see his rolling walk back again but for now it was pushed away by the stiffness of his injuries. Oh God, there was so much that was different, but last night in bed it had been the same. She must hang on to that; and there had been no dreams for him. But then, they had not slept.

That afternoon they saddled up three horses and rode out to

the house which was being repaired for them. It had been built by his grandfather, Ed told them, out of pine logs from the slope above them and had two bedrooms but would be big enough for now though it would not be finished until next spring. They stood and looked but somehow it wasn't her house, though it had windows and a door. There was no roof, just bare rafters which looked pale against the seasoned pine of the old walls. She smiled at Ed.

'It's going to be splendid, isn't it, Chris?'

Chris nodded and then urged his horse on up the rutted track and his hoofs sucked and slurped at the mud.

The horse was gentle beneath Helen and she felt confident while Ed pointed out the cabin hundreds of feet up the slope where the sheep herders based themselves in the summer and where you could hide from the world in the winter. She watched his hands as he pointed, his face which she loved, and she pushed the words of the old man and Heine's pain away because her husband was here and therefore Little Fork must become her home.

The next day she sat in a chair in the lounge looking through the window at the men hurrying from the bunk-house to the lambing sheds. She saw Ed walking stiffly to meet them, his hat sat back on his head as he nodded to his father and sent one of the men into town. He had taken Chris with him, saying that Helen had done too much for too long but she was restless and walked around the room, smoothing the settee covers, flicking open books and then shutting them. The newspapers were there but held no news of England, only of America.

She walked into the kitchen and baked alongside Mrs McDonald who told her how ill Ed had been, how bad the nightmares were until he knew that Helen was coming.

'That's when I knew I loved you, my dear. I feared for him you see. I didn't know what was in his head, why he screamed out like he did. We haven't been in the war, out here. How can we know? But you know. You've been through it.'

Helen put her arm round her shoulder. 'Don't worry, he'll be fine. He's such a good man.' She mixed the flour with the butter, squeezing it through her fingers, wondering how long she could keep the darkness out of Ed's eyes. She rolled out the pastry, shaking flour on to the board, wanting to be busy, but using her body, not just her hands because there was too much time to think about how little she really knew of the horrors, the reasons for the dreams. And how could she help unless she knew?

'I guess you might like to come down and take a look at the creamery, honey,' Mom said.

They went after lunch, a large meal which was served in the kitchen to the men and the family. No one spoke very much as they crammed food into mouths then left, busy, purposeful, and Helen wanted to be with them, but instead walked with Mom down across the red shale track towards the bunkhouse and beyond. There were no flowers, no colour and Helen thought of the daffodils and tulips at Laura's but then she must not think of things that were English.

It was damp in the creamery and her hair hung limp as she asked questions, shouting to be heard above the clatter of the churns and machinery. She saddled up her horse at four and rode out across the edge of the hayfields, missing John and the horses, missing the hoeing, the weeding, the feeding, and so the next morning she rose with Ed, pulling on her riding trousers and shirt and going with him to the lambing sheds because, she told him, she had come to America to be with him, not to get in his mother's way.

He looked at her, then stooped and kissed her hard, calling to Chris to come too and roll his goddamn sleeves up or his mother would beat them both to it.

All day they worked because the lambs were coming thick and fast. In the lambing shed board pens about four feet square stretched row upon row and the bleating and curses of the men mingled with the smell of iodine, manure, wool and alfalfa. Helen's hair hung in her eyes and Ed threw her his bandana to tie up around her head. Chris stayed with her, watching the lambs nuzzle the sheep, pointing out ones which were not suckling, then climbing into the pen with his mother to work the teats to make sure that the milk was flowing before putting the lambs on to suckle.

Again and again Helen did this and the heat in the shed built up until sweat poured down her body but this was work she understood and for the first time since she had left England she felt at ease. Ed called to Chris and showed him how to stamp the ewe and lamb with the same number to show that they belonged to each other.

297

After a lunch eaten in haste and with little conversation as they had done in the English fields they were out again, though this time Helen went with Ed to the pasture where they had to wrestle the ewes into the jugpen pulled by horses and then take them back to the shed. The sheep fought and Helen tussled them, holding them firm or snaring them by the hind leg with a sheep hook to snake them in backwards.

That night Chris and Ed tallied the numbers. It was mid April and now they had numbered over a thousand head of sheep and his father laughed and winked at Mom.

'I guess we got a good bargain, didn't we, Momma?'

That night Ed made love to Helen and it was not gentle but filled with passion as hers was and later she whispered, 'I need to work alongside you, my love. We have had too many hours taken from us.'

He kissed her and said, 'I love you and hate every second away from you.'

The next day a lamb died and Ed showed Helen and Chris how to skin the dead lamb, snipping four small leg holes and a head hole. Then he took a twin from another ewe, fitting the skin to the lamb.

His hands were smeared with blood and Chris looked away. 'Now you have to present this to that ewe over there. The one whose lamb has died. She'll accept it in a coupla days because she'll recognise the smell as her own.' He nodded at Chris and Helen. 'You got that?'

Helen nodded and Chris too but he was pale. Later Helen found a dead lamb and called Chris to grab one of triplets from a pen higher up. He did and then watched his mother do a job he felt he could not attempt and later that evening he went and put his arms around her and said, 'I love you, Mum.' But what he wanted to say was, I respect you. You are so brave and so strong and I don't know what I would do without you and I wish I could accept my German part but I can't.

On Friday they went in the car to the house behind the drug store taking two casseroles with them to place on the table as Ed's mom said they must. Mrs McDonald introduced Helen to the younger women first and they were kind and friendly and kissed her when the British would just have shaken hands. They also heaped presents on them for the new house.

They talked of Ed as a child, how he had fired arrows at targets and missed, breaking the drugstore window. How he had ridden his horse down the main street on Independence Day, firing his pop's old gun. Helen looked across at him as he talked to a ring of men, throwing his head back and laughing, his arm on Chris's shoulders and she loved him more than ever.

Two of the women talked of working in factories during the war, of leaving home while their men served in the forces. They spoke of how small the town seemed now. Of how they had been hated by the men in the factories and feared by them because of their abilities. They put their hands on Helen's arms.

'I guess it must be the hardest thing in the world, to come over to another country. It was sure bad just moving to a bigger town,' Susie said, her blonde hair swept back in a pony-tail, her blue eyes sympathetic. 'Come see me sometime, anytime.'

Though their heads ached the next day from too much to drink they were up at daybreak as usual because lambs did not stop being born to accommodate a hangover, Helen groaned, as she pulled on her trousers. But now she felt as though she had a friend in the small town and that made her feel safer somehow.

In the evening she wrote to Germany to try and find Frau and Herr Weber and Chris watched her but said nothing. They packed up a parcel of tins to send to Laura and Mary and next year Mary was coming, they decided, even if they had to go and fetch her, because Helen was looking forward now.

In June the mosquitoes were rising from the creek and the sheep had to go through the gate and be counted but Chris was not here during the day now because he had gone into the town along from Little Fork where the High School stood and he talked of pitching and batting, chewing gum as he did so. He handled the work well and liked the kids, he said, and Ed and his father chuckled when Helen told him to take that disgusting stuff out at once.

Chris lay in bed feeling the heat of the summer which he had never before experienced. Life was good but he missed Mary. He had not thought he would quite so much, but there was a difference between these kids and those back home. These ones were fresh and bright-eyed and knew nothing of bombs and death. He was thirteen and he did. He knew its sounds and smells.

He lay with his hands behind his head. Mary had written to say she would come next year, definitely, and Laura too, and he wanted to show her the jackpines, the creek and his horse, Sorrel. He wanted to show how he could lasso a calf, hauling back on the rope. He wanted to show her the calluses on his hands.

Would she like his friends? Roy with the broken tooth because he was a fighter; Ted with his red hair. And what about the coach who said he'd make a great batter one day? He turned over in the bed. Gee, it was hot. He lifted the sheet, waving it up and down.

The coach was German but nobody minded. He should tell them he was too, but he couldn't and he didn't know why. Chris turned over towards the window. He needed to tell. He knew he did but he couldn't because he hated the Germans. He still hated them.

In mid June Helen and Ed drove with Mom and Pop to the High School game because Chris was playing. Helen sat in the stand and watched the girls dancing at the edge of the pitch, heard the school band and ate popcorn which Ed handed to her in a cardboard carton. She wanted to wave to Chris when he ran on to the field and the supporters stood and cheered their team but she did not. She just watched and wondered at how American he had so easily become and how English she still was.

She watched the battle between the pitcher and the batter, heard the screams and cheers as runs were scored and home base was reached. She listened as Ed explained that each team had nine innings and that each team's inning lasted until three men had been put out.

'The visiting team is always the first to bat,' Ed's father told her, roaring as another run was scored then groaning as a batter hit an infield fly.

Helen didn't understand but shouted when Chris hit a homer and scored a run and the rest of the team went wild.

'I showed him how to hit that, Christ almighty. I told him,' Ed said, grabbing her and kissing her and she laughed, feeling free tonight, and happy. She looked along the rows of people watching, seeing their faces, hearing their voices drawling and

American, but not seeming as strange as they had two months ago and she settled back for the rest of the evening. She would write her monthly letter to Claus tomorrow and he would laugh at all this.

On 15 June, while Chris was off on a baseball tour, Helen and Ed went into the timbered slopes to herd sheep for two weeks with a wagon full of groceries, opening fence line gates on the rutted tracks leading up into the mountains, feeling the coolness of shade which could not be found in the valley.

The wagon sat high on the spoked wheels and the leather reins were soft in Helen's hand from years of use. She propped her foot up on the weatherboard and smiled at Ed, feeling the lurch of the wagon over roots and stones, hearing the yap of the herd dogs as they ran round and round the wagon as it moved along, so slowly.

'I'm looking forward to this sheep herding your mom's been talking about.'

He smiled and his mouth was lazy. 'I guess I am too.'

They looked back down into the valley. Smoke rose from the farmhouse chimney and the creek moved sluggishly through dried banks. They could see the shimmer of the heat and Helen relaxed in their shaded cool, bringing out her camera, taking shots of the valley, the mountains, the darkness of the pines.

'It's a bit more like England up here,' she murmured, leaning over and kissing him.

'I guess so, honey. Do you miss it so much?' His hands caught at hers and held them loosely and he watched the horse as it picked its way along the track.

'No, not at all,' Helen said but she did. She still did, though not with the sharp pain of the first days of strangeness. She looked up picking out the sky through the branches. It was a dull ache which never left her. But she loved him so much that it filled every other part of her and it was this that she tried to think of each day.

They stopped beneath sun-splashed pine boughs before the day ended, knowing that the sheep were all around, hearing their bleats and the whine of the dogs. They unhitched their horses from the tailboard and rode out; checking, laughing, listening and just sitting with their hands on the saddle, looking together up at the mountains, breathing in the pure air, hearing nothing of the world beyond the timber and it was a

301

touch of heaven. A soundless time which they each sucked in after the screams of the last few years.

That night they lay together on the soft pine needles and loved beneath a sky filled with the smell of jackpines and clear mountain air, and Helen felt that this was what she had been waiting for all her life and the ache for England would subside with each day that passed for this was her home, here in the cool of the mountains, in the silence of its skies.

She kissed his mouth and told him this; that here they were together and there was no past and no future, just their love and he held her then and told her of the dreams he had when the war still roared and crashed across the world. He told of the blood on his face, on his body, of Joe, and she held him as he told her it was not his guilt for Joe that made him scream but his guilt for those beneath his bombs. He told her of London that day, of the crosses in the rubble and she kissed him and said that war asked strange things of people and that it was all over now. He held her.

'Dear God, I hope so,' he murmured.

They followed the sheep along the range for the next two weeks and Helen grew to love the wagon, its storage bins which doubled as seats, a table which hinged down from the wall. There was a bunk bed which fitted across the end of the wagon but they lay beneath the stars or used a canvas tent which they folded each morning and set up again at a new site every evening.

They sat in the wagon with the Dutch door half open watching the sheep, listening to coyotes and Helen thought of Ed as a child, coming up here with his father, shooting grouse as big as hen turkeys, eating half at night, putting the other half in a jar, dangling it in the stream and having it for breakfast.

He told her of the small cabin which he loved to camp in, the winter he had spent guarding the sheep and just existing and how it had honed him as a man.

They talked of the child they would have when their own house was finished and Helen called it their home and said that maybe they'd have to divide the larger bedroom into two.

She learned to balance a cup of water on the table at each night stop to check that the wagon was level and to dig beneath the wheels if it wasn't, and for those two weeks there was nothing and no one in the world but them, and there were no words left unsaid, no thoughts and fears left unspoken, and Helen prayed that the darkness had left Ed for ever. But sometimes his hands still trembled and tightness gathered round his eyes.

CHAPTER 21

In late June they were back in the valley, joining in the heaving and raking of the late wild hay after Helen had fed the chickens and checked the seed potatoes which she had bought from the store and set behind the unfinished house, digging in the cool of the evening, and after Ed had ridden round the cattle, checking the fences, repairing wire where it had sagged and posts which had loosened.

They set half the bunkhouse on one of the fields and took two other men, sending the others out to the pasture to guard and move the cattle. Helen laughed because Pop wouldn't use 'new fangled machinery' for harvesting when he had good horses and idle men. She tossed loads up to Ed who pulled his hat down hard and worked to keep up. His back and leg were looser now and his stride was almost easy.

The smell of the hay filled the air and midges danced along with the seeds which scattered and blew on the wind, and as Helen drove the wagon through the field she thought of all the young men who had helped in East Anglia and whose parents would never again see the sun on their backs as she was seeing it on Ed's. They worked with the men for two days transporting the hay to stacks which looked like loaves and on the third she dragged the stetson which had been Ed's when he was young well down, grateful for the shade across her face, feeling the heat beating down on to the ground and then rising in waves from the parched earth. The creek was almost dried out and the willows rattled in the slight breeze which gave no relief because it too was dry and hot. The dampness of England seemed a miracle, one which she could almost no longer imagine.

Helen wiped her parched mouth. Ed threw down a leather flask from the wagon where he was stacking the hay, outside first moving inwards as John had shown her.

'Drink this, honey, you'll be losing a heap of moisture.'

She lifted it to her mouth. The water was warm but she needed it. God, how she needed it. She looked across to the other field seeing it fragmented by the blazing heat. She drew up her leather gloves so that they met her cuffs, unbuttoned to allow a draught. Her arms had burnt on the first day and now she kept them covered and her hands too.

The letter from Claus crackled in her pocket. He had sent bulbs for the fall and three rose bushes which he said she must bury deep down beneath the earth for the winter and then dig up for next spring. A little bit of England, he had said, and Ed had promised that he would help. They would plant them round the new house and even if they were still not in by then, at least it was as though their souls were there.

She smiled up at him. His hair had bleached under the searing heat and his moustache too. His skin was burnt dark brown and he was beautiful. They sent the two men back to the range in the afternoon for they were almost through with the field and they wanted to be alone, lifting, heaving, throwing, hearing the breaths they each drew, speaking words which only they should hear. Helen leaned on her rake as Ed stretched back his shoulders, standing above her on the wagon, ankle deep in hay, balancing, then falling, sinking into the green grass and laughing deep down in his body.

It was darker now, though it was only four o'clock and Helen raised her arm, shading her eyes as she looked towards the mountains to the west. Dark clouds were forming, tumbling on top of one another, grey, then black, and she shouted to Ed to look. He did, then stopped, his head lifted. He jumped down, picking up the tools throwing them on top of the load, calling to her to do likewise.

'There's a storm coming.' His voice was tight and his movements quick. 'Get up on the wagon, Helen, let's get this load back.' He took the reins and shook them out and now it was humid, heavy and wet, and just as hot as before.

Helen saw his hands trembling as the thunder rumbled in over the mountains, coming before the rain, before any lightning that they could see.

He shouted at the horse now. 'Get your goddamn butt moving.'

She looked at him and then back at the storm, swirling in,

filling the valley with darkness and noise and now the lightning flashed, tearing jagged through the clouds and the thunder clapped above them, rolling round and round, trapped within the mountain range, and then the rain, heavy and hot. So hot.

The horse was nervous, edgy, side-stepping within the traces. Ed clutched the reins with white-knuckled hands, shouting above the storm.

Helen gripped the sides of the seat, water running off her stetson, crouching as the lightning sliced through the air again and the thunder rolled and banged.

'For Christ's sake,' she heard Ed say as the roan staggered and side-stepped. 'For Christ's sake.'

Helen looked ahead, knowing the farm was along the road, but she could not see through the steam and the rain and the darkness. The noise went on and on and the lightning was like the searchlights seeking and the gunfire probing and the noise was the noise of bombs.

The lightning ripped the skies apart again and Helen gripped Ed's arm, rising as he was doing as he slapped his reins on the horse, shouting at him. She felt the roughness of his shirt, it was full of water. There was water everywhere, in her face, her mouth and in his too.

'For Christ's sake,' he said again tightening the reins as the horse moved faster, balancing as the wagon shifted from side to side.

'Hang on to these,' he shouted, passing them to her, leaping down from the wagon, running to the horse's head, dragging him forward as he side-stepped again and Helen could hardly see him through the torrent and was afraid.

'Don't leave me,' she cried and he looked up at her, his arms pulling at the horse, effort stretched across his face and then the lightning seared again, close, too close, and thunder crashed, cruel and consuming, and she screamed as the horse reared in the traces, striking out at Ed who was knocked to the side. Helen saw the roan's ears flatten as lightning again and again stabbed across the blackness and then he ran; his legs fully stretched, his head wrenching at his bit and she heard Ed's cry.

'Helen. Helen.'

But she could hear nothing but the rain and the thunder and she thought of the raven and the gods and knew that the wagon was tipping, lurching, straightening and rushing forward

306

again. And then it hit the boulder and flew high and sideways. She heard the wood tearing and the thunder and it was as though bombs were coming down and crushing her into the ground and there would be dust and bricks and death and she screamed into the darkness of the cupboard.

She wasn't hurt, she kept telling him. Not hurt, as he pushed the broken wagon from her legs but he was crying and holding her and that night, after they struggled home he went into the bedroom and drank whisky until he passed out and then he screamed all night as the darkness closed in on him because he had nearly killed Helen as he had killed so many others.

As summer turned to fall and the leaves shone orange, red and gold, he saw none of it, only the shadows of his mind and at night he could not scrape off the dried blood which belonged to Joe and the rest of the people he had killed. Helen lay and listened and wept because she could not reach him, could not help him any more. But could the whisky either?

He would not let Helen drive the wagon again and so she rode her horse out across the valley, taking photographs of the trees, the creek, and the men as they cut out the calves from the mothers, and stooped and wrestled in the bright air, their chaps dust covered, their hats sodden with sweat. She used black and white, and created clear true images and sent them off to Claus who sold them, ploughing the money back into the agency for her and sending her the half-yearly statement of accounts. Business was good.

And then Ed slapped her one night with a drink-clumsy hand because he said she was going to leave him here while she ran away to New York. She put her camera away and held him and said she would never go. Never ever go. But it did not stop her from viewing her world with a photographer's eye because, when all this was past, she would work again.

She told Chris that Ed was not well but he knew that already. He had heard the words which tracked from Helen to Ed's parents as evening followed evening and seen the strength which had been Ed become sodden and fumbling. But sometimes Ed laughed for a moment like he used to, and Chris would sit with him then because he loved him and he had saved him from the bullies all that time ago.

But as October became November there were no more

307

smiles, just shouts. No kindness, just tension and he knew that somehow the war was not going to leave Ed again as it had done, briefly, for the summer. Each night he would listen for the stumbling feet on the stairs and grieve for the man who had pitched at him and his hate for the Germans was fuelled.

Mr McDonald sold a hundred head of cattle in the first week of November, and Helen worked with him and the men, driving them to the shipping pastures where they milled and worried until the train came in, and then she and the hands pushed the shoulders of their horses at the cattle, moving them forward, feeling their heat, breathing in their dust until finally they were on board. Ed did not come. She did not look at Wilton's Bar as they passed and neither did Pop but all the way back they talked about the man she loved. But their words did no good. Pop's son, her husband, did not want a clear mind.

At the ranch she manhandled the sheep up the chutes into the trucks, gripping their fleeces; her fingers thick with their oil, not feeling the chill of the autumn until she stood back and watched the truck leave. She drove the pick-up into town, following on, Mr McDonald at her side guiding her with the gear shift, praising her until they reached the railroad shipping pens, and she wondered if her husband would ever be sixty with hands as calm and eyes as clear as this dear old man's for he was becoming the father she had hoped for.

Again she wrangled the sheep up into the boxcars when the train came in, cursing as the men did, but not loudly, coughing too and falling, grazing her arm but rising and smiling, bearing Ed's share of the family labour. The days passed, busy, empty, because Ed was not with her but a million years away, fighting the war again, drinking until he could no longer stand and somehow she must stop it, but did not know how.

Mr McDonald told her as the chill wind blew across the valley that soon she must take her driving test and she nodded but said to Ed the next morning as he lay in bed, his breath sour and his skin too, that she must dig a trench for the roses before the winter froze the ground.

'You promised to help, my darling,' she said.

He looked at her with eyes grown dull and dark, then turned away and so she bent and kissed his head, his cheek, and thought of his hands which never stroked her now.

'It will pass,' she whispered. 'This is just a fragment of time.'

308

She rode her mare to the house which would one day be theirs and dug the trench, wrapping the rose roots in sacking, covering the plants with layers of newspaper and earth. She then sliced the spade into the ground around the house, digging once, twice. Counting as she struck stones, rocks and thick clay but never stopping until the sun was low and the beds were finished.

She looked up as Chris rode along the track towards her, halting, his arms folded on the saddle horn.

'Why, Mum?' he said pointing to the ground.

Helen looked up at him, seeing the man he was becoming, hearing the voice beginning to crack and deepen.

'Because it's going to be our home and I'm staking my claim.' She straightened her shoulders, passing the spade up to her son. I'm staking my claim to my husband's life, she thought, staring up into the sky, seeing ravens where there were none. The gods are not going to get him, somehow I shall make sure of that, but she couldn't speak the words because if she did, the pain would flow from her in a torrent which would drown them all.

On 1 December Chris was fourteen and Mr McDonald drove him and his friends to a movie in Rider's Halt, the first big town, and she sat and joked beside him, listening to Ed's father laugh with his son's laugh.

They ate hamburgers thick with a relish which could still not wipe out the memory of the English sauces and the boys were happy and whistled 'Little Brown Jug' all the way home.

Helen and Mr McDonald checked the sheep in the lower pastures in the early evening and Pop said that there would be snow that night, he could smell it on the air, and Helen remembered all that Ed had said of the Montana winters and pulled her padded jacket closer around her body.

When they returned to the house Mom sat by the stove, her face worn into deeper lines.

'Ed took Chris into town,' she said. 'Because it's his birthday.'

Helen stood with her hand on the door, listening to the wind rising, seeing the first big flakes come down beyond the window, thickening until there was almost no darkness between them. He couldn't have taken her son there, Heine's son there? Surely not. But he had. For God's sake, he had. She made herself smile at Mom and Pop who did not smile back, their shoulders tense as they sat, legs crossed before the stove. There was only the crackle of burning wood, the wailing of the wind to fill each minute until the clock on the shelf struck eleven and then she could bear it no longer.

She took the truck, driving in along a whitened road which was indistinguishable from the meadows, the headlights probing the falling snow. There was nothing to hear but the straining of the wipers, silting up with snow and then free again. The only thing which indicated her path was the fence, snowed up four inches and it was like the German winter with the trees and shrubs foreshortened and she felt Heine with her again. She drove into the skids as Pop had said she must, not afraid though he had been, as he watched her from the door, wanting to come. But this was her job.

Ed's pick-up was there, slewed in at an angle to the sidewalk as she had known that it would be. She drew up her hood, stepping out into cold which dug long-fingered into her lungs. She shouldered her way up the steps, across the sidewalk where snow had drifted against the walls and in through the wooden slatted swing doors like some mockery of an old western.

Cigarette smoke was thick and heavy in the room and the colours of the juke box which played 'Chattanooga Choo Choo' spun across the ceiling: blue, red, green. Blue, red, green. She walked into the room and the men stopped talking. Chris was there sitting on a stool at the mahogany bar. She watched herself in the mirror which stretched behind the bar, walking so slowly towards the man she loved whose face sagged in the dim light and her son who held a glass of Scotch to his mouth. She looked old.

She saw the labels on the bottles of whisky ranged in front of the looking-glass and the glasses which rested mouth down on the shelf.

She looked at the nuts in neat packets and the naked woman on the calendar which hung from a rusty nail. She watched the barman pulling the spigot, steadily, carefully, and now she had reached them and took the glass from her son's hand, took it away from his mouth. The saxophones were playing in perfect time as she put her sodden son's arms around her neck and heaved him from the stool. He was coming home.

She saw her husband turn now and look at her, his eyes narrowed, his glass to his mouth. She passed by, saying nothing, dragging her son back out to the truck, pushing him in, propping him in the corner. She used the clutch with the gearshift, crouching behind the wheel, hearing the wipers, seeing the snow which had stopped falling but now drifted in waves like the sea and ripples like the shore. She drove back carefully, saying nothing to Mom and Pop as she dragged her son to his room, lying him on his stomach.

In the lounge their faces were grey with shock and shame but Helen came up to Mom and hugged her. 'Don't worry, it will be all right. Now go to bed and don't get up, whatever you hear.' Remembering that she had once said this before, long ago.

They did go, and alone, in front of a stove that she replenished with logs every hour, she waited. He came home at two in the morning and stood in the doorway, bourbon spilt down his shirt, his eyes sunken, his lips loose.

'You are coming to the mountains with me tomorrow,' Helen said, full of love for him, wanting to take him in her arms because he was in so much pain, but she did not. She kept a hardness in her voice, a command.

'For goddamn why?' he said, still slumping against the doorframe.

'Because I say so,' Helen replied, not standing, just sitting up straight, her hands on her knees. 'Now go to bed.'

He didn't move to the stairs but walked towards her, standing in front of her. 'Don't you go giving me orders, you little bitch. You little English bitch. We came and saved your little two-bit country.' He was shouting and the smell of alcohol reached her. 'We came and saved you and now you take your boy away and he was only having a drink, a little friendly drink.'

'I know you came and saved us. But you've lost something of yourself and I won't let you go on without finding it. We are going to the mountains.' Her voice was level and she never took her eyes from his face even when he reached down for her, gripping her arm, pulling her up to him. She felt his spittle as he shouted.

'I don't need you.' He shook her then and her head rocked back. He slapped her and her lip cracked.

311

Again she said, 'We are going to the mountains, to the cabin where you once found peace, because I love you more than life itself.' Her voice was still level. 'And I don't care how many times you say no, you are coming with me. I won't leave you to fight this alone.'

She tasted the blood from her lip, felt it run from the corner of her mouth, felt the pain.

Ed stumbled back, looking at the red on her chin and reached out his hand. He touched it, then started to wipe it on his shirt, again and again and again, and now he was crying and Helen held him, rocking him as though he were a child. Listening as he choked out words, sentences, curses. She pulled him down on to the settee, feeling his tears, until at last he slept. She stayed with him, sitting before the stove, listening as he dreamt and mumbled and groaned but tonight he did not scream and she dared to hope that the cold hardship of the winter would bring release.

At seven they left, Helen and Pop harnessing the workhorses to the hay-sled, working the stiff webs of leather across each wide back, fastening the ice-cold buckles with numb fingers before passing the reins to Ed who sat bowed and limp on the driving seat. They drove off into the white shadowless snow, heading up for the homestead which was hidden behind the frozen jackpines.

She had left him at five to stock up the stores, to wake Chris and explain and ask him to come, if he wanted to. He was pale. His head ached, his mouth was sour, and anyway, he said, he did not want to come because Ed must get better. Besides, he had things to do. She had kissed him, holding him, telling him she loved him and that it would only be for three months and she could come back at any time, or he could come to her. That there were no bombs keeping them apart, no bullies hurting him. He had smiled and so had she, but the guilt at leaving him was great because he too needed to be freed from the hate which he carried like a torch.

She had taken pen and paper and written once more to Germany before she left.

Chris took the schoolbus the next day, carrying his lunch in his bag, lugging it over his shoulder, his earflaps down, his hat low. It was cold and the air was sharp in his chest and on the bus he

312

waved to his buddies but did not talk because he had
something to do.

All morning he listened in class, answering questions,
chewing gum until the sugar was gone, then he unwrapped
another strip and chewed again. At lunchbreak he ate in the
dining-hall, eating peanut butter and jam sandwiches and
cakes.

'Which you guys call biscuits. Crazy Americans,' he said to
his friends and then threw the ball in the sports hall but he
didn't talk to the coach; not yet.

At recess he listened to the talk all around; the ball game
scores, the high school prom, but he was thinking of his mother
and Ed. Her face had been swollen this morning when they left
and he had heard the shouting last night, though his head was
swimming from the bourbon.

How far had they gone? Up beyond the timber line? Why
should they have to go? It wasn't fair. Ed had fought his war
but it wouldn't leave him. He knew that now because Ed had
cried last night after he had shaken his mother. He had wept
and said, I can't wipe it out. I can't forget the missions, the
blood. It's all over my body, my face and I can't wipe it off. And
now I have yours.

Chris sucked on his straw. His Coke was almost finished. He
put it to one side and walked down corridors lined with lockers to
the sports hall. His coach was there, bouncing a football, up and
down, up and down. Chris walked up to him. He wasn't a very
big man really, he thought, as he hit him where his abdomen was
soft and unprepared. It was the same punch that Ed had shown
him when the war was raging and the gang was taunting. He hit
him again and chopped his legs from under him.

The coach lay on the floor and Chris turned and walked
away, but before he did so he said, 'You're a German bastard.
You people killed my real dad and now you're trying to kill Ed.'

He spent the afternoon in the Head Teacher's office waiting
until old Mr McDonald came. He didn't mind. He sat on the
chair thinking of the air raid sirens, his father's face when he
had kissed him goodbye. The letter from Willi. He thought of
Mary and Laura and it all seemed so long ago and far away.
His head hurt and he missed his mother and somehow life had
gone wrong again.

He sat nursing his sore hand as Mr McDonald explained to the Head Teacher about Heine and Ed. Chris looked at the picture on the wall. It was of the school's winning ball game last season. He would never play for the team now but he'd had to do it, whatever they said or did, he could have done nothing else.

The snow was falling again outside the window, great thick flakes as the talk flowed to and fro between the old man and the younger one and Chris felt older than fourteen. How far had his mother got, he wondered. Were they there yet?

The Head was talking to him now, his voice dry and angry, his fingers picking up and putting down a wooden rule.

'Well, Chris. I guess that you've been through some things in England that we must make allowances for. I shall delay all action until your mom returns and then we shall decide what to do with you. You have until the spring to settle in again. No one knows about this but you and the coach. It shall remain this way. You may not practise for the team. You will take sport under another teacher. So. We shall wait until the spring.'

Chris nodded. It didn't matter, it wasn't as though bombs were falling, as though anyone was getting killed. He looked out of the window again. Would his mum save this dad? Would she save him from the Germans? He knew he had to wait for the coming of the spring.

He looked out of the window again. How far had they got?

CHAPTER 22

Helen slapped the reins against the horse's back with numbed hands. She sat next to Ed on the planks which Pop had lashed on to the front pair of sled runners and there were blankets heaped beneath and around them. She pulled her hat, tugging it down and her collar up. There was more snow now but at last she could see the cabin in the distance, though all she could hear was the sliding of the tracks, clean and clinical, and the jangle of harness.

Ed sat with his head down on his chest saying nothing. They had travelled all morning with the dog leaping in and out of the deeper drifts, then jumping up on to the seat, its hot breath on Helen's face. The provision boxes were heaped with snow, their weathered rawhide a stark contrast where they speared through settled flakes at the corners. They didn't stop to eat but swished along behind the horse which heaved and leaned against the harness, pulling steadily uphill towards the pines which were laden with frosted snow. There had not been one word between them.

It was three in the afternoon before they reached the cabin, its varnished logs coated with blown snow on the east side, its roof hung with icicles as they would hang on the roofs in Hanover – if there were any roofs left. Helen dug her chin deeper into her coat as she tied the reins around the brake. Would Frau Weber receive her latest letter?

She pushed aside the blankets. The temperatures were lower than any she had imagined. The blanket was encrusted with iced snow and it cracked and fell in large clumps on to the sled.

'Come on, my love,' Helen said, touching his arm. 'Let's get the things inside.'

She moved towards the unlocked door, opening it, hearing the creak of the hinges. It was dark inside but not as cold and the wind could not pierce her body as it had been doing. The stove was where Pop had said it would be, the logs too and coal and kerosene. She pulled her mitts with her teeth, shaking the snow to the wooden floor, letting them fall at her feet. She turned and kicked the snow from her boots on to the step and then walked, hearing each step, and then there were his behind her. She did not look but opened the black stove door, soaking the coal with kerosene, throwing in a lighted match, hearing the burst of flame through the closed iron door.

She turned and watched as Ed put the rawhide boxes down and went out into the cold for more. Still they had not spoken. She picked up logs and threw them into the stove, lifting the metal jug from the first of the boxes, walking back out into the cold, heaping snow into its mouth with her bare hands and then she felt his around her waist.

'Let me, honey. And get those mitts back on. I don't want you to lose your fingers.' He didn't look into her face, just crouched where she had been and rammed in more snow.

He carried the jug on to the stove and she heard the hiss as the snow which clung to the base melted and was then heated into steam. She fought her way back out to the sled through the wind, bringing back the saws and wedging them in the corner. One fell and the noise was loud, though the wind was wailing as he left again to rub down and stable the horse. The dog was in front of the stove and its smell rose dankly from its coat.

The sky was darkening now, sucking the daylight from the room. She lit the kerosene lamp and put it near the window. Its yellow glow would reach the valley and Pop and Mom would sigh and so would Chris. She moved heaped dry blankets from one of the boxes on to the bed, and sheets too because for the next three months they would live and eat and sleep in here.

He came in then, his moustache ice-encrusted, his hat thick and white. He knocked it against the doorpost, kicking his boots off and then coming to her, taking her hands in his, breathing on them, rubbing until the feeling burned in her fingers and in her heart because he had touched her. After so long he had touched her.

That night they lay together though passion did not rise. He dreamt and cried and called but there was no bourbon and so he did not breathe sourness into her face.

As dawn settled into the day they used a pick to cleave an

earth closet behind the cabin and ate oatmeal cooked on the stove. His hands were shaking and his face was pale but they took the saws and the sled and worked on the pines one hundred yards beyond the cabin. They chose one that was long and straight and nicked one side of the trunk, then sawed the other, one on either end, pulling and pushing, hearing the teeth driving and tearing, feeling the snow drop around them and on them from the tree's branches. When the saw stuck they eased in a wedge. Her breath was cold in her chest and her back ached and so did his, but they didn't speak, just worked.

The tree fell where he had intended it should and then they lopped the branches; neatly, efficiently, while the dog ran around, yapping and barking and chasing his tail. Helen laughed but Ed did not.

He tramped back to the cabin and she could see his breath billowing in great gasps as he brought the chains and the ropes. Together they pushed the chains through the packed snow beneath the tree, wetting their sleeves but not noticing. Round and round they wound it and now Helen went back for the horse, into the warmth of the dark stable, harnessing her, easing her out into the dazzling white silence of the day, hearing the crunch of the snow packing beneath her hoof. She steadied her up as Ed hitched the rope to the harness and then they led her as she dragged the tree to the skidway, plodding down the slope, leaving great sliced marks in their wake. Down they inched to the flatness of the ledge and the saw bench where they released the tree, slipping off the chains, sawing it into sections, heaving them on to the bench, then sawing again. One two, one two, one two, while the horse waited for the hour it took and the sawdust mounted, the logs too.

Then back up to the stable and another tree and so each day they worked and the logs grew and Helen slept with the smell of pine in her clothes and her skin and her hair and it was the same smell as the pines in Heine's forest so long ago.

Each day too they checked the bawling cattle which drifted on the lower slopes amongst a whirling mass of whiteness, searching for buried sage. As mornings turned to afternoons they carted hay from the barn behind the cabin, carrying it between them to the hay sled, tossing it with pitchforks towards the cattle before returning to the saw which became hot to the touch as they pulled backwards and forwards.

317

*

Christmas came and went but they did not stop and each night Helen looked down into the valley, seeing the lights where Chris slept and woke and played, and missed her son and longed for him, but Ed would have been lost if they had not come. She could not have allowed that to happen as it had happened to Heine. And so she worked and watched and hoped, but the days went by and the dreams continued and no contact was made between this man and herself.

In January the sun was bright on the last day of the first week and they tossed out to the cattle hay which they had harvested in the valley, in the long hot summer and Helen talked as she always did; this time of the harvest in East Anglia. He looked at her and she saw him smile and he replied in a voice ragged and unused.

'I love this kind of a day,' he said. 'Nothing bad can ever happen when there's this feeling in the air.'

He told her then of the winter when the cattle had eaten the willows by the creek and died of starvation, lying in dark heaps, like mole-hills on an English lawn and she hardly dared to breathe as, slowly, he came alive.

'We brought in hay and saved them but it damn near broke us,' he said, wiping the breath which had frozen to ice on his scarf.

That night he did not dream but held her and in the morning he touched her face and kissed her.

As they worked that day he told her of the square dances they had held in the town with his pop calling, 'Now swing your corners, twirl your partners and mosey on down.' And then his mom had dished up the punch.

'They were good days,' he said. 'Good clean days.'

The next week, as they slid a long tree down the slope he slipped and gashed his knee and the blood was vivid against the snow. The cut was deep and clean, Helen saw, as she cut the trouser from his leg in the warmth of the cabin.

'In the Fortress the blood froze before it spouted,' he said, as he sat on the chair and looked into the open stove. 'Except in the cockpit where it was warm, and then it flowed like Joe's all over him, all over me.'

Helen laid the scissors quietly on the table, taking the cotton

318

wool, bathing the cut gently, listening as he told her again of the blood and of the guilt.

'The bloody, bloody guilt and the cross stuck so goddamn crooked in the rubble,' he said, looking at her as she took his hand. 'Help me, Helen. I'm going kind of mad. I can't get it out of my head.'

She came to him, holding his head against her breast. 'I'm here. I'm always here. You did the job you had to do. What else could you have done?' She was stroking his hair, wiping the tears from his cheeks, feeling them soaking through her blouse. And then he pulled away, jerking his finger at the lint on the table.

'Come on then, Helen. For Christ's sake, we've got work to do.'

He wouldn't look at her again, wouldn't listen to her voice and so she knelt and dressed his knee, sewing up his trousers again, knowing he would go out again into the cold because his face had closed. He would not talk any more of the darkness today, but perhaps tomorrow? Oh God, she hoped it would be tomorrow and that the darkness would escape for good.

It did not. Instead he talked of the tadpoles he had scooped into his hands in the pools of the creek when he was barely six and the summers were long and hot. The water had run through his fingers and dripped back into the pool and it had been so cool and so clear.

He talked of the igloo he and Pop had built, hacking out February snow which had frozen so hard it was ice. How white and cold it had been to build but so warm inside, and silent.

All day they sawed but then the dog barked and called and they found a cow by the barn toiling with a breech birth. They moved her into the barn. Ed heaved and pulled until the calf slipped into the straw, slippery but warm and alive and then he turned to her, his face gleaming with sweat.

'I would like a child, Helen, a daughter that looks like you.'

She stood still as the cow nuzzled the calf and Ed rubbed it with straw, and they shared the cry of the newly born.

He came to her then and they walked back to the cabin, to the bed, and he held her but did not love her, not then, but that night he held her and stroked her.

'I love you, I love you,' he said, his mouth finding hers and every touch of his body against hers was tender and all that

319

night he loved her and then he talked of the raids, the bombs, the people, and again the next night and the next. Each day the lines grew less and the trembling left his hands and Helen knew the taste of happiness again.

In February the cold was at its most intense, deep and bitter, and now they sat before the stove, talking and listening, and she told him of the cupboard and her own fears, her own guilts. He told her of his first loves, his first kisses. They checked the cattle in short bursts, pinching their own cheeks to make sure that there was no frost-bite. She drank coffee, her hands around the tin mug as he took the hay sled to the cattle by the lower pasture, hearing the wind whipping round the cabin. It grew worse as the day got older and then she blocked out the draughts with old sheets, newspaper, anything, and the smell of beet came back to her; over the miles, over the years.

He came back as the afternoon ended and she rubbed his hands and feet, listening as he told her of the horses he had broken, how he had worked them gently until they understood, how he had been tossed and hurt but had come back again, gripping with his knees, never shouting, never hitting, as his father had shown him. She learned of the hill horses who were not mongrel mustangs but pastured and forgotten ranch horses who had grown stronger from their wildness. And these were his first love. They looked gentle and kind but were too proud for a saddle, too proud for a man.

'Until they understood that you weren't about to own them, just use their greatness,' he said, his face ruddy from the stove, his voice gentle as it should always be. Each night they lay in bed, loose limbed and free from the shadows.

'For now, free from the shadows,' Helen whispered against his skin while he slept. But would it last? She looked round the one-roomed cabin in the yellow warmth of the kerosene lamp, smelling its scent, hearing the breathing of the dog. Snow had built up at the windows and the wind was blowing drifts whichever way they looked but in here was warmth and love. For now there was love which reached out and held them both. She looked at the rawhide boxes which held two more weeks' provisions.

It was the next week that the calf drowned, down by the great pine where in the summer the mountain stream turned and followed the boulder path. They were laughing, holding the horse by its harness as the sky rose, clear blue above them when they heard its mother's bellows across by the stream.

They ran then, across the skidway's packed solid snow, slipping, falling, rising, then plunging through the drifts up to their knees and out again until they reached the snow path the calf had taken.

He was gone when they reached the broken ice, and there was just jagged blackness scythed out of the frosted ice where he had jumped and broken, then died. They followed the stream down but never found him and Ed remembered that he had left the barn door open. There was no laughter again, no loving, just the dreams and the calling of the cow, night after night after night as he slipped relentlessly from her grasp.

On the first of March they came back down through the forest because there was no point in staying any longer. She steered the horse through the lower pastures, seeing the road from the ranch to the town stretching away like a dirty ribbon. It had been cleared by ploughs and the snow heaped like swollen waves on either side.

She drew up the horse before they reached the ranch, holding his hand and kissing it where the mitt ended and his sleeve began, smelling his skin.

'I love you,' she said. 'But I am not enough. You need something else. You need absolution and I don't know how I can give it to you.'

He kissed her lips and looked towards the house where his parents waited. He loved her so much but she was right and he despaired, because how could anyone here give him that?

Chris hugged his mother and then Ed, knowing his new father was not better. He could tell it from the tension in their bodies, their faces which were drawn and tired. He stood as they pulled off their clothes and hung them in the laundry. He stood as they sat and drank coffee and talked of the cattle, the calf, the logs but not of themselves. He stood as Mrs McDonald told Ed and Helen of Chris and the coach and in his mother's face he saw despair and anguish.

She took him into the lounge, holding his hand, listening as he told her that he had to do it, and he couldn't understand why she ran to her bedroom and wept until the next morning;

321

not eating, not speaking, but howling as a dog would do when there was nothing but horror all around. She didn't see the rose wallpaper, the new curtains. She didn't think of the bulbs she had planted, the rose bushes she had buried because the darkness of the cupboard was in her and outside her.

It was then that Chris took her up the letter which had come in February. It was from Germany, from his father's father and he read it to her, loudly above her tears, shouting it into her face.

Hanover
December 1946

My dearest Helen,
It is with such relief that we receive your letter and forgive my language. I do not use English since you left but now I must begin again to practise and I shall.

We have not received others of your letters and thought that war had taken you also, as well as Heine.

Yes, we survive. Oma is thin but lives. That is all we can do, is it not? There is hunger here and nothing, not even a bird sings but we deserve nothing more.

It is glad news that you have another man you love. Perhaps it is a time for new beginnings.

I cannot ask you to come to see us because our shame is too great, such terrible things have been discovered. Did we know? No, but perhaps we guessed and did not wish to know? But I wish you peace, my dear. Peace for you and your husband and your child.

With loving thoughts from your father.
Wilhelm Weber

Helen stayed in her room all day, holding the letter, listening to the sounds of the farm, seeing the sun reflected off the snow lightening the room, and then she rose, sitting on the bed,

322

feeling old now, hearing again the news of her son and his
hatred, his confusion. She grieved for his lost youth. She heard
again the screams of her husband and the years which had
gone from his life and which perhaps would never be regained
and then she read the letter again.

CHAPTER 23

Helen drove into town that sunless day, down the sanded and salted road, between high drifts where no shadows carved and cut. She rang Claus from the old hotel lobby, talking in a low voice, listening as he agreed. She drove back then and into the yard, through the kitchen, past Ed and Chris who looked at her, but she did not stop.

She walked up the stairs, going into Chris's room, throwing open his cupboard, heaping clothes on to the bed, hauling out the case they had brought with them from England, because Chris was going home. She folded the clothes, knowing that now her son and husband were at the door, watching, but still she said nothing. She put in his baseball mitt, his ball and then looked at Chris.

'Do the case up.' It was an order but she did not wait to see him force it down and click the locks. She marched instead to her own room and took Ed's clothes and hers, folding them, pushing them into her case and his, then she looked at him as he stood silent in the doorway.

'Do the cases up.' It too was an order and again she did not wait to see him zip his own and lock hers but went down into the kitchen, sorting through cupboards as Mom watched, bringing out elastic which she knew would be needed where they were going. She put toothpaste, soap, cotton, needles, cigarettes, cans of ham, sugar, coffee and flour into a rucksack which she pulled out from the drawer in the laundry room. She told Mom and Pop where they were going then and they nodded, for what else could help?

Helen showered then, raising her face to the jetting water, letting it drench her hair and her skin, letting it take her breath and her thoughts away, just for those few moments. She felt it sting her skin and ease heat into her body. The towel was rough

324

and the mountains clean and snow-laden as she rubbed the condensation from the window with her hand, her tiredness gone now because she knew now where they were all going.

She told them that it was to Germany that they were travelling as they stood on the platform, stepping backwards as the Pullman roared in, so loud and large. She and Claus had arranged that her share of this year's profits from the agency would pay, but she didn't tell them and no one asked. She took Chris's arm as he spun round away from her, from the train.

'You will come because you need to, and I insist.' That was all, and her voice was hard and angry, but there was love in it too. She looked at Ed and there was shock in his face.

'You will come because I can think of no other way of clawing back your life and if you don't then I will go alone and never return.'

They both boarded the train with her, heaving up the cases, then sitting, watching the white valleys and mountains merge into night. They slept and woke and ate and slept again but did not speak. The train rattled and jerked and Helen felt Ed's arm against hers but it was stiff and afraid. Chris watched America, not her. He read comics which they bought from the stations they halted at, flicking the pages, his head down. Helen did not try to reach him. She could wait.

They reached Chicago and changed trains and travelled again and slept again until New York loomed, cutting out the light, its tall skyline one of the few left in the world which was untouched by the war.

They caught a cab to the docks where Claus met them in the shadow of the liner. He held her and his body was warm, and she wanted to lean into him, rest on him, but she could not. There was no time. Until they had been home, there was no time.

'So, my dear Helen. You have heard at last.' His smile was kind and his face no thinner than it had been last year.

She nodded. 'And you?'

He shook his head. 'There is nothing. I never will, I think. But you, at least you have heard.' His eyes were deep with distress but there was a certain acceptance. 'It comes in the end, a sort of acceptance,' he said. 'It has to.'

He looked at Ed and Chris. Chris looked away but Ed put out his hand.

'I'm grateful,' he said. 'It's good of you to do this for us.' His hand trembled and there was stiffness in his every movement.

Claus smiled and shrugged. 'My friend, it is so little. You did so much for us. Do not forget that as you travel back.' He turned now to Helen. 'I have the press pass. You have your camera? Good. Present it if you need to bypass the occupying regularities.'

Helen took the pass, stepping to one side as a passenger pushed past them up the gangplank. There was movement all around and the noise of traffic and ships and tugs. Their liner hooted, long and low, and she looked at the ship and then back at Claus.

'I will try to find out what I can, my dear friend,' she said, holding his arm and kissing his cheek. 'Really I will.' A steward was beckoning to them, his face red as he gestured from the deck.

'*Auf wiedersehen*, my friends,' Claus called as they started up the gangplank and Helen turned, her eyes meeting his, both wondering what she would find in the Germany they had once known.

The voyage to Liverpool lasted ten days and the weather was rough. They lay in their bunks for the first three days and then walked the decks and still Chris would not speak, though Ed held her arm and they breathed in the air together, feeling the cold on their skins; the wind whipping their salt heavy hair. As the days went by she felt him loosen and his walk became his roll. He bought more cigarettes to take as currency but smoked some too. They sat in deckchairs and talked a little and his hands grew still as his face took on the look of someone who could not turn back now. His cigarette glowed in the wind and the smoke was brushed away before it became visible, and its smell with it. He did not drink. But he did dream.

They docked in Liverpool and drove by taxi to the airport through drizzle-drenched streets, passing women in head-scarves and streets gouged by bombs, the ruins laced with rosebay. There were queues outside shops and now Chris turned to her.

'Remember what they did,' he said. 'And you are making me go back.' His face was set and his lips were thin.

'I am making you go home,' Helen said. 'Because you have to face yourself, you and Ed have to face yourselves.' She reached for her son's hand and held it, though he tried to pull away.

'Listen to your mom,' Ed said. 'She loves you. Listen to her. She's right. We've got to face it.'

But Chris would not listen and so Helen looked from him out to her homeland, its smallness, its hardship. It looked broken, like Ed, but it wasn't, she knew England better than that. But what about Ed? Was he broken?

She sat back, feeling the streets and rubble pressing in on her as they followed behind small cars driving on the left-hand side. She had forgotten how comforting such closeness was, how England clustered, keeping the great vast spaces out of view. She loved it, but she loved Ed too.

She reached for his hand and he squeezed hers and smiled but there was a distance between them which would always remain until he had come to terms with the past. Would Germany do that for him? Would there be absolution?

'Anyway, I want to see Laura and Mary,' Chris said, looking out at a park with no railings, his breath misting the window. The drizzle had turned to rain and it jerked down the window as the taxi rattled along the pot-holed road.

'We shall see them, on the way back,' Helen replied, looking at her watch. Claus had arranged for a flight at four and it was now two o'clock. She looked up into the grey sky. We shall also visit Heine's grave, she said to herself. This was something they must both do at last.

The arrived at the airport at three-thirty and as Helen strapped herself into the small Dakota she looked at Ed who was at the front talking to the Captain. He was investigating the controls, sitting in the pilot's seat, getting the feel again, and she saw life in his face, in his hands which moved quickly, competently and knew that she was frightened. She had never flown before.

Chris sat next to her with Ed in front and Helen couldn't speak as they took off, rearing up into the air, the bucket seats hard, the air pockets bumping her so that she was lifted from the seat. She gripped at Chris and screamed.

Chris and Ed turned and saw her face, so pale and fraught, and they laughed, looking at one another and then at her, and Chris put his hand on hers while Ed explained the rudiments of flight, though she heard not a word. She did feel her son's hand, though, and feigned fear long after it had gone.

There was a steady drumming of sound in the plane and they looked down through the narrow window as they skimmed over the North Sea, seeing the waves rippling and breaking.

'Just like the snow, Mum,' Chris said, leaning across her to see more easily and she liked his closeness and touched his hair where it stuck up at the back. He didn't feel it and so did not pull away. She looked up and Ed was watching. He smiled and for a moment there was no distance at all between them.

The plane bumped its way through the overcast sky and the sea seemed to last for hours. Helen looked around at the plane. It was small and cramped and seemed to be held together by wire, but it was quick because she could see a sandbank ahead already.

'This is the coast of the Netherlands,' the pilot called.

They flew over the island of Walcheren, most of which had been under water, though the floods had now receded, the pilot told them, as the gaps made in the dykes by the RAF had been closed.

'The fields will be barren though because of the salt,' he added and Helen looked at Ed but couldn't see his face because he had turned towards the window.

They flew over bomb-damaged woods, in one of which a wrecked plane still lay. There were bridges and railways sprawled beneath them, some still useless and in disarray. Long stretches of electric railway lay grass-covered and unused. The pilot brought the plane down lower so that they could see.

'The Nazis looted miles of copper wire which was needed for the cables,' the pilot explained and now Helen looked at Chris who just stared at her.

They landed and drove through the once flood-ravaged streets of Holland, sometimes breathing in the smell of sea-saturated earth and there was magenta rosebay here too on the ruins, though clearing and rebuilding had begun. They stopped to buy milk and the Dutch pastor told them how the Dutch had eaten tulip bulbs to survive but that Canadian rations had entered and the children were beginning to put on weight.

Helen looked around at the scabied legs and the hand-made shoes that the thin children wore.

Ed said, 'In Little Fork they grouse because they had to pay heavy taxes for the war. They don't understand.'

Helen took his arm. 'How can they? It is only those who've seen and been amongst it all, like us. We are the only ones who can understand.' He looked at home now, relaxed as though there was no conflict, no battle. Would he still dream tonight?

They stayed in an old inn and he did dream.

They drove the next day along roads which were full of Allied vehicles. They reached the border and this time there were no Nazis holding them up, no red and black flags, and no hidden camera. Helen looked at Chris as they were waved through and his face was tight and cold.

'We brought in a camera for your grandfather. Do you remember? We brought it in so that he could blackmail the Nazis and save some people. He is a man to be proud of.'

But Chris turned away and did not reply.

They drove through the west German countryside, along roads carved through heathland, dotted with pines. Some snow remained where clumps shadowed it from the sun. They passed through decimated towns where hardly a building remained and the people pushed prams from ruin to ruin, searching for fuel. Rosebay grew here too, though clearance had begun.

Helen watched Ed's face as he looked at the crosses which were still planted in the rubble so long after the war. He stopped the car and walked across and stood near one and she joined him and could smell the dust. It was the same dust as in England.

They travelled along the great Nazi *Autobahn* from then on which bypassed all the big cities, and now the three of them were quiet, filled with their own thoughts.

Helen counted the steel-helmeted military motor-cyclists which wove in and out of the Army lorries, the small military cars, the German farm carts pulled by thin horses. They passed the flat beet fields and there were women bending and walking, bending and walking. Helen asked Ed to stop and she stood by the car, taking photographs because Heine had done this once.

She told Chris to come and see. He stood next to her and was almost as tall. She told him of his father; how he had taken photographs and exhibited them, how he had thought life would be simpler if he lived as one of these workers, hoeing and weeding and harvesting.

They stood in silence and then he turned to her.

'I guess maybe he was right.' There was not the earlier hardness in his face, there was doubt and this is what Helen had wanted to see.

At last they drove into what remained of Hanover. The Kröpcke was destroyed, its glass dome gone and cleared away along with the smart women and their cigarette holders, along with a world which had once glistened and glittered. In its place there was ruin and devastation, and rosebay too.

They parked and watched labourers, thin and with sacking tied to their backs for warmth, clearing piles of melted lead and stonework. There were people here too who pushed prams and sorted in the rubbish and Helen wondered where the old Jew dressed in black was now. Had he survived? Had Claus's family survived? They were also Jews.

They passed broken bridges and bomb-proof shelters which had saved thousands of people, but not enough, because thousands had also died. Now a policeman told Helen they housed the homeless. She took photographs and Chris stood with her, while Ed walked to the ruins, picking up rubble, turning it over and over in his hand.

They drove to the Headquarters of the British Occupying Army and Helen presented her press pass to the commanding officer, explaining why she was here, the real reason why she was here and the officer nodded and turned away, saying he had not seen her, because fraternisation was not allowed.

Helen smiled. 'Thank you,' she said and left the room which was solid and full of photographs of his wife and children and very English.

Her footsteps sounded on the steps and on the road and an old woman glared at her.

'*Engländerin*,' she hissed but Helen did not mind because she would feel the same if the Germans were marching all over her ruined land.

They reached the village as dusk was falling and now there were no Nazi flags, no blonde girls with coiled hair, no windowboxes, and only six houses left standing in this main street. The church was still there and Herr Weber's house, or part of it. Helen walked up to the front door. There was ash on

330

the path, left over from the snow which only lay now beneath the stumps of the limes which was all that remained of the trees that Heine had loved, and for a moment she thought she could smell their summer scent.

She knocked, knowing that Claus had telegraphed ahead for her but she was nervous. Perhaps Oma would hiss at her too. She knocked again, feeling the hardness of the wood on her knuckle. She did not recognise the woman who opened the door until she spoke, and then she knew it was Oma, and she held the small thin body in her arms, hugging her, crying because this was Heine's beautiful mother, and she had no teeth and her once thick hair was thin and white and limp.

She held her saying, 'I'm so glad to see you. So sorry that Heine died,' and together they wept for the man they had both loved and then Chris was there, standing and looking, until Helen turned, her arm around Oma.

'This is your grandmother, Chris. This is Oma. You have come home.'

He didn't move or speak, just stood with his face closed and then Herr Weber came, walking slowly on two sticks out from the darkness of the hallway. His hands were gnarled and his fingers crooked. Oma told them the Nazis had beaten him when he had been betrayed; all over his body, including his hands and fingers. Still Chris just stood with Ed behind but Oma and her husband smiled.

'Come, my child,' they said to Helen, drawing her into the house, drawing them all in. 'Come. It is hard for him. It is hard for us to forgive ourselves.'

That night Helen lay in the room that had been Heine's. The lead soldiers were still on the shelf but the blue tiles of the stove were cracked from the blast of the bomb which had taken off the corner of the house. The brass knobs of the stove no longer gleamed and the body beside her was not Heine but Ed, and she loved them both.

They slept in their clothes because it was so cold and there was no fuel for the stove and only one blanket. She lay looking at the ceiling lit by the moon; a bomber's moon and she wondered if there would ever be a time when they stopped using the language of war.

She tucked her arm beneath her head turning to look at the clouds scudding across the sky.

331

'Will you lay your ghosts too?' Ed said.

She turned to him, not knowing until he spoke that he was awake.

'My ghosts? she queried.

'Sure, Helen. You have Heine to set down quietly in your life. He died alone. That's why you are trying so hard with me.'

His voice was gentle and he reached out and wound her curling hair round his finger.

Helen grasped his hand, loving it, loving him. He was right, she needed to lay her ghost, but she was fighting because she loved him, not just because Heine had been alone. She told him this, pulling his head down, kissing his lips, his eyes, his cheeks.

'I love you, I love you and I always will.'

He put his arm around her and pulled her to him and she felt the buttons of his overcoat against her throat.

'Even if I don't stop this goddamn war inside me?' His breath lifted her hair and it was warm on her skin.

'We'll stop it. It might take a while but one day it will all end.' But it did not end that night because the dreams were there as usual.

Chris lay in his room with his Oma's old duvet over him, dragged down from the attic which he had remembered as smelling of apples, but which was now open to the sky, the roof sliced open by a bomb; a British or American bomb. He was warm, though the stove was unlit, and he remembered now how his father had carried him from the dining-room when they had arrived that last time. There had been the scent of honey candles and heat from the stove. There had been the taste of venison in his mouth and the feel of his father's arms about him as they came upstairs into this bedroom where the stove was unlit. There was frost on the window and he could remember the mark his mother's nail had made where she had run it down, scraping at the ice.

He lay in bed and smiled and thought he heard his mother's voice. 'In my family, children sleep in warm rooms even if it means the adults go into the cold one.'

His father had laughed and said, 'My darling girl, do not prepare to do battle.' Chris looked round because the voice had been so clear but there was no one there. His mother had always been prepared to do battle for him. She was doing it

332

now and he knew that she was winning because he had seen the ruins, the despair, his Oma and his grandfather. The Germans were just people like him and their houses had been ruined and their children killed and he knew now that all Germans were not monsters, only some had gone mad. He knew that he was not from a family which had done that.

The next morning they ate ham from the cans and a few potatoes but not many and Helen was hungry as she had not been for over a year.

They sat in Wilhelm Weber's study because it was smaller to heat, Oma said, her voice tired. There were still old shirts laid against the gap in the bottom of the door but it was not against the prying ears of Hans but against the draught which whistled through the damaged house. There was the same lamp on a cupboard which had lit the room when she and Heine had come before and the same chairs, but they were ripped and torn and the horsehair protruded.

All morning they talked and Chris listened. Herr Weber told them how Hans had betrayed him but that they had never found the camera. They had taken him, the local *Blockwart*, to the cells and beaten him.

He told Chris and Ed how the Americans had come before the Nazis could kill him. The Americans had destroyed every house not flying a white flag and any resistance near a village meant retribution by United States artillery fire and the people knew this.

'Soon,' he said, 'there was a forest of white flags. Some still died though because the Nazi guerrilla fighters shot the first to put up the white flag. In our village it was the pastor who died. The madness, you see, lingered even until the last moments of the war. Perhaps it still exists.'

Helen watched Chris who sat, his head on his hands.

Wilhelm Weber looked at Ed. 'You were a bomber pilot. Well let me thank you. During the last months the Allied bombing smashed the transport systems faster than they could be repaired. Aircraft parts could not be moved from the factories.'

Now he tapped Ed's knee. 'So you see, my dear young man, in this war you served a purpose.'

Herr Weber nodded then to Helen because she had told him of her husband and the nightmare he lived through each day.

Ed shrugged. 'I guess maybe that's good of you to say bu there's still an awful lot of death beneath the bombs I dropped. His voice was unsteady and he clasped his hands together Helen heard the creak of his chair as he hunched his shoulders.

The old man nodded. 'Yes, that is true. There was so much death everywhere and mistakes were made. Of course they were made. We played a game which was so big, so ugly that no one knew what the results would be.' He sighed. 'Did you ask for the war?'

It was a question he wanted answered and Ed shook his head.

'No, I guess I never really gave it a thought.'

'Of course, my boy, no one really knew that any of this would happen, even we Germans. In the early days the Third Reich was going to bring us, oh, how do you say ... I know, employment, stability, grandeur. Your wife will have told you that Heine saw other things. I did not. I supported Hitler.'

He coughed and Oma went to him, patting her own mouth and sucking in her lips. Helen went to the kitchen and brought back aspirin for him, glad that she had packed three bottles.

'The Nazis gave us work though it became work in support of war. They improved housing, promised equal pay for women, gave marriage loans, increased family allowances, built roads. Things we had thought we would not see again after the First World War, the poverty of the twenties, the street fighting of those years. He gave all this to us, he gave us order and we looked away from the sickness we should have seen.'

Helen watched Chris. He was still resting his chin in his hands and Ed put his hand on his shoulder and together they learned about another side of the war. Oma left to brew real coffee brought from America and the smell invaded the house, bringing a smile to the old man's face.

'Ah, that is good. We have used acorns for so many years I had forgotten that there is such a thing as a coffee bean.' He laughed but there was still a deep sadness in his eyes.

She looked around the room. Two prints remained on the walls. The glass was cracked. The telephone had gone.

'Willingly we turned aside, you understand? At that stage, no black boots kicked at us. That, my fine young pilot, is our guilt. We allowed this to happen, all this.' He swept his stick towards the village, then sucked at his lips, rubbing his age-spotted hand over his mouth.

'It was only later I realised the truth and then I did something, but it was so little.'

Helen began to speak but Chris interrupted. 'You did not do little. You risked your life day after day like Ed did. That is more than I've ever been asked to do. Perhaps more than I ever will be asked to do.'

His voice was adult, his words too, and now he looked at Helen and smiled and she knew that he had seen, and was on the way to accepting, his heritage.

Herr Weber tapped Chris's leg lightly with his stick. 'You are very like your father, and your mother too. My son would be proud of you.'

He turned to the door as Oma brought in the coffee and they curved their hands round the mug because the stove was burning small bits of the dining-room furniture and there was very little heat.

'Before the war Hitler talked to his people. He travelled amongst them. But afterwards it was different. No. Seldom did he go to his soldiers. Never did he go to the bombed cities to talk to his people. But, my dears, the people still trusted him to win the war.' He threw up his hand, spilling some coffee on to his patched trousers but he didn't notice. 'And do you know why? Because they had so much suffering they had to have victory to justify it all.'

Helen thought of Churchill and the King and Queen, stepping over rubble, their faces compassionate, sharing the danger.

'I guess victory makes it better,' Ed said, sipping his coffee. Helen could see the steam rising from his mug.

'Defeat makes it all a mockery. But it is a mockery anyway. It was a game of the Nazis that went so wrong and we did not oppose it in time. That is our crime. That is the crime of the people, and your task for the future is to make sure you never let that happen in your lives. That must be your expiation. You must make every day of your life count for something good.'

There was silence and then Chris said, 'But what about the camps? That is what is so terrible.'

Oma wept now and Wilhelm Weber looked at her and then at Helen, Ed and Chris.

'And do you imagine we can forgive ourselves?' He looked at Ed. 'You dream at night because of the job you did.' His face was fierce now and his voice that of a younger man.

Ed looked at him, listening intently, his eyes fixed on the old man as he continued. 'We have to live with the knowledge that, as Germans, we allowed this murder of innocents to happen. We read *Mein Kampf* but we thought it too outrageous.' He was talking quickly now. 'But it happened. It was a state secret and knowledge of that secret was punishable by death. The secret was preserved.' He stopped now and looked at them all; one by one.

'But each night and every minute of every day I ask myself the question. Did I know? Had I guessed and turned from the truth?'

He sat back now, his coffee forgotten, his old damaged hands limp on his thighs.

Oma took one and held it, sitting on the arm of his chair. She said, 'You see, it makes anything that we did seem so little. Can you understand that?'

Again there was silence which was not broken by anyone until Helen touched Ed's hand and they left the room, walking out to the car, hearing Chris behind them.

They drove to the forest, walking amongst the trees, away from the paths, picking up kindling and carrying it back to the car, loading the boot, then the back seat. They drove and emptied it into the corner of the kitchen where newspaper was laid on the floor and chairs were dumped, waiting to be burnt.

They went back again, but only Ed and Helen now because Chris wanted to stay with his grandparents. They walked amongst the oaks, the beech, past the woodsman's cottage where there were no tables any more. She showed him where once logs had been stacked. They gathered what they could find but many had been here before them. It was grey and the cold seeped through their clothes and into their bones but there were too many thoughts for them to speak.

That night there were no dreams but they were there again the night after that, though not so vivid nor so loud and he woke when Helen touched him and wept in her arms and it was the first time he had been able to leave the blood and climb out of the darkness. She stroked his hair and kissed his eyes and they talked, slowly and carefully until the sun began to rise.

In the fresh dawn Helen took him to the woods, making him walk on the soft pine needles which had eased the ache in Heine's leg and would help his too. The sun was filtering through this time and now Helen remembered that soon there would be wild anemones and violets beneath the spreading branches. There were buds on the trees which must have been there before but they had not noticed.

'I kind of forgot for a while that the sun comes out and trees bud,' Ed said, reaching for her hand. 'I guess I've forgotten a lot of things.' He stopped and pulled her to him. 'Maybe your bulbs will be out around our house, and we should dig up your roses when we get back.' He kissed her with lips as soft as she remembered.

'Our bulbs and our roses,' she said against his mouth.

They walked again, mud clinging to their shoes as they walked on paths which had become overgrown and unkempt beneath the trees, and looked up through the branches at the sky.

The next day Ed began to seal up the roof, taking the asbestos off the sheds in the garden, dismantling their wooden joists and resettling them across the damaged corner of that attic, wrenching rusty nails out, sawing, chiselling, using Heine's old tools. He did not use those of Herr Weber because it was the son who had been denied the right to live long enough to do this for his parents and so Ed would do it for him.

He dug out slates from the nearby ruins, knocking and tearing his hands, seeing his blood in German dust, sifting where others had been before but always finding more as the days wore on, until at last there was a shape to the roof and that night he did not dream nor the next nor the next until he no longer dreaded the end of the day.

Helen drove round, taking photographs, asking questions about Claus's family. She took Wilhelm and Chris with her and together they worried and urged the authorities and saw the poverty all around, the children without shoes and little flesh. The meagre rations which were dependent on employment.

In the third week the old man took Chris to the end of the garden and asked him to dig three feet down, and there in an oilskin was the camera that they had brought through the border just before the war. He gave it to Chris and there was still film left and so Heine's son asked his mother to drive him to the beet fields and stood where his father had been, and took the same photographs.

In bed, two nights before they left the village, Ed held Helen and they talked about America and whether the dreams would come again when they were back where people could not understand.

'I guess not,' Ed said. 'I've got too much to do. I'm thirty-six, Helen, and Wilhelm said that we were the ones who have time. We do. I don't want to go back and just farm. I want a plane. I want to start an airline and Little Fork is as good a place as any.' His voice was eager and he pulled himself up on his elbow and looked down at her. 'There's more business setting up there all the time and the train's so goddamn slow. That war taught me too much and I reckon I'm going to take something out of it other than dreams that keep us both from our beauty sleep. We both need that too much.' He grinned. 'You want to learn to fly a plane or are you going to play around with your camera like I kind of think you are?'

Helen lay back in his arms, looking at his face which was so beautiful even though the lines remained and the scars from the crash were there beneath his hair. 'Why can't I do both? And while you're about it, you can teach Chris too.' She kissed him, feeling that now there was the hope that he would push the images to one side if they returned; when they returned.

The curtains were wide open because there had been too many years with the light blacked out, too many years of restrictions. She lit the candle by the bed, then carried it to the window, leaving it on the sill wanting to see its frail light seeping out into the sky.

The next night she did the same, and Ed laughed and kissed her as they watched the flame flickering in the draught.

Helen said, 'You can't just let your parents down, Ed,' because the thought had played in and out of her mind all day as she scrubbed the floors, washed windows, beat rugs. 'They have the ranch and farm to run and expect you to share in it.'

He sat up, taking a cigarette from the pack by the bed, lighting up, blowing the smoke up to the ceiling. 'I don't intend to leave them stone cold. It'll take a while to get set up, won't it? We'll be living in the house and we can amalgamate the ranch and the airline. It'll all work out, honey.'

And now, tonight, Helen began to believe that it would, and felt the darkness released from deep inside at last. And later, while Ed slept, she finally allowed herself to listen to the sounds of the house which had been Heine's home and grieved gently for the plans he would never make, the dreams he would never dream, and said goodbye.

As night became day and Ed woke they talked gently, deeply, about what could be done over here in the village, and Ed said they would send goods – food and clothing – and come back and finish the house. It was something that he owed these people.

Wilhelm and Oma did not want them to go; it was in their eyes as they stood on the doorstep with the scent of spring all around and the tips of bulbs green against the earth, and as Oma held Helen's hands they promised to go on searching for Claus's parents; it was something they wished to do, they said.

Helen asked if they would try and locate others that Claus knew and they nodded, knowing that she knew it would give them peace. She left the cigarettes for them to use as currency for information and she would bring more when she came again, she said. They would all come. She kissed them both then walked down the steps from the front door. The sky was deep blue today and at last there were violets in the shelter of the garden wall.

She waited while Chris stood before his grandfather.

'I shall see you again soon, Grandfather. Will you come to us too? There's someone I would like you to meet. He's my coach.'

Helen turned then and walked towards the car where Ed waited, smelling the violets, feeling the sun on her skin. When they came in the summer they would bring lime trees.

Also available in Arrow

After the Storm

(Previously published as *Only the Wind is Free*)

Margaret Graham

War can end more than one life, and break more than one heart.

Born into hardship in a Northumbrian mining village, it takes all
Annie Manon's spirit to survive the bleak years following the First
World War. Through hard work and determination she eventually
leaves the poverty and despair of her childhood behind her.
But then war breaks out once more, taking her further away from
her dreams and those she loves most. And it is all she can do
to keep hope alive.

Annie's Promise

Margaret Graham

It was a time when family values meant more than empty words.

It's the 1950s and Annie Manon has come home to the North-east
to keep a promise. And with her fledgling fashion business she
looks forward to providing work for the women of Wassingham. But
Annie has much to cope with and when her daughter Sarah leaves
home for London, Annie is torn between love for her only child and
the need to keep her promise to Wassingham's womenfolk.

arrow books